ONE KISS ALONE

the PENN-LEITHS of THISTLE MUIR
BOOK THREE

NICHOLE VAN

Fiorenza Publishing

Published by Fiorenza Publishing
Print Edition v1.0

ISBN: 978-1-949863-18-5

One Kiss Alone is a work of fiction. Names, characters, places and incidents are the products of the author's imagination or are used fictitiously. Any resemblance to actual events, locales or persons, living or dead, is entirely coincidental.

To the lonely and lost,
Hold fast. You will find home.

And to Dave,
For ensuring I never need to look for home.
Wherever you are, there I belong.

PROLOGUE

A MOUNTAIN ROAD NORTH OF VENICE, ITALY
AUGUST 1846

The lady was hauntingly beautiful.

Ethan Penn-Leith hated the mundanity of the thought—the uninspired diction, the lack of poetic creativity.

However, the loveliness of the woman before him scattered his wits so thoroughly, it took all his willpower not to stare in slack-jawed stupor.

He felt stunned.

So stunned, in fact, that the flimsy sentence appeased him with its accuracy.

The lady sat opposite him in the jolting hired coach. A gauzy black veil consigned her eyes to glittering shadows, leaving only a pert nose, the elegant slash of a jaw, and the lush pout of her red lips visible. The severe cut of her gown revealed an enticingly curved figure, the sort designed to draw a man's attention.

A fairytale bound in tight-cut silk.

The line of poetry flitted through his mind.

Aye, the lady was that and more.

Her presence in a hired carriage on a perilous mountain road implied she possessed courage and pluck.

The maid at her side indicated she was a noblewoman of some means.

The unrelenting black of her clothing suggested she was in mourning. Was it too cruel to hope the deceased had been her husband?

Heaven should strike Ethan down for such a thought.

And yet . . .

The carriage rocked over the rugged roadway, jostling his shoulder into a rotund man-of-business who sat sleeping beside him. The man snorted and half-opened his eyes before drifting off once more, head tilted back against the squabs.

Opposite, the beautiful lady demurely lowered her head. What color were the eyes hidden beneath her veil? Ethan's poetic soul thrived on details, and he detested that this wee one eluded him.

Ye are still staring, ye eejit.

Right.

Ethan tugged a pencil and leather-bound notebook from his coat pocket, hoping to distract his thoughts by cataloging impressions.

Briefly, he wondered how his older brother, Malcolm, might describe the scene. No doubt, Malcolm would say something deeply philosophical about the fleeting nature of external beauty and the importance of inner virtue. However two years ago, Ethan had stopped looking to Malcolm for inspiration, vowing to rely on his own thoughts alone.

To that end, Ethan imagined recounting his current situation before a blazing fire in the taproom of the Lion Arms in his home village of Fettermill, Scotland.

I was in Italy, riding in a vetturini. *Imagine it like a yellow bounder—an*

Italian post-chaise. Only in Italy, ye can share a post-chaise with strangers. The coachman, the vetturino, *sees tae everything for the passengers—arranging the coach, horses, lodging, and food. 'Tis more comfortable and safe than a* Diligenza, *the public stagecoach.*

I had been traveling in the vetturini *alongside a man-of-business from Padua when we stopped in Belluno, a wee village surrounded by granite peaks. Travelers fear bandits in the high Alpine passes, but I had come prepared.*

While in Belluno, a bonnie lady and her maid joined us. The lady was exquisite. Imagine a Renaissance Madonna without a gilded halo—

No. That wasn't quite right.

Perhaps—

She was a Mediterranean siren, akin to the one Odysseus faced as he—

"You appear to be a devotee of *la penna, signore.*"

A contralto voice in heavily-accented English halted Ethan's pencil with an audible *scritch.*

He raised his head and sucked in a startled breath.

The lady had lifted her veil.

Gray eyes framed by velvety long lashes met his gaze.

Aye . . . stunned stupid.

Those were literally the only words that Ethan Penn-Leith could string together.

It felt nearly cliché that he—a poet the *London Times* had recently heralded as a 'writer of endless invention'—should be robbed of adjectives by a pretty face. And yet . . .

He sat up straighter, mentally reaching for that roguish part of himself—the one that had charmed bullies at Eton and made friends of enemies at Oxford.

And then . . . Ethan smiled. The very smile Malcolm dubbed *The Swooner,* as it had a tendency to cause ladies to faint when deployed.

For the record, Malcolm was not wrong.

This lovely Italian lady did not swoon, more's the pity.

She did, however, blink. Twice.

So perhaps she was not entirely unmoved.

That slight tick bolstered Ethan's confidence.

What had she asked him?

Oh, right.

"My pen?" he replied. "I do feel compelled to write when I am inspired, madam. A beautiful vista often does the trick."

"Ah." The lady leaned forward to peer out the window. The movement pulled her bodice tighter against her torso and sent a heady breeze of exotic perfume wafting over him. Jasmine, perhaps, with undertones of ambergris and rose. Ethan breathed in deeply. The lady's dress was well made, but with its puffed sleeves and rounded waistline, the garment was decidedly five years out of fashion. Had she dyed an older dress black for mourning?

Unruffled by Ethan's gaze, she merely studied the soaring mountains surrounding them.

They had finally reached the beginning of the *Dolomiti*, the craggy granite mountains that stretched for hundreds of miles within the Kingdom of Lombardy-Venice and the Austrian Empire. The rugged terrain rendered the region a bit of a no-man's-land, an endless expanse of peaks and valleys that hid charming Alpine villages and enterprising bandits in equal numbers.

Should adventure find him, Ethan had come equipped. A Belgian pin-revolver rested in the satchel at his feet—a gift from his brother-in-law, Captain Fox Carnegie. Engraved with Ethan's name, the gun was the latest in modern weaponry, able to fire off six rounds in rapid succession.

In looking at the elegant lady across from him, he had to wonder—why had *she* braved the danger of the Dolomites?

"I have always adored the mountains of the *Südtirol*," she said, as if responding to his unasked question. The husky timbre of her voice abraded Ethan's skin, causing all the fine hairs to stand at attention. "The view is remarkably inspiring."

"I agree," he grinned. "But that vista is not what inspires me at the moment."

The lady tilted her eyes back to his in surprise.

Ethan allowed the warmth of his gaze, a brief up-down glance, and a flash of The Swooner to communicate his meaning.

Instead of blushing or lowering her head, the lady merely raised an eyebrow. "*Bravo*. Cleverly done, sir."

"Thank ye."

Beautiful *and* a quick flirt.

Ethan was in love.

She returned his frank appraisal with one of her own, eyes casually skimming his person—lips, chest, thighs.

Heaven help his heart. It thundered beneath his sternum like a Highland waterfall after a summer storm.

"Your English is excellent," he continued.

"As is yours," she replied sardonically, ignoring his implied question as to *how* she knew English. "Though I cannot quite place your accent."

"I am a Scot, madam."

"Ah."

A pause. Her lady's maid joined the businessman in snoring.

The lady spared a sideways glance for her servant and then brought her cool, gray eyes back to his. Something about the movement struck Ethan as bizarrely familiar. As if he had been on the receiving end of her gaze before.

Surely that was impossible. He would never forget this woman's face.

His sense of recognition had to come from Fate. That he and this unknown lady were intended to meet one another.

Perhaps they had been born under the same predestined star.

Och, that was rather good.

He penciled the romantic thought in his notes.

"And yourself, madam?" He lifted his eyes from his notebook. "From whence do you hail?"

"Venezia."

"*La Serenissima.*" He stated Venice's nickname—The Most Serene. "And your . . . husband?"

"*Morto*, I am afraid." If she found her husband's death a trial, her tone did not convey it.

"Ah, you have my condolences." Ethan's intonation implied the opposite of his words.

Her answering faint smile said she did not miss his meaning.

"What is your destinat—" he began.

"You are a writer then?" she interrupted, nodding toward his notebook.

"*Sí*. Un poeta," he replied. His Italian wasn't excellent, but he knew the basics, particularly words that were essentially English with an Italian flourish.

"A poet?" She spared a glance for his pen. "That explains much."

Part of Ethan wanted to legitimize his work. To explain that he wasn't merely an aspiring poet or some wealthy nobleman who fancied himself a wit with a pen.

No. He was Ethan Penn-Leith. The man one reviewer had recently described as, "the most celebrated poet since Milton." A writer so well-known, he could scarcely walk down Bond Street in London without being mobbed by enthusiastic acolytes.

But he said nothing. He liked that this unknown Italian woman knew as little of him as he did of her. That his name would likely mean nothing.

"Do you like poetry?" he asked.

"*Sì, mi piace.* But I prefer Dante to your Shakespeare."

"Is that so?" He raised his eyebrows in a challenge.

They spoke of poetry for nearly an hour, arguing over Shakespeare's love of metaphor and Dante's use of meter.

This woman . . .

Beautiful, flirtatious, *and* educated?

Bloody hell.

Ethan wanted to know every wee thing about her. Every detail of her history—her upbringing and parentage, her deceased husband and her life with him, why she was traveling on this dangerous mountain road and where she was headed.

Lines of poetry thrummed through his brain.

. . . *ruby-soaked lips* . . .

. . . *a raven of grief rimmed in angelic light* . . .

He would pen scores of poems in her honor.

She could be Beatrice to his Dante, Laura to his Petrarch.

He itched to begin. To immortalize this lady in words.

But first . . .

"And your name, madam?" he asked when their conversation lulled. "I have been so lost in our conversation, I neglected to perform an introduction."

A wee smile touched her lips. Instead of answering, she relaxed back in her seat and removed her gloves, tugging at each finger in turn. Ethan stared in fascination, helpless to look away. Like the rest of her person, her hands were fine-boned and elegantly made. She folded the gloves neatly before tucking them into a pocket in her skirts. From that same pocket, she produced a fan, waving it to cool herself.

Bright August sun beat upon the roof of the carriage. Had they been traveling through the swamplands inland from Venice, they would have been red-faced and dripping in the humid heat. Thankfully, the climb into the Alps had lowered the outside temperature to more tolerable levels.

Still, several beads of perspiration gathered at her temples, damp jewels sparkling in the dim carriage.

"*Il mio nome*?" she repeated in Italian and then slowly shook her head. "*Penso di no.* I believe I prefer to remain a mystery."

"I see." He heaved a sigh. "I fear I shall have tae name ye myself then." A pause. "*Bellissima.*"

"*Bellissima*?" she sniffed. "I am more than a pretty face, *signore.*"

"Of that, I have no doubt, *Bella Mia.*"

"*Bella Mia?* My beautiful one? You repeat yourself, sir, and show little creativity. Are you sure you are a poet?" She pointed her fan at his notebook. "Or perhaps your *abilità* with the pen fails when challenged?"

Ethan mimed picking up and dusting off the gauntlet she had just figuratively laid at his feet. "Challenge accepted, *La Mia Sirena.*"

His actions startled a throaty laugh from her. "A siren? Are we to speak of Homer next? Or do you fear I shall lure you to your death?"

"Perhaps." He leaned forward, bracing a hand on his knee in the swaying coach and permitting his gaze to drop to her mouth. "But what a sweet death it would be."

The lady's gray eyes flashed. She looked at him steadily as she fanned her face. With a quick grin, Ethan bent to tuck his notebook into the satchel at his feet.

When he lifted his head, the lady was in the process of removing her bonnet and veil, revealing a wealth of dark hair coiled atop her head.

The maid at her elbow stirred at the movement before sinking back into slumber.

"*Fa caldo, no?*" The lady set her bonnet and veil in her lap and then fanned herself more vigorously.

"Aye, 'tis quite warm today. Is that what I should call ye, then? *Focosa?*"

Yes, the word suited her—fiery, spirited.

"Are you always so relentless?" She cocked her head.

"Pardon?"

"The charming grin? The dashing attire?" She motioned her lovely hand up and down, indicating his tightly-cut brown coat over a green silk waistcoat and linen trousers. "The endless flirtation?"

Ethan leaned into The Swooner and deepened his brogue. "I have yet tae receive any complaints, lass."

She tapped her lips with one long finger. "I struggle to decide if I should commend your dedication or feel appalled on behalf of womankind."

"I would be delighted tae receive any praise ye should like to give me, the more personal the better, *mo leannan.*"

"You are truly *incorreggibile. Non so cosa da*—"

CRAAACK!!!

The sound of a gunshot split the air.

Shouting in rapid-fire Italian immediately followed.

The maid woke with a scream.

The businessman beside Ethan jerked upright.

The coach lurched to a stop, horses whinnying, tackle jangling. Ethan and his fellow travelers swayed with the motion.

Another shot cracked through the mayhem.

"*Banditi,*" the businessman hissed.

Ethan pulled wide the satchel at his feet and tore out his Belgian pinfire revolver.

He met the *bellissima* lady's wide gaze, her eyes dropping to the gun. Twisting, he hastily tucked the weapon into the waistband at the small of his back, covering it with his coattails. The press of the revolver against his spine promised some hope of protection from whoever was outside.

The carriage door opposite flew open.

A masked highwayman aimed an old single-shot pistol into the interior of the carriage. Ethan quickly counted five more armed bandits beyond the first man's wiry frame—three standing and two on horseback with rifles trained on the coachman and postilion. Pine trees and granite peaks towered behind them.

Ethan cataloged the men's positions and weaponry. They might be highwaymen, but their guns were at least thirty years out of date. None of their weapons would fire more than one shot.

That evened the odds a smidgen.

The highwayman at the door smiled, his eyes flashing behind the black slits of his mask.

The dreamlike quality of the situation washed over Ethan, as if he had abruptly become an actor in a mawkish melodrama.

First, traveling through breathtaking mountain scenery.

Second, flirting and conversing with the most fascinating lady he had ever met.

And third, being accosted and held at gunpoint by armed, masked highwaymen.

The poem I write about this will be epic, he thought.

One of the bandits shouted at the coachman and fired another warning shot, quickly reloading his pistol. The weapon might be outdated, but the highwayman packed the powder and shot blindingly fast.

If I survive, Ethan amended.

Please let me survive. He glanced at his lady—the pinch of her mouth, the tense muscles of her cheeks. *And, perhaps, save the damsel as well.*

Ethan was, after all, a devout optimist.

If he could extricate them, perhaps they could continue their conversation this evening. Over a bottle of red wine. Alone.

The highwayman at the carriage door barked orders in sharp Italian, motioning with his pistol for the passengers to descend.

The businessman exited first, but the maid shrank back, blubbering in fear and clutching her mistress's arm. Ethan intervened, placing his body between the highwaymen and the ladies.

Clambering out of the coach, he turned and extended a hand to the maid. The terrified girl stumbled down the steps only to collapse against the rear wheel of the carriage, sobbing hysterically.

Ethan's lady, however, was made of sterner stuff. She remained stoic-faced as he reached for her. The weight of her fine-boned hand burned his palm.

"Stay behind me," he whispered as her feet hit the ground.

She met his gaze with her own tremulous one and nodded, her gray eyes wide, before turning to comfort her maid.

Such a *braw* lass, his lady.

Ethan pivoted to face the robbers, still keeping his body between the highwaymen and the women, shoulders held high, the revolver a comforting weight against the small of his back.

Noting his chivalry with a sneer, the lead bandit rattled something in quick Italian that Ethan did not understand.

Ethan lifted his chin in reply anyway.

He felt the gentle press of a hand between his shoulder blades.

"You will get yourself hurt with such bravery, Poet." His lady's low voice reverberated from behind. "Do not be a fool."

"I won't be rash," Ethan murmured, keeping his gaze trained on the highwaymen. "But I will protect your bonnie self."

Her soft hand skimmed down his spine, coming to rest at his waistband, the touch igniting goose-flesh.

Bloody hell.

The threat of the highwaymen combined with the delicious touch of the lady's hand set Ethan's heart to a mad gallop.

Had he ever felt so piercingly alive?

Every sense was heightened. The sharp definition of white clouds against the summer-blue sky. The panicked nickering of horses. The feel of the lady's body pressing closer behind him.

Two highwaymen on foot pulled luggage off the back of the coach, rifling through trunks. The businessman protested, only to fall silent when the lead bandit menacingly cocked his pistol.

Would the highwaymen be content with robbing them only? Ethan wondered. Or would his lovely lady be a physical target, as well?

Ethan had meant what he said—he would protect her.

The highwaymen with the luggage shouted in triumph, hefting two bags that clanked with coin from the businessman's trunks. The man wrung his hands in distress.

The lady's palm moved slightly at Ethan's waist, as if pleading for protection.

Aye, lass. I'll protect ye, he thought.

The bandits remained focused on the trunks, gathering to examine the goods.

It was now or never.

"When I move," Ethan said softly, "I want yourself and your maid tae crouch down. Get as low as ye can."

The lady hummed in agreement and murmured, "Be ready," in quick Italian to her maid.

Tensing, Ethan shifted his weight, elbow bending to reach for his revolver.

But nimble fingers pulled it from his waistband first and pressed the barrel of the gun against his spine.

The revolver cocked, causing Ethan to freeze.

What the ever-loving hell?!

His lady moved from behind him, his own gun pointed at his chest. Her gray eyes snapped with fiery hauteur, a calculating smile on her lips.

With a laugh, her maid—miraculously recovered—scampered to join the highwaymen, clearly another player in the plot.

The lead bandit swiveled round at the commotion and cackled in delight. "È sempre un piacere averti con noi, Signora."

"*Grazie*, Fabrizio," Ethan's beautiful lady replied with a saucy toss of her head, gesturing with his pistol. "I am glad to be here, too."

Ethan stared, suspecting he resembled an Atlantic salmon after spawning in the River North Esk—red-skinned, open-mouthed, gasping.

Surely he would be reliving this moment with vivid clarity for the rest of his life.

The gut-punch of surprise. The jolt of shock.

His lady had been a plant—a willing ally to the robbery.

The plot twist in his unwritten poem he had not seen coming.

He couldn't help but chuckle in dumbfounded astonishment.

"Well-played, *la mia piccola ladra* . . . my wee thief." He swept her a lavish bow. Ethan was, as ever, a gentleman to his core. "*Bravissima*."

"Even with your back against the wall, you still charm," she replied in her throaty, Italian-accented English. "I fear it is an illness with you."

"If it means gazing upon your fair self, lass, then heaven forfend I ever feel well."

She smiled at that . . . but not a true smile. Her gray eyes remained dull—obdurate chips of gray Aberdeen granite against her golden skin.

What catastrophe had forced such a fine lady to ally herself with highwaymen?

"Was there ever a husband?" Ethan had to ask.

His *ladra*—his thief—laughed. "No. Never. I prefer my life . . . unencumbered." She waved his revolver in a circle. "*Libera.* Free."

The leader of the highwaymen—Fabrizio, he supposed—snorted, his gaze narrowing as he looked between Ethan and his wee lady-thief.

Fabrizio was not un-handsome, Ethan noted. He supposed that some women might find the man's dark curls and Grecian nose appealing. The devil-may-care glint in his eye didn't hurt either. And Fabrizio had spoken to Ethan's *ladra* with the familiar *tu* in Italian—the form reserved for close friends . . . or lovers.

Ethan swallowed against the thought.

And why, in heaven's name, was he more concerned about Fabrizio's possible romantic involvement with the lovely highwaywoman than the guns currently aimed at his head?

The highwaymen made short work of the rest of the belongings. Ethan's trunk was searched, though he carried little of value. Then both he and the businessman were trussed with their hands behind their backs. Ethan stood tall throughout the ordeal, his gaze trained on his *ladra*.

Wee things stood out to him.

She grasped his revolver with ease and was obviously comfortable with firearms. Ironically, he found that thought reassuring. His *ladra* was a fighter, clearly able to defend herself.

And yet, conversely, she held herself upright and unbending. Ethan recognized that self-preserving stance—the sort of rigidity born of shouldering blow after blow from life.

Unfortunately, Fabrizio took note of all of Ethan's noticing. The man's eyes narrowed, and the grip on his pistol tightened.

Finally, as the other bandits mounted their horses, Fabrizio stopped in front of Ethan, gaze raking him from head to toe. He barked in Italian, the words undecipherable.

With a frown, Ethan looked to his *ladra*, standing beside Fabrizio's mount.

With an oath, Fabrizio cracked Ethan across the face with his palm. Ethan's head snapped back, his ears ringing from the blow.

"Keep your eyes off *la mia signora,* Englishman," he snarled, his accent thick.

Ah.

So the man spoke English.

"I'm a Scot," Ethan lazed in return, tasting blood in his mouth. "Not English."

Fabrizio's hand raised again, fisted this time.

"*Basta!*" Ethan's *ladra* stepped between them, a restraining palm pushing on Fabrizio's chest.

She said something in clipped Italian.

Fabrizio spat a reply.

She waved Ethan's revolver in the air, arguing some point.

Fabrizio's face turned red. He glared at her, lungs heaving, before shooting a murderous glance at Ethan.

"*Vai.*" She flicked her fingers, ordering Fabrizio to leave.

"*No,*" he replied, continuing to glare at Ethan.

The lady rolled her eyes. She and Fabrizio sniped back and forth for another two minutes.

Finally, his *ladra* huffed and slipped the revolver into her pocket.

Pivoting back to Ethan, she did the last thing he expected—

She grabbed his lapels in two fists, raised onto tiptoe, and pressed her lush mouth to his.

Surprise jolted him.

Her kiss scorched, hot and punishing.

Ethan could taste his blood on her lips, feel the sharp desperation in her touch.

Leaning into the kiss, he returned her fury, straining against the bonds that tied his hands.

She reciprocated with a breathy gasp, a hand around his neck, her chest pressing into his.

Electricity crackled between them. Ethan's blood turned to lava.

Dimly, he heard the highwaymen hooting and shouting.

He was too lost in his lady's plump lips to care.

When she finally pulled away, he chased her with his mouth, refusing to lose the connection.

Stepping back, she pressed her palm to his cheek, wiping the blood from the corner of his mouth with her thumb.

His lungs heaved. Over her shoulder, Fabrizio sent Ethan a death stare as he mounted his horse.

"God's speed, *la mia ladra*," Ethan murmured. Swallowing hard, he planted a kiss on her palm.

"You, as well, Poet," she said softly.

And then, she straightened her shoulders, her gray eyes hardening to tempered steel—a huntress donning her armor.

Chin high, she turned round to her comrades and, placing a foot in Fabrizio's stirrup, pulled herself up to ride pillion in front of him. The highwayman wrapped a possessive hand around her waist before sending Ethan a sneering look and kneeing his horse into a gallop. The rest of the gang followed after.

Ethan's wee *ladra* did not look back.

She was a thief in every way, he realized . . . his pocketbook, his watch, his revolver, and—devil take her—a sizable wedge of his heart.

Ethan was quite sure he would never be the same.

He watched until the highwaymen had disappeared into the surrounding forest, leaving only the chirp of cicadas and the lone call of a circling hawk.

Aye.

He may have lost the lady, but in a sense, that scarcely mattered.

Every experience, he knew, provided fodder for writing.

And this particular turn of events?

Well, he intended to shape them into a poem so epic, Shakespeare himself would writhe in jealousy.

ALLEGRA BAROZZI DREAMED of a different life.

One in which she had enough coin to be free of constant worry. A place where she did not have to depend upon someone else—translation: *a man*—to support her.

In short, she yearned for freedom.

But for all her dreaming, Allie was a cold-eyed realist.

And realistically, she was currently as liberated as she was likely ever to become.

She sat on a cushioned window seat, slowly fanning herself and staring sightlessly out over the twilight mountain landscape. The setting sun painted the gray granite peaks of the Dolomites in shades of pink and orange. The *Rosengarten,* this particular grouping was called in German . . . a rose garden for the colorful beauty of the mountaintops at sunset.

Tonight, Allie scarcely registered the stunning vista.

Outside her door, the raucous noise of her comrades celebrating echoed up the stairwell. Of course, the extra bottles of wine Allie had gifted them likely contributed. She enjoyed sharing any largess that fell her way.

"You did well today, *cara,*" Fabrizio Sacci said for easily the tenth time, his Italian laced with the crisp staccato of his Lombardian roots. He stood near the unlit fireplace, twirling the Scotsman's expensive revolver with one hand and holding a glass of fine *chianti rosso* in the other. Their mountain villa may be rustic, but it was well-provisioned.

Allie did not acknowledge Fabrizio's words.

He had to know he had crossed a line with the poet today—striking the Scot and then threatening more. In hindsight, she should have anticipated Fabrizio's temper.

Allie, Fabrizio, and their band belonged to *La Giovine Italia*, a political uprising determined to consolidate all of Italy into a single, unified republic. After all, the Italian peninsula had not been united since the fall of the Roman empire. *La Giovine Italia* wanted to see a *risorgimento*—a resurgence of the grandeur of Italy's past achievements.

The robberies were merely a way to shuttle needed funds to the movement.

For her part, Allie was less interested in the cause and more dedicated to her own personal freedom—keeping her stomach full, her wardrobe in decent repair, and enough coin in her pocket to prevent having to become an old lady's paid companion or some arrogant lordling's mistress.

Being treated as a valuable cog in *La Giovine Italia's* organizational machine was merely a lovely bonus.

Consequently, over the past five years, she had assisted Fabrizio in scores of heists.

With her ladylike bearing and knowledge of upper-class society, Allie always ensured potential marks were wealthy individuals who could easily afford financial losses, and given the ill-gotten nature of their own funds, were unlikely to report the theft to the authorities.

For example, today's target—Signore Carrerra, a man-of-business from Padova—had been secretly carrying nearly ten thousand *lira* to a bank in Innsbruck. The coin came from murky trading deals with pirates off the coast of Morocco. So to Allie's equally murky moral calculations, two wrongs made a right in this instance.

But she had not intended for an innocent poet to be caught up in the fracas. Their robberies rarely resulted in injury, but as a precaution, the *vetturino* had been ordered to refuse passage to any other travelers. Of course, the Scot had likely charmed his way into a seat regardless.

The man was too attractive for his own good. His handsome face, silver tongue, and careless disregard for his own safety could land him in serious trouble. Even hours on, Allie fretted for him. The poet had regarded the world with a wide-eyed optimism that, to her view, bordered on naiveté and innocence.

He certainly doesn't kiss like an innocent, a dry part of her noted.

Yes, well . . . the kiss had been necessary.

She had seen how Fabrizio assessed the Scot, as if looking for reasons to harm him. Her colleague was impulsive and had no qualms about hurting anyone he perceived as an obstacle to his goals.

Fabrizio saw himself as her would-be lover, no matter how many times she refused his advances. And so when the Scot protected and flirted with her, Fabrizio had become a bomb in search of a fuse.

At that point, Allie had done the only thing she could:

She had claimed the Scot as her own.

It was rather like a dog marking its territory—an unsavory, though accurate, comparison.

By kissing the Scot, she had tagged him for herself, effectively stating to the rest of her band, even the enraged Fabrizio, that the Scot's life belonged to her and her alone.

Honor among thieves and all that.

Not that she would ever see the Scot again.

And how odd . . . that simple fact pricked like a sliver in her heart—a sharp twinge of agitation.

She shook her head. Harboring regrets for a charismatic Scotsman would serve nothing. Sentimentality had only ever brought sorrow and hardship to her door. Her twin brother had thoroughly schooled her in that painful truth.

Though perhaps she would claim the Scot's revolver for herself. Fabrizio had taken it before she had a chance to examine it, but she would like it as a souvenir.

Outside, the sky had faded slowly into a dusky purple, the sunset having spent its glory.

"I say we celebrate another successful venture." Fabrizio crossed to her, a second glass of red *chianti* in his hand, the Scotsman's revolver forgotten on a table. "Mazzini will be pleased with our efforts."

Allie nodded and took the goblet from Fabrizio.

Yes, Giuseppe Mazzini would be ecstatic over the rush of funds into *La Giovine Italia's* dwindling coffers. Mazzini was the leader of their movement, a man who rubbed shoulders with the kings and queens of Europe, using his smooth charm and clever tongue to raise money for his cause.

Devoted acolytes such as Fabrizio resorted to baser methods of securing funds. *Rash, fanatical, mercenary* . . . those were the words she would summon to describe her friend.

Allie knew Fabrizio had dreams of grandeur. Of raising enough money—either through theft or gambling—to be appointed Mazzini's right-hand man and travel around Europe with the dashing revolutionary.

"To our success." He leaned a shoulder on the wall beside her window seat and lifted his glass.

Allie followed suit, clinking her goblet against his.

She swallowed half the cup's contents in one swallow and then frowned.

"This wine has gone off. It tastes far too acidic. Where did you get—"

Realization came quickly.

Fabrizio had spiked the wine with laudanum.

Her goblet tumbled from fingers gone numb.

Porco miseria, how much laudanum had he put in her glass?

She looked up at her supposed friend.

The world spun on its axis, turning one Fabrizio into three.

"W-why?" she whispered.

The three Fabrizios smiled in unison, an unpleasantly hard expression on his handsome face.

He saluted her with his own glass. "Your brother sends his regards, my lady."

Of course.

That bloody bastard.

But before Allie could muster the energy to scream her frustration and anger, darkness claimed her.

E than Penn-Leith had not set out to become the most famous person in London.

His ambitions had always been modest in scope—appease his uncle, write poetry, marry a suitable lady . . . goals listed in that particular order.

Instead, his fame had arrived like flood waters rising along the River Dee, a slow trickle that had increased gradually until—like a heedless fisherman—Ethan had found himself floundering in the rushing tide of his celebrity.

Take this evening, for example.

He sat on the first row of a large assembly—the gathered *hoi polloi* of the London *ton* thronged around him—preparing to give a reading of his most acclaimed poem to date, "Auld MacDougall in His Cups Reminisces; or One Kiss Alone."

Ethan's escapade with his lovely wee thief the previous summer had indeed been material for the most monumental of poems. Why, even Queen Victoria herself was to have attended tonight, but Her Majesty had cried off at the last minute due to a megrim.

Granted, Her Majesty's withdrawal had done nothing to dampen enthusiasm for the evening. The Earl of Aberdeen's crowded ballroom vacillated between sweltering and stifling despite the May rain pattering against the windowpanes.

A distant relative, Lord Aberdeen had been eager to host one of Ethan's rare public recitals. White-haired and standing rigidly on a small dais at one end of the room, the earl greeted his guests, introducing Ethan in resounding terms.

"I have never been more proud to call a gentleman kinsman than tonight," Lord Aberdeen intoned, voice carrying easily due to his years of giving speeches in Parliament. "Mr. Penn-Leith is a credit to our family line, and I have long looked upon his accomplishments with great pride. His first book of poetry, *Poems from the Highlands*, astounded us all with the fluidity of his words and the profundity of his ideas. His second book, *Of Lovers and Madmen*, solidified Mr. Penn-Leith's place as one of the most gifted poets of our age. However, it is his latest slim volume, *Romances from Italy*, that will ensure Mr. Penn-Leith's place alongside Shakespeare, Milton, and Wordsworth as one of the most celebrated writers of the English language. And to think, he has accomplished all this before the age of thirty years. Tonight, I am pleased to have coaxed Mr. Penn-Leith—the Highland Poet himself—from his home in Scotland to grace us . . ."

The earl droned on, lauding Ethan and simultaneously taking credit for his successful rise from obscurity. Ethan understood that the evening was one of political posturing for Lord Aberdeen. After all, the man had just finished a term as Foreign Secretary, and it was no secret he wished to replace Lord John Russell as Prime Minister.

At Ethan's side, his uncle, George Leith, shifted in his seat, clearly chafing at Lord Aberdeen's credit-taking. After all, it had been Uncle Leith who had seen the potential in his sister's son and plucked Ethan from a lowly farm in rural Angus to raise him as a gentleman. It was no exaggeration to say that a large portion of Ethan's current success originated from Uncle Leith's largess.

Of course, in exchange, Uncle Leith led Ethan about like a prized sheep, leveraging his nephew's fame and social connections to further his own business ventures. Tonight would be no different.

Despite Uncle Leith's current discomfiture, he and Lord Aberdeen had much in common regarding how they viewed Ethan himself—

Everyone wanted something from him.

Nobles, like Lord Aberdeen and the frighteningly-ambitious Duke of Kendall, sought to exploit Ethan's popularity to further their own political aims. Uncle Leith expected Ethan to use his renown as the charismatic Highland Poet to prosper his business endeavors. Ethan's publisher wished to line his coffers with the profits from Ethan's writing. Ladies, both noble and otherwise, courted his attention, his body, and optimistically, his heart. The adoring public wanted his time, his voice, and at times, torn bits of his clothing.

It was all a sort of madness.

Some days, Ethan felt as though he would give up all his successes to find one person who wished nothing from him other than his own company.

Tonight, however, was not to be one of those occasions.

"Remember, you must speak with Kendall," Uncle Leith whispered in Ethan's ear. "I am counting on you to help secure a contract to ship saltpeter from the Salzi Mine in Austria."

As if Ethan could forget.

His own acquaintance with the Duke of Kendall was loose at best but more than Uncle Leith could claim. George Leith, Scottish minor gentry and distant relative of Lord Aberdeen, was not lofty enough to rub elbows with the likes of Kendall. But Ethan, in his fame, *was*.

More to the point, three years ago, Kendall had attempted to use Ethan's popularity to garner public support for some proposed legislation. Because of this, Kendall might be willing to entertain Ethan's request for the shipping contract—an opening that Uncle Leith intended to exploit with single-minded determination.

Lord Aberdeen finished his introduction to thunderous applause.

Ethan rose from his chair, the pleats of his kilt swaying. As usual, he wore the tartan of the Leith clan—a red-maroon background shot through with soft green and gold.

Nodding his thanks to Lord Aberdeen, Ethan took his place on the dais, the weight of over a hundred eyes pressing into him. Lord Aberdeen's London residence, Argyll House, was not located in fashionable Mayfair but rather sat on the outskirts of Westminster. Consequently, his lordship had yet to invest in gas lighting for his home, leaving the ballroom rather dim. His staff had perhaps overcompensated for this defect by placing a staggering number of candelabras between the stage where Ethan stood and his audience—turning the gathered aristocrats into murky shapes.

Ethan was glad of it. The vague shadows beyond the dais made it easier to perform, to sink into the persona of the Highland Poet.

Standing nonchalantly, he placed his left arm behind his back and moved his right foot forward, knowing the pose made his shoulders appear broader in his tightly-cut evening coat.

He might be a poet, but Ethan had long ago intuited a simple fact—the force of his persona could enhance the power of his verse.

It was the oddest thing . . . fame. He craved and loathed it in equal measure.

"Thank ye all for coming tonight," he began, loosening his Scottish brogue. If it was a wee bit thicker than usual, well, that was all part of his Highland Poet role. "It is a privilege tae find myself amongst so many illustrious ladies and gentlemen."

Ethan rattled on for a moment and then recited several poems from his latest publication. The crowd listened attentively, save for an elderly lord in the front row who kept coughing. Ethan would pause and allow the coughing to subside before continuing.

As usual, he saved his most popular poem for last.

"I ken that I can't leave tonight without reciting my most successful work tae date, 'Auld MacDougall in His Cups Reminisces; or One Kiss Alone.'"

A wave went through the crowd at his words. A female voice let out a high plaintive sigh, causing a ripple of soft laughter. The elderly lord coughed again. Three young bucks came rushing through the door, perhaps having been alerted that the highpoint of the evening's entertainment had arrived. Air swept in behind, blowing out several candles at the front of the stage, affording Ethan a clearer glimpse of the audience.

Of course, his gaze collided instantly with that of Uncle Leith, impatiently tapping his foot beside Ethan's empty seat on the front row. His uncle fixed him with a stern frown.

Right. Getting on with it then.

"As ye may already know," Ethan continued, "this work is a dramatic monologue, a poetic form popularized by Mr. Tennyson with the publication of his poem, 'Ulysses,' some years past. Permit me tae set the scene for my own poem. Imagine ye are sitting in the Lion Arms, an inn and public house in Fettermill, Scotland. Ye have just ordered a steak and ale pie, and as ye wait for your food tae arrive, ye can't help but overhear two men blethering at the table behind your own. *Auld MacDougall is at it again*, ye think, *telling his tales*. Ye lean in, curious tae hear what Auld MacDougall is saying:

> Nae, let us not leave yet. I would sit awhile
> Longer and enjoy MacKay's fine whisky.
> I am in earnest, my good man. Ye doubt
> My account and yet—What is that? Ye say
> I am one for tall tales? Bah! Perhaps.
> But in this, I swear the truth . . ."

Ethan continued reciting the long poem from memory, Auld MacDougall describing his encounter with bandits in Italy.

As he spoke, Ethan's eyes roamed the room, the occasional familiar face emerging from the shadows now that several of the candles were extinguished.

Ah, there was His Grace, the Duke of Kendall, sitting three rows back. The shock of light gray hair atop his tall head shimmered even in the dim light. The fact that the man was at least three years Ethan's junior rendered his aged coloring all the more striking. Ethan noted Kendall's position, knowing he would need to approach the duke before the evening ended.

Words tumbled from Ethan's mouth, even as he squinted to see other acquaintances and marked the audience's reaction to his poetry.

In the poem, Auld MacDougall described the precise sequence of events as they had occurred: the beautiful woman, the highwaymen, the hidden pistol, the double-cross, the kiss.

Ethan had decided *not* to write the tale as himself. Partially because his chosen poetic form, the dramatic monologue, required him to adopt a persona. Partially because he didn't wish his *ladra* harm. If the world merely thought the poem a fanciful story, then no one would issue an arrest warrant for a lovely dark-haired thief operating in the Dolomites of *Südtirol*.

But mostly, Ethan had chosen to tell the tale from another's perspective because he wished to treasure the memory instead of selling out every last aspect of it.

When the world owned so much of you, it was lovely to hold a piece back. A brilliant happenstance that sparkled like a jewel in his mind's eye alone.

Granted, Ethan did share the physical details of his *ladra* through Auld MacDougall's point of view:

> "Should I describe her as the poet doth?
> With hair of darkest jet, quicksilver eyes,
> And lips vermilion red? A fairytale
> Bound in tight-cut silk. Yet such pedantry
> Would mock her beauty. She appear'd a siren
> Of the night, and I, the helpless traveler,
> Caught in her snare . . ."

As usual, the words conjured her in his memory—the animated spark in her gray eyes as they bantered in the carriage, the haughty toss of her head as she turned his revolver on him, the startling press of her mouth to his—

Had she been born a lady? Or had that, too, been a fiction?

Truly, Ethan thought about her far more than was wise. Far more than those brief hours of conversation warranted.

And yet . . .

Perhaps it was the romantic in him, but the events of that afternoon felt momentous. A portent of sorts.

Had he the money, Ethan would hire an investigator to find his *ladra*. To assuage his curiosity and ensure that she had actually existed, that she had a name and a history. That those hours in the *vetturini* hadn't been some dazzling fever dream—a hallucination that he had confused for reality.

The poem continued onward. He described the wit of bantering with his *ladra* to a scattering of laughter and more female sighs. The arrival of the highwaymen elicited gasps.

He recited how his *ladra* snatched the revolver from his waistband—

"The metal, cold and firm, pressed to my spine
In her fair grip did find a hold . . ."

His eyes wandered back to the rows of the audience he could see, unerringly guided by Kendall's tall, gray head.

And there . . .

As if conjured by some meddling divinity—

His *ladra*.

In the very flesh.

Seated beside the Duke of Kendall.

Her dark hair was curled in the latest fashion, shoulders creamy-white above the violet silk of her evening gown.

Her wide eyes bored into his.

Shock jolted Ethan's spine, his voice trailing off.

No.

How could she be here? In England? In London?

Surely, he was mistaken.

Such a reality was impossible.

The words of his poem had merely bewitched his eyes, causing him to see his *ladra* in this unknown lady.

The elderly gentleman in the front row coughed again.

Spell broken, Ethan blinked and, looking away, resumed speaking.

But his eyes couldn't resist returning to the woman, searching for reasons to dismiss her as his wee thief.

How could it be her?

In his mind's eye, his *ladra* had grown and morphed from a mere

Italian lady bent on highway robbery to something more like an enchantress. A pagan goddess of mischief, as beautiful and dangerous as she was unattainable.

No part of him had ever expected to see her again.

And yet . . . the more he studied the unknown lady, the more he was convinced he was *not* mistaken.

It had to be her.

Somehow, some way . . .

His *ladra* was here.

Sitting beside the Duke of Kendall, looking as innocent and benign as an angel.

LADY ALLEGRA GILBERT was robbed of voice.

Truth be told, she scarcely breathed.

The Scot had recognized her.

Damnation.

This was a wrinkle she had *not* foreseen.

Allie had suspected it might be him when he had first taken the stage. That devastating grin lingered in her memory. Not to mention the looming breadth of his shoulders and tousled shock of chestnut-brown hair.

Then he had begun to recite the tale of their meeting.

Auld MacDougall reminisces, indeed. She mentally rolled her eyes.

Though her forbidden Scot hadn't lied about being a poet.

Mr. Ethan Penn-Leith.

She knew the name. His fame had even spread to rural Wiltshire and Hawthorn—the primary seat of the Dukes of Kendall—where her brother had condemned Allie to rusticate for the past six months. Her maid there couldn't speak the name *Ethan Penn-Leith* without blushing. Allie had teased the girl more than once over her infatuation with the Highland Poet.

Though speaking of blushing . . .

Allie forced herself not to squirm. Was this genuinely how Mr. Penn-Leith had seen her? A "fairy tale bound in tight-cut silk"?

Her aunt, Lady Whipple, shifted in her seat to Allie's right, adjusting her lorgnette and studying the Scottish poet with avid interest. Her aunt was not one to squander an opportunity to ogle a handsome man.

Kendall remained stock-still on her left, his hand fisted on his thigh, the ruby glint of his ducal signet ring flashing in the dim light.

Did her twin brother know that *she* was the woman in Mr. Penn-Leith's tale? And regardless of the answer, how could she use that fact to her advantage?

Mr. Penn-Leith's gaze returned to hers, though he didn't stumble over his words this time.

Instead, he held her eyes, as if they were the only two in the room and his poem were entirely for her ears alone.

He had accused her of being a "siren of the night," but at the moment, he was the bewitcher. And she the bewitched, snared by the rise and fall of his voice, dragged into the rhythm of his words.

Allie's pulse quickened. Heat warmed her cheeks.

Drat. She owed her maid an apology.

Worse, would Mr. Penn-Leith's presence here impact her plans?

No. She refused to scuttle everything due to his untimely appearance.

But then—*madonna mia!*—the Scot described their embrace, his eyes unerringly finding hers as he spoke. The intensity of his gaze—the intimacy of his words—scalded her.

She looked away, but his voice carried on:

> "Her lips a mulled wine kiss, velvet warm and lush—
> A soldier's greedy buss of leave-taking,
> Pouring breath and life into lungs bereft
> And weighted with fevered longing.
> Her cheek at my palm, silken and flushed.
> The beat of my heart, an anvil ringing."

Behind her, a lady let out a tremulous, "Ooooh!"—half gasp, half yearning sigh.

Allie nearly did the same.

Velvet warm and lush . . .

His words conjured the memory. The Scot's startled hitch of breath. A split-second hesitation of surprise. And then his ravenous reply, lips owning her own, branding, claiming—

The beat of my heart, an anvil ringing.

Fire and frost warred for dominance in Allie's chest.

Was she . . .

Was she . . . *blushing?*

She had thought blushing a reaction lost long ago . . . right along with her naiveté, hope, and belief in the goodness of the human race.

"Scandalous," Kendall muttered.

Allie glanced sideways. Her brother sported a formidable dent between his eyebrows.

"We should not have come tonight. I should have sent our regrets when Her Majesty declined to attend," he continued on a whisper. "Mr. Penn-Leith goes too far."

Well, if Allie hadn't liked Mr. Penn-Leith already, he would climb in her estimation simply for having irritated the mighty Duke of Kendall.

"You mean you regret not keeping me chained in my cage, Kendall?" she breathed in return.

Allie would never forgive him for kidnapping her as he had, not to mention the laudanum. Surely Saint Peter had reserved Kendall a special place in hell for that offense alone.

"Enough of this recalcitrance. I provide boundaries for your own good."

"I do believe that is precisely what any gaoler would say."

"You are not my prisoner."

"Truly, Kendall? Then you will deed over the Salzi Mine and permit me to return to Italy?"

"Cease this absurd obsession, Lady Allegra. Your future is here in England . . . with me."

Allie gritted her teeth and shoved the pain of his words down, down, down.

Once upon a time, her twin had been the other half of her soul. Their minds so attuned, they could complete one another's sentences.

Once upon a time, they had been Tristan and Allie to one another, not the stilted, formal *Kendall* and *Lady Allegra* of now.

As Tristan, he had been the brother who held her hand on nights when their dark nursery felt too oppressive. The one to dry her tears when their mother had ridden off again for London or Paris or whatever place their father demanded. The one to soothe Allie when their father lashed her with the caustic edge of his tongue—or worse, his fist.

As Allie, she had been the sister to coax Tristan outside when he had become too lost in a book. The one who had raced him from the home farm to the mill pond, seeing who could undress first before diving into the frigid water. The one who had fiercely defended him against anyone who mocked his shy nature, even their cruel father.

Now, it was as if the Tristan of her memory had been replaced by a terrifying automaton who resembled her twin but sounded and acted like their tyrannical sire.

She and her brother had become pugilists in opposing corners of a boxing ring—figuratively bludgeoning and bruising at every turn—all traces of their former connection erased.

Allie loathed Kendall. She would never forgive him for his perfidy. Years ago, in her greatest hour of need, he had spurned her cries for help and betrayed her to their father. Then last summer, Kendall had the audacity to have her drugged and kidnapped from Italy. When she finally landed on English soil, he immediately imprisoned her at Hawthorn. Before coming to London last week, she had only seen her twin three times since arriving in October.

For a woman who craved freedom, her existence was as constricted as possible without being in a literal prison. Her life's goal had devolved into ridding herself of Kendall's controlling leash. To seizing the reins of her own future once more.

Allie looked at the dais . . . which was probably a mistake.

Mr. Penn-Leith snared her gaze once more.

Truly, the Scot's attention was akin to cheery sun on a January day. Allie longed to bask in its captivating warmth, letting the warm rays soak into her winter-weary soul.

More the fool her.

Such an instinct would only hamper her plans.

And yet, she didn't look away.

From the corner of her eye, she noted the dent in Kendall's brow deepen. His fisted hand opened and closed on his thigh—practically a conniption fit for one so restrained.

Her twin glanced at her and then looked back to Mr. Penn-Leith.

Was he finally connecting the poem with her exploits in Italy?

Allie bit her lip. Her night had only needed this one final complication. No matter. She would persevere.

Allie had a plan. Kendall would rue the day he double-crossed her.

Mr. Penn-Leith finished the poem with a dramatic couplet:

> "But oft still I wonder, I must own,
> How Fate can turn on one kiss alone."

The room erupted into thunderous applause. The crowd surged to their feet.

Allie reluctantly followed suit.

Mr. Penn-Leith bowed, elegant and precise, his kilt swaying.

The man truly was far too attractive for his own good.

The crowd surged forward, everyone eager to speak with the charismatic Scot.

Lord Aberdeen hailed Kendall to her left.

A friend bent to say something to Lady Whipple on Allie's right, distracting her aunt from her chaperoning duties.

Perfect.

Expression polite and bland, Allie slipped behind two giggling débutantes and strode with purpose toward the servant's door hidden in the wall to the left of the dais.

H is *ladra* had escaped.

Again.

Ethan had been acutely aware of her every breath, noting with avid interest the blush darkening her high cheekbones as he described their illicit kiss.

It *had* to be her.

But how?

And . . . why?

She passed not ten feet from him before slipping through the servant's door hidden in the damask wallpaper of Lord Aberdeen's third-floor ballroom.

Ethan had tried to capture her attention, but she had steadfastly ignored him.

And now, he stood on the dais, surrounded by enthusiastic well-wishers—aristocrats that Uncle Leith expected him to woo and charm.

What to do?

Scanning the crowd, Ethan smiled at an elderly lady—who chirped her appreciation of his use of metaphor—while simultaneously searching for a way to hasten after his *ladra*.

"You seem distracted, lad." Uncle Leith appeared at Ethan's side, his voice a low murmur. "I need you focused. As soon as Lord Aberdeen lets Kendall go, you must be at His Grace's side."

Ethan spared a glance for Kendall and Aberdeen. Given how emphatically Aberdeen was speaking—his gnarled finger pointing and white head bobbing—the two men were going to be at it for a while.

Ethan had a moment or two of time still.

If only . . .

Bending down, Ethan whispered to his uncle. "I *am* a wee bit distracted. I shouldn't have had that second glass of wine with dinner. I must seek out the water-closet."

Uncle Leith shot him a monstrous frown. "Truly?"

His uncle surveyed Ethan as if he were ten years old again and too gauche to survive genteel life.

Ethan did as he always had—he smiled his most winning, sheepish grin.

"Be quick." Uncle Leith jerked his chin toward the servant's doorway in the corner. "I'll give your apologies."

Wasting no time, Ethan slipped through the door. The passageway was dimly lit, extending from left to right along the length of the ballroom. A spiral staircase stood in the right-hand corner.

Where are ye? he thought.

The soft shush of silk skirts reached his ears from the right.

Ah. She had gone down the stairs.

Ethan rushed after, round and round the spiral staircase, descending toward the servants' domain in the basement. Once he reached the bottom, he turned down a long, shadowy corridor, his *ladra* a rustle of fabric drawing him forward.

Finally, he ran her to ground before a delivery door. She was bent over as if peering into the lock.

What the devil was she up to? And how could she see a blessed thing in this dim hallway?

He cleared his throat.

She gave a startled "Eeep!" and whirled around to face him, chest rapidly rising and falling in her surprise.

They stared at one another for a long, breathless moment, her gray eyes glinting in the darkness.

Unbidden, Ethan's eyes skimmed the vast expanse of her creamy skin on display—bare shoulders, elegant collarbones. The purple silk of her dress shimmered even in the low light, the deep V of its fashionable waistline accentuating the glorious curve of her nipped waist.

Heat expanded his lungs.

Just as in that carriage last summer, she clubbed his senses.

And just as then, he felt an unbidden sense of familiarity, as if he had seen her before.

"You," she said, hand pressed to her bare décolletage, lungs still heaving.

"Aye. Me." He leaned a shoulder against the wall to his left, crossing his arms. "Imagine meeting yourself like this."

"Yes. Imagine." Her dry tone was all the confirmation he needed of her identity.

He grinned.

She blinked.

"So, it *is* you," he murmured.

She shrugged, lifting that delicate jaw of hers.

How was she even more lovely than his memory?

"Ethan Penn-Leith, at your service, *la mia ladra*." He sketched a brief bow.

"Hmm, I gathered as much, Mr. Penn-Leith. Do you always command such fanfare?" She waved a hand, indicating the fuss in the ballroom three stories above their heads.

"I did tell ye I was a poet," he replied . . . and then frowned. "Your English is remarkably aristocratic. You seem to have misplaced your Italian accent."

Her hand dipped into the poof of her voluminous skirts. A wee furrow dented her forehead as she rummaged through her pocket.

"Thank you. It *is* my native tongue." She paused her searching, raking him up and down, eyes lingering meaningfully on his kilt. "I am not sure I can say as much for yourself."

Her dry teasing startled a laugh out of him.

"*Och*, insulting the Scot for his accent, are ye, lass?" Ethan deepened his brogue, leaning forward. "Say no more, my lady. I believe ye tae be English now. Though I'm well-puzzled as tae why ye were pretending tae be an Italian lady of dubious origins and accosting—"

"Would you be so kind?" She pulled a candle and candlestick from her skirts and extended them both to him.

He hefted the fine brass candlestick in his hand. "You hid this in such a lovely dress?"

"Of course." She flashed him a grin so sunny it caused his breath to hitch. "It has pockets."

With a flourish, she produced a box of lucifer matches, carefully extracting one.

"Why do ye need light?" Ethan asked, placing the candle into the holder. "I'm more than willing to describe my handsome face for ye."

Though it was too dark to tell, he suspected she rolled her eyes.

"Your flirtation is relentless, Mr. Penn-Leith."

"Thank ye."

"But I can't very well pick this lock in the dark now, can I?" She motioned to the delivery door at her back.

"Pardon? The key isn't already in the lock?" Reaching around her, he inspected the bare lock and then tried the handle to no avail. "How odd. Why lock a servant's door from the inside?"

"I assume because the Duke of Kendall ordered all the exterior doors locked or guarded tonight. This door should be one of the last areas he will search."

She struck the match and, shielding the flame, lit the candle in Ethan's hand.

He blinked, the sudden illumination bringing the planes of her face into focus. The candlelight loved her, lending her skin a soft pearlescence and catching in her silvery eyes.

Bloody hell, but she was bonnie.

It took him a moment to process what she had just said.

"Search? And did ye say *Kendall*?" Ethan squinted at her. "Why would the Duke of Kendall order Lord Aberdeen tae lock all his doors?"

Her fine eyebrows winged upward. "To prevent me from escaping, of course."

"Pardon?"

"Tristan is a controlling arse at the best of times." She twisted and began to rustle through another pocket.

"Tristan?" Ethan struggled to follow the thread of her conversation. "Who the devil is Tristan?"

She paused and then, rolling her free hand, continued on a sigh, "Tristan Gilbert. Duke of Kendall. The boorishly arrogant halfwit with whom I once, unfortunately, shared a womb. You know, *that* Tristan."

She pulled a long pouch that clanked with tools from her pocket and, leaning into the light, began rifling through it.

Ethan stared at the crown of her lovely head for several seconds, his mouth slightly ajar.

He counted to six before his brain managed to fit all the puzzle pieces together.

"Ye be Kendall's twin sister." Ethan could hear the surprise in his voice. "Lady Allegra Gilbert."

"In the flesh, unfortunately." She turned to the locked door. "Give me five minutes, however, and I will be but another memory for a poem to make women swoon." She tapped the door frame beside her head. "Would you be so kind as to hold the candle just here?"

Stepping into the fullness of her skirts, Ethan obliged. Her perfume intoxicated him, exotic jasmine and ambergris. No pedestrian rose water or lavender oil for his *ladra* . . . ehr, Lady Allegra.

His mind whirled, trying to merge the persona of his wee *ladra* with what he knew of Kendall's twin sister. Uncle Leith had mentioned something last week about Lady Allegra having accompanied her brother to London. For years, she had been living with her mother's relatives on the Continent, but that was all anyone knew. This was to be her first London Season.

For her part, Lady Allegra began expertly setting pins in the lock.

"I do admire the expansive education you have received, my lady." He nodded toward her tools. "Ye are a woman of many talents, I suspect."

"*Grazie,*" was the only reply he received.

Studying her profile as she worked, he realized why she had felt familiar the first time they met.

"Ye have the look of your brother," he said without thinking.

She froze and, lifting her head, fixed him with such a *glare*. "And here I thought you charming. Why would you say something so mean-spirited?"

Ethan spluttered for an answer, because with her eyes narrowed and jaw set, the resemblance to Kendall was almost uncanny.

"He might be an arse, as ye said, but he's not an *unhandsome* one."

With a sniff, Lady Allegra turned back to the lock. "That could win a prize ribbon for the most backward compliment ever delivered."

Ethan smiled.

Lady Allegra labored in silence for a few moments, her fingers working adeptly.

"Why not go out a window?" he asked, conversationally.

"In this dress? I cannot see my feet without assistance." She peered up at him. "Why? Are you offering to help?"

"No. I would prefer not tae displease His Grace at the moment."

She snorted. "You and the rest of London."

"My uncle requires a shipping contract, ye ken, and—"

"Let me guess?" she sighed. "The saltpeter mine?"

"Aye, the very same. Kendall's mine will prove—"

"Kendall's mine?!" She glared up at Ethan. "The Salzi Mine belongs to me. Or it would . . . if my cursed sire and domineering brother hadn't taken it for themselves. And now Kendall holds me prisoner—"

"Wait—ye are a prisoner?" Alarm zinged Ethan's spine.

"Yes. Keep up." She rattled the door, as if to emphasize her point, before bending to her lock picks again. "Kendall has me guarded day and night. This evening marks the first occasion His Grace has permitted me to mingle with others of the *ton*. I've put my dearest brother in a pickle, you see. He cannot auction me off in marriage to the highest bidding lordling without trotting me out to balls and soirées, showcasing the goods on offer, as it were. But every excursion affords me opportunity to escape or see myself properly ruined. Or both, truthfully. Kendall should have anticipated that I would be three steps ahead of him tonight. I will be far gone before morning."

If Lady Allegra thought to stem Ethan's concerns, she was utterly mistaken.

His alarm grew.

"Does Kendall know about your exploits in Italy?"

"I assume so. We don't speak of it, of course. Kendall rarely condescends to converse with me. But I am quite sure he does not know of *our* connection." She brightened, darting a glance up at him. "You should tell everyone I am the woman in the poem. Do you think that would ruin me sufficiently?"

This woman. She would be the death of him. "Ye don't want tae be ruined."

Ethan knew the grim lot of noblewomen who found themselves outside the fold of the *ton*.

"Permit me to be the judge of that. Ruination would make me useless for Kendall's aims, which in turn, would force him to cast me off, hopefully back to Italy. Tonight has been my first chance to see it properly done, and I am seizing the opportunity."

Again, not comforting. Much as it pained him to admit, Ethan could understand why Kendall was so intent on restricting Lady Allegra's movements.

The woman seemed hellbent on self-destruction.

"So where will ye go tonight?" he asked.

"I shall not tell you. You would run right back to my brother with the information. Or worse, he would extract it from you in some unsavory way."

"I don't ken that Kendall stoops tae torture."

"Of course not. Torture would sully his kid-leather gloves. He is much too Machiavellian for such bourgeois behavior. He would merely threaten to see your elderly Aunt Sara evicted from her cottage. Or ensure that your publisher drops your works." The lock clicked. "Ah-hah!"

Lady Allegra began tucking her tools back into the pouch with startling alacrity.

"Meeting you like this has been lovely, Mr. Penn-Leith," she said, "but here we must part ways."

She held out her hand for the candle. Ethan lifted it higher and stepped between her and the door. "Ye cannot mean to rush out into

London in that absurdly expensive dress, hail a hansom cab, and dash off tae heaven knows where. Ye will be robbed and assaulted faster than it took ye tae pick this lock."

Crossing her arms, Lady Allegra scowled at him. "Really, Mr. Penn-Leith. Our time together has always been delightful. Do not taint our memories with hysteria. You know perfectly well I am more than capable of taking care of myself."

Och, she would drive him mad. "Have ye spent any time in London, my lady? Do ye know the city at all? At least, permit me tae escort ye tae wherever ye have arranged lodging for the evening. If something were tae happen to your bonnie self, I cannot think—"

"I am hardly your concern, Mr. Penn-Leith," she snapped. "Please return my candle and remove yourself from the doorway!"

"Lady Allegra, the gentleman in me simply cannot—"

"Well, this is quite the scene." The aristocratic tones of the Duke of Kendall resonated down the dim hall.

Ethan peered over Lady Allegra's head to see her brother emerging from the dark passage, gray head gleaming in the candlelight.

Both Kendall and Lady Allegra looked about two seconds away from skewering Ethan.

Truly, the resemblance between the siblings was remarkable.

"Your Grace." Ethan inclined his head. "Pleasure tae see ye again, as usual." His breeding was too reflexive to do anything but greet a duke with formal politeness. Besides, if Ethan made an enemy of Kendall, his uncle would disinherit him.

"Penn-Leith." Kendall looked at Ethan, dark eyes blazing. "How odd to find you here."

"Simply trying tae help," Ethan replied, faintly. He was surely seconds away from receiving a blistering set-down.

However, Kendall's attention moved to his sister, dismissing Ethan entirely.

Lady Allegra morphed before Ethan's eyes—gaze hardening, chin lifting, shoulders tensing.

Here was a woman prepared to battle.

"How charming," she hissed at her brother. "My prison warden has arrived."

Ethan's eyes widened at her tone.

Kendall, however, did not so much as flinch.

"Lady Allegra." He nodded. "I do believe the coachman is awaiting our departure."

"Eager to return me to my cage, are you, Duke? Maybe include some shackles this time?"

Ethan barely stifled a gasp.

Lady Allegra was high-spirited and forthright, but baiting Kendall so vociferously could only harm herself.

The duke visibly stiffened.

"As always, your comfort is my only goal, my lady," Kendall replied, the urbane smoothness of his voice belying the anger crackling in his gaze.

"Of course, it is." Lady Allegra's words dripped acid.

"If you please." Kendall motioned back down the dark hallway.

With an Italian curse, Lady Allegra pushed past him, head held high, silk skirts rustling as she retreated.

Kendall stared at the candle in Ethan's hand for a long moment, his breaths labored, hands clenched at his sides.

It was odd to see the duke so motionless.

Mentally, Ethan equated Kendall with a temperamental stallion—a volatile animal best handled with caution.

And possibly sugar cubes and the occasional carrot.

Given the taut tension in the air, Ethan scarcely breathed, fearful that his slightest gesture might elicit a sharp response.

Though only an inch taller than Ethan, the duke loomed. The man's preternaturally gray hair glowed in the dim light, contrasting starkly with his youthful face and dark eyes. It was said his sire, the former Duke of Kendall, had sported a shock of white hair by the time he was thirty. The current duke appeared on track to perhaps best his father's record.

Swallowing hard, Ethan handed Kendall the still-lit candle in its elegant brass holder.

"Your sister is . . ." Ethan trailed off, desperately searching for an innocuous adjective.

"Elegance and poise?" Kendall finished for him, the words clipped.

"Aye," Ethan agreed, thankfully erasing any trace of sarcasm from his tone.

"Lady Allegra is the soul of discretion and all that is proper in one of genteel birth," Kendall continued, glancing back at his sister's retreating shadow. "As I would hope you yourself to be, Mr. Penn-Leith."

Ah.

This, Ethan understood. He hadn't survived Eton and Oxford by being a lackwit who disregarded clear warnings.

"Of course, Your Grace. I am a gentleman to my core." Lady Allegra might hate Ethan for interfering with her escape into the streets of London, but he did not regret his decision.

Besides, it never hurt to have a carrot to dangle when hoping to coax Kendall into a certain course of action.

The duke wasn't the only one capable of Machiavellian stratagems.

"If you will excuse me." Kendall dipped his head at Ethan, pivoted, and walked a wee bit too quickly after his sister.

3

Allie could feel Kendall seething at her side as he escorted her down Lord Aberdeen's front steps toward the waiting town coach, their family coat of arms gleaming on the door.

Oh, her ducal brother hid it well behind a banal expression, but the clenched fist against his thigh gave him away.

He was furious over her attempted escape.

Good. *Bene.*

Let him stew, the blackguard.

"I sent Lady Whipple home ahead of us," he said *sotto voce*, words clipped. "You will not need her chaperonage for this."

This, Allie suspected, was to be a thorough dressing down.

"Yes. Let us spare dear Auntie Whipple having to witness a scene." Allie's own tone was as dry as day-old toast.

Lady Whipple adored a scene—the louder and gossipier the better. Assuredly, she had vehemently protested being sent home alone.

Reaching the carriage, Kendall motioned for Allie to precede him. He might be holding her prisoner but heaven forbid his manners slip.

Allie smiled and nodded to the footman, Thomas, waiting at attention beside the open coach door. She had been on a mission to charm Kendall's servants into giving their devotion to her. Unfortunately, her brother paid well and expected allegiance and loyalty in return.

It had been a slow battle.

But as Allie placed her gloved hand in Thomas's to be assisted into the carriage, she felt the telltale rasp of foolscap against her fingers.

Hah!

Without missing a beat, Allie palmed the scrap of paper as she settled onto the carriage seat.

I will win over the servants yet.

Behind her, Kendall looked up to speak with the coachman. Allie took advantage of his momentary distraction to glance at the foolscap, tilting it into the lamplight just outside the carriage window. An inky scrawl jumped off the white paper.

> *Tu sei stata avvisata. Ed ora, ho fatto come ti avevo detto. Aiutaci o rivelerò al mondo il tuo passato.*
> *—F*

Allie barely suppressed a sigh as she slipped the message into her pocket.

Of course.

Like squawking homing pigeons, the events of that momentous day last August were returning home to roost this evening.

First, Mr. Penn-Leith.

And now, another attempt at blackmail from Fabrizio.

Staring sightlessly out the carriage window, she replayed the note in her head.

You were warned. And now, I have done as I said I would. Help us, or I will reveal your past to the world.

Honestly, Fabrizio and his Italian flare for the dramatic.

The man did not understand how little she cared. His threats and demands for money were pointless. She had nothing left to lose. Any information he revealed about her time in Italy would only aid her and plague her ducal brother.

Why wasn't Fabrizio blackmailing Kendall? Her brother was the one who cared about protecting her reputation as a pristine lady. And his deep pockets had clearly paid for Fabrizio's services in the past. Allie could still taste the laudanum on her tongue.

Likely, Fabrizio saw her as the easier target.

More the fool him.

The coach rocked as Kendall finished speaking with the coachman and climbed into the seat opposite her, facing against the flow of traffic.

Again, beautifully mannered, her brother.

Pity it didn't extend to his soul.

The carriage lurched into motion.

Allie noted Kendall's tight fist now resting on the seat beside his thigh. Did his knuckles ache at night given how hard he clenched them when in her presence?

The Tristan of her childhood had been a shy, quiet boy who listened to her monologue about the travels she intended to take, his dark soulful eyes attentive. She had never called him Lord Hawthorn—the courtesy title of the Dukedom of Kendall. Instead, from her earliest memory, she had insisted on being his equal in everything, including using their proper Christian names with one another.

Back then, Tristan had been the brother who had sat beside her sick bed reading *Fabulous Histories* and *Tales from Shakespeare* to stave off her boredom. The boy who had wiped her tears whenever an encounter with their father became physical.

But the autocratic, cold gentleman sitting opposite her now was none of those things.

The Tristan Allie knew had perished at some point. And in his place, a hard man had emerged—power-hungry, arrogant, and despotic. Now reigning as the mighty Duke of Kendall, her twin aimed for the Prime Minister's seat and a role in governing the country.

Allie had no doubt he would succeed eventually. The man was too bloody single-minded to do otherwise.

But for now, Queen Victoria considered Kendall, at barely twenty-seven years of age, a bit too young for the title of Prime Minister. She preferred more seasoned statesmen like Lord Aberdeen for the position.

That didn't stop Kendall from campaigning, however—collecting political favors and governmental influence the way other men amassed horses or lovers. Every duke needed a hobby, she supposed. Kendall had chosen his.

"I instructed the coachman to drive an aimless route through the city," Kendall said into the coach's silence. "I will inform him when we are to return home."

Ah. "Giving yourself adequate time to castigate me?"

"There is no need for the servants to overhear our private business."

"Is that what you call my captivity now? Our 'private business'?"

Was it her imagination, or did Kendall sigh at her words? His right knee bounced in the dim light.

Allie jerked her chin away and stared out at the gaslit streets passing by, the cobblestones glistening with evening dew.

Why did her foolish heart still faintly pang at the sight of her twin's distress?

He kidnapped you, she bitterly reminded herself. *He has spent the last eight months ensuring you have no options other than the paltry ones he offers you.*

"I know you are angry with me—" he began.

"Understatement that."

"—but matters do not need to be like this between us. We can be allies—"

"Allies?! *Porca miseria!* Do you even understand the meaning of that word?"

"Watch your language, Lady Allegra."

"Like *hell* I will! Would you prefer I use the English *dammit* instead?"

"I would prefer for you to cease this endless waspishness. United, we could—"

"We will *never* be allies, Kendall. You left me a prisoner at Hawthorn for nearly eight months—my every move watched around the clock and scarcely a word from yourself. London has been no better. My entire existence is a cold misery at present. Those are not the actions of an ally."

Kendall's back stiffened, his eyes black pools in the darkness. "I clothe you in silks, and instead of gratitude, I receive accusations of—"

"*Bah!* You dress me in silks for the same reason a horse merchant brushes out a filly's coat—you wish to attract a high-bidding buyer when the brood mare goes to auction. Only the venue, Tattersall's or Almack's, marks the difference."

"I grow weary of your recalcitrant behavior and crass tongue." Kendall gave her his profile, staring out the window. "You would be wise to not provoke me."

Allie nearly snorted in reply.

Misbehavior was the only weapon she had at her disposal. She would continue to make his life a living hell until he set her free.

"And as I keep repeating, you do not have to tolerate my 'crass tongue.' Merely return the two things I prize most—the Salzi Mine and my freedom—and you shall never see nor hear from me again."

"Your absence is not my aim, Lady Allegra. I value your comfort and happiness." He whipped his gaze back to hers. "Besides, our mother deeded the mine to our father, and well you know it. The mine belongs to the dukedom now."

"Mamma signed it away under duress. To save her life and possibly my own. Could you truly have forgotten how those events played out? I remember you raging about it at the time."

The guttering street lamps rimmed a muscle twitching in Kendall's jaw. "Those events occurred in another life, Lady Allegra. Do not think me the soft boy I was then."

Tossing her head, Allie turned away, gazing out her window once more. The yellow glow of the gaslight reflected off the low-hanging clouds and the spires of Westminster Abbey looming ahead.

She *hated* thinking upon their parents' grim history and the gaping wound of Tristan's loss that had resulted. And yet, with her brother following so closely in their father's vile footsteps, the pain of the past blazed bright.

Their sire, the old Duke of Kendall, had been a revolting excuse of a human being. Convicted of bigamy nearly thirty years prior, he had found himself fifty years of age, divorced, and lacking a legitimate heir. Undaunted, he had wasted no time in courting the twins' mother, Lady Beatrice Barozzi, a young Italian beauty of Venetian descent.

Allie and Tristan were born within ten months of their parent's marriage.

As her dowry, their mother had brought the oldest salt mine in Europe into the marriage—the Salzi Mine in southern Austria. As per family tradition, the salt mine passed from mother to daughter, trailing the maternal line down through the centuries. Therefore, the mine was listed as Beatrice's separate personal property in the marriage contracts, leaving it under her sole control.

Allie supposed their overbearing father had assumed he would cow his young wife into turning control of the mine over to himself.

In that, he had erred.

Their mother had been fierce in her defense of herself, and by extension, her children. She held on to the mines with an iron fist, using the wealth they produced to extract concessions from her husband, to temper his autocratic demands and cruel tendencies.

But as the years passed, the elder Kendall's behavior grew more and more violent—his caustic words usually punctuated with his fist—until Beatrice feared for her life. After all, if she met an unfortunate 'accident,' Kendall would automatically receive the salt mines in their entirety.

And so, when the twins were ten years of age, a final deal was struck.

Kendall would grant Beatrice a divorce: a *divortium a mensa et thoro* to use the precise legal phrase—a separation of bread and board. In short, Beatrice would no longer be Kendall's financial responsibility, and he would no longer contribute to her upkeep. In return, the old duke would have no further legal claim on her. She would be free.

In exchange for such freedom, Beatrice agreed to sign full ownership of the Salzi Mine over to Kendall.

But Beatrice wrung one last boon out of her husband: she insisted Allie accompany her. The duke would never have released Tristan, his heir, to her care. But he did permit Beatrice to take 'the girl.'

Allie flinched away from the memories of that day.

Of those last hours together with her brother, huddled in her bed—ten years old and aware that the only life she had known was about to change forever.

"This is not addio*," Tristan had whispered, eyes red-rimmed like her own. "We will not wait until we are before God to see each other. This goodbye is* arrivederci—*until we see one another again."*

"*Father is so angry,*" Allie had hiccupped in return, swiping away her messy tears. Tristan handed her his handkerchief. "*He will never permit Mamma or me to return to Hawthorn. He won't even let us write letters. We will be lost to you!*"

Tristan shook his head, gaze earnest and so stubbornly determined. "*Nothing will stop me from seeking you out once I am of age. As soon as I am able, I will hunt the world over for you. You and I . . . we are forever, Allie.*"

How fierce he had appeared in that moment. So confident that his love for her would never abate, never change.

But change . . . everything had.

Not even an hour later, Allie had followed Mamma down the steps to a hired coach waiting before Hawthorn's front doors. Only Tristan came to see them off. The Duchess of Kendall spared a few words and an embrace for her son before climbing into the carriage.

But Allie held him firmly and whispered a watery, *I love you,* into his ear before following their mother. Pressing her nose against the carriage glass, Allie had watched until Tristan's tear-streaked face faded into the distance.

We are forever, Allie.

That vulnerable ten-year-old girl hadn't known then that their good-bye had actually been *addio* in the end—*to God.* Never to be seen again in this life.

An ache lodged in her throat.

Allie ruthlessly swallowed it back.

She was made of sterner stuff now.

Paradoxically, the belief that Tristan—*her* Tristan—waited for her had given Allie the strength to forge her soul into steel over the intervening years.

How bitterly ironic, as she now wielded that same inner steel against him.

Allie adjusted her skirts, watching Westminster Abbey roll past as the carriage turned onto Whitehall.

"If you could control your harpy tongue for even five minutes, Lady Allegra," Kendall's voice cracked over the clatter of the coach wheels on flagstone, "you would learn that I will, in fact, be returning the salt mines to you."

Allie looked at her brother, expression surely stunned and incredulous. Was this . . .

Was this *finally* a faint glimmer of the boy she had known?

"Truly?" Allie could hear the hope lacing her words. "When? And how?"

"Upon your marriage to a man of my choosing. As your dowry."

Allie's spirits plummeted.

Marriage. Of course.

More the fool her to soften toward her twin for even one second. Kendall had kidnapped her for this very reason, after all. She was to be a marital pawn in his bid for power.

"As my . . . *dowry*." She inflected the word *dowry* with the same disdain as *taxes* or *a pox*. "If so, the mines will belong to my husband, not myself. So they are not my own, but instead the carrot you will extend to see me married off like the brood mare I am. You speak lies, Duke."

Kendall's chest heaved.

"The Salzi Mine has made you the most eligible of heiresses," he snapped, "and this despite your advanced years and—"

"Advanced years?! You call me *una zitella* . . . a spinster." Her eyes narrowed. "I know this may be difficult for you to recall, Your Grace, but we are, in fact, the same age. That makes you *uno zitello,* a . . . a . . ." Allie floundered, searching for the male equivalent of a *spinster* in English, but came up empty. ". . . an old bachelor," she concluded lamely.

As a language, English was sometimes decidedly lacking.

"Must I now explain to you how life is different for men than for women?" he asked, voice dripping with condescension. "Surely you are intelligent enough to grasp that?"

Allie was fairly certain her eyes had devolved into flames.

Uffa. Was fratricide legal if one were sufficiently provoked?

"As I was saying," her twin continued, "despite your age, many have already petitioned me for the privilege of courting you. The value of the recent saltpeter discovery cannot be underestimated."

The saltpeter.

Of course.

Several months past, a vein of pure mineral saltpeter had been discovered in a section of the Salzi Mine that hadn't been worked since the medieval age. Typically, saltpeter manufacture was an arduously slow process involving vats of dung and ashes left to rot for years on end. But in a select few places, saltpeter could be mined.

The discovery of such saltpeter had been a revelation. Why, even Mr. Penn-Leith had mentioned it this evening—his uncle sought a contract to ship the saltpeter to market ports in England.

Heaven knew Kendall didn't need the financial gains the saltpeter offered. But he did crave the connections and power it promised, particularly in wooing potential suitors for herself.

However, there was delicious havoc to be wreaked as a lauded heiress on the marriage mart. If Fabrizio's promised retribution didn't destroy her reputation, Allie would still have ample possibility to see the task done. And with her reputation in tatters, Kendall would cast her off as useless. She wouldn't receive her salt mine, but she would be a free woman.

Her mind whirred with plans.

"Gentlemen have petitioned to pay me court?" she asked, her voice all curious innocence. "That means I will have to attend more social events in order to meet them properly, will I not?"

"Knowing your general recalcitrance, Lady Allegra, I have calibrated my plans accordingly," Kendall said, tone far too casual for Allie's liking. "This will perhaps overset you, but—"

Allie scoffed in contempt.

"—just yesterday I finalized negotiations with your future husband. There will be no busy social calendar or opportunities for mischief. This entire affair will require nothing more than your presence before a vicar. I hope to have the marriage contracts signed in the next few weeks."

At the age of twelve, Allie had stumbled while disembarking from a *traghetto* after crossing the Grand Canal in Venice. She had pitched forward, the bow of the gondola cracking into her sternum and knocking the breath from her lungs as sure and true as her sire's fist.

Kendall's words landed a similar blow.

Allie's lungs refused air for several seconds.

The bars of her cage clanged.

"You have already found me a husband? And so quickly?" she hissed. "You couldn't wait for a ripping good day at Tattersall's to do the deed?"

"Lady Allegra, despite everything of which you accuse me, I *do* wish to see you properly settled and your future secured."

"By selling me to a man I do not know and was not permitted a single opinion in choosing? Do not attempt to turn your high-handed domineering into some sort of martyred goodness."

"You are hysterical, and such language is most unbecoming of a—"

Oh! "You auction me off, body and soul, to some unknown man who will take me to his bed and *rut* his pleasure on my body, very likely against my will—"

"Enough with your vulgarities!"

"—a man who will then own me like chattel for the rest of my life, all for the sole purpose of furthering *your* political aims. And if I protest this treatment, I am then branded as hysterical! You learned our father's lessons well, Duke. Will you strike me now to ensure my compliance?"

She and her brother glared at one another, their harsh breathing filling the coach.

Kendall's nostrils flared. His hand flexed.

Would he strike her? Their father had been a violent man, but her brother, despite Allie's relentless attacks over the past week together, had yet to raise a hand against her.

Was this how their father had begun? Intimidation and demands evolving into threats and physical violence as the years passed?

Allie watched the slow bob of Kendall's Adam's apple.

With a frustrated *click* of his teeth, he whirled to stare out his window once more.

They rolled across Trafalgar Square and turned onto Pall Mall, gas lamps blinking past the carriage windows. Gentlemen stumbled out of their clubs, leaning on shoulders and calling to one another.

Allie licked her lips. "Who is this paragon of manhood you expect me to sacrifice myself to like a meek lamb?"

Silence for another beat.

"His name is Lord Charswood." Kendall turned back to her. "He is a good match for you, Sister. I would not—" Here he broke off with a jerk, swallowing again. His fingers drummed on the leather seat. "I am appalled at the thought of striking a woman, much less yourself. More to the point, after suffering through our father's behavior, I would never subject you to a cruel husband."

Interesting.

Allie didn't believe him on either account, but . . . interesting.

"Ah yes, what every young woman dreams of—a husband who doesn't beat her bloody. I cannot wait for such marital bliss!" Allie clasped her hands to her bosom and batted her eyelashes in a mockery of maidenly delight. "Pray tell me about this man so I may bask in giddy rapture over this blessed event. Is he handsome? Witty? Kind? Capable of intelligent conversation?"

Unbidden, the image of Mr. Ethan Penn-Leith rose in her mind's eye. The low rumble of his laughter. The way he looked at her with curiosity and amusement, but also . . . Allie had to grasp for the word . .. kindness. The memory of his mouth on hers, the way her whole body had thrummed to life, eagerly rising to meet his—

She brutally batted the thoughts away.

"Lord Charswood is a man of mature years," Kendall said, caution edging his tone.

"Old, you mean. He's old. How old?"

A long pause and then, "I believe his lordship has recently celebrated his sixtieth year."

"Sixty?! You are proposing I marry a man old enough to be my grandfather? Have you an ounce of compassion left in your black heart?"

"Charswood is a good man."

"Of course he is. And let me guess." Allie tapped her lips with a finger. "He also has business ties to saltpeter you wish to exploit and political power you are desperate to add to your own."

Kendall's dark glare and ringing silence were answer enough. "Do not dismiss this out of hand, Lady Allegra. You are being unreasonable. We will be traveling to Scotland within a fortnight for—"

"Scotland?!"

"Yes, Scotland. The Earl of Hadley is hosting a political gathering at his estate. Lord Charswood will be in attendance, giving you the opportunity to come to know his lordship."

The carriage turned sharply off Pall Mall and onto St. James Street. Allie braced a hand against the door.

"And then what?" she said. "I will certainly refuse to go along with your plan. We live in a modern age. No matter how you threaten or browbeat me, you cannot force me to marry."

"Lady Allegra—"

"I will not comply with your wishes, Kendall. You have removed every choice from me. My back is against a wall with nothing to lose. I will find a way out of my prison."

Allie's harsh breathing filled the coach's interior.

The wheels rocked over the cobblestone streets, braces squeaking.

"And yet . . . ," Kendall said slowly, ". . . you are still here. You are far too intelligent to have *not* escaped your 'cage,' as you call it, were you truly determined."

Allie hated him in that moment. Hated that her twin, even now, knew her so well. That enough of Tristan remained within his cold heart to see through her so clearly.

Yes, she did want her freedom. But part of her was still that little girl curled up in her twin brother's embrace. Still the sister who ached to reunite with him.

When would she finally permit that dream to die?

"Do not let that thought lull you into complaisance, Your Grace." She folded her hands in her lap.

"I am not wrong, Lady Allegra. The stunt you pulled tonight with Mr. Penn-Leith was merely that—a stunt. You allowed him to thwart you."

Silence again.

Allie said nothing, as Kendall was correct—damn him. She *had* permitted the Scot to waylay her plans.

"Or is there perhaps more I should know about your relationship with Penn-Leith?" Kendall continued. "I could have sworn you had no prior acquaintance with him before tonight and yet . . ."

Innuendo dripped off the end of her brother's ellipses.

Allie laughed. "What are you suggesting, Kendall? That Mr. Penn-Leith and I are lovers?"

"Hardly. I have known Mr. Penn-Leith for a number of years, and the man is far too honorable to seduce a young lady. But you cannot deny his poetry affected you. You were practically hanging off his every word.

Moreover, I have only once seen Mr. Penn-Leith show genuine interest in an eligible lady. He tends to flirt outrageously but nothing more. Yet, he broke free of his uncle's tether to run you to ground."

A thrill chased Allie's spine.

She immediately quashed the emotion.

Ethan Penn-Leith had merely been eager to confirm her identity.

Yet . . . how differently would she feel about Kendall's machinations if Mr. Penn-Leith were the groom who awaited her? And who was this other woman Mr. Penn-Leith had shown interest in?

But perhaps most importantly, how could it help her if Kendall knew *she* was the woman in Mr. Penn-Leith's famous poem? Could she threaten to go to the press with the information? Or would that merely encourage her brother to tighten his grip on her cage?

She would have to ponder the ramifications carefully before she acted.

"Penn-Leith is not for you, of course," Kendall continued. "A fact I shall be sure to inform him of when next I see him."

Of course.

"No need to go to such effort. Someday soon, you will turn around and find me gone for good."

"Or you could see that I truly *do* want what is best for you."

"Does that lie help you sleep at night?"

"No, Lady Allegra, it does not," her brother snorted, soft and low, before pinning her with his dark eyes. "As I said at the beginning of this conversation, we could be allies, you and I. Bury our hatchets and embrace a more harmonious relationship."

"Become your docile, obedient handmaiden, you mean? No, thank you," Allie sneered. "Despite your faint protestations, you are a man like our father, forcing others to grovel and scrape before your egotistical whims. I repeat—find another sacrificial lamb!"

Did Kendall sigh at her words?

Her brother rapped on the carriage roof, signaling to the coachman to finally return them home.

Allie pinched her lips shut and turned to look out at the gaslit streets of Mayfair crawling past her window.

Fabrizio's note sat heavily in her pocket.

Yet one more man making demands of her.

Yes.

It was past time to be gone from Kendall, to cut all ties with her twin. Sentimentality and a longing for the past had only ever caused her heartache.

E than passed a restless night.

The image of Lady Allegra's bonnie face would not leave him be—her gray eyes reflecting the candlelight as she spoke, her nimble fingers easily picking Lord Aberdeen's lock.

How angry had Kendall been with his sister? Was Ethan's wee thief in danger? And even if she were, what could he do about it? Scale the walls of Gilbert House in Grosvenor Square and steal Lady Allegra from her bedchamber?

Mmmm. The idea appealed to both his sense of drama and romantic chivalry . . . but he couldn't afford to make an enemy of Kendall.

His uncle would disown him, for one.

And secondly, Ethan might be the most famous man in London, but Kendall was one of the most powerful.

And Ethan well understood the difference between the minor power he held and the true economic and political authority that Kendall wielded.

Ethan had spent his life navigating that divide.

The knowledge didn't prevent him from recalling Lady Allegra's reaction to her brother's arrival the evening before. How she had morphed into a cornered animal, metaphorically hissing and spitting.

While at Oxford, a friend of Ethan's had kept a parrot in his rooms. Generally, the bird hopped from person to person and gamely attempted to mimic the words they taught him. But after a holiday break, they would often return to find the parrot plucking out its own feathers and butting its head against the wall.

Ethan had found the bird's behavior baffling. Why hurt itself?

And yet . . . Lady Allegra reminded him of that parrot—a self-harming creature of exotic beauty. A trapped woman turning her impotent rage inward, injuring herself.

And like his friend's parrot, Ethan felt helpless before Lady Allegra's obvious distress.

All he could think to do was continue their conversation from the night before . . . without Kendall or Uncle Leith finding out.

To that aim, Ethan washed and dressed, donning his favorite kilt. Then he slipped down the stairs of his uncle's Mayfair townhouse, intent on summoning a hansom cab and embarking on some reconnaissance.

Uncle Leith leased this townhouse for the London season. Though ostensibly in Mayfair, it sat on the fringes of fashionable society. The poet in Ethan saw the metaphorical similarity between the house's location and his uncle's standing in the *ton*—within sight of greatness but lacking true grandeur of his own.

Ethan nodded to the butler and had just set his hat atop his head when his uncle's voice reached him.

"I would think twice before leaving today, lad."

Frowning, Ethan handed his hat back to the butler and walked into the dining room to the right of the wee entry hall.

His uncle sat at a burled mahogany table, a breakfast of eggs, blood pudding, and rashers of bacon before him. A large painting of horses and hounds chasing a fox hung above his head—their rented townhouse was staunchly hunting-themed in its decor. The usual stack of newspapers lay folded at his uncle's elbow. George Leith liked to know exactly what was being said about his nephew at all times.

In short, Uncle Leith appeared utterly in his element for a Thursday morning.

"Pardon?" Ethan conjured a smile for his uncle.

Uncle Leith nodded toward the window which faced the busy street outside. "I awoke to a phalanx of reporters camped upon our stoop this morning."

Ethan froze, unsure from his uncle's tone *how* he was to react.

Were reporters a good thing in this particular instance? Or . . . no?

A quick mental review of his activities over the past few weeks turned up nothing of import. Ethan had learned long ago to keep his behavior strictly in line with his uncle's parameters.

Life was easier that way.

Chasing after Lady Allegra last night marked the first time in three years that Ethan had done something contrary to his uncle's edicts. But even then, a reporter would hardly consider that action newsworthy.

Stepping over to the window, Ethan parted the gauzy curtains and looked out to the street.

One, two, three . . .

He quickly counted six reporters pacing the flagstone pavement.

Even for Ethan, six reporters appearing on the doorstep before breakfast was unprecedented. But, again, was it a positive development?

"Has something happened?" Ethan crossed to the sideboard—a painting of a Highland stag rimmed against a red sunset hanging above— and dished himself some eggs.

He had planned to forgo breakfast, but now that he was here . . .

Sitting at the table, he placed a napkin on his lap and nodded his thanks to the butler who poured coffee from a teapot.

Uncle Leith did not keep Ethan in suspense.

Tucking the broadsheet into a roll, his uncle sent it skimming down the table to Ethan. "*The London Reveler*, third page, top of the society column."

Ah. So something *had* happened.

Lifting his eyebrows, Ethan flipped to the appropriate section.

The headline jumped out immediately.

Is Mr. Penn-Leith's Celebrated Poem Autobiographical?

Frowning, Ethan leaned over the page.

> *It has come to the attention of this newspaper that Mr. Ethan Penn-Leith's celebrated poem, "One Kiss Alone," might be based on a real-life adventure. In speaking with an anonymous source, we have learned that the events Mr. Penn-Leith details in his famous poem—namely a stagecoach ride where the main hero is robbed at gunpoint, double-crossed by a beautiful woman, and then scandalously kissed by that same woman—are true events which befell Mr. Penn-Leith on his last trip to Italy. Why the Highland Poet has chosen to cloak the story in fiction, we cannot say. Perhaps it is due to his own sense of poetic form. Or, could it be to protect the lady in question? Our source tells us that the infamous Italian woman in the poem is, in fact, English and currently residing at a fashionable address in London. We wait anxiously with the rest of the English-speaking world to hear if Mr. Penn-Leith will confirm or deny these reports.*

"Bloody hell." Ethan pressed two fingers to the bridge of his nose.

"Language, boy," his uncle countered.

Who had uncovered this secret? Ethan himself had realized only last night that his *ladra* was Lady Allegra. How had someone else managed to unearth the truth so quickly?

No wonder reporters were on the prowl this morning.

Tossing *The London Reveler* onto the table, Ethan looked at his uncle.

"So it's true then." His uncle did not frame the words as a question.

Ethan nodded.

"Is the lady in London?"

Another nod.

Ethan closed his eyes, waiting to see if Uncle Leith would put it together.

Damn and blast.

Had anyone other than Kendall realized Ethan had bolted after Lady Allegra last night? Or . . . had Lady Allegra placed the story herself in a bid to ruin her reputation, as she had alluded?

"Does this relate to why you disappeared for a solid thirty minutes last night when I expressly requested you petition Kendall on behalf of our shipping interests?"

Ethan picked up his fork, mind racing, parsing how to best answer the question. Telling his uncle that Lady Allegra was the woman involved would be a disaster. And yet, withholding the information was equally problematic.

"Out with it." Uncle Leith beckoned with his fingers. "You know you must tell me eventually."

"Ye willnae like it." Ethan stirred his eggs around his plate, his Scottish brogue deepening due to his distress.

It was said Uncle Leith had the look of his sister, Isobel, Ethan's mother—brown hair, green eyes, a strong jawline. As Isobel had died shortly after his birth, Ethan had no memory of her. But he knew he had inherited many of the same physical traits. People often mistook Ethan to be Uncle Leith's son.

In that, they were wrong.

Ethan remembered his own father well. A rugged gentleman farmer of soft manner and even softer voice. A kind, good man. The sort who would put Ethan on his shoulders as he trudged out to check on the oats in a far field or cuddle him against his side as he read a book of an evening.

Not once had Ethan doubted his father's love for him.

The same could not be said for Uncle Leith.

"I'm already apprehensive if this situation causes your language to slip so," Uncle Leith said sharply. "What have you done, lad? What is the sorry truth behind that poem of yours? As I have told you a thousand times, that trip to Italy was a mistake."

Ethan had heard that refrain more than enough over the last year.

Uncle Leith had been livid when, on the heels of a romantic disappointment three years past, Ethan had fled Britain for the Continent. His uncle relied on Ethan's popularity to grow his merchant fleet empire and solidify trade contracts with men in power. However with Ethan gone to Italy, his uncle had found himself on the outside of the highest echelons of Polite Society.

A fact George Leith would never let Ethan forget.

With a sigh, Ethan glanced toward the hallway and the butler standing at attention there. Pushing back from the table, he crossed and closed the dining room door.

Uncle Leith frowned. "As bad as all that?"

"Aye," Ethan answered. "I don't want the lady's identity to leave this room. And trust me, neither do ye yourself."

Ethan sat down beside his uncle, fixing him with his sternest stare. The expression felt almost foreign on Ethan's face—pulling his lips down and furrowing his forehead.

No wonder he smiled all the time. 'Twas much simpler than frowning.

"Now ye be frightening me, lad." His uncle's accent tended to slip as well when agitated. Morning light filtered through the windows to their right, highlighting his uncle's graying head and the wealth of wrinkles stacked around his eyes.

Leaning forward, Ethan said on a whisper, "The woman in question is Lady Allegra Gilbert, Uncle. That is why I bolted last night. I didn't realize it was her until suddenly, *poof!*, there she was, in the flesh, seated beside Kendall."

Uncle Leith literally stopped breathing for the count of four seconds.

"Ye be sure, lad?"

"Aye. I spoke with her."

"How the *bloody hell* did ye get wrapped up in a scandal with Kendall's twin sister?" Uncle Leith hissed.

"Hush, Uncle." Ethan glanced toward the closed door.

"Of all the *bampot, eejit* ways tae disgrace our family name, ye had tae go and involve yourself in the scandal of a century with the twin sister of one of the most powerful men in Britain. Have ye not an ounce of common sense left in that poetry-addled head of yours?"

Ethan sat back in his chair, arms folded across his chest.

Och. His uncle had gone a bit too far.

"Were ye no' listening tae me? I didnae ken it was her until last evening at Lord Aberdeen's. She never gave me her name in Italy, and quite frankly, she seemed entirely Italian at the time. So ye cannae blame me for this turn of events."

And yet, long experience told Ethan that his uncle would, indeed, blame him.

Uncle Leith tipped his forehead into his hands, head shaking back and forth.

"What will become of our hopes for a pact to ship the saltpeter now?" he nearly moaned. "I was counting on ye facilitating that for us. Europe faces political turmoil at the moment, and the potato blight in Ireland has now spread to Scotland. These are uncertain times, my boy. We require the extra financial security that such a shipping contract would bring."

"I can and will speak with Kendall about it, Uncle. That avenue is not lost to us yet. I dinnae ken that Kendall knows of Lady Allegra's exploits in Italy, nor my involvement." Ethan may have crossed his fingers under the table.

"You must stay far, far away from Lady Allegra," Uncle Leith said, wagging a finger at Ethan. "If the press catches a single word of this . . ."

Ethan readily understood the rest.

Kendall would be apoplectic if his sister's identity leaked to the public. And knowing Kendall as Ethan did, the man would likely fault Ethan for the slip.

The question, of course, was who had already told the press about that afternoon in Italy? And would that person strike again?

"I will be careful, Uncle," he promised.

"See that you are, lad." Uncle Leith turned back to his breakfast and newspaper. "I would hate for there to be consequences from your indiscretion."

Ethan managed a grimacing smile in reply before returning to his seat and his now cold eggs.

Consequences. That was always his uncle's vague threat.

Those consequences, of course, being Ethan's disinheritance.

Why didn't his uncle simply trust Ethan's loyalty? After all, the man had provided handsomely for Ethan's education and upbringing, a gift that he valued and respected no matter how condescendingly it had been given. Threats were unnecessary and turned Uncle Leith's patronage into a millstone around Ethan's neck.

Poetry provided Ethan with a decent income. But it was a minuscule amount when placed beside Uncle Leith's coffers. If Ethan wished to marry a lady of good family and upbringing—and he had hopes of doing so—he would need Uncle Leith's largess.

It was as simple as that.

And so, Ethan and his uncle continued their odd dance. His uncle browbeating Ethan into compliance instead of merely asking in trust. And Ethan, diligently obeying but growing increasingly frustrated over being treated like a wayward child.

With a sigh, Ethan sipped his lukewarm coffee and stared sightlessly ahead at a painting of a hunting dog standing proudly beside a brace of pheasant.

How ironic he found his existence at times.

He was one of the most famous men in London. His face so readily recognized, he had to be wary of where he went and with whom. A mob could form at a moment's notice, poetry enthusiasts eager to snatch any wee piece of Ethan Penn-Leith that they could.

Why just a month past, he had attempted to purchase a new watch fob from a shop on Regent Street and had made the monumental mistake of, firstly, wearing a kilt, and secondly, stepping out from the shadows of the Quadrant Colonnade. A group of young ladies had spied him and, shrieking along with their mammas, had immediately circled round, harassing him with requests for a poem and, quite frankly, their wandering hands.

He had barely escaped with his pocket watch and dignity intact.

The same could not be said for the outer layer of his kilt.

In all, he found it a decidedly lonely existence—recognized and sought by everyone, yet known by very few.

To the masses, he had become an object more than a person.

And yet, as Ethan sat in the silence of his uncle's dining room, he rather thought his uncle might consider him an object, as well.

For Ethan, affection and love had largely been transactional emotions. Love, in particular, had often felt like a commodity that could be removed and bestowed elsewhere on a whim.

Just as his thoughts threatened to become maudlin, a knock sounded on the dining room door.

"Come," Uncle Leith called.

The butler entered, the morning post on a silver salver. Uncle Leith collected his letters and then motioned for Ethan to take his.

Quickly sorting through the messages from admirers and friends, Ethan smiled to see a letter from his sister, Leah.

Ah. Praise be to the Universe for having an uncanny sense of timing.

Despite the paradoxical reality of his everyday existence—constantly surrounded by people and yet persistently lonely—there were those who *did* love him unconditionally, namely his older siblings, Leah and Malcolm.

At sixteen years his senior, Leah had been more mother to him than sister—quick to rap his knuckles when he stole shortbread cooling on a kitchen worktable, but even quicker with a cuddle.

To him, Leah was home . . . a hug in human form.

Married now, his sister lived ten miles up a Highland glen in drafty Laverloch Castle with her husband, Captain Fox Carnegie, and their two children, Madeline and Jack.

Ethan scanned the lines of her letter:

> *. . . the rain has been relentless the past few weeks. Jack has resorted to practicing his lure casting in Fox's study, much to the dismay of both Fox and Mr. Dandy, who has not ceased his feline yowls of protest. But Jack is determined to accompany you fishing when you next visit Laverloch, and so practice he must. How is that for a subtle hint? Meanwhile, tell me how you are faring under the weight of Uncle Leith's demands. Know that you are missed and loved, wee brother . . .*

Ethan's heart gave a painful thump.

Fishing with wee Jack? He longed for that.

Ethan could practically hear the rushing of the River North Esk and the rustle of wind through the Scots pines along its banks. A hawk's lone call echoing off the walls of Corrie Finn as he cast his line across the water. And best of all, his six-year-old nephew, Jack—with a shock of blond curls and eyes as vividly blue as the water itself—asking endless questions in his high voice.

Ethan missed Leah and Jack and, well . . . all of them.

Uncle Leith coughed, the sound reverberating around the dining room. Ethan studied his uncle's profile, noting the wrinkles that time and a fondness for scowling had etched there.

Yes, Uncle Leith did not supply much warmth, and Ethan often felt alone and isolated here in London, but knowing that he would always find welcome at his siblings' doors was enough.

Did Lady Allegra have people who loved and supported her? Her mother's family? The highwaymen she associated with in Italy, perhaps?

He prayed that if she *had* managed to bolt from Lord Aberdeen's townhouse last night, she would have found friends waiting in some raucous inn with open arms.

And yet . . .

The tightness in Lady Allegra's eyes and the grim set of her jaw made Ethan doubt such an outcome. Perhaps that was why he had so vociferously questioned her decision to leave.

Because the lady's strained expression had mirrored, in the brief moment before she left, the loneliness and isolation that Ethan himself felt.

E than intended to keep his promise to stay away from Lady Allegra. Truly, he did.

Yes, Lady Allegra Gilbert was the most fascinating woman he had ever met.

Yes, Ethan wanted nothing more than to call upon her and spend hours talking over tea, on a walk, throughout dinner. And then immediately call again the next morning.

The memory of her clung to him, as enticing as the scent of Leah's bannocks fresh from the griddle and drizzled in honey. And just as he did with his sister's cooking, Ethan longed to greedily feast on Lady Allegra's company.

But no good would come from pursuing her. Ethan's attentions would only upset his uncle, anger Kendall, and risk exposing Lady Allegra's identity as the highwaywoman from "One Kiss Alone."

If that happened, she would be ruined, shunned by Polite Society.

No. He would never forgive himself for harming her so.

And so, Ethan forcibly set Lady Allegra from his mind and went about his week.

Well, as much as was possible.

The report in *The London Reveler* spread like wildfire. The crowd of reporters had grown from six to nine to twelve at last count and prevented Ethan from leaving the townhouse.

His celebrity was like a slowly expanding prison, restricting his movements one golden chain at a time. It felt almost blasphemous to bemoan his fate. After all, his fame fueled sales of his books which, in turn, lined his pockets. And yet, the lonely days spent in the silence of his uncle's drawing-room—the mantle clock ticking away the hours—weighed upon him.

Finally three days after the report in the broadsheets, Ethan could suffer his isolation no longer. Aside from being desperate for fresh air and a change of scenery, he had meetings with his publisher and tailor that could not be postponed.

To that end, he slipped out the servant's entrance of the townhouse at first light, a hat pulled low to hide his face.

Hours later, his tasks completed, Ethan walked back through Mayfair toward his uncle's residence, head tucked down, every movement of his body saying, *Ignore me. I am no one.* The experience on Regent Street had been harrowing enough and that had occurred before this latest *on dit.*

All was going well until he crossed Grosvenor Square—the heart of Mayfair.

Here, the city mansions of the most powerful families in Britain stood at attention around a wide, fenced garden. Naturally, Gilbert House—the town residence of the Dukes of Kendall—occupied a prominent position with its impressive three-storied portico and imposing pediment.

Skirting along the edges of the large square, Ethan stared at Gilbert House, pondering against his better judgment what Lady Allegra might be doing today. Was she lonely, like him, in her marble cage? *Was* Kendall keeping her prisoner?

And was she the informant behind the information leaked to the newspaper? Or was she, like Ethan, fearful that her identity would be uncovered?

As he stood staring at the edifice, a furtive movement to the right caught his eye.

A man with dark hair and a foreign air slipped into the narrow alleyway beside Gilbert House.

Ethan couldn't say why the man's actions struck him as sinister. The sun sat high in the sky, and maids and footmen in livery rushed to and fro on their employers' business.

But the man's manner and dress were decidedly not that of a servant, and, well . . . he slithered. There was no better word to describe the motion.

Squinting, Ethan watched for a long moment as the man crept forward, *slithering* along the wall of Gilbert House.

Was he . . .

Was the man familiar?

Ethan rather thought he was.

In fact, the man bore a strong resemblance to the *bandito* who had slapped Ethan before galloping off with Lady Allegra that day in Italy.

What had been the man's name? Fabrizio?

As Ethan watched, the man tentatively opened an iron gate that led to the back garden of Gilbert House, giving Ethan a clearer view of his face.

Yes. It had to be the same man—Fabrizio.

Frowning, Ethan hesitated.

He knew he should keep walking. Lady Allegra was none of his concern. The Italian had been her compatriot in the past and was perhaps intent on helping her escape Kendall's opulent prison.

And yet . . .

Shouldn't that garden gate have been locked? If Lady Allegra had the key to let the man in, she likely would have already used it to escape under the cover of darkness. So why was the Italian entering in broad daylight?

The facts did not add up. Something felt off.

Crossing the street, Ethan walked down the alleyway. The sounds of the square retreated, the cool damp of the stone walls absorbing them.

The man had left the gate ajar—an open invitation.

Ethan approached the iron bars slowly . . . as if they were vipers waiting to strike.

Dinnae do it, his inner voice whispered. *Just go on your way.*

Brazenly entering the back garden of Kendall's London residence would break at least half a dozen rules of etiquette, not to mention the Queen's Law.

Yes. He must abandon this course. It would serve no purpose. Lady Allegra and Kendall were more than capable of solving their own problems. They did not need his meddling.

Half-pivoting, Ethan turned to leave when voices reached him.

A murmuring rush of Italian.

A man's tenor, low and sharp.

And a woman's alto, soft but enraged . . . almost hissing.

Lady Allegra.

Blast.

Ethan's Italian was rudimentary at best, but the cadence of an argument sounded the same in any language.

He simply couldn't walk away. Not without ensuring Lady Allegra was well.

With a sigh, he pushed open the gate—it pivoted soundlessly on well-oiled hinges, thanks surely to the duke's equally well-oiled staff— and crept into the garden. A wild riot of trees and shrubbery lined a graveled path before him. Soundlessly, Ethan stepped off the walkway and hid himself between an obliging rhododendron bush and a tall yew tree. If anyone came up the path, they would be unlikely to see him.

Unfortunately, it also meant he could see little of the garden himself. He bobbed his head, searching for a glimpse through the thicket but saw nothing more than a wee flash of red. Lady Allegra's skirt, perhaps?

Fabrizio was speaking at a clipped pace. Ethan strained to make out the words, but only caught the occasional snippet.

. . . *dovevo farlo* . . . *perdonami* . . .

Something about 'having to do it.' And . . . 'forgive me'?

Grimacing, Ethan crossed his arms and leaned back against the yew tree. He darted a glance at the iron gate.

He should leave. He understood little of this man's relationship with

Lady Allegra. They could be lovers or even married, for all that Ethan knew.

Still . . . he waited, shoulders pressed to the tree trunk, Italian and the occasional bumblebee buzzing around him.

ALLIE GLARED AT Fabrizio.

He propped one arrogant foot atop an obliging stump to the rear of the garden, a vibrant forsythia bush at his back.

Had this man—one she had once called friend—always been such a conniving, traitorous worm?

Excuses continued to roll off his tongue in staccato syllables.

"*Ma dai, cara.* As I keep saying, I only sold you to your brother because I knew you would wish the payment to go to our cause." Fabrizio smiled at that—the *idiota*—a roguish lock of hair tumbling across his forehead.

How had she once thought him handsome? At the moment, he resembled a disreputable conman . . . which, she supposed, he had always been.

She had merely ceased finding it attractive.

Allie had resolved to never speak with Fabrizio again. But the stubborn man had become more brazen in his attempts to contact her, including bribing a servant to unlock the back garden gate while Allie enjoyed her morning *passegiata*—strolling back and forth along a narrow path under Aunt Whipple's watchful eye.

Kendall didn't permit her to walk in the garden at the center of Grosvenor Square, fearing she would bolt . . . which was precisely what she would do, but still . . .

She would have liked to roam in a larger space—a park or a meadow, perhaps. Or best of all, an Italian mountainside a thousand miles south.

Furthermore, how annoying to discover that servants who were hesitant to be bribed with her smiles and shiny coin readily succumbed to an unsavory reprobate.

"Charming bit of logic there," Allie retorted. "So you're now claiming I would have *wanted* to be sold?"

A loud snort sounded behind her. Allie whirled to look at Lady Whipple. Thankfully, her elderly aunt remained as she had for the past hour—head back and snoring in a heavily stuffed armchair that two footmen had set on the grass beside a purple flowering azalea.

Lady Whipple did not always sleep in the garden. Usually, Allie had to contend with her aunt's relentless questions as she relished hearing about drama. And Allie's war with Kendall was the very definition of such drama.

But today, the sun had worked its warm magic, setting her aunt's eyes to closing. More helpfully, her aunt's hearing had deteriorated as of late, so slight noises would not rouse her.

Thankfully, Kendall himself was absent, having climbed atop his favorite stallion this morning and headed off to attend to ducal duties.

"*Madonna!*" Fabrizio exclaimed. "Why must you twist my words, *cara mia?*"

"I am *Lady Allegra* to you," Allie bit out between clenched teeth. "You lost the right to call me anything else when you drugged me with laudanum and handed my unconscious body over to my brother's hired thugs."

Fabrizio at least had the decency to flinch.

"I assisted *La Giovine Italia* for years," she continued, stabbing a finger at him, "and the only request I made was to be treated as a colleague-in-arms. Your quick defection to Kendall's demands demonstrated louder than any sworn oath that you did not value me. So why have you approached me, Fabrizio? As far as I'm concerned, you are my brother's minion now."

"Kendall has forbidden me to speak with him!" Fabrizio threw his hands in the air in a decidedly Latin gesture of exasperation. "The payment for handing you over came with the stipulation that I never contact him again. If I do, he will give my identity to the authorities in Südtirol. Kendall also refuses to speak with Mazzini."

Mazzini was in London attempting to drum up support, specifically monetary, for *La Giovine Italia*. Allie had yet to see the man, mostly due to the fact that Kendall never permitted her to leave the house. The evening recital had been a notable exception.

"And because Kendall is no help," Fabrizio continued, "we have turned to you."

Allie sighed. Of course they had turned to her—a woman they saw as weak and easily manipulated. A woman who had done their bidding hundreds of times in the past.

Never again.

When would she *finally* learn that men were not to be trusted? That they would always play her false?

Taking a step back, she crossed her arms over her chest.

"This is me saying *no. No, no, no!*" she continued in crisp Italian. "Tell the whole world what you know. Ruin me. I. Do. Not. Care. I have no money to give you, and even if I did, I would not spare a *lira*. Besides, how do I know you aren't gambling again instead?"

Fabrizio inhaled sharply. "I am firmly Mazzini's man. All that gambling nonsense is in my past, *bella*. Mazzini would have my head otherwise."

"What if I *want* Mazzini to have your head?" Allie asked conversationally. "That sounds rather appealing at the moment."

Sighing, Fabrizio pressed his palms together in an attitude of prayer. "*Per favore, mia signora.* Please."

Oh yes, she would make this blackguard grovel before she was done.

"Instead of blackmail, you should have begun with negotiation, Fabrizio. I might be able to procure the funds you seek in exchange for assistance with my own troubles." Allie's mind raced with possibilities. Could she trust Fabrizio to help her escape Kendall's clutches? Or would that just toss her from the skillet into the fire?

"Truly?" The hope on his face was almost comical.

She would have to ponder the idea thoroughly. But in the meantime, let the scoundrel hope.

At the very least, denying him later would prove deliciously rewarding.

"Possibly. I must think upon it. Now, go away." She made a shooing motion with her hands. "If you are caught here, I will scream and turn you over to the constable. Or worse—to Kendall himself."

Fabrizio didn't quite blanch, but he swallowed a bit too audibly.

And given the crimes she had witnessed Fabrizio commit in the past without so much as a flinch, the fact that Kendall inspired such fear was . . . well . . .

To be expected from a Duke of Kendall, she supposed.

Her brother had certainly become a cold beast of a man.

With a terse nod, Fabrizio slipped down the path and out the garden gate.

The garden gate that some kind servant had unlocked for him.

The same garden gate that now stood ajar.

Mmm . . . perhaps she wouldn't require Fabrizio's assistance to escape after all.

Allie glanced back toward Aunt Whipple, still snoring contentedly in her plump armchair.

Well, this might prove a bit too easy.

With a shrug, Allie lifted her skirts and walked briskly toward the open gate.

She had one foot in the alleyway when a Scottish voice stopped her:

"*Och*, making a dash for it again, are ye, lass?"

Allie barely stifled a screech.

She spun around, hand on her bosom, heart a stampeding bull in her chest.

Searching the dim shadows, she tried not to contemplate why she instantly recognized the man's voice.

"Really, Mr. Penn-Leith, I'm starting to think you have a rather unhealthy relationship with secretive behavior. First Lord Aberdeen's dark hallways and now my brother's garden?"

A lovely low rumbling chuckle was the only reply she received. The sound brushed her skin like a lover's caress, coaxing every fine hair to stand at attention.

He stepped from the shadows, his broad shoulders emerging like a thick tree branch and blocking the sun just as effectively. Even dressed simply in black trousers and a green coat, he exuded a sort of elemental charisma. As if an Olympian god had somehow made his way to Earth. Apollo, perhaps, as the god of poetry.

Allie stopped her rambling thoughts right there.

Was she . . .

Was she . . . *flustered*?

Oh, gracious.

She was.

Ethan Penn-Leith *flustered* her.

Lady Allegra Gilbert could genuinely not remember the last time an attractive man had so thoroughly scattered her wits.

Which could be the only explanation for the sharp tone of her reply: "What do you wish, Mr. Penn-Leith?"

If he found her words curt, he didn't show it.

Instead, he smiled, the wretch.

That devastating smile of his that pulled his cheeks wide and stacked wrinkles beside his eyes and nearly rendered Allie's knees weak.

Madonna mia.

Apollo, indeed.

"Nothing, lass. I want nothing." His smile deepened as he performed a nerve-tingling skim up and down her person. "Except perhaps tae gaze upon your bonnie face once more."

Her knees truly did tremble at that.

Locking the traitorous joints in place, Allie lifted an eyebrow. "And *that* is why you have hidden yourself in my brother's back garden?"

"Well, that and I saw a rather familiar, rag-mannered Italian man duck through your garden gate, and the gentleman in me insisted I come to investigate."

"Thinking to rescue me? You attempt that every time we meet. Unfortunately, you have yet to succeed."

Did he sigh at her words? "Aye, my lady. 'Tis a source of vexation."

A small silence ensued.

The foolish girl in Allie's heart clapped her hands in giddy excitement. *The handsome man noticed you. He cares what happens to you!*

The battle-hardened realist she had become rolled her eyes at that girl.

Surely Ethan Penn-Leith, like every other man on the planet, had an agenda. The Scot was merely waiting to exploit her in order to achieve his goals.

Whatever those may be.

He smiled far too readily, too magnetically, to be trustworthy.

And she had an escape to make.

"As I said at Lord Aberdeen's not three days past, I am not your concern, Mr. Penn-Leith. Therefore, I bid you good-day and assume you will show yourself out of my brother's garden."

Giving the Scot an aristocratic nod of her head, Allie passed through the gate and into the alleyway.

She walked ten paces down the narrow passageway before pausing. Behind her, the garden gate remained ajar, Mr. Penn-Leith presumably still inside. Thirty feet ahead, footmen in livery and maids carrying baskets mingled with ladies in bonnets and gentlemen in top hats.

Now what?

The chance to escape had come so unexpectedly, she hadn't a moment to plan.

Thankfully, she was wearing a walking dress and bonnet. However, she lacked a pelerine or a shawl or any other accoutrement of a lady.

Worse, she did not have a single farthing to her name.

Drat.

In the past, she had *always* had a plan.

Was she going soft? Had months of being waited on hand and foot by Kendall's servants dulled her sense of survival?

Perhaps she could slip back into her bedchamber and retrieve the small cache of coins and expensive baubles she had purloined over the past few months. But if Aunt Whipple awakened. Or Kendall returned home. Or Fredericks, her brother's stodgy butler, noticed the unlocked gate before she could exit again, then—

"Are ye sure ye don't require some aid?" Mr. Penn-Leith said at her elbow. "Ye appear tae be dithering far too long for a person who doesn't need assistance."

Allie suppressed another *eeep!* of surprise, spinning to glare at him. How did he sneak up on her like this?

He leaned against the stone wall of the alleyway with irritating insouciance, hands raised as if begging for her forbearance.

"I'm merely pointing out why I keep thinking ye might be in a wee bit of distress," he continued, nodding back to the garden. "Who is that Italian thief tae yourself? I didn't understand all of what was said, but I did gather that he expects something from ye."

"My affairs are my own, Mr. Penn-Leith."

"Of course they are." That grin teased his lips. "But if I knew more about your aims, perhaps I could at the very least provide directions. I ken that ye be new tae Town and . . . well, London can be a bit overwhelming."

In the diffused sunlight of the alleyway, his eyes were the deep green of an Alpine grassland in August. Not a hint of blue or gold. How was such a color possible?

Allie shook her head.

No mooning over the Scottish poet.

Escape. She needed to escape.

"Are you offering to assist me in fleeing Kendall?" she asked.

Mr. Penn-Leith froze before her. Something wary and hesitant flitted across his face.

Was there *any* man in London who did not fear her brother?

"Why don't ye tell me of your plans," he hedged, "and I can perhaps advise ye from that point. It would be particularly helpful to understand what the Italian wants of ye."

"Fabrizio is no one to me."

"Are ye sure?" Mr. Penn-Leith cocked his head, the motion genuinely curious. "Because why would an Italian thief lurk about the Duke of Kendall's back garden if not to extract some sort of promise, at best, or perhaps blackmail, at worst—"

"Did you deduce this?"

"— after all, he knows everything about our scandalous . . . hmmm, what would ye call it? Our *encounter* in Italy?"

A long silence met the end of that sentence.

Allie stared up at the Scot.

Well, she had never doubted his intelligence.

His tenacity, however, was a new discovery.

"Are you always this obnoxious?" If Allie thought to quell his inquisitiveness with her curt tone, she was sadly mistaken.

The wretch only grinned wider and, predictably, weakened her traitorous knees in the process.

Honestly.

This had to stop.

Allie had an escape to bring off, a despotic brother to thwart, and an Italian blackmailer to disappoint.

Engaging in getting-to-know-you banter with a famous Scottish poet was not on her list of tasks.

And yet, her feet remained rooted in place.

She blamed his pretty eyes.

"*Och*, I would use the word *persistent* instead of *obnoxious*, but aye," he replied. "'Tis the youngest child in me, I suppose."

The unexpected bright *pop* of information startled her. It was a lightning-brief glimpse at the man behind the persona. At the human being who surely had parents and siblings and, well, history.

Odd that she hadn't thought of him in that light before now.

Who was Ethan Penn-Leith truly—the man that the adoring public didn't know?

A coal wagon clattering along the street jolted her to her senses.

Uffa. Ethan Penn-Leith was doing it again: bewitching her away from her goals.

His charm was potent. Did he don it the way she donned confidence: a mask to keep the world awa—

No. Stop.

She refused to be enticed into analyzing Ethan Penn-Leith.

The man was a menace. Full stop. She need know nothing more than that.

He clearly was hesitant to help her; Kendall's shadow loomed large.

Shaking her head, she backed away from the poet.

"Enough distraction, Mr. Penn-Leith. I must be on my way." She nodded at him. "*ArrivederLa.*"

Pivoting yet again, Allie walked purposefully down the alleyway to the cobblestone street circling Grosvenor Square. Coaches with gilded crests rolled past, a curricle or two zipping between them. A group of gentlemen and ladies on horses walked down the middle of the hubbub, laughing and chatting. Children shrieked with nannies in tow.

A group of débutantes strolled past with their mothers, curious heads turning in her direction.

Mmmm.

Allie keenly felt the lack of a chaperone and a shawl.

Not that she needed or wanted either item, but her lack of them made it harder to blend into the masses. Her red silk dress with its fine Venetian lace collar and acres of black velvet trim did phenomenal things for her figure but was more akin to a bullfighters cape than a monk's cloak for one who wished to remain inconspicuous.

She looked precisely what she was—a wealthy, aristocratic heiress. *Bother.*

But she hadn't participated in five years of Fabrizio's scheming without acquiring some pluck. She merely needed a few minutes to think through her options and formulate a plan. Preferably out of sight of the front windows of Gilbert House. The trees and shrubbery in the fenced garden in the center of the square suited that goal.

Undaunted, Allie lifted her skirts and carefully picked her way across the street to the park, her movements purposeful and direct.

More heads turned her way.

A tall black iron fence surrounded the garden. She followed the pavement until coming to an imposing gate which, unfortunately, stood precisely opposite her brother's townhouse.

She raised her hand to unfasten the latch.

"Permit me, my lady." Large gloved fingers reached past her shoulder to unlatch the gate.

Allie looked up into Ethan Penn-Leith's mossy eyes and barely resisted the urge to stamp her foot.

"A piece of advice, Mr. Penn-Leith." Allie could hear the exasperation in her voice. "When a lady requests you quit her company, it is decidedly rag-mannered to continue to foist your presence upon her."

"Understood, Lady Allegra." The dratted Scot dipped his head in acknowledgment. "Let me state that I merely wished tae take in the greenery of Grosvenor Square and, therefore, I am mercly acting the gentleman in assisting ye with opening this heavy, iron gate. I was not, as it may appear, following ye."

Allegra narrowed her eyes. "You are playing with semantics now."

"I would call it *poetic* license,"—he lifted his eyebrows—"but far be it from me tae contradict your fair self."

A long beat of silence.

Shadows of passersby moved in and out of her peripheral vision.

"I suppose you consider yourself humorous," she deadpanned, stepping away from the gate and placing his large body between herself and Gilbert House across the street. Anything to avoid attracting the watchful eyes of Kendall's servants.

"Oh, aye." He matched her monotone cadence, though his lips curved slightly at the corners. "The best poets are."

Unbidden, a burble of laughter escaped her throat.

A lightness filled her lungs, like balloon gas taking flight.

Mr. Penn-Leith stared down at her, his green eyes wide and, if she were to label the expression, nearly stunned.

"If *I* may offer a word of advice—" he began.

"Please do not."

"—ye really should laugh more, Lady Allegra. I fear ye haven't laughed enough in your life."

Allie lifted an eyebrow. "You are surprisingly terrible at taking a hint."

"Alas, my talents lie in other areas."

A murmuring rush of sound finally broke through Allie's consciousness.

"It's him," a voice said to her left.

"'Tis hard to tell without the kilt," another answered.

"Mr. Penn-Leith!" a third person called.

Allie peeked around the Scot's shoulder.

A phalanx of faces greeted her.

Ladies in feathered bonnets that eagerly bobbed in time with their heads. Gentlemen wearing black top hats and curious expressions. Maids in pinafores, giggling and clutching one another's hands.

A veritable mob of people, eyes somewhat glazed and transfixed on Ethan Penn-Leith.

Allie resisted stumbling back, her initial sense of surprise rapidly morphing into alarm.

And then . . .

. . . the crowd surged forward, trapping herself and the Scot against the iron railings of the garden fence.

6

Ethan turned around to face the crowd, keeping Lady Allegra behind him, praying his body protected her from the gathered throng. His heart pulsed against the back of his tongue.

Damn and blast.

His *ladra's* throaty laugh had taken a battering ram to his intelligence. And, quite frankly, every sensible cell in his body.

His chest still sparked and popped like a damp log over a red-hot fire.

How had he forgotten his surroundings so easily?

The masses were gathering by the second.

A Greek chorus of "Mr. Penn-Leith!" and "Read us a poem!" rose in the air. A few hands from the crowd grabbed at him.

He and Lady Allegra were pinned in place—the iron fence at their backs, a half-moon mob blocking escape to the sides and front.

Only one option remained—he would need to woo the multitude into complacency.

Ethan held up his palms in a placating gesture.

Was this how the Pied Piper of Hamelin had felt when facing a hoard of rats? Hadn't Mr. Browning written a poem on that very topic not two years past?

Regardless, Ethan pasted on The Swooner, flaring his charm as brightly as possible.

At the sight, two maids sighed and a débutante fainted rather dramatically onto her companions.

Truly, this was all a bit ridiculous.

"Friends!" he said, smile deepening with his brogue. *Charm, charm, charm.* "How lovely tae see so many supporters out and about on this bonnie aftern—"

"Oy! Who is the lady behind ye?" someone called.

"Is she the one from the poem?"

"Look at her hair. Is it jet black?"

"Does she have gray eyes, too?"

Ethan's smile morphed into a plastic expression.

It was one thing for a mob of acolytes to accost him.

It was something else entirely for them to unmask Lady Allegra.

"Come now." He spread his hands. "My companion is of no concer—"

"Give us a poem!" a footman yelled.

"Can you make one up on the spot? Right this instant?"

Sweat turned the band of Ethan's hat sticky.

How had his day gone so sideways?

Uncle Leith was going to disinherit him.

Right after Kendall broke every bone in his body for exposing his twin sister to the censure of the *ton*.

Assuming Ethan could get them out of this *fankle*.

A firm wee hand shoved Ethan's shoulder, sending him lurching sideways.

Lady Allegra stomped forward, hands on her hips.

"Enough! How disgraceful!" Her voice rang over the gathered throng. She stood at militant attention, a thousand years of aristocratic breeding apparent in her posture and cut-glass vowels. "Mr. Penn-Leith is neither a monkey to dance to your bidding, nor an automaton to be wound up on command. You should all be ashamed!"

The crowd shuffled backwards in the wake of Lady Allegra's fury.

"Now, if you will please excuse us. Mr. Penn-Leith has an appointment with my brother, His Grace, the Duke of Kendall. You there!" Lady Allegra pointed at a particularly burly coachman. "You seem an enterprising fellow. Could you help clear a path to Gilbert House?" She waved a hand to indicate the imposing pillared edifice towering across the street. "I am sure Kendall will be displeased to find his guest has been accosted on the pavement before his very abode."

The man blushed and, with a bob of his head, jumped to do her bidding.

"Ye heard the lady!" he bellowed in a voice that could likely be heard in Westminster. "Make way!"

Like Moses with the Red Sea, the crowd miraculously parted.

Lady Allegra wrapped her gloved hand around Ethan's left elbow and all but dragged him across the street toward the Grecian facade of Gilbert House.

Voices rose around them as they passed,

"She does have gray eyes!"

"I could see her as a highway woman."

"The Duke of Kendall's sister? How scandalous. Wasn't their mother Italian?"

Ethan and Lady Allegra had just reached the stoop with its run of six stairs when the mob's forbearance broke.

"Wait!" a female voice shrieked. "We didn't get a poem!"

Abruptly, hands grasped at Ethan's coat, tugging on his right sleeve, pulling on his coattails.

Ethan swung his left arm forward, forcing Lady Allegra in front of him.

No slow-top, her ladyship raced up the stairs to the door, red skirts a poof of shimmering silk.

For his part, Ethan yanked his coattails free of the grasping hands and followed Lady Allegra through the front door of Gilbert House.

He slammed the door behind them, spinning the key in its lock for good measure.

Lady Allegra rested her back against the door, chest heaving.

Ethan joined her, slouching against the cool oak, trying to catch his breath.

Standing shoulder-to-shoulder, their panting echoed off the gleaming marble of the impressive entry hall and mingled with the muted calls of the mob outside.

"That was . . ." Lady Allegra began, swallowing hard.

"Aye. No need . . . to expound. I ken . . . the feeling."

"Are your excursions . . . about London . . . always like this?"

"Nae?"

Lady Allegra turned her head to peer up at him with those lovely gray eyes, her breathing still labored. "How is that . . . a question?"

Ethan swallowed, attempting to catch his breath. "I usually garner some attention . . . and admirers can be insistent, but this . . ." He waved a hand to indicate the rabble-rousers beyond the door at their backs. "This is another level altogether. That article three days past has all but trapped me at home."

"I see."

"I had nothing tae do with the informat—"

"I know."

"Ye do? How?"

"Fabrizio."

"Ah." Ethan frowned. So *that* was the source. "That man is a wee bit of a troublemaker."

Lady Allegra snorted, an indelicate, guttural sound. Ethan smiled in delight.

"Says the man who is in desperate need of a bodyguard," she shot back. "We should organize a Praetorian Guard for you."

"Like some pampered Roman emperor?" Ethan laughed, his lungs easing. "I think not."

"Well, you cannot continue to live like this." She tossed a thumb over her shoulder.

"True. Though I am rather surprised ye saved my hide instead of escaping into London as soon as the mob was upon me."

"Yes. Me, too." Was that sarcasm in her voice? "Unfortunately for me, the only way out of our situation was through the crowd. So I did what I must to survive."

Ethan suspected that might just be her life's motto: *I did what I must to survive.*

"Is that so?"

"Yes. Do not mistake this for any sort of compassion on my part." She fixed him with an exasperated look. "Though I *do* save your person more often than not. Granted, I'm not sure that is due to my own skill as much as your poor choices and bad luck."

"Me? Now, my lady, I would not—"

Ethan cut off as a dignified butler in fussy livery all but raced into the room, nearly skidding across the marble floor in an effort to control his speed.

"Lady Allegra!" the man panted. "What is all this? A footman notified me of some commotion? And a celebrated guest?"

"Ah, Fredericks." Lady Allegra pushed off of the door. "There seems to have been a bit of an incident with Mr. Penn-Leith here."

Fredericks nearly cricked his neck he turned toward Ethan so quickly.

"Mr. Penn-Leith." The butler bowed, deep and precise. "It is *such* a pleasure to welcome you to Gilbert House."

Ethan nodded, placing his top hat and gloves into the butler's outstretched hands.

"I am a devout reader of your works." The man's eyes were radiant.

Wait? Was that a tear? Was Kendall's butler about to . . . cry?

"Thank ye." Ethan donned his 'sincerity' face, the one he used with sobbing widows and, apparently, ducal butlers.

"I must tell you, after my mum died,"—the butler tucked Ethan's hat under his arm and, yes, his eyes were suspiciously glassy—"I read 'On Grief' at least once a day."

"Aye?"

"Your words soothed my soul more than I can ever express." Fredericks pressed his free hand over his heart.

"I am humbled tae hear it."

"I owe you such a debt of gratitude . . ."

"Nonsense. Merely knowing ye have read my works is sufficien—"

"Thank you, Fredericks." Lady Allegra removed her bonnet and slapped it against the butler's chest. She flounced between the two men, aiming toward a door to the right. "Mr. Penn-Leith will wait with me in the small drawing-room until the enthusiasm of the crowd outside wanes or my brother returns home, whichever occurs first. If the mob outside becomes unruly, send a few grooms to knock heads about."

Frederick's eyes widened, and he reverted to the role of a staid house servant. "At once, your ladyship."

Ethan smiled at the man before following Lady Allegra into the small drawing-room.

He paused in the doorway.

Many adjectives could be used to describe the room. However, the word *small* or any of its relatives—*little, tiny, wee*—would not have made the list. Ethan would have chosen *opulent* or *sumptuous* himself.

Rich blue curtains draped two imposing windows to the right, while a gilt fireplace topped by an imposing mirror engulfed the left wall. Lady Allegra sank into one of two large settees that flanked the hearth, sagging her weight against the back in an unladylike neglect of posture.

She motioned for him to shut the door.

With a quick grimace, Ethan closed it only partway as a nod to propriety.

Lady Allegra gave Ethan a moue of displeasure and then shifted left, indicating that he should sit beside her.

Ethan wavered, fearing she was coaxing him down the path to ruin.

Did he dare indulge his fascination with her? Kendall was due home soon. And the duke would likely be displeased to find Ethan ensconced in the *small* drawing-room. The wise course of action would be to inquire about using a discreet servant's door to exit Gilbert House altogeth—

"Trust you to flap the most unflappable butler I have ever known," Lady Allegra said on a smirk, interrupting his dithering.

"Flap?" Ethan asked.

She patted the sofa cushion to her left, arching an elegant eyebrow in challenge.

He swallowed.

Perhaps . . . perhaps there would be no harm in permitting himself five minutes of indulgence. Kendall was not home yet, after all.

Ethan sat on the sofa, leaving a chaperone-approved amount of space between his trousers and her skirts. However, he did angle his body sideways to face her.

"Yes. You spread your bird-of-paradise wings and reel the poor fools in." She mimed spinning a fishing reel.

"How does that work, precisely? I'm not sure ye understand metaphors, my lady. Or, quite frankly, fishing."

"Perhaps not. But I do recognize potent charisma when I see it."

Her words conjured a genuine grin on his face.

"Why, Lady Allegra, was that a compliment? I *knew* ye found me attractive." He rested an elbow on the back of the sofa. "I predict we will be great friends, yourself and I. Just ye wait and see."

Rolling her eyes, she lolled her head against the sofa cushion. "I consider a friendship between us *highly* unlikely, Mr. Penn-Leith."

"Well, with an attitude like that . . ." he *tsk*ed. "Why such pessimism?"

"You keep rudely interrupting my escape attempts and flirting with me. Neither of those actions is particularly friend-ish."

"*Och*, that isn't kind, my lady."

"Pardon?"

"Ye be making me choose between friendship with your lovely self and the enjoyment of teasing a blush to your bonnie cheeks."

"Mr. Penn-Leith, you are relentless."

"Thank ye." He leaned toward her, darting a glance toward the ajar door before whispering conspiratorially, "However, my *friends* call me Ethan. And I must respectfully disagree with your assessment of our future friendship. I fear it is imminent."

He said the words with a suggestive lilt to his brogue, hoping to tease her into a smile.

Instead, she merely raised that same challenging eyebrow.

Perversely, he adored that she was not easily swayed by his charm. Lady Allegra would make him earn her regard, and he respected her all the more for it.

"I categorically refuse to call you *Ethan*." She looked away from him on a scowl.

His Christian name on her lips sent gooseflesh flaring up his arms.

He spared another glance for the door. How much warning would he have if Kendall *did* return home? Surely, he had a few minutes yet, right?

He turned to study Lady Allegra's profile.

Sunlight streamed through the windows at his back and highlighted the elegant slash of her cheekbones, the porcelain smoothness of her complexion.

Attraction and yearning ballooned, swelling his lungs.

The poet in him searched for adjectives he could use to describe her.

Silken, perhaps, for her skin.

Sinuous for the curve from her bosom to her narrow waist.

Striking for the difference between her silvery eyes and olive Mediterranean skin.

Magnificent for everything else—the fire of her personality, the soft plump of her lips—

He released a slow breath.

"What did our Italian acquaintance—Fabrizio, is it?—want with ye?" he asked, needing to distract his thoughts.

"Back to that are you?"

"Aye. Friends share with friends. It's my personal motto."

She lolled her head sideways to look at him, her eyes narrowing. "You just made that up."

"Anything for a friend," he replied with a wink.

She smiled . . . reluctant . . . but a smile nonetheless.

Ethan would take it.

And still, she remained silent, gaze looking past him to the window beyond. Again, her sense of loneliness, of isolation, struck him.

He spared a third glance for the door. He really should be on his way . . .

The thought scattered as Lady Allegra fully turned her body to face his on the sofa, bringing them that much closer together.

"You wish to hear of my troubles. Very well." She spoke with an edge to her tone. As if in challenge. As if she expected him to bolt.

Well, Ethan certainly wasn't going to leave now. The offer of information had its own gravitational pull.

"Go on, lass."

Pursing her lips, she said, "When you and I encountered one another in Italy, I was working as an operative for *La Giovine Italia*."

"I've heard tell of them. They are a revolutionary group fighting tae unite Italy into a single democratic country, are they not?"

"Yes. Fabrizio claims to be raising money and assisting the organization financially. Hence his presence here."

"Ah. He wishes ye to contribute tae the cause, willingly or otherwise."

"You have the right of it."

Ethan frowned. "Why isn't Fabrizio blackmailing Kendall? Your brother would be a much more lucrative target."

"My thoughts precisely," she snorted. "But apparently Kendall forbade Fabrizio from ever approaching him again. And, of course, Fabrizio fears my brother while simultaneously seeing me as an easy mark."

"Then Fabrizio is a bigger fool than I had supposed."

"You say the kindest things," she said expansively, her lovely eyes blinking in a slow up-down swoop.

"Only the truth, lass."

Did her gaze drop to his lips?

Their tingling clearly said *aye.*

She studied the two feet of chaperoning space between them, and then on a sigh, she halved the distance, sliding so close that Ethan could see flecks of dark gold in her gray eyes.

He was torn between jumping to standing or closing the small gap entirely.

"I believe I am finished discussing my past for today," she said.

"Why is that?" he asked, voice suddenly husky.

"Because I have a question of my own."

"Do ye now?"

She nodded.

"I was merely wondering, you see," she began, "if this is who you truly are, through and through?" She waved a hand to indicate his person. "Or do you habitually wear the mask of a charming, ever-affable gentleman?"

The question caught Ethan off-guard, like the icy water Malcolm used to flick onto his face to wake him on a frosty morning.

Ethan blinked, sitting upright.

She wasn't done. "I only ask because you appear adept at playing the persona of Ethan Penn-Leith, as you did with your mob of admirers outside. And given that you seem determined to orbit my sphere, it leaves me wary as to your true self and, hence, your true motives. In short, I find you difficult to trust, Mr. Penn-Leith."

Well, he had never doubted her forthright manner.

Lady Allegra was not the sort to censor her thoughts out of politeness.

Though the underlying cynicism of her question felt like a lash of nettles against Ethan's skin. Did she expect everyone she met to betray her in some way?

She continued, "For myself, personally, if this"—here she waved a hand to indicate his face and person—"is a mask, I would prefer to interact with Ethan the Scot rather than the famous Highland Poet."

Lady Allegra's words conjured a knot of emotion in Ethan's torso. The jumbled mass called to mind Leah's knitting basket—a multitude of snarled threads that were impossible to untangle.

Surprise surfaced as the most readily recognizable sensation.

He truly could not remember the last person who had intuited the nature of his life. His respect for Lady Allegra's intellect grew hourly.

And so he met her candor with his own.

"Ye are correct. I am not often merely . . . Ethan," he began slowly. "Most people read my poetry and assume they know me . . . all of me. I am generally affable. And of a certainty, I do leave wee bits of myself in my writing, but that is not *all* that I am. Of course to many, poetry *is* my most compelling attribute, so why discuss anything else?" He gave a low, self-deprecating laugh.

Lady Allegra frowned at his words. Ethan couldn't decide if it was a good or bad thing.

"And I must agree with such opinions," he continued. "I *am* more interesting as the Highland Poet. So . . . I wonder . . . why do ye wish tae know me as mere Ethan?"

7

Allie had made an enormous mistake.

She stared at Ethan Penn-Leith, his head rimmed in golden sunlight and green eyes gazing at her so earnestly.

As if expecting a reply to his question.

A question prompted by her own far too personal one.

She hadn't intended for him to actually *answer* it.

Her aim had been to drive him away. To ask something ridiculously impertinent and, therefore, cause him to retreat. To halt his relentlessly prying questions and ludicrous talk of friendship.

But instead of a polite retreat, the wretched Scot had figuratively turned onto his back and presented her with the soft underbelly of his sincerity.

The unexpected trust jolted her. She was torn between the urge to race from the room or grab hold and kiss him just as she had on that road in Italy.

She found herself genuinely . . . *liking* him.

Uffa.

How utterly absurd.

There would be—could be—no 'friendship' between them. As in the *vetturini* last summer, she and Ethan Penn-Leith were merely travelers passing one another on very different paths of life. Her, on the way to freedom from her brother. Him, to a life full of . . . whatever famous Scottish poets did.

And yet . . .

Were circumstances different, would she have liked claiming Ethan Penn-Leith as a friend? The question prickled, like a sprig of holly held too carelessly between her fingers.

Worse, he continued to regard her with those summer-green eyes that caused her breathing to splutter.

She couldn't give him the truthful answer to his question. And so, as was her wont, she dodged it entirely.

"You mentioned you are the youngest of your family?" she asked.

Ethan paused, those mossy eyes narrowing, as if trying to understand the unexpected bent of her conversation.

His eyes drifted toward the ajar door and then came back to her.

"Aye," he finally nodded. "I have an older brother and sister who delight in tormenting me."

Again, the spare facts glittered in Allie's mind. Part of her heart lunged at its restraining tether. The part that missed Tristan and their mother, that ached for whispered confidences and late-night cuddles.

She pulled the tether tight, silencing those longings.

"Something tells me ye haven't had much teasing in your life," he continued.

Similar to his earlier remarks, the comment was a probing one.

"I am the first-born twin." Though even as she said those words, Allie thought of the older step-siblings she had never met. The children of her father's first bigamous marriage, those who had been raised to rule the Kendall dukedom only to find themselves abruptly declared bastards and disinherited.

Didn't one of them live in Scotland? Sir Rafe Gordon, or some such?

Allie shook her head.

"I am the tormentor, not the tormented," she continued. "I believe it is a hard fast rule of elder siblinghood."

"Unrestrained tormentation?" he asked, lips twitching with amusement.

"Aye," she drawled, mimicking his accent.

That earned her a smooth chuckle.

Allie felt a small smile tug the corners of her lips, coaxing them upward.

This man . . .

He was a walking, talking sphere of sunshine, radiating warmth to everyone he met.

Like summer in a kilt.

She felt herself swaying toward him, seeking some of that warmth for her own chilled heart.

And she very well might have, had his next words not halted her.

"I enjoy fishing," he said.

Though master of a good non sequitur herself, Allie still blinked. "P-pardon?"

"Just returning tae your question from earlier. I ken that ye want tae know more about myself. It's part of what would make me an excellent friend, my ability tae anticipate your needs."

"Back to that, are you? And so you mention . . . fishing?"

"Aye. There is nothing as fine as flicking a line over the River North Esk on a July morning, mist rising off the water. 'Tis the best way tae commune with nature." He paused, gaze turning inward. "Mmm, perhaps I should write a poem about that."

"An Ode to Fishing?" Allie asked, not even attempting to keep the dry humor out of her voice.

"Aye. I ken that you be thinking tae mock me over this, but ye forget, lass, I am Scottish. We Scots keep our pastimes simple." He ticked off on his fingers. "Hunting. Fishing. Getting *fou* off of whisky and then challenging one another to lift heavy things."

Laughter burbled up her throat. "Lifting heavy things?"

"Aye, like boulders or coos. 'Tis a national sport." His eyebrows lifted, as if daring her to gainsay him.

"I would have thought the landscape itself would provide a pleasant way to pass an afternoon. Your poetry makes it sound beautiful."

"Hah! So you've read my poetry, have ye? Now the truth outs."

"Well, I did take pity on your poor self and force my way through *Poems from the Highlands*."

She may have read through it a time or three over the past several days.

Ethan Penn-Leith *was* a remarkable poet. His acolytes were not misguided in their adoration. Merely a bit too excitable.

"And?" he grinned softly, the merest hint of his dazzling smile popping out.

"Please." Allie held up a staying hand. "You do not need my opinions to prop up your obviously-sufficient ego."

"But as a *friend*," he leaned into the word, "what would you say, Lady Allegra?"

"Again, we are not friends, Mr. Penn-Leith. Case in point, a friend would have been granted permission to call me Allie. You, sir, have received *no* such privilege."

"Allie . . . ," he repeated slowly, as if savoring the mere two syllables. "So it's not *Bellissima*, as I had presumed."

His words stirred an entire flock of shimmery-feathered birds in her stomach.

"No." Her eyebrows drew down. "Moreover, friends don't flirt with friends, Mr. Penn-Leith. I thought we already discussed this."

"Well, ye clearly have never been friends with the right gentleman then. I couldn't stop flirting with your fair self even if I tried." He heaved a rather put-upon sigh. "I fear it will be a trial of our friendship that ye will simply have tae endure."

Uffa! The man was shameless.

Shifting his weight, Mr. Penn-Leith faced her more fully on the sofa, arm extending along the back, fingers mere inches from her slouched shoulders.

Would he touch her, she wondered? Or was he too much of a gentleman for such forward behavior?

Granted, she could simply close the remaining foot between them, cup his cheek in her right hand . . . and bring his mouth to hers.

But . . . he came no closer.

Instead, he spared another glance for the door. The sun behind him caught the reddish highlights in his light brown hair and accented the breadth of his shoulders.

Even without his dazzling smile, he was a striking man. His rampant popularity rested on the force of his poetry, to be sure. But some of it was tied, inextricably, to the power of his personal charisma.

Many compared Ethan Penn-Leith to Lord Byron. To Allie's purview, they were not wrong.

He canted toward her, as if ready to impart a secret. "Now I have a pressing question for yourself."

Unbidden, Allie matched his motion, angling her body toward his. He smelled intoxicating, something woodsy and exotic.

The birds in Allie's stomach swooped.

"Yes?" she murmured, eagerly anticipating another flirtatious exchange.

He darted another look at the door and then asked on a whisper—

"Does Kendall truly keep ye prisoner?"

Allie froze, the sincerity in his gaze and unexpected question pinning her in place.

"You do realize this is one of the reasons I am refusing your friendship," she said, sitting taller. "Acquaintances do not ask such impertinence."

"Ye be avoiding my question," Mr. Penn-Leith clicked his tongue, "which means that the answer is *Yes,* Kendall *does* keep ye a prisoner here."

"Very well," Allie huffed, relaxing back and running her hands down the red silk of her skirts. What information would satisfy the inquisitive Scot? She decided on, "I am a prisoner of a sort. Kendall wishes me to bow to his will. I refuse. He expects me to be an extension of his political power. I merely want my freedom."

Mr. Penn-Leith stilled at her words, his very breath seizing. The charismatic fire in his eyes dimmed. His green eyes searched her face, expression solemn. Did his gaze drop to her mouth, too?

"Ah," he finally breathed. "Kendall requires certain behaviors of you. And as I witnessed earlier, Fabrizio is now making demands, as well."

"Precisely."

He nodded, eyes going distant, shoulders slumping slightly. "I ken that."

Abruptly, he appeared not as the lauded Highland Poet or the charismatic Ethan Penn-Leith.

But instead, merely a man . . . exhausted and lonely and too far from home.

A flash of understanding illuminated Allie's mind.

Oh.

They were the same, the two of them. They each existed in a cage of a sort.

Hers was a literal cage of Kendall's construction.

His cage was forged of expectations—overly-exuberant devotees, publishers, literary critics . . . even the Queen herself it was rumored. Mr. Penn-Leith couldn't walk the streets of London without being mobbed.

A sense of kinship unfurled in her breast—a bright summer rose, sweet-smelling and dew-soft.

Was Ethan Penn-Leith an *anima gemella,* as the Italian's called it?

A soul twin?

She liked him. The way his head tilted as he listened to her. The lopsided quirk of his lips when he smiled. The eager intensity in his person. His relentless hunger for life, as if he awoke each morning brimming with enthusiasm to think and explore.

In particular, she admired his physicality. The way she had fit against him during their brief kiss. The leashed power in his muscles—

No!

Cease this!

Allie mentally reached within and crushed the emotions swelling beneath her sternum, squeezing that imagined rose of kinship in both fists, heedless of the thorns cutting her palms.

Liking Ethan Penn-Leith would serve nothing. Despite the brevity of their acquaintance, he had already thwarted her escape plans twice. She would be safely lost in the pandemonium of London by now, moving ever farther from her ducal brother's reach, if Mr. Penn-Leith hadn't accosted her.

The man was no soul twin, no friend.

You are far too intelligent to have not escaped, were you truly determined.

Kendall's words from the carriage four nights past arrowed through her mind.

Enough.

This was why she needed to cease all interactions with men—Ethan Penn-Leith, Kendall, Fabrizio . . . all of them.

She *would* escape.

She merely needed to sever all sentimentality.

Starting now.

"I may face demands, Mr. Penn-Leith, but I also make them of others." Allie gave an agitated laugh. "I have saved your skin twice now—once in Italy and again today. You owe me a debt, Poet. And be warned—a daughter of a Duke of Kendall always collects her debts."

Speaking of Kendall . . .

She heard the tell-tale *clack* of the door leading in from the mews.

Perfect.

Allie made a split-second decision, one calculated to antagonize—both Kendall *and* Mr. Penn-Leith.

If she appalled Mr. Penn-Leith, he would leave her be for good.

If she engaged in sufficiently improper behavior, Kendall would cast her off as useless.

And she could do both within the next minute.

"Mr. Penn-Leith," she said, erasing the space between them, "I fear that I am about to give you a rather pointed lesson as to why a friendship with myself would be ill-advised. Consider this a debt collected."

Angling her head, Allie trailed fingers down his cheek, slid her fingers between his neckcloth and throat, . . .

. . . and pulled his mouth to hers.

Madonna mia!

Her eyes nearly crossed at that first heady taste of him—soft lips and leashed power.

His kiss was every whit as potent as her memory had painted it.

No slow top, Mr. Penn-Leith eagerly leaned into her, his own hand rising to cup her face. His thumb skimmed her cheek, pressing into the corner of her mouth.

Yearning thrummed between them, a pulsing current that propelled Allie to run her palm from his throat to his hair, threading her fingers into the thick mass.

She could taste the loneliness on his lips, the hunger for connection.

Her own hunger rose to meet his, each press of their lips a soothing balm to the loneliness within herself.

This was the feeling she remembered from that dusty Italian road. A matched pair to the kiss she had relived a thousand times.

His touch scorched her skin.

To her eternal embarrassment, she moaned.

She felt him grin against her mouth.

Even unseen, his smile made her chest ache.

Oof! She would punish him for making her feel so—

Crash!

The sound of a door slamming shut sent Allie jerking back in surprise.

Turning, she met the eyes of an enraged Kendall. He stood rigidly in front of the closed door—still vibrating on its hinges—gray hair tumbled across his brow, nostrils flaring in suppressed fury.

"What . . . the *hell* . . . are you doing?!" he asked, his tone glacial enough to freeze the Thames in July.

A sensible person would waver before such rage.

Allie, of course, had stopped wavering long ago.

8

E than feared his heart would give out.

First . . . that kiss . . .

And now, Kendall looking about two seconds away from tearing him limb from limb.

Had he likened the duke to a stallion? Presently, the man more closely resembled a lion eager for his blood.

As for himself, Ethan was rightly an *eejit* to end all *eejits*.

He had known he should leave. Instead, he had eagerly followed Lady Allegra down this primrose path to sure destruction.

Ethan shifted his weight to stand, but Lady Allegra clutched his hand, pressing it into the sofa, silently pleading with him to stay seated beside her.

He dared a look at her face. And then blinked.

The thoughtful woman he had been speaking with just moments before had vanished.

In her place sat the woman he had last seen in that dim hallway at Lord Aberdeen's—closed, haughty, insouciant. A brilliantly plumed parrot in a gilded cage, intent on its own destruction.

"I asked a question," Kendall snapped. "I do not like to repeat myself, Lady Allegra. What are you doing?"

Yes, what was she about? Did she think to goad Kendall into setting her free?

Ethan had no desire to become a puppet in Lady Allegra's war with her twin.

Or rather . . . *more* of a puppet.

"What am I doing?" Lady Allegra huffed as if the answer to Kendall's question were absurdly apparent. "Why, breaking commandments, obviously."

"Pardon?" Kendall's two eyebrows drew down into one.

"By my estimate, I've smashed through at least four in the last hour. Chastity, clearly." Lady Allegra paused to turn and drag the thumb of her free hand over Ethan's lips, trailing fire in its wake. "But I also coveted Mr. Penn-Leith's poetic skills and experienced a tremendous amount of hate for my father. Oh! And I stole Mr. Penn-Leith's watch."

Despite the tension in the room, Ethan nearly laughed when Lady Allegra reached around and lifted his pocket watch from beside her skirt. She handed it back to him.

How could Ethan be so wary of this woman and yet so intrigued at the same time?

Lady Allegra Gilbert was catnip to his poetic soul.

Astonished bewilderment was the only explanation for his next words.

"Ye be fair brilliant, lass," he said in awe. "We're going tae be tremendous friends, yourself and—"

"Do *not* finish that sentence, Penn-Leith," Kendall warned. "Lady Allegra is not for the likes of you."

At Ethan's side, Lady Allegra tensed. "Hah! Truly, Kendall? Who am I *for*, then?"

"The gentleman I choose!" Kendall clapped back.

"But I have been caught in an indecent situation, Your Grace." She motioned to Ethan beside her, voice taunting. "Surely, I am ruined goods now?"

"Hardly." Kendall gave a humorless laugh. "I will not say a word about what I witnessed today. Nor will Mr. Penn-Leith." He shot Ethan a stern look. Ethan hastily nodded in agreement. "I would say you will have to try harder, Lady Allegra, but I hate to encourage such sinful—as you termed it—behavior."

Swallowing, Ethan looked between the twins. How odd to see them together in the daylight. The family resemblance was evident in their high cheekbones, wide-set eyes, and matching expressions of hostility.

The longer Ethan sat beside Lady Allegra, the more the harsh reality of the afternoon's events intruded.

Och, this was a bloody disaster.

He needed to appease the duke and make a hasty exit.

To that end, Ethan gave Lady Allegra an apologetic glance, tugged his hand away from hers, and stood. Affixing The Swooner to his face, he sank forcibly into his role as the Highland Poet.

"Your Grace," he bowed, "please accept my most humble apologies and—"

"Spare me your clichéd groveling, Penn-Leith. I know my sister has dragged you into this," Kendall all but snarled. "And stop brandishing that ridiculous smile of yours. It sets my teeth on edge."

Ethan instantly dimmed his smile but leaned harder into projecting charisma and charm. Amiability, after all, was his weapon of choice. 'Kill them with kindness' could be called his life's mantra. He might as well have the concept carved into a coat of arms.

He certainly felt like a knight when he donned it—weaponed-up and ready for war.

"Really, Kendall," Lady Allegra drawled, lounging back into the sofa once more. "Is cheer so unwelcome in your own life that you must now police it in others? Is that where you were this morning? Pushing for legislation that will restrict bonhomie and tax laughter?"

Ethan was fairly sure he heard Kendall grind his teeth. It seemed *this* version of Lady Allegra was calibrated to test the duke's patience at every turn.

"As much as I enjoy verbally sparring with you, Lady Allegra," Kendall said, swallowing audibly and lowering his shoulders in an attempt to rein in his temper, "I feel compelled to discuss the mob which materialized on my stoop not an hour past."

"Oh, yes!" Lady Allegra noticeably brightened. She leaned forward, as if explaining something to a wee child. "You see, when someone is personable and congenial—as Mr. Penn-Leith most assuredly is—people are drawn to them. Sometimes, a crowd just magically appears to cheer on the kind pers—"

"I gather, Penn-Leith," Kendall interrupted his sister and fixed Ethan with his black stare, "that Lady Allegra is the mysterious woman in your latest scandalous poem?"

Why Ethan experienced a jolt of astonishment at the man's astute guess, he didn't know.

Kendall could be called many things—and heaven knew Ethan had used many pejoratives to describe His Grace over the course of their acquaintance—but *unintelligent* was not one of them.

Sparing a glance at Lady Allegra's equally surprised face, Ethan answered truthfully.

"Aye," he nodded. "She is."

Lady Allegra crossed her arms over her chest.

"I see." Kendall rocked back on his heels.

"Please understand, Your Grace," Ethan said, "that I was unaware of the connection between my poem and your sister before the evening at Lord Aberdeen's. I would never have risked her reputation in such a way, had I known."

"As you say," the duke replied, tone cold. "Regardless of intent, Penn-Leith, your actions have landed us in a particularly thorny predicament. If word of Lady Allegra's involvement gets out, she will be ruined. Given the delicate nature of this situation, I rely on your honor as a gentleman to ensure this information remains secret."

"Naturally, Your Grace."

"I am also certain I do not need to indulge in melodrama to make clear that you are not to speak with Lady Allegra again. Your short association with her has sufficiently tempted scandal."

Ethan's tongue stuck to the roof of his mouth.

"*Madonna mia*, Kendall"—Lady Allegra surged to her feet—"I am hardly some precious flower in need of your protection. I'll associate with whomever I wish and—"

"You are dismissed, Mr. Penn-Leith." Kendall pointed toward the door. "I would like a word with my sister."

NOT FIVE MINUTES later, Ethan slipped out a side door of Gilbert House and into the mews. Devotees of his poetry still milled about in front of the townhouse, so Fredericks had suggested he leave by another route.

Hat pulled low, Ethan walked away from Grosvenor Square—shoulders hunched, gait purposeful—praying no one recognized him.

The cold reality of his situation weighed heavier and heavier with each step.

For a man who had awakened determined to avoid Lady Allegra at all costs, he had monumentally blundered. Any hope of petitioning Kendall for a shipping contract was now dead. Uncle Leith would be bitterly disappointed.

Did Ethan regret his actions? Was he discomfited in knowing Lady Allegra had used him for her own aims?

Unfortunately for both his pocketbook and his future, the answer was truthfully . . . *no*.

No, he did not regret stepping into the back garden of Gilbert House and speaking with Lady Allegra. He did not regret their verbal sparring or listening to the throaty timbre of her laughter. And despite the consequences, he most certainly did not regret enjoying the plush feel of her mouth on his once more.

His blood heated at the thought.

Ethan had often wondered if the circumstances of their initial kiss— the thrill of the highwaymen, the surprise of his *ladra's* defection—had been the source of the kiss's power. That it had lingered in his memory as this electrifying moment due to the perilous situation, not necessarily because the kiss itself was pleasure and awe and heat on his lips.

In that, he had been mistaken.

Today . . . kissing Lady Allegra . . . the press of her body against his, the husky catch in her throat at his touch—

Ethan bent his head lower and took in a slow, steadying breath.

Aye. He had not exaggerated the power of her kiss.

He wanted more of them. An endless number.

A star-scape of kisses shimmering onward to eternity.

The line of poetry drifted through his mind.

Hmmm. That was rather good.

He pulled his ever-present notebook and pencil from an inside coat pocket and scribbled the line down.

Of course, nothing led him to assume Lady Allegra had felt the same about either of their kisses.

Tucking the notebook away, he crossed Oxford street and slipped into a wee alleyway, cutting through the narrow lanes of mews that backed larger houses.

As he wended his way back to Uncle Leith's townhouse, one awful, glorious thought occurred:

In the end, he had never promised Kendall that he would cease all communication with Lady Allegra.

They *could* still speak with one another.

Not that Ethan would. But he *could* . . . and still keep his honor as a gentleman.

Ostensibly, Lady Allegra Gilbert was trouble. He knew this. She was a chameleon, practiced at assuming whatever role would best serve her needs and protect her interests. Behaviors Ethan understood only too well.

The spare confidences they had shared spoke to their similarity of thought, to parallels in their lives despite their different circumstances.

I would prefer to interact with Ethan the Scot rather than the famous Highland Poet.

His heart panged to remember her words.

Lady Allegra Gilbert had seen past his own adopted roles and wished to know Ethan. Not the Highland Poet. Not Ethan Penn-Leith with The Swooner on his face.

Simply Ethan.

A Scotsman who missed his homeland at times with a feral ache and yet also reveled in exploring far-off lands. A man who relished fishing on a bonnie July day. Who enjoyed sitting beside a cozy fire on a winter's evening, swapping philosophical ideas with his brother. And yet, a man who also loved attending the theater or shopping along Bond Street.

A man of contradictions and paradoxes.

A man who Lady Allegra noticed.

Ye must let her go, he pleaded with his heart. *As Kendall clearly stated: she is not for yourself.*

She would have to face Fabrizio's harassment and Kendall's imprisonment alone.

The very thought hurt, and yet, there was no other option for him.

A quick glance down the street to his uncle's townhouse showed that the number of reporters had only grown in the hours since Ethan's departure.

Blast.

With a sigh, he walked down an obliging alleyway and made his way to the servants' entrance.

"Is that you, Ethan?" Uncle Leith called from his study as Ethan climbed the stairs to his room.

Closing his eyes in a bid for inner strength, Ethan took a deep breath and tucked his philosophizing-traveler-angler self away.

"Aye, Uncle," he replied, voice convincingly chipper and at ease.

By the time Ethan stepped into his uncle's study, The Swooner was firmly in place.

His uncle sat behind a large desk, the room's solitary large window at his back. Sunlight illuminated the desktop and rimmed his silver head.

He appeared . . . haggard.

But then, his uncle had seemed perpetually haggard since Ethan's return from Italy last summer. Ethan could only suppose that the death of Aunt Leith nearly two years past had precipitated the change.

As Uncle Leith saw things, it had been bad enough for Ethan to leave Britain for parts unknown. But then to remain abroad for three years in the face of his uncle's loss and subsequent grief . . .

Ethan had expected to be disinherited.

(He was constantly expecting to be disinherited.)

However at the time, his heart had been too sore and his ego too bruised to care.

Ethan had fancied himself in love with Miss Viola Brodure, a popular authoress. The whole country had known of their courtship and urged them to marry. Uncle Leith had been ecstatic at the prospect. But then Ethan discovered that his older brother, Malcolm, had been courting Miss Brodure in secret. Miss Brodure returned Malcolm's affections and chose to marry him instead of Ethan.

In the months following Miss Brodure's rejection, Ethan had been desperate to escape. To bury the pain of Malcolm's betrayal. To leave behind Britain and his hordes of acolytes demanding to know *why* he had let Miss Brodure slip through his fingers. To flee his uncle's recriminations and disappointment. And to forget Miss Brodure's radiant smile whenever she looked upon his brother.

Ethan's entire soul had felt bruised purple—pain pulsed with each breath.

Of course, time and distance had helped Ethan to realize that he had never truly loved Miss Brodure. He had been caught up in the public nature of their relationship, enamored with her writing, and charmed by the idea of marrying a successful novelist. In hindsight, he understood that he had never loved *her* specifically. Certainly not as Malcolm loved her.

Ethan's brief acquaintance with Lady Allegra had already shown him how wrong he had been about Miss Brodure. The authoress had never dominated his thoughts, his heart, his very breath, as Lady Allegra did.

And Uncle Leith hadn't disinherited him . . . *yet*.

"The reporters are becoming bolder. They've doubled over the past hour," Uncle Leith said without preamble, expression taut. "One of them knocked and informed the butler you were involved in an incident outside Gilbert House earlier today. Worse, the incident apparently involved Lady Allegra herself. Word has it Kendall was incensed."

Only years of practice kept Ethan from flinching at his uncle's words.

For not the first time, he wished he had been graced with doddering relatives. The sort who gave a blank face to most news and were too lazy to poke at his secrets.

What to say?

After all, his uncle's information was absolutely correct.

Forcing bravado that he did not feel, Ethan broadened his grin and sank into the chair before Uncle Leith's desk.

"Aye," he nodded. "I was on my way to tell ye."

"About the incident?" Uncle Leith pinched the bridge of his nose. "Or Lady Allegra, the woman whom I distinctly remember ordering you to avoid at all costs?"

"Both?" Ethan gave a deliberately casual shrug, all the while, mentally scrambling to decide how to weave the threads of truth into a cloth that would soothe, rather than chafe, his uncle.

He settled for the barest sketch of the events—encountering Lady Allegra outside her house, the mob forming, escaping into Gilbert House, Kendall's arrival. He did not, however, mention the kiss.

Uncle Leith's brows drew down, down, down as Ethan spoke.

"So to clarify," his uncle said when Ethan had finished. "You entered Gilbert House . . . in the company of Lady Allegra . . . in front of an entire mob as witnesses. Many of whom, the reporter was kind enough to point out, noted the similarities between Lady Allegra and your beloved thief from 'One Kiss Alone.' And then Kendall discovered your presence in his home and was, understandably, overset."

Yes, well, when put that baldly, things did appear dire.

Ethan forced himself not to squirm under his uncle's green gaze, eyes so like his own. Even so, his knee bounced in agitation.

"You literally had only two tasks to accomplish, Ethan." Uncle Leith massaged his temples. "One, do not inspire even a wisp of rumor regarding Lady Allegra. And two, do not anger Kendall. And yet, somehow, you accomplished both in record time this afternoon. How are we to secure a shipping agreement with Kendall now, I ask you? We need this contract, Ethan. Our coffers cannot continue to support our current lifestyle—" Here, his uncle waved a hand, indicating the townhouse and city at large. "—without an infusion of cash."

"There is still a chance, Uncle," Ethan rushed to say. "I cannot call at Gilbert House and risk Lady Allegra's reputation." *Not tae mention that Kendall has banished me,* he did not add. "But I will see if I can speak with Kendall at White's, as we occasionally cross paths there."

Uncle Leith had been beside himself with joy when Ethan had been elected a member of the exclusive gentlemen's club. It was unusual for someone of Ethan's lower social standing to be admitted, but his popularity and close association with members such as Lord Hadley had ensured it.

His uncle stared sightlessly ahead for a long moment, thoughts far away.

Ethan frowned. Something was not quite right.

Uncle Leith should be raging, voice loud and opinions cutting.

Alarm skittered down Ethan's spine.

"What is it, Uncle?" he asked.

Uncle Leith's shoulders sagged. "I fear, Nephew, that I have made several bad investments over the past few years, particularly after your aunt died. As I've intimated, the political upheavals in Europe at the moment have proved perilous for banks and financial ventures. Many have gone bankrupt, taking our money with them. We are not paupered. Not quite yet. Our ships are still sound and seaworthy, and we do have cargo to transport. But our financial situation is . . . precarious. Without a lucrative shipping contract, I fear I will need to sell off the fleet. And you and I both know that will spell the beginning of the end."

Ethan's heart stuttered. No wonder Uncle Leith had been so insistent. Ethan should have realized there was more at stake here than just his uncle's typical fussing over profits and market shares.

"I will speak with Kendall," Ethan vowed. "I will repair the damage I have caused."

"See if you can, lad." Uncle Leith scrubbed a shaking hand over his face. "You are my heir, but if matters continue as they are, there may be precious little for you to inherit. Heaven knows, relief cannot come quickly enough."

9

"We cannot continue like this," Kendall said, crossing to the empty hearth of his private study.

Allie didn't give her brother the satisfaction of a reaction, choosing to remain standing just inside the closed door.

Mr. Penn-Leith had departed a quarter-hour past.

She refused to think of him as *Ethan*. The familiarity of his given name rendered his exit from her life too personal. How quixotic, knowing she would never speak with him again even as her lips still thrummed from the feel of his mouth.

And now, Kendall had ushered her into his private study. Would her ducal brother finally upgrade her captivity to a locked cell and shackles?

At the very least, meeting in his study precipitated a sound tongue-lashing for herself. The room was nestled behind his bedchamber and dressing room, ensuring a buffer between their voices and the keen ears of servants.

For not the first time, Allie wondered why her brother took privacy so seriously it bordered on paranoia. What past event had precipitated such caution? Knowing their bastard of a sire as she did, it had assuredly been traumatic. At least Allie and their mother had escaped the man's influence, though they had only traded one hardship for another in the end.

Her brother had not been so fortunate.

Allie stomped on the pity that threatened to expand under her breastbone.

He keeps you prisoner, she reminded herself. *He expects you to marry some domineering, elderly lord.*

She would break Kendall first. Her unruly behavior had to eventually crack his armored resolve.

To that end, Allie crossed the room and, opening a small cabinet to the left of Kendall's desk, poured herself a solid two fingers of French brandy from a crystal decanter.

For the record, she detested brandy.

But given Kendall's hiss of breath behind her, she had no regrets either.

Turning back toward the hearth, she sat in one of the leather armchairs before the fireplace, slouching into the chair's back and looping one leg over the arm, her red skirts sprawling. Meeting Kendall's dark gaze, she took a belligerent sip of her brandy.

Uffa. How could men drink this abominable stuff? Particularly when wines like an aged *chianti rosso* existed in the world?

Regardless, the awful taste was worth it as she watched a muscle twitch in Kendall's left cheek.

"As I was saying," her brother continued, "we cannot continue like this."

"Like what?" Allie asked, setting her tumbler down on a side table to her left and reaching for a humidor full of cheroots.

With a grunt, Kendall closed the space between them and snatched the humidor out of her hands.

Allie suppressed a gleeful grin.

Hah! She would break him yet.

"I see what you are about, Lady Allegra." He crossed the room and slid the humidor into a drawer in his desk. "You seek to provoke me into tossing you from my residence. That will never happen, mark my word."

"You always were unconscionably stubborn." Allie slumped back in her chair once more. "It will be your downfall."

"And overconfidence will be yours." He slammed his desk drawer shut. "I have noticed the disappearing trinkets. A pair of ruby earbobs and matching bracelet. Three silver candlesticks from the library. A set of spoons from an old cutlery chest. A cache of coins from my bedside table. My favorite cravat pin. The list goes on."

Allie stilled, unsurprised that Kendall had noticed. She had hardly been circumspect in her pilfering. Every move had been carefully calculated to enrage him.

"If you would grant me pin money or, heaven forbid, the portion due me as your sister," she replied, tone annoyingly sweet, "then I wouldn't feel the need to pinch items from our late father's estate."

Kendall poured himself a matching tumbler of brandy before sitting in the chair opposite her, his long legs stretched out before him. Gray whiskers already stubbled his jaw, though he had surely been clean-shaven this morning. His similarly gray hair grew long over his ears, wavy with a hint of curl, while his broad shoulders strained the seams of his immaculately cut coat.

Allie detested the lingering ache in her chest. That she had missed witnessing her shy twin transform into this indomitable beast of a man. That somehow, had she been present, she might have prevented the worst of their father's imprinting upon him.

But, like herself, he had been thrown to the wolves.

Unlike her, he had lost most of his humanity in the ensuing carnage.

Kendall took a healthy swallow of his brandy.

"You are fortunate I haven't accused one of my innocent servants of theft," he said, crossing his feet at the ankle.

"Why *not* accuse a servant? From yourself, such behavior would surely be apropos."

He gave a mirthless chuckle. "Because despite your lowering opinion, I am not, in fact, a cruel man. And I *do* know you." He pinned her with his dark gaze, looking so much like the boy she remembered and yet unutterably altered. "So I comprehend why the items are disappearing. Though for the record, I would appreciate the return of my cravat pin."

"If you truly *knew* me and were indeed *not* a cruel man, as you claim, then you would grant me freedom." Allie picked up her tumbler once more, swirling the amber liquid. "If your black heart held even an ounce of brotherly love, Your Grace, then you would set me free instead of forcing me to bend to your will. You save your kindness for your servants and spare none for the sister with whom you once shared a womb. Such actions are the very definition of cruelty."

She took a long swallow of the brandy, fighting a wince as the liquid scalded her throat.

Kendall picked at a speck of lint on his trousers. Fastidious as ever, her brother. If he felt any twinge of emotion at her words, he didn't show it.

"We leave for Scotland and Lord Hadley's house party in six days," he said, moving on as if he hadn't heard her. "Lord Charswood will be in attendance, so it will afford you the opportunity to become better acquainted with his lordship. As you have noted, I cannot force you into a marriage, no matter how advisable I deem the match. But I wish you to genuinely consider Charswood's suit. He would make you an excellent husband, Sister. You scoff at his advanced years, but age will surely render him indulgent. I anticipate he would grant you the freedom to do as you please."

Allie snorted in derision. "Do not be obtuse, Kendall. No old goat marries a woman young enough to be his granddaughter because he longs for a costly pet. Charswood wishes to marry me because I offer him money and access to my bed. Any man in that circumstance would be well-contented to keep me chained to his side—an unpaid servant to his every whim, no matter how base. This marriage has nothing to do with me or my wants. *You* wish me to marry the earl because he will lift you one step closer to the office of Prime Minister."

Kendall's jaw tensed, the muscles in his cheek twitching yet again.

"I expect you to weigh Charswood's offer carefully," he repeated, voice clipped.

"That will never happen. You are delusional."

He ran a hand over his face, again speaking as if he hadn't heard her. "Additionally, the house party will include some of the most notable politicians of our day. Therefore, I will need you to be immaculately behaved, something I know you are fully capable of doing. No cursing, no ruinous behavior, no attempts to abscond, et cetera." He sighed, long and deep. "What will it take for you to cooperate willingly? To travel to Scotland and genuinely consider Charswood's suit?"

Ah-ha. At *last.*

Allie nearly crowed in triumph.

She had finally broken through Kendall's stalwart resolve and forced him into the position she had been maneuvering toward for months— bargaining . . . the first step of many along the road to her brother's complete capitulation.

Had the kiss with Mr. Penn-Leith done the deed? Allie hoped so. Some good needed to come from her abuse of Mr. Penn-Leith's offer of friendship.

"My freedom," Allie countered without hesitation. "I wish a guarantee of freedom once the trip to Scotland is over."

"I cannot promise you that." Kendall gave a decisive shake of his head. "You belong here, with me, even if you reject Charswood."

"Then I will not accompany you. Why would I? You are the enemy I know. This Charswood is not. I prefer my chances here."

"Such ridiculous melodrama." He tossed back the remainder of his brandy. "You are so like our mother with your—"

"I would tread carefully with how you speak of our mother," Allie warned. "She was the brightest part of my life and never once hesitated to come to my aid. That is more than I can say for yourself."

Kendall looked away, his teeth clicking shut. He breathed in and out, lungs swelling his ribcage.

It was the closest they had come to discussing his broken promise to come for her . . . to the awful betrayal that had shattered Allie's world.

"If you do this for me . . ." He turned back her. "If you go willingly to Scotland and behave like the picture of elegance. If you listen to Lord Charswood, permit him to court you, and *genuinely* consider his offer of marriage. If you keep your behavior and manner above reproach and do nothing to soil our family name, then . . . I am prepared to offer concessions."

Allie was skeptical Kendall even understood the meaning of the word *concessions.*

But as their conversation was headed in the right direction . . .

"Very good," she replied.

"Before you get too cocky, let me reiterate: I cannot turn over the Salzi Mine to your care. Too much is at stake."

"For *you*," she pointed out. "Too much is at stake for *you*."

Kendall closed his eyes for a long moment, hopefully praying for patience. Allie intended this to be as trying as possible.

He opened his eyes.

"I cannot grant you *freedom*"—he leaned mockingly on the word—"as you term it. If you were to live outside my protection, I should fear for your safety, not to mention the irreparable damage to your reputation."

"My safety and reputation?" Allie scoffed. "You certainly didn't care about either after tossing me aside six years ago when our mother died."

"Enough, Lady Allegra." He sat back with a huff. "I am willing to offer you six months of reprieve."

"Six months?" Allie frowned. "And . . . *reprieve*?"

"Yes. Should you decide against Lord Charswood—which I strongly suggest you do not—I will give you six months of respite. Six months in which I will not pursue another marriage for you. Six months in which you may have pin money and enjoy Society to your heart's content without my constant surveillance. Provided, of course, that you behave with the utmost propriety. Any more incidences like the ones this week with Mr. Penn-Leith, and I will consider our contract void. Most importantly, you will do everything in your power to ensure that no one ever learns of your deplorable behavior in Italy, particularly the link to Mr. Penn-Leith and that ridiculous poem. To that end, you will not converse or interact with the Scot again."

Allie stared at her brother, mind racing, trying to decide how to approach his 'offer.'

"So to sum up, in exchange for my impeccable behavior—the adjudication of which you alone will be judge and jury—you offer me a paltry six months of false freedom?" She gave a mirthless laugh. "Why should I accept such a proposal?"

"I will grant you a hundred pounds a month in pin money."

That brought Allie up short.

She could do much with a hundred pounds a month. It was a significant sum.

Thoughts flitted through her head, ideas and plans—a furtive escape under cover of darkness, an overland journey to Italy, a small cottage in a mountain village . . .

"I want a year of respite and three hundred pounds a month," she countered, merely to give herself time to think through the ramifications.

How silly that her mind snagged on abandoning Mr. Penn-Leith as the most painful stipulation of her brother's proposal. She wasn't even sure she *wished* to continue fraternizing with the poet, but it smarted to think of surrendering that possibility entirely.

"I cannot agree to a year, as that would take us partway through next year's Season. And as we have already discussed, you are a bit long in the tooth. Let us say nine months and"—here Kendall heaved a weary sigh—"*two* hundred pounds a month. That is my final offer."

Allie mulled over his words. It was a decent proposition. Eighteen hundred pounds for nine months of proper behavior . . .

She could live for quite a while on such a sum, provided she was frugal. Particularly if she continued to nick things from the estate.

"And what happens at the end of the nine months?" she asked. "Are my chains reinstated?"

"I have faith that by then you will have seen the wisdom of my sensible requests."

"Sensible?!"

"Yes. I am being excessively indulgent and reasonable here, Lady Allegra."

Allie snorted in derision. "We have *very* different opinions of indulgent and reasonable, Your Gra—"

"What will your answer be, my lady?" Kendall's voice cracked. "Nine months of peace for myself and freedom with pin money for you, assuming you are not swayed to accept Lord Charswood before then. What say you?"

Was there truly any other answer to give?

She was a realist, after all. Even Ethan Penn-Leith would be sacrificed.

"Very well, Kendall, you have yourself an agreement. I will go to Scotland and meet your earl. I will converse with him and flatter him—I will even dance with him. And when he asks me to be his wife, I will weigh my options," Allie said, keeping her tone chilly. "But I want all this put into writing."

"Writing? You do not trust my honor?"

"Oh, I trust your honor, but not your sense of ruthlessness or fair play. I give you six weeks before you begin adding additional requirements or hedging your promises. Write it up precisely as we've agreed, and I will sign it. Any adjustments will have to be renegotiated. This is not up for debate."

Kendall stared at her for a long moment.

Finally, his shoulders sagged. The tiniest capitulation, but Allie felt it as keenly as the walls of Jericho collapsing.

"As you wish." He pushed out of his chair and walked over to his desk, retrieving a clean sheet of foolscap from a drawer. "Let us clearly outline these terms. But you are on notice, Lady Allegra. I do expect your behavior to be unimpeachable."

Allie saluted him with her glass and finished the last of her brandy in one grimacing swallow.

"Of course, brother dearest." She managed a facsimile of a smile. "I shall be a paragon of virtue to everyone we meet."

Thankfully, she managed not to punctuate her sentence with an echoing belch.

Kendall visibly relaxed at her words, dipping his pen into an inkwell. "I look forward to experiencing a softer version of your tongue."

Allie continued to loll in Kendall's armchair as he bent over the paper, pen nib scritching. Her thoughts, however, were a whirlwind.

Like her brother, she also possessed a streak of ruthlessness.

Unlike her brother, her sense of honor was loose at best. She owed him no loyalty.

This gambit of his bought her time. If she behaved herself over the next few months, Allie could lull Kendall into a false sense of security. And then, when the ideal moment arrived, she would take his money and abscond.

Yes, she would play the perfect lady. After all, she had done so with her mother in Venice all those years. Not to mention when *La Giovine Italia* needed a noblewoman to help acquire information.

However, her heart thump-thumped to ponder Ethan Penn-Leith.

Would she have enjoyed his friendship, had she decided to accept it?

The Scot was relentless. He would pick and pester until he had all her secrets. And though she wasn't afraid to be known, per se, she doubted her ability to open her heart to a man again. Such trust had only ever brought her heartache.

And how could she form a true friendship without trust?

She couldn't.

Ethan Penn-Leith's status as a potential soul twin, an *anima gemella*, would forever remain just that—potential.

Watching her brother's bent gray head, she forced herself to not mourn the past. To not remember Tristan, who had once been her literal *anima gemella*.

Yes, it was for the best that Mr. Penn-Leith was lost to her now. After all, her history with *anime gemelle* had only ever caused her pain and suffering.

And if experience had repeatedly taught her anything, it was this—

Life was less perilous for a woman when she kept her heart locked firmly in her chest.

10

Over the next four days, Ethan endured the sharp edge of Uncle Leith's worry and frustration.

"Have you spoken with Kendall yet?" his uncle asked repeatedly.

No, Ethan had not.

The duke had been elusive.

Ethan escaped to White's whenever he could, hoping to catch sight of Kendall's gray head.

Instead, such outings only resulted in mobs of reporters and fanatical admirers accosting Ethan, everyone demanding to know the identity of his Italian lady.

The members of White's were not much better, requesting private readings of his poems or giving unsolicited advice on what he should write next. Though one or two impertinent gentlemen had asked if Lady Allegra were indeed the woman in 'One Kiss Alone.'

True to form, Ethan smiled and charmed and laughed his way through all their prying questions.

And the one time he finally *did* see Kendall from across the library at White's, the duke had studiously ignored Ethan's gaze and left soon after, his stiff shoulders making it clear that he did not wish to exchange even one syllable.

If Kendall refused to speak with him, how was Ethan to ever reconcile matters with Uncle Leith?

The only bright spot in his week had been a letter from Malcolm. After a rather dry summary of the progress of his cow herd—his brother ran a prosperous cattle farm—Malcolm moved on to more personal matters.

As usual, he waxed voluble when speaking of his two-year-old daughter, Kirsty.

> *. . . Ye must come see your wee niece, Ethan. She changes from day to day. Why just yesterday, she learned the word 'naughty' (which comes as no surprise, as she hears it often in relation to herself), and she informed Viola that she was a 'naughty mamma' for refusing to lift her up. As Viola is close to her confinement, hefting a wiggly two-year-old is a bit beyond her ken—*

> *Och . . . Viola has just entered the room and requested that I ask if ye will be attending Hadley's house party in a few weeks' time? Ye ken how Lord Hadley is. Every couple of years, he hosts England's mightiest lords in order to remind them of his own economic might. 'Tis a rather devilish way to wield political influence . . .*

Malcolm's words lifted Ethan's spirits. His brother deserved every happiness.

As for his question—

No, Hadley had not invited Ethan to the house party. Uncle Leith would be beside himself with joy were Ethan to secure such an invitation. But Hadley's gatherings had always been about political influence and power, not literary entertainment.

The day after receiving Malcolm's letter, Ethan was climbing the stairs to his room after yet another fruitless excursion to White's when his uncle's voice reached him.

"Any luck with Kendall, Nephew?" he asked again.

Stifling a sigh, Ethan turned his feet toward his uncle's study.

"Unfortunately, no." Ethan stopped in the doorway, hoping to keep his report brief.

"Sit." Uncle Leith pointed at the chair opposite his desk.

Of course Ethan obliged, closing the door behind him. Any other choice would be futile.

Uncle Leith stared at him for a long moment, bushy gray eyebrows drawn down, account books spread across his desk.

The pall of his uncle's disappointment hung in the room like a death shroud.

Ethan forced himself not to squirm.

"Is Kendall our only hope?" Ethan asked. "Surely, there are other shipping contracts to be had . . ."

"Perhaps." Uncle Leith sat back with a huff. "But none as potentially lucrative or as consistent as transporting saltpeter. Unfortunately, that plan appears to be rubbish now, thanks to your actions."

Ethan managed a grimacing facsimile of a smile.

For not the first time, he wondered why his uncle put so much upon him.

No matter how high Ethan climbed, no matter how many accolades he garnered, there was always something further that his uncle required—

Learn more. Write faster. Charm admirers. Befriend the nobility.

Would Ethan ever arrive at a place where affection was not transactional?

Case in point, Uncle Leith sat back in his desk chair and revisited his anger over Ethan's reckless behavior.

"Why did you go within a mile of Gilbert House? Why not simply walk away once you encountered Lady Allegra?"

How vitriolic would Uncle Leith be if he knew what had happened *inside* Gilbert House?

He listened in mute silence as his uncle continued listing the litany of Ethan's failures. His mind, however, longed for escape. To retreat to Scotland and Thistle Muir.

Though not Thistle Muir as it currently was, where Malcolm and Viola enjoyed connubial bliss and doted on wee Kirsty.

No, Ethan longed for the Thistle Muir of his childhood. For those rare months when he would shed the restrictions of Uncle Leith's household and return to his father's warmth and Malcolm's teasing and Leah's care.

In those moments, Ethan had been the center of his family's attention—Leah, in particular. The wee motherless brother who needed her desperately.

Now, Leah had found purpose and love and so much happiness, and Ethan rejoiced with her in those gifts. He had even written her a poem to that effect. Similarly, Malcolm had his Viola and a rich, full life.

But it still saddened Ethan to hover at the fringes of their lives.

He recognized the thought for the ungrateful one that it was. How could his days be so full and yet so lonely?

A world, full and green, atop a hollow sphere.

Mmm, there might be a poem in that line. He must remember to write the thought down before—

"Ethan!" His uncle slapped the desk with his palm. "Stop your daydreaming and attend to the gravity of my words. Is Kendall deliberately avoiding you? Did something more serious happen in your wee escapade at Gilbert Hou—"

Tap, tap, tap.

A sharp rap on the door stopped his uncle's inquisition.

"Come!" Uncle Leith barked.

Their butler opened the door, the usually stoic man nearly wringing his hands. "Sir, the Duke of Kendall would like to speak with Mr. Penn-Leith."

Ethan sucked in a startled breath.

Kendall? Here?

Uncle Leith sat back, mouth agape and salmon-like, for a long five seconds.

"P-pardon?" his uncle stuttered.

"The Duke of Kendall has called. I took the liberty of informing His Grace that Mr. Penn-Leith was at home to visitors and placed the duke in the drawing-room. I hope I did not overstep?"

Uncle Leith's eyes grew three sizes.

"Not at all." Ethan rose.

Why, in the name of all that was holy, had Kendall come to call? Given the tenor of their last interaction, his presence was an ill omen.

Uncle Leith, naturally, saw the duke's arrival differently.

"His Grace has come!" Uncle Leith crowed in triumph. "This can only mean salvation."

Ethan very much doubted that.

He crossed to the window and peered down at the street.

A black, nondescript carriage stood at the curb.

Ah, Kendall had come incognito, not wishing to advertise his presence here.

Yes. This was decidedly not a polite social call.

A wee tremor started in Ethan's hands.

He turned back to the butler. "I shall attend His Grace immediately."

Smiling broadly, his uncle stretched out his hand to Ethan. "You must secure the contract, lad. Promise me that—"

"I will, Uncle," Ethan interrupted, blood a punishing hammer against his ribs. "I have always understood what you expect of me."

As he walked toward the drawing-room, Ethan felt like a French aristo climbing the stairs to the guillotine.

Silver lining?

There was likely a poem in that thought, too.

ETHAN FOUND KENDALL standing before the barren hearth in the drawing-room, his shoulders to the door, hands clasped behind his back, gaze fixed on a painting of hounds tearing into the haunch of a wild-eyed Highland buck.

The duke turned around at the *snick* of Ethan closing the door. Whatever the duke had to say, Ethan was quite sure they both wished to keep it from prying ears.

"Penn-Leith," Kendall nodded.

"Your Grace," Ethan returned.

"This painting is wretched." The duke pointed to the artwork with a shake of his gray head. "Please tell me this house is rented, and therefore, neither you nor your uncle had any say in its decor?"

Ethan managed a genuine smile at that, despite the vise banding his lungs. "We have indeed let the house for the Season." He motioned to the chairs before the hearth, indicating His Grace should sit. "To what do I owe the pleasure of your company, Your Grace?"

Kendall, of course, waved away the offer of a seat with a ducal flick of his hand. Which meant that Ethan had to remain standing as well. Decorum demanded no less.

The duke began pacing in front of the hearth, hands clasped behind his back once more. "I shall simply come to the point, Penn-Leith. You and that dratted poem of yours have placed me in the most dire of straits. The press continue to sniff around Lady Allegra, despite my denials of her innocence. My threatening letters to various newspaper editors are all that stand between my sister and ruin. I am sure you understand the seriousness of this situation."

"I do, Your Grace." Ethan folded his own arms across his chest, perhaps to hide the faint shake of his hands. He could taste his pulse on his tongue. "I hope ye are here because ye ken I can help in some way."

There. That was polite and helpful *and* diplomatic.

Assume the best until you were told the worst.

Kill them with kindness.

"Yes, well, you might have the right of it." Kendall moved to pace in front of the windows opposite the fireplace. "I have looked at this state of affairs from all possible angles, trying to find a way to prevent my sister's ruination. Blackmailing, paying off, or bloodying every newspaperman in Britain, aside from being tedious, would hardly bolster the claims of my sister's innocence. And realistically, I have recognized that our family history is far too salacious to silence the rumors. Our mother was Italian. She divorced my father quietly and privately, but the matter is still discussed in hushed voices nearly sixteen years on. Add in gossip about my own sister's time in Italy . . . and well, it is simple to weave a captivating narrative."

Here, the duke paused, releasing an enormous sigh.

Kendall was right, of course. The very idea of Lady Allegra's history was simply too scandalous, too romantic, too fantastical *not* to spread like wildfire.

Ethan could scarcely feel the breath in his lungs. What did the duke wish from him?

Taking two steps, Kendall sank into an armchair, the seat groaning faintly right along with him. He pressed three fingers to the bridge of his nose, as if his head ached.

Cautiously, Ethan took the chair opposite.

"After several days of thought," His Grace continued, lifting his gaze to Ethan, "I have realized that the only solution to this problem is to seize the story's momentum for myself."

"Pardon?" Ethan frowned.

"I need to make it appear—*convincingly* appear—that I know there is nothing to the rumor. That it is the height of absurdity to suggest that my twin sister, the elegant Lady Allegra Gilbert, would have ever plied trade as a highwayman in the mountains of the *Südtirol* and held the famed Ethan Penn-Leith at gunpoint."

"When stated so baldly, such an idea does beggar belief," Ethan agreed. "So what do ye propose?"

Here, Kendall heaved another sigh and returned to pressing the bridge of his nose. "To be exquisitely clear, I do not like what I am about to suggest, but it is the only solution I see. Lady Allegra and I will be leaving to attend a house party in Scotland in two days. I would like you, Penn-Leith, to accompany us."

Shock cemented Ethan's tongue to the roof of his mouth.

He blinked. And then blinked again.

What? And . . . why?

"P-pardon?" he finally managed to say.

Ethan's mind raced, attempting to connect all the points of the duke's logic.

"I know," Kendall gave yet another weary sigh. Which, for the stoic duke, had to be a record. "It seems utterly counterintuitive, and yet . . ."

"Nae," Ethan slowly nodded, the picture forming in his mind, "I can see the logic of it. If I am invited to travel with ye to Scotland, as a hanger-on or even guest of sorts, then it makes it harder for the press and Society gossips tae argue that ye be concealing something. The action proclaims louder than words that their scurrilous claims have no credence. Why would ye allow me within a mile of your sister if she were the highwaywoman of my poem? Of course, ye would not. Your own reputation for propriety is unimpeachable."

The plan was rather diabolical, actually.

No wonder the man succeeded in politics.

Ethan may not have liked Kendall as a person, but the duke's mind for strategy was rapier sharp.

"Precisely." The duke nodded in approval. "A Duke of Kendall would never risk his own sister's reputation in such a manner. We are above reproach. Therefore, by admitting you into my inner circle, I am showing plainly and clearly to the entire world that I—that you, that my sister—have nothing to hide. That the story regarding Lady Allegra is an utter falsehood."

"And thereby taking the wind out of any gossip rag that chooses tae perpetuate the idea that Lady Allegra is the woman from 'One Kiss Alone.'"

"Exactly," Kendall said. "In turn, I will encourage several of the more favorable newspapers to report on our journey together to Scotland. Perhaps weave it into a tale based on the rumors—I found it appalling that anyone could presume such behavior of my own beloved sister, but it did spark a desire to explore Scotland. And who better to guide us than the Highland Poet himself."

Despite himself, Ethan was impressed.

It was clever. Very Clever.

More than anyone, he understood the power of words and a good narrative.

Kendall continued, "You will agree to accompany us, of course."

Not a question.

Och, there was the duke that Ethan knew. Autocratic and demanding.

How could Ethan turn this to his own advantage? He quickly thought through options.

"Of course," he replied smoothly. "Though I do have four questions."

"Four? That seems rather excessive."

Kendall stared him down. Ethan met his gaze, unflinchingly.

After a moment, the duke relented.

"Very well." His Grace waved a hand. "Proceed."

Internally, Ethan celebrated the wee victory. "Where are we going in Scotland?"

Kendall smiled faintly. "Well, if I have the Highland Poet as my guide, then we should retire to the place Ethan Penn-Leith knows best— Fettermill and the Angus Glens."

Ethan raised an eyebrow. "My home?"

"Muirford House, to be precise. You likely already know that Lord Hadley is hosting another of his political gatherings."

Ah. Of course, Kendall would have been invited to Hadley's house party.

"I would prefer you to stay at Muirford House," the duke continued, "and not the ramshackle affair you call a home, even if that overbearing brother of yours insists."

"Malcolm? And Thistle Muir?"

"The very same." Kendall brushed lint off his trousers.

Ethan barely suppressed a smile. The few times Kendall and Malcolm had met, they had gotten along about as well as water and oil. Or perhaps more accurately, coal gas and a lucifer match—bilious and explosive.

"My sister-in-law is nearing her confinement—"

"Again?" the duke sounded scandalized. As if Viola's descent into motherhood were a personal affront. Viola had grown up on Kendall's estate in Wiltshire, so His Grace was well-acquainted with her.

"Yes. So I expect I would be *de trop* at Thistle Muir, regardless. As for my second question—"

"Do you truly have four?"

"Aye. Why are ye trusting me with this task? Despite what ye want the press tae believe, ye did witness me kissing your sister. Is it wise tae throw us into one another's company for an extended length of time?"

"Firstly, Lady Allegra obviously initiated that kiss to provoke me. She kissed you, not the other way around," Kendall snorted. "Do not take my sister's actions to mean anything. To Lady Allegra, kisses are currency. They are simply one more tool in her arsenal to mold and manipulate. And though she may seem friendly enough, you are hardly the sort of man to tempt her into true ruin."

Oof.

Ethan disliked how his stomach plunged and swooped at the duke's words. However, he was honest enough to acknowledge the truth behind Kendall's assessment of his sister.

Lady Allegra *had* deliberately kissed Ethan to elicit a specific reaction. Twice.

And yet . . .

He couldn't help but relive the very real passion in her touch. The sparks that had arced between them.

Had all that been manufactured as well?

"Your reputation when it comes to the fairer sex precedes you, Penn-Leith," Kendall continued. "You flirt and charm, but I know you are not the sort to risk harming the reputation of an unmarried woman. That said, I expect your own behavior to be above reproach with regard to my sister. You will speak to her only when necessary and avoid her whenever possible. You will be merely another traveler with my valet, man of business, and secretaries."

Man of business? Secretaries? How many people traveled with Kendall?

And though Ethan disliked the idea of avoiding Lady Allegra, he begrudgingly acknowledged the wisdom in Kendall's request.

"As ye wish." Ethan nodded. "My third question—are ye holding Lady Allegra prisoner?"

Kendall stilled, fixing Ethan with a long, dark look.

Ethan maintained his gaze.

Finally, the duke looked away, regarding the distressed stag above the fireplace. "I fail to see how my personal interactions with my own sister are any of your concern, Penn-Leith."

Ethan's eyebrows lifted.

Kendall *was* holding her prisoner then. If not, he would simply refute the possibility.

Ethan kept his expression carefully blank.

"I shall only say that my sister has a rather Italian tendency to over-dramatize events," Kendall continued. "I view myself as a caring, protective brother. Lady Allegra, however, chooses to see me as a selfish man of heavy-handed control. That is all."

Ethan barely suppressed a snort of his own. *A selfish man of heavy-handed control* might as well have been printed on the duke's calling card.

"Your last question, Penn-Leith?" Kendall asked.

Now it was Ethan's turn to brush a speck of lint off his trousers. "My uncle wishes a contract tae ship your saltpeter from Austria to market here in Britain."

"I rather suspected he might."

Ethan allowed the silence to build for a few moments. "And?" he finally asked.

"Several gentlemen have already approached me about it, Hadley included. His lordship's merchant fleet out-sails your uncle's three to one."

Kendall was not wrong.

"However, my uncle is known for his reliability and dependability," Ethan countered.

"So is Hadley."

Again, Ethan couldn't argue.

Another long silence.

"I shall consider it, Penn-Leith," Kendall finally conceded, rising from his chair, "but I make no promises. Show some zeal in rebuilding my sister's honor and do nothing to excite the press again, and perhaps I will change my tune."

Ethan nodded, standing as well. Considering the circumstances, the concession was a gracious one.

"The sooner we move our plan into place, the better. I would hate for some scoundrel from Lady Allegra's past to surface and cause trouble." Kendall turned for the door. "I shall send you the details of our travel itinerary."

Ethan nodded and saw Kendall out.

As he climbed the stairs to report all to Uncle Leith, Ethan couldn't pinpoint what precise emotion he was feeling.

Excitement to see Malcolm and Leah and spend time in the vicinity of Lady Allegra.

Apprehension that he would do something to destroy his uncle's chances of winning the shipping contract.

And terror that this entire charade would come tumbling down like a house of cards.

A llie stared at the note a street urchin had shoved into her hand as she stepped from Kendall's carriage at St. Katharine's Dock.

> *Non dimenticarci mentre viaggi in Scozia. Ci aiuterai*
> *ancora, o la nostra punizione sarà veloce.*
> *—F*

Good grief.

She rolled her eyes.

Do not forget us as you travel to Scotland. You will help us still, or our retribution will be swift.

Fabrizio had grown impatient waiting for Allie to respond and had reverted to threatening her.

Kendall had been true to his word. For the past several days leading up to their departure for Scotland, he had permitted Allie the same freedoms as any woman of her rank. Unfortunately, her newfound freedom had also made it easier for Fabrizio to hound her. This was the second note she had received in as many days.

But this morning, Allie, Kendall, and Lady Whipple had boarded Kendall's private steamship, the *SS Statesman*, for the voyage to Montrose, Scotland.

Fabrizio would find it hard to continue his attempts at intimidation, thank goodness. This was both a positive and a negative.

Though Allie appreciated the reprieve, she now had to heed Fabrizio's threats. If he told a gossip rag that she was the thief from Mr. Penn-Leith's infamous poem, Allie would find herself in dire straits with Kendall.

Holding the foolscap in her hand, Allie analyzed her options and came to an unfortunate realization—she needed to tell her brother about Fabrizio's presence in London and his blackmail attempts.

Kendall would be incensed and likely blame her for Fabrizio's indiscretion. But telling her twin was preferable to him deciding she had broken their agreement.

Allie would tell him when they stopped for the evening.

Looking up from Fabrizio's scribbled note, Allie braced a hand against the ship's railing, eyes scanning the busy dockyard. The boat rocked in its moorings, sailors tossing ropes and calling orders to set sail.

To her left, flags fluttered over the walls of the White Tower and the Tower of London. Sunlight gleamed anemically overhead, trying to break through the perpetual haze that blanketed the city. Tilting her head back, she reveled in the feel of faint sunshine on her skin. After so many years of Italy's bright skies, she craved the sun.

"Will you come below deck, girl?" Aunt Whipple asked at her elbow. "Kendall has promised that there is comfortable seating to be had in the stateroom. And I should hate for the sun to spoil your complexion." Her aunt looked pointedly at Allie's raised chin and the useless bonnet atop her head. "Besides, I had a lovely chat with Mr. Simpson yesterday that I believe you shall find diverting."

Aunt Whipple loved sharing gossip about people Allie knew not at all.

"Thank you, Aunt, but I believe I will stay here and enjoy the views once we set sail."

Aunt Whipple lifted a solitary eyebrow, before pointedly surveying the ramshackle St. Katharine Docks around them—longshoremen calling to one another as they rolled casks down gangplanks, drunken sailors staggering along the quay, the ever-present scent of excrement that plagued the Thames hovering in the air. Lady Whipple pursed her lips, clearly weighing the miserable whole against the golden jewel of gossip on her tongue and finding it lacking.

"As you say." Her aunt gave a disapproving sniff and retreated down the stairs.

The steam engine rumbled underneath Allie's feet, and the smokestack belched black smoke, adding to the London haze.

The *SS Statesman* was Kendall's pride and joy. Though her brother was not necessarily an enthusiast of the sciences, he found modern technology fascinating. He could wax eloquent for hours about the utility of steam power, and he never tired of discussing the *SS Great Western,* the first steamship to cross the Atlantic not even a decade past.

Such curiosity was the only significant remnant of the Tristan of Allie's childhood.

Therefore, it had not surprised her to learn he had purchased this ludicrously expensive boat, named it the *Statesman* in honor of his own ambitions, and insisted on sailing it to Scotland.

Granted, the ship did not offer suitable accommodations for ladies—Kendall's words, not Allie's—and so they would dock at ports along the way and spend their evenings at a proper inn with proper food and proper beds—again, Kendall's words, not hers.

For her part, Allie would be perfectly content with a hammock aboard ship—heaven knew she had slept in shoddier conditions over the years—but Kendall had merely clenched his jaw, then his fist, before walking off when she had mentioned as much.

So given his irritation . . . the suggestion hadn't been a complete failure.

Currently, Kendall was closeted with the ship's captain somewhere, likely barking orders and making a general nuisance of himself to men who knew full well how to run the ship. Or perhaps he was dictating missives to one of his two secretaries. Or consulting with his man of business in the solitary stateroom.

As a duke, Kendall never traveled anywhere without an entourage in tow—two secretaries, a man of business, and a valet, not to mention Allie's own maid and another to wait upon Aunt Whipple.

To Allie's purview, they only required a trumpeter and standard bearer to form a procession.

With a blare of a whistle, the *SS Statesman* pushed out of her dock, the round paddle wheels on either side of the ship—one to port, one to starboard—propelling it toward the river lock that led to the Thames proper. Tall masts with sails furled stretched overhead, enabling the ship to utilize wind power when it was advantageous and steam power when it was not.

Allie watched the Tower slide past, teeming masses of humanity scurrying along the docks, walking the streets, sailing the river . . .

Was Ethan Penn-Leith currently among those throngs, hat pulled low to hide his handsome face? Or had he gone to ground, determined to wait out the scandal that dogged them both?

She had tried not to think upon Mr. Penn-Leith too much over the past week.

Of course, the task had proved difficult. Partly because, she acknowledged, Kendall had forbidden their acquaintance. And Allie instinctively aimed to behave in the precise opposite manner of Kendall's demands. Even if in this case, all she could do was allow herself an illicit thought or two of Ethan Penn-Leith.

But she also mourned the loss of possibility. That she might—possibly, maybe—have enjoyed exploring a friendship with the Scot.

Which only served to illustrate the strength of the man's pull on her and why her existence was better off without him. Safer. Easier to control.

Because if they had been thrown into one another's orbits with more frequency, she might have found herself tumbling into—

"Rather bonnie day for a wee sail, I ken," a familiar Scottish voice said behind her, as if summoned by the God of Mischief himself.

Yet again, Allie let out an *eep!* of surprise and whirled around.

Ethan Penn-Leith stood before her—tall, feet braced against the ship deck, that signature smile of his stretching from ear to ear.

Allie mirrored it back to him.

"Mr. Penn-Leith!" she exclaimed before remembering to wipe the far-too-happy grin off her face.

What was he doing here?

Kendall would have the poet's head.

Right after he relocked her cage for speaking with the rogue.

"*Och*, I thought we had decided tae forgo formalities between ourselves? Friends, remember?" Mr. Penn-Leith bent toward her, a scented cloud of sandalwood and heather following and nearly causing Allie's eyes to roll into the back of her head.

Must he prove so lethal?

"We decided no such thing," she countered, looking to see if Kendall were nearby.

"I cannot call ye Allie, then?" He said her given name as if it were a bonbon on his tongue, honey-sweet.

She merely stared at him, too stunned to speak for the space of two heartbeats.

Thump. Thump.

The man was at risk of immediate death or dismemberment the moment Kendall sighted him, and *this* was the question he asked?

Mr. Penn-Leith continued to regard her with that breath-stealing smile, his green eyes crinkling at the corners, hair poking out from the brim of his top hat and tempting her to right it with her fingers. He wore no kilt today, but a blue coat clung to his broad shoulders with all the attention of a lover's caress.

In short, he looked *delizioso*.

And cavalierly unaware of the imminent danger in which he found himself.

Ignoring his question, Allie leaned to the side, scanning the deck more thoroughly for Kendall.

"What are you doing here?" she hissed. "Kendall made me swear off all contact with you. And you swore an oath to my brother that you would never speak with me again."

"Ah! But if ye will recall the scene, I didn't actually swear as much. Kendall sent me packing before I could give my oath."

Madonna, this dear, sweet, obtuse man.

Kendall was going to use his bloodied body as shark bait.

"Such pedantry will hardly matter to Tristan Gilbert, Duke of Kendall."

Without thinking, Allie took Mr. Penn-Leith's arm and tugged him into the space between the paddle wheel and a high stack of rope, attempting to shield him from her brother's eagle eye. The ship lurched as it settled into the river lock, waiting for the water to equalize before sailing into the Thames proper.

"Why would you be so idiotic as to board my brother's ship?" she continued. "If he finds you here, Kendall will have you pitched into the river."

Instead of showing the least bit of alarm, Mr. Penn-Leith merely grinned wider. "Your concern for my person is delightfully touching." He shot a bemused look at her hand wrapped around his upper arm. "Very much so."

Allie released him with a slight flinch. Though, for the record, not before noting how firmly muscled his arm was. How did a poet come by such a honed physique? Didn't he merely sit with a feathered plume in his hand all day? Was all of him similarly brawny? And if they traversed the narrow corridors of the ship together, could a rough sea assist her in finding out?

She shook her head, tossing the maudlin questions aside.

Mr. Penn-Leith continued to look at her with an unconcerned, bemused gaze. "Ye know ye can place your wee hands on my person whenever you would like, aye? No excuses necessary. Consider it a privilege between friends."

Allie's eyes narrowed, her mind whirring to make sense of the Scot's nonchalant presence aboard her brother's ship.

Idiota.

Of course.

"Kendall knows you're here," she said flatly.

Uffa. Speaking of men who would soon be shark bait.

Her twin topped the list.

A heated look lit up Mr. Penn-Leith's face. "Is it inappropriate of me tae express how much I admire your singular intelligence?"

"*Sì.* It is. Friends don't flirt with friends, remember?"

"*Che peccato*," he murmured, gaze dropping to her mouth and making her lips tingle. "I thought we had decided that flirting was acceptable."

And to think . . . she had kissed that mouth. Twice, in fact.

"No, we decidedly did not." Allie took a step back and crossed her arms, hoping somehow to ward off the allure of him.

"Are ye sure? Because I seem tae remember that—"

"Why are you here, Mr. Penn-Leith?"

That grin flashed again, here and then gone. "Why am I not surprised Kendall didn't inform ye that I would be joining yourselves for the voyage tae Muirford House?"

"Why indeed. Pray enlighten me."

Allie listened in stunned silence as Mr. Penn-Leith explained Kendall's plan to stay ahead of the gossip-mongers.

"It is a rather brilliant scheme, ye must admit," Mr. Penn-Leith said as he finished.

Nodding her head in begrudging agreement, Allie sighed, "It is diabolical. I would expect no less from Kendall."

It appeared that her brother had already neutralized the threat that Fabrizio posed, which meant Allie did not need to tell him about her would-be blackmailer. If Fabrizio went to the press now with his information, his claims would batter futilely against the powerful reputation of the Duke of Kendall. And despite their personal differences, Allie could not disparage Kendall's character as a gentleman of honor. His stalwart reputation was well-honed.

She glanced at Ethan. Granted, she didn't approve of *everything* her brother had done.

"Of course," she continued, turning to look at the shoreline, "his lofty dukeness couldn't be bothered to share his plans with me."

For all of Kendall's talk of a ceasefire between them —a wish for more amicable interactions—he still didn't understand that any meaningful relationship required trust as its bedrock. But he had shattered their mutual trust years ago and obviously would make no attempt to rebuild it.

Frowning, she left the shelter of the paddle wheel and returned to standing at the ship's railing. The ship floated out of the river lock and slowly merged with the crowded boat traffic on the Thames. Heads turned to stare at the *SS Statesman* as it churned past, seafaring steamships being an uncommon sight.

Allie watched the city drift by, a fetid wind tugging at her bonnet.

Mr. Penn-Leith nudged her elbow with his.

"It was *numpty*-headed of your brother not tae tell ye of his stratagems," he said quietly.

This was the problem with Ethan Penn-Leith, Allie decided.

Yes, he was the Highland Poet—charisma wrapped in a kilt—saying charming things like '*numpty*-headed' in his Scottish brogue.

But he was also Ethan . . . an insightful, kind man who slid behind her emotional defenses as smoothly as a Borgia *stiletto* through fresh mozzarella.

It was equal parts unnerving and gratifying.

She longed to sink her head onto his shoulder. To allow him to support the weight of her heavy heart. To find an island of respite in his sympathy.

Swallowing, she shoved the urge down, down, down. In her experience, weakness had only ever led to heartache. Trusting anyone other than herself ended in disappointment.

So instead, Allie laughed, hating the bitter edge to it but helpless to tame it either. "A *numpty*, you say?"

"It is a *braw* Scots term. Your brother is a wee bit of a fool to abuse your affections so."

Allie's breath caught in her throat. "Affection? What possible affection could I hold for that overbearing, rude—"

Mr. Penn-Leith turned and fixed her with such a disbelieving *look* that Allie broke off speaking.

She glanced away from him, watching the metropolis as it continued to scroll past—wharves and docks, warehouses and tenements.

Something unbearably aching and hard caught in her throat. Surely it was just smoke from the steam engines that rendered her eyes tender and stinging. Not the memories of Tristan giggling as they played hide-and-seek in Hawthorn's attics or conspired to pinch treacle tarts from Cook.

Uffa. When would Tristan's loss cease hurting?

In her peripheral vision, Mr. Penn-Leith leaned both elbows on the railing, hands hanging limp at the wrists.

All traces of Ethan Penn-Leith, lauded poet and shameless flirt, had fallen away. In his place was a quiet, steady man. The sort to exchange whispered confidences with on a dark night. To wipe the fevered brow of a fussing babe or to share outrageous gossip over an intimate dinner.

The sort of man with whom to build a life.

A life that would never be hers, even if she could bring herself to love and trust any man to that extent.

And didn't that simple thought make her throat ache all the more?

How cruel of Kendall to rob her of such a simple pleasure. To coerce her into allying her future with some crotchety old man who would attempt to dominate her just as their father had their mother. And how bitter that every man she had ever known had only ever administered lessons in betrayal and distrust.

"My brother, Malcolm, is my best friend. He always has been." Mr. Penn-Leith clasped his hands together. "But it is that closeness which gave him the power tae betray myself."

Allie looked at Mr. Penn-Leith, startled by his unexpected and unprompted personal admission. "Betray you? How?"

He waved a hand. "'Tis not much of a tale, I suppose. Unbeknownst to me but *not* to him, we both courted the same woman. She chose him over myself. Suffice it to say, it may have taken me a couple of years and a thousand miles of travel, but I no longer harbor anger toward Malcolm."

Allie's mind snagged on those simple facts. Mr. Penn-Leith had courted another woman—the same woman Kendall had mentioned? And she had chosen his *brother* instead? Was the woman mad?

"That is noble of you," Allie replied.

The smallest grin flashed across Mr. Penn-Leith's face. "My point is this—love that was once there simply doesn't die. It may become battle-worn and weary, but it always remains. It merely takes time for hurt to heal."

"Unless one party continually injures the other. In such a case, love becomes a bludgeoning weapon."

"Perhaps. Though that is a rather grim way of—"

"There you are, Lady Allegra." Kendall's aristocratic voice sounded from behind them.

Allie stiffened and gave Mr. Penn-Leith a long-suffering look before turning around to face her twin.

Her brother loomed. "Providing a bit of a show for the crew, are we?" He glanced meaningfully between Allie and Mr. Penn-Leith.

"A show?" Allie peered around Kendall and noted that, yes, a number of the crew appeared to be loitering about, eyes and ears bent their way. She had been so engrossed in her conversation with Mr. Penn-Leith, she hadn't noticed.

"Precisely," her twin said, jerking his chin at the Scot. "You are dismissed, Mr. Penn-Leith. I believe there is an extra chair in the cabin where my man of business has set up. As I said when we discussed this trip, I expect you to limit your interactions with my sister. You are meant to dispel rumors, not create them. Do not make me regret inviting you along."

Mr. Penn-Leith smiled, tight and controlled. "Of course, Your Grace." He bowed. "Lady Allegra."

Allie watched the poet's broad shoulders as he walked purposefully across the deck, the confident set of the hat atop his head, the way the wind tugged at his coat—

"I expect you to abide by the contract we signed," Kendall intoned.

Allie whipped her gaze to his. "I have. I cannot be blamed if your actions throw Mr. Penn-Leith into my path."

"Ah. And that is why you spent a quarter-hour just now chatting with the man? He was in your path?" Kendall snorted in derision. "Of all the women in London, I would have thought you above making calf eyes at Ethan Penn-Leith."

That dropped Allie back into reality with a jolting thud. "Pardon?"

Kendall spared a glance to where Mr. Penn-Leith had disappeared below deck. "Every woman in Britain adores that man. It's practically a rite of passage these days. A young lady arrives at adulthood when she trades her plaits for a chignon, buys gowns for her first Season, and procures an unrequited tendre for the Highland Poet. Congratulations. You have accomplished all three tasks in less than a month. As a Gilbert, such perspicacity is to be expected. On the whole, however, I would have hoped you to be less pedestrian than other young ladies."

Allie stared at her twin for a long moment.

Was her softening toward Ethan Penn-Leith so readily obvious? Or was her brother merely being cruel and needing to assert himself?

And how much did she care?

"Unlike some gentlemen I know," she said, "Mr. Penn-Leith is unfailingly gentle and kind to me."

"Every lady thinks so. It's part of the man's legendary charm—his ability to make each woman feel seen and valued."

Yes, but one woman had chosen another man over Mr. Penn-Leith. His own brother had played him false. Wounds that had cut deep and required years to heal.

The sort of pain that Allie herself well understood.

The dratted Scot weaseled his way under her formidable emotional defenses with terrifying ease.

Anima gemella, indeed.

"Do you even hear yourself, Kendall?" she said in return. "Disparaging another man for the talents you so clearly lack? Mr. Penn-Leith, at least, had the courtesy to explain to me why he was on your ship in the first place. Something you yourself declined to do."

Kendall's nostrils flared. "I do not habitually tell you of my dealings with inconsequential servants or hangers-on, my lady. Why should the matter of Mr. Penn-Leith be any different? It never surfaced as important enough to bring to your attention."

Mmm. Allie wasn't sure she bought that arrogant logic. It was just as likely that Kendall had wanted to assert his supremacy over her.

"And now that you have closeted me on a ship with Mr. Penn-Leith, how am I to avoid him?"

"You are clever. I am sure you will figure it out."

"How typical." Allie glared up at him. "You place me in a nearly impossible situation and plan to crow victory when I slip up."

"Avoid the Scot, and there will be no issue," he shot back. "But heed my words of warning, Lady Allegra. Ethan Penn-Leith is nothing more than a showman. An actor playing a part. Do not confuse such superficiality with genuine sincerity. Charswood will be the gentleman for you." He waved a hand for Allie to precede him. "Lady Whipple has requested your company below deck."

Ah, yes. Her aunt's promised gossip awaited.

With a grimace, Allie allowed Kendall to lead her away.

Her brother was wrong, of course.

Yes, Ethan Penn-Leith was a performer of a sort. He had to be, reciting and dramatizing his writing. And if the persona of the Highland Poet were the sum total of his substance, he would be easy to dismiss.

But, no.

It was the brilliance of Ethan, the man himself, who held her captive.

ALLIE HEEDED HER brother's directive and attempted to avoid Ethan. She did not approach or speak with him for the rest of the day.

But the close quarters of the ship thwarted her nonetheless.

Mostly, as Allie acknowledged, because Ethan Penn-Leith was just so damn likable.

After being summarily dismissed, instead of licking his wounds with Kendall's man of business, Mr. Penn-Leith set about charming the crew.

And so, for the rest of the day, Allie watched Mr. Penn-Leith laugh with the first mate and captain. He regaled the officers with a story of his time in Rome. Something about a pickpocket, a lemon, and a monkey that involved a lot of screeching and flapping of his arms.

Allie had looked on, helplessly bewitched along with the crew.

It wasn't that she was unaware of Mr. Penn-Leith's magnetism. Her mother had cultivated relationships with similarly engaging men during their years in Venice.

It was more that Mr. Penn-Leith, for all his brilliance and success, didn't take himself or his craft too seriously. Though he was easily the most famous person in London, he hadn't let the fact go to his head. Instead, he laughed at his own foibles. He took the officers' ribbing with a chuckle and self-deprecating grin.

Case in point, after a lunch of cold meats and cheese, Allie found him in the midst of a group of midshipmen. The men were ostensibly repairing ropes around the main mast, but two sailors begged Mr. Penn-Leith for a story. Ever amiable, Mr. Penn-Leith recounted a garden party he had once attended where an amorous ram decided that Mr. Penn-Leith was to be his next conquest. Though hilarious, the account would have been mortifyingly embarrassing to any other human being.

But not to Ethan Penn-Leith.

No, he told the tale with verve and expressive hand gestures.

"And there I was," he said, arms spread wide, "racing back and forth across Lady Stewart's garden party, Fergus in pursuit and bleating his displeasure at my lack of *amour*. Every chance he got, the sheep would pinch another article of my clothing between his teeth—my coat, a shoe, my left shirtsleeve. I was half-naked before I managed tae scramble atop a wall. Of course, I cursed enough tae make a sailor proud—" He paused while the men rolled with laughter. "—sufficiently horrifying the ladies present and causing no end of trouble."

As the men cackled around him, Mr. Penn-Leith turned and unerringly found her gaze where she stood at the ship's railing. His grin softened slightly and he winked before turning back to the gathered sailors.

Kendall snorted at Allie's elbow.

Allie glanced up at her brother, leaning back against the railing.

"I find it amusing that Penn-Leith attracted a literal sheep given how people follow him around." Kendall sent Allie a rather pointed look.

"Are you now insinuating that I am a sheep?"

Kendall crossed his arms. "If the cap fits . . ."

"Ah, meaning I am also a dunce? How lovely of you. I have kept my promise. I have not spoken with Mr. Penn-Leith since your interruption this morning. You cannot fault me for looking at him." Turning to her twin, Allie tapped her chin. "But I must say, Kendall, I find the inner mechanics of your mind to be fascinating. Do you honestly believe this tack will work?"

"Pardon?"

Allie placed her palms to her cheeks and adopted an expression of mock horror.

"Oh no!" she rasped, mimicking Kendall's deep bass. "Lady Allegra appears to find the Highland Poet interesting. I know! I shall attempt to turn my sister's sense of individuality against her and imply that she is a simpleton to fall for Mr. Penn-Leith's chicanery. That will certainly embarrass her into compliance." She dropped her act and gave her twin a deadpan stare. "Really, Kendall. You are cleverer than this. At the very least, give my own intelligence more credit. You know Mr. Penn-Leith is considerably more than the sum of his charm and handsome good looks."

"And now we're adding *handsome* to his list of adjectives? I'm starting to think I may have made a grave mistake in allowing Mr. Penn-Leith to journey with us. It might not have been my finest decision."

"Yes, well, if the cap fits . . . ," she parroted back to him.

Kendall clenched both his fists, a clear sign that Allie was besting him.

Which meant that his next words were all too predictable.

"Tread lightly, Lady Allegra," he said, looming over her. "As I've repeatedly noted, the poet is not for you. Do not think that this . . ." He waved a hand. ". . . this rapport that is growing between you can ever be anything more than that. An alliance between yourself and Ethan Penn-Leith will never happen. I can and *will* ruin him before I permit it."

Waves lapped against the hull of the ship.

"Careful, Kendall," she said softly. "Your ducal pedigree is showing. It's rather alarming how thoroughly you channel our sire's spirit."

Her brother pushed off the railing.

"We have an agreement, you and I," he said. "See that you abide by it."

Kendall stalked off.

Allie looked back to the main mast to find Mr. Penn-Leith regarding her with raised eyebrows.

Do ye require any assistance? his expression said.

Allie shook her head.

Mr. Penn-Leith lifted his chin in acknowledgment and turned back to the group of men around him.

The simplicity of the moment felt transcendental.

A lightning bolt of realization.

That tiny action was what differentiated men like Kendall from a gentleman like Ethan Penn-Leith.

Kendall saw her as a commodity to be conquered and leveraged in his never-ending quest for power.

However in his small reaction, Mr. Penn-Leith showed himself to be cut from a different cloth. He trusted her to sort her own problems. To know her own mind. To be a person in her own right.

He wished to be her partner, her equal. Her friend. Ethan Penn-Leith would never view Allie as a shiny bauble to acquire for his own gain or to soothe his vanity.

Something cracked beneath Allie's breastbone. One of the braces, possibly, that encased her distrust of men.

Perhaps . . .

Perhaps, she would consider trusting *this* man.

Not an ocean of trust or even a lake. But a thimbleful?

Yes. Maybe that she could conceivably manage.

E than didn't speak with Lady Allegra for the remainder of that first day.

Kendall ensured it.

His Grace shot Ethan warning looks anytime he got within twenty feet of Lady Allegra.

It was all for the best, really. The duke had made his position exquisitely clear, and Ethan knew Kendall would crush him like a gnat should he disrupt His Grace's orderly universe.

So instead of attempting to circumvent Kendall's strictures as he desperately wished, Ethan spent the day aboard ship charming his way through the ranks. The more allies he had, the better.

At dusk, the *S.S. Statesman* docked in Cromer along the Norfolk coast for the evening, and the passengers made their way to a quayside inn. There, Ethan dined with Kendall's secretaries in the inn's taproom. Soon, the entire dining room was listening in, travelers and local tradesmen alike eagerly asking questions.

After a request from an elderly farmer, Ethan climbed atop a table in order to be better heard. At one point, he looked up and caught Lady Allegra staring at him inscrutably before following Lady Whipple up to their rooms.

The sight caused a painful hitch in his chest. As if a string were stretched between them, connecting his ribcage to hers, and it pulled too tight, pinching his heart as her skirts disappeared up the staircase.

Ethan rubbed a fist over the ache and could have sworn the candles dimmed in her absence.

THE OCEAN GREW fitful the next morning. By mid-afternoon, it was throwing a tantrum.

Dark clouds rolled in. Rain lashed the rigging in blinding sheets. In response to the downpour, the North Sea roiled and lurched, seeming determined to either send them to the bottom of the deep or dash them atop rocks.

The sails creaked and midshipmen called back and forth as they fought to keep the paddle wheels in the water. The steam boiler and mechanical gears clanked, the noise rattling ominously through the ship.

Ethan retreated to his tight quarters along with Kendall's man of business and two secretaries, each clinging to their seats and praying they didn't need to lunge for the chamberpot. Lady Allegra and Lady Whipple were closeted in the small stateroom, likely fighting a similar battle.

The ship shuddered and creaked around them. After hours of being tossed about like a toy boat in a barrel, a loud crack sounded and the entire ship tilted alarmingly to port.

Too queasy and unsteady to even attempt to discover what had happened, Ethan and Kendall's men remained in their quarters until the vessel docked in Whitby with a tired thud. Here, the ocean break-wall and surrounding cliffs offered a respite from the worst of the storm, permitting the rain to fall in a more orderly fashion, straight down and soaking.

Emerging onto the rain-lashed deck, Ethan figured he looked similar to Kendall's men—wild-eyed, wobbly-kneed, and bedraggled as a nearly-drowned cat.

Only Kendall himself appeared unaffected. He stood beside the captain at the mizzenmast, talking in a clipped voice, only pausing for the captain to bark orders to the crew. Phrases like "cracked beyond repair" and "taking on too much water" rang across the deck.

"Penn-Leith!" Kendall called as Ethan walked toward the gangplank. Ethan crossed to the duke. "Your Grace?"

"We will be staying in Whitby for the night. Unfortunately, the storm has damaged the steam propeller, and we are taking on water far too rapidly for my liking." Kendall had lost his hat at some point. His gray hair clung to his forehead and dripped over his ears. He blinked water out of his eyes. "We need to see to repairs immediately. Would you escort my sister and aunt to the inn? It is far too dangerous for them to remain aboard, and I would see them comfortable for the evening."

Ethan nodded in surprise. "I should be honored, Your Grace."

The duke narrowed his eyes. "Do not read too much into this request. I require my secretaries' assistance, and my man of business—" Here Kendall spared a glance for said gentleman, currently losing what was left of his lunch over the side of the ship. "—is rather indisposed. I trust you to behave with the utmost propriety."

Ethan tipped his head, barely suppressing a delighted grin. He pivoted around and headed toward the ladies in question before Kendall could change his mind.

TWO HOURS LATER, Ethan found himself sitting in the private dining room of The White Horse and Griffin, enjoying a fine steak and ale pie in the company of Lady Allegra and Lady Whipple.

Ethan and Lady Allegra ate in silence as Lady Whipple recounted tale after tale of the people she had once known.

"I knew the Duke of Wellington in my youth, you see," Lady Whipple said on a laugh. "At one point, I remember saying to my dear friend, the Duchess of Marlborough, that Arthur Wellesley would become *Someone Important*. He cut far too dashing a figure to *not* rise to great heights." She punctuated this comment with an appraising look at Ethan.

The coal fire in the hearth radiated warmth through the room despite the continued patter of rain on the paned window. The occasional clank of cutlery or crack of laughter drifted in from the public dining room beyond their door.

Ethan dared a glance at Lady Allegra. Dressed simply in a dark blue gown impeccably tailored to skim her glorious curves, hair pulled into a thick chignon, she truly was the siren of his poem. Worse, at some point over the past day, she had ceased being the stilted, aloof *Lady Allegra* in his thoughts and had become *Allie*—a wary, wounded woman with secrets and a treasure trove of brilliant thoughts he longed to unearth.

For her part, Allie clearly noticed his noticing. When Lady Whipple bent over her dinner, Allie sent him a raised eyebrow.

Nothing escaped his wee *ladra*.

Finally, after a delicious dessert of treacle tart, Lady Whipple pushed back from the table.

Ethan immediately shot to his feet.

"I am for bed. My old bones are not quite used to sailing through violent tempests such as that of today," her ladyship announced, turning for the door. "You have been a delight, Mr. Penn-Leith. I am glad we have your company. Will you see me upstairs, Lady Allegra?"

"Of course, Aunt." Allie rose too, her meek behavior marred by the smirk she sent Ethan.

His eyes followed his *ladra* from the room, noting the wee nip of her waist and helplessly imagining how it would feel under his palms.

> Silken warm, an infinity contained
> Beneath fingertips sure yet trembling.

Unhelpful thought that.

With a deep breath, he sat back down and poured a glass of port, nursing it while staring into the fire.

This infatuation with Allie was rapidly becoming a hydra—every wee attempt he made to stem his admiration merely spawned a new behemoth of affection to be conquered.

It was the veriest madness.

Mmm, though the comparison might make an excellent poem.

So . . . not all was lost.

He was contemplating jotting down his ideas and seeking his own bed when the dining room door opened—bringing with it a burst of noise from the public taproom—and Allie slipped in.

His stupid, foolish heart leapt as he rose to his feet.

She closed the door, muting the sound.

"Is that wise?" He nodded toward the latch.

"Probably not," she said, sliding into the chair opposite him. "But the noise is dreadful and who here in this inn will report our indiscretion? Kendall and his men are still with the ship, and Aunt Whipple all but shooed me away."

Ethan sat back down.

They stared at one another for the space of two deep breaths.

He knew he should open the door. Propriety demanded it.

And yet . . .

"Why do I sense that your aunt wishes tae stir up trouble?" he finally said.

"Aunt Whipple?" Allie's eyebrows rose. "Of a surety. She would love nothing more than to have delightful morsels of gossip to tell her friends. I should hate to disappoint her." She pointed to the decanter of port. "May I?"

Ethan poured her a glass and passed it across the table. "Lady Whipple appears tae be a rather ineffective choice of chaperone."

"Not at all. She is usually militant in her chaperonage." Allie sipped her wine. "I merely think she has taken a rather strong liking to yourself. You are, after all, deadly charming."

Ethan toyed with his own glass of port. "Should I be flattered or alarmed?"

"Both."

"Ye are doing a rather poor job of easing my fears, lass. Will your brother kill me if he catches us closeted together?" he asked.

"Most probably."

"Pistols at dawn, do ye ken?"

"Unlikely." Allie laughed, sipping at her wine. "Kendall would hardly stoop to something so tawdry, particularly for a gentleman of no rank. He would merely hire a pair of thugs to, and I quote, 'Teach you your proper place in society.'"

"Ouch." Ethan mimed taking a fist to his chin.

"I have never been one to sugarcoat reality."

"Nae, ye have not." He saluted her with his glass. "It's one of the reasons I let ye call me a friend."

"I'm beginning to think you don't have many of those, given how often you bring it up. Desperate, are you?"

His lips quirked. "The number of people who wish something from me is endless. But the ones *I* call friend are few."

That was his bare truth.

"And you have chosen me. I am honored." She saluted him with her glass before adding, "Ethan."

His Christian name on her lips loosed a stampede of emotions—elation, relief, desire. *Finally* he was making measurable progress in winning her trust.

"The pleasure is mine . . . Allie," he replied, clinking his glass with hers.

She smiled and sipped her port.

"The innkeep mentioned that Captain Cook himself used to hire crew from this very room." She surveyed the space with its low timber ceiling and smoke-stained fireplace. "Plucking friends from the masses, as it were. I gather that is what you have done with me."

Ethan clasped his hands on the table, admiring how easily she threaded ideas through their conversations.

"I suppose, after a fashion," he said. "I ken that the entire wealth of Britain has been built on meetings in rooms just like this one."

"True."

"Do ye wonder if powerful aristocrats ever think of all these people?" He waved a hand to indicate the inn and the working-class men and women who had passed through its doors over the years. "How the labor and industry of the masses fund the lifestyles of the wealthy?"

"Aristocrats like my brother, you mean?" She quirked an eyebrow at him.

"Well, I suppose I do."

"You sound like a revolutionary," she said. "Are you quite sure you don't have sympathies with *La Giovine Italia*?"

Ethan took a sip of his port. "Their ideas? Of a surety. Their methods, however? Perhaps not so much. For example, I find your Fabrizio to be a rather suspicious person. He seems the sort to have scarce loyalty for anyone but himself. Everything he does appears to have a selfish aim."

"You are not wrong on that score. Fabrizio is a gambler and swindler at heart."

"Ah! The kind tae sell you out for a farthing," Ethan continued, leaning forward on his elbows.

"Oh, he already has." She gave a mirthless snort, gray eyes snapping in the candlelight.

"Pardon?" Ethan's neck prickled with alarm.

"Do you not know?" Her head canted to the right. "My beloved brother paid Fabrizio to have me drugged and delivered to his hired henchmen—thugs who promptly transported me back to England. I never even properly learned the men's names. They trussed me up and stood guard day and night until finally passing me along like a postal parcel to Kendall at Hawthorn. All I lacked was a wrapping of brown paper and jute twine." She narrated the events casually, as if recounting the weather.

Ethan's brows drew down, his breath tight in his lungs.

"You look appalled," she continued.

"I *am* appalled. I didn't know ye had been forced back tae England in such a barbaric fashion."

"Yes, well, from Kendall's point of view, it was necessary. If he wishes to become Prime Minister, he cannot have me rabble-rousing across the Continent. And if I am in England, then he can use me as a pawn in his ruthless quest to consolidate power."

"Through marriage?"

"Sì." She nearly spat the syllable, as if marriage were a bitter gooseberry on her tongue. "Such has always been the way of the Dukes of Kendall—marry off their womenfolk, willingly or not, for political gain."

Ethan waited for her to expound upon the topic.

She said nothing more.

"Did your father attempt to arrange a marriage for ye?" he finally asked.

She sipped her port, looking into the fire. "What do you think?"

Ah.

So the old Duke of Kendall *had* attempted to bend her to his will.

"I would hear the story, if you would tell it." Ethan longed to know every last crumb of her history.

"No," she shook her head decisively. The motion knocked loose a tendril of her dark hair, sending it tumbling over her ear. Ethan's fingers ached to smooth it back. "I have merely agreed to a tentative friendship with yourself. Only true friends are privy to my history with the former Duke of Kendall. Better luck next time."

Ethan's lips quirked at her tone. "Do ye fear your brother will constrain ye tae marry?"

"Of course he will. He is a Duke of Kendall, after all. My groom has already been chosen, have you not heard?" Allie stifled a bitter laugh.

Ethan's stomach somersaulted into a dive.

His lovely *ladra* was already affianced and promised to another? Kendall was entirely the sort to arrange a marriage with or without her consent.

Ethan felt an *eejit* in every whit.

They often made light of Kendall's control of her, but that did not remove the very real consequences of that control. The duke hadn't gone to such machinations—kidnapping his sister from Italy and restricting her movements—to permit her to marry where she wished.

No. Kendall would use her marriage to bolster his own political aims.

"I had not heard. Who is tae be the lucky groom?" Ethan took a sip of his port, but it did nothing to quell the riot of his thoughts. They tumbled and shouted like unruly school children, rendering his rational thinking chaotic.

"Lord Charswood," she replied, her expression feigning indifference, but the white knuckles of her fingers wrapped around her glass said otherwise. "I have yet to meet him."

"Ye haven't met him? So you are not *officially* betrothed?"

"Not yet, thank heaven. Are you acquainted with Lord Charswood?"

"Charswood?" Ethan had met his lordship once or twice—a gray-haired, wiry man with sharp, blue eyes. But surely that couldn't be the correct gentleman. "I know the elder Lord Charswood, but I haven't heard anything of his passing. I assume Kendall wouldn't expect ye tae marry someone quite so . . ." He trailed off.

"Old?" Allie supplied. "In that, you would err. My dear brother does indeed expect me to marry a man ancient enough to be my grandfather."

Ethan let out a harsh breath.

Kendall was a right bastard.

And so Ethan said as much, "Forgive me, but your brother is a right bastard."

Allie saluted him with her glass. "On that point, we can easily agree."

"Why Lord Charswood?" Ethan wondered aloud.

"Kendall has declined to illuminate that point. I assume Charswood offers some specific political benefit."

"Aye. That, he would." Ethan plumbed his memory for what he knew of the earl. "From what I can recall, Lord Charswood is a respected statesman. As Kendall's brother-in-law, he would likely bolster your twin's appointment to a cabinet position . . . and eventually Prime Minister. But I am sure Charswood already has an heir from a prior marriage, so why would he pursue yourself, particularly as you have never met?" Ethan thought further and then snapped his fingers, quickly connecting the dots. "*Och*, of course. Charswood also owns the largest gunpowder factory in Britain."

Allie froze for the space of three seconds before thawing, her shoulders slumping.

"Naturally, he does," she murmured, draining her port and motioning for Ethan to pour her more. "The missing piece. No wonder Charswood is eager to acquire me, sight unseen. My dowry includes the Salzi Mine and provides him with a ready-made source of saltpeter for his factory. 'Tis a match made in heaven . . . for Kendall and Charswood, that is."

Ethan snorted, filling her glass. "While your own personal desires and well-being are merely an unfortunate inconvenience to be swept aside."

She sipped her wine, eyes narrowing at him. "Do you ever tire of feeling like a prize to be won?"

"Pardon?"

"Kendall has ensured that I am a pretty, expensive parcel to be purchased."

"He did have you posted from Italy, as you say."

"Precisely." She pointed a finger at him. "I am nothing more than the sum of my looks, my pedigree, and my dowry. While you, Ethan Penn-Leith, I imagine are often viewed as the sum of your talent and persona as the Highland Poet. The public feels that they know you, and therefore, own a part of you, as it were."

"Haven't we already touched on this topic?"

"Perhaps obliquely. I guess what I am asking is . . . do you ever tire of having to play the expected part?"

Och. That was the question, was it not?

Of course he tired of playing the Highland Poet. Just as she was restless in her role as Lady Allegra Gilbert.

"At times," he admitted. "But unlike yourself, it is a role I chose. Which I suppose sums up the difference between being born a man or a woman. As a man, I can at least select my cage."

"A rather grim but accurate assessment," she replied with caustic bitterness. "I needn't tell you that any courtship Charswood musters will receive a resounding rejection from myself."

Allie lounged back in her chair, swirling the ruby-red liquid in her glass and studying it in the candlelight.

Huh. Her lips truly were vermilion red, lush and petal-soft. For easily the thousandth time, Ethan relived the memory of her mouth on his, the punishing urgency of those lips.

He shook the thoughts free. "So what will ye do about Kendall's demands?"

"At the moment? Nothing." Her gaze locked with his, gray eyes sparking. "Unless, that is, you are planning on kissing me again? Perhaps in front of his ship's crew this time? It definitely riled him last week."

Ethan choked on his port, coughing loudly. "P-pardon? Kiss ye?"

"You keep staring at my mouth like a man dying of thirst, so what else am I to think?"

She punctuated her words with an arched eyebrow and a lingering survey of his own mouth.

Bloody hell.

She set him afire.

But then . . . he had known this woman was trouble from those first moments aboard the *vetturini* in Italy.

Abruptly, all he could think was that it would be so easy . . .

So simple to merely reach across the table, thread his fingers into her hair, and create another memory of the gentle give of her lips under his. The hitch in her chest. The soft exhale of her warm breath against his mouth.

Or maybe . . .

. . . he would just write a poem about it instead.

That was the safer option, was it not?

If Allie found his lengthy silence unnerving, she didn't show it.

She continued to regard him with a casual insouciance.

Which, in its own way, revealed her feelings on the prospect of a kiss.

"Aye, I'm a man. Of course, I want tae kiss yourself," he finally said. "But I don't think ye genuinely wish me tae kiss you."

"Whyever not?"

Och, so many ways to answer that simple question and none of them good.

"Because ye would be kissing me merely tae spite Kendall. Because ye may have already had a wee bitty too much port tae think clearly. Because Kendall claims that ye use kisses like currency, spending them tae bend men tae your will, and I don't wish to be counted among that number."

She set down her wine glass with a thud, causing the remaining port to slosh in a rollicking circle. "I thought we already agreed that my brother is a bastard?"

"Aye, but an intelligent and perceptive one."

His implied question—*well, do you use your kisses as currency?*—hovered between them.

She stared at him, declining to answer.

"Contrary to my past behavior with regards tae yourself, I don't make it a habit tae kiss women willy-nilly. When a lady kisses me, I want it to mean something." Ethan paused and held her gaze. "Because when I kiss a lady, it *will* mean something."

That was the raw truth.

Though he wanted this woman more than his next breath, he also desired more than just her lips or her body under his—things she appeared ready to bestow on anyone she deemed useful.

No.

Ethan was greedy.

He wanted the wee bits she kept stowed away. The guarded pieces of her soul no one else knew existed.

Allie sucked in a long, stuttering breath, as if his words had rattled something loose.

And then she let it out again, just as quickly.

"Your poetic nature is showing, Ethan," she said, eyes dropping to her wine glass on the table. "Always wanting everything to mean something. Sometimes a kiss can just be a kiss."

"I disagree. A kiss is a communion. An exchange of spirit right along with breath."

"Again, that is the poet Ethan Penn-Leith speaking."

"It is, but then, I am that man, too. Words are my craft."

"And sometimes, I suppose, you feel that Fate can turn on one kiss alone?" A sardonic humor tinged her tone.

"Aye." He tossed back the rest of his port and shot her a wry smile. "As an acclaimed, dashing young writer once said, sometimes it very well can."

She sent him a faint smile and then looked away, staring into the low fire burning in the hearth. Rain continued to drum against the window.

He continued, "I'm afraid, as a friend, ye will simply have tae accept me in my complexity."

"I'm still on the fence regarding our friendship, Ethan," she said primly. "Do not take more rope than I have permitted."

"I think we are more alike than ye care tae admit, lass," he replied, voice soft. "As ye said earlier, both of us know what it is like tae be viewed as trophies. I want to be the man ye let inside the armor ye don to fend off the world. Just as I wish tae let yourself inside my own armor. To be a *true* friend, not merely a sometime kissing partner or a companion of convenience."

Allie had gone preternaturally still opposite him. "And what if I don't wish for that?"

"Well, that is for yourself tae determine. But I have faith I can win ye over." Ethan rapped his knuckles on the table. "And then, after we have become *true* friends, should ye ever decide ye want more than friendship . . . if ever ye look at me without calculations going on in that lovely head of yours, if ye can meet my yearning gaze without glancing away . . . then and only then, will I kiss ye. But be warned, lass, if I kiss ye at that moment, I'll be kissing ye for keeps."

13

Allie had a rather restless night's sleep.

She attributed it to Aunt Whipple's snores echoing from the adjoining room.

But she knew that for the lie it was.

Ethan's words would not let her be.

I want to be the man ye let inside the armor ye don to fend off the world.

Goose-flesh pebbled her skin at the memory of his green eyes, sincere and brimming with intensity.

His words were a challenge.

A call to change. To trust.

Yet . . . her armor, as Ethan termed it, was born of betrayal and self-preservation.

In the past, every person she welcomed inside her walls turned traitor.

Tristan, as her twin brother.

Fabrizio, as a companion in her quest for purpose and survival.

She needn't look far to see how *those* relationships had come out.

So . . . why would she let Ethan in?

He offered her nothing but his friendship in return. And she had never had a friend . . . just to have a friend.

When a lady kisses me, I want it to mean something. Because when I kiss a lady, it will *mean something.*

She shivered. If she had been ambivalent about Ethan's kiss before—which, for the record, she had *not*—those two sentences would have changed her mind in an instant.

Their previous kisses had, in a sense, been hers. She had initiated them, demanded them.

But . . . how different would the kiss be if *he* were claiming it of *her?*

Madonna.

The very thought rendered her lightheaded with want.

And yet . . . it was his parting words which had landed hardest.

If I kiss ye at that moment, I'll be kissing ye for keeps.

Allie couldn't even envision how that sentiment would play out.

How could she ever trust enough to permit a man like Ethan Penn-Leith—optimistic, cheerful, buoyant—to kiss her for keeps?

And even if she *wished* to be kept, Kendall would tear them asunder. Her brother had made that more than plain.

Allie awoke to rain drizzling out her window and Kendall rapping incessantly on her bedchamber door. When she opened the door, her brother barged into the room—fully dressed, hat in hand, and drafting damp sea air in his wake.

"The ship's engine suffered damage yesterday," he began without preamble. "We stemmed the inflow of water last night, but critical repairs must be made. The captain, the engineer, and I will work to fix what we can, but we require a part from Manchester to render the ship seaworthy once more."

"I see." Allie pulled a dressing gown around her shoulders. "Will such repairs take long?"

And how could she finesse this turn of events to her own advantage?

"Not too long," her brother said. "We should have the ship running in about four or five days, but I feel the need to oversee the repairs myself."

Ah. How delightful to discover an instance in which Kendall's overbearing need for control actually assisted her. With any luck, the repairs would take so long, they would miss the house party altogether.

And wouldn't that be tragic?

She should have thought to sabotage the ship herself.

"Unfortunately," Kendall continued, turning his top hat in his hands, "I shall be unable to attend to you or Lady Whipple in the interim, as the repairs will command my time, and I must send a secretary and my man of business to collect the required parts."

Gracious, this entire situation simply kept improving—possibly avoiding Lord Charswood, missing the house party, *and* being left to her own devices with Ethan Penn-Leith about?

Allie felt like she had just been dealt a winning hand in *vingt et un.*

"*Che peccato.* Aunt Whipple and I shall simply have to make do with one another's company," she replied, careful to keep her expression neutral.

On the inside however, a trio of fairy sprites named Elation, Hope, and Optimism had formed a circle and were currently dancing a wild jig of joy.

"Yes. See that you do," Kendall nodded. "Let Lady Whipple guide your behavior as to how you spend your time. I shall arrange a private sitting room for you both, so you may have a place to embroider and read at your leisure. I will speak with our aunt about the arrangement right now. I will also inform Lady Whipple that you are not to spend too much time in Mr. Penn-Leith's company. We needn't set tongues to wagging on that score. Remember the contract you signed." He glared at her in warning before shoving his hat atop his head. "Meanwhile if you need me, I shall be at the wharf."

Kendall shut the door with a sharp *snick.*

Rain pattered against the window pane.

But not even the dreary weather or her brother's smothering authority could dim the brilliance of Allie's smile.

TRUE TO HIS word, Kendall did arrange a private sitting room for Allie and Lady Whipple.

Aunt Whipple, however, seemed less enamored of the arrangement.

"Why should I leave the comfort of my warm bedchamber to sit in a drafty room?" the lady had intoned when Allie visited her an hour after Kendall's departure. "This trip has already been ruinous to my health."

Allie stared down at her aunt as she lay in bed, propped up against a mountain of pillows and enjoying an excellent fruit scone with a cup of hot chocolate from the inn's kitchen.

The lady's health appeared anything but ruinous.

"I am sorry to hear that, Aunt," Allie said contritely. "I guess I shall have to while away the hours in the sitting room by myself."

"Are you content to do so, girl?" Aunt Whipple's expression was far too innocent to be believable. "You will likely need some sort of companionship, will you not?"

Was her aunt suggesting what Allie *thought* she might be suggesting?

"I . . . I suppose I could see if Mr. Penn-Leith were about," Allie offered. "I am sure he would be willing to keep me company."

"Excellent idea, child," her ladyship nodded her head. "Just ensure you leave the door open, as propriety demands."

"Of course."

"And do not mention this to Kendall." Lady Whipple peered up at her. "You know how your brother can be."

Allie nodded. "I shall be quiet as the grave, Aunt."

"See that you are." Aunt Whipple took a bite of her scone, dabbing at her mouth with a fine linen napkin. "Enjoy your time with Mr. Penn-Leith. And then please return and tell me about it."

TEN MINUTES LATER, Allie paused in the doorway to the private sitting room Kendall had arranged. She was still trying to come to terms with her aunt's easy dismissal of her chaperonage.

If Allie had known that a charming poet was all it took for Aunt Whipple to forsake her duties . . . well, she might have dredged one up long before now.

Though she did not mind her current freedom, given the view before her.

The private sitting room featured a bank of cheery paned windows overlooking the street, several stuffed armchairs, a writing desk, a table for cards, and a large fireplace. Most importantly, it was up a flight of stairs and on the opposite side of the inn from the noise of the public dining room.

But all of this she noticed merely in passing.

Ethan Penn-Leith held her riveted.

He sat at the desk before the windows, profile to the door, writing quickly in a notebook, a pair of spectacles perched on his nose. Dressed only in a waistcoat, shirtsleeves, and neckcloth with his chestnut hair falling in loose waves across his forehead, he seemed . . .

Well . . . he seemed like Ethan. The hard-working, humble man behind the famous Highland Poet.

Allie couldn't look away. Witnessing him like this . . . so unguarded and authentic . . .

Once, her mother had taken a lover who was a benefactor of La Fenice, the popular opera house in Venice. Before the opening night of a performance of Mozart's *The Magic Flute*, the gentleman had led Allie and her mother on a tour of the stage and backdrops, showing them *how* an opera was made.

It had been a revelation.

Seeing Ethan like this was much the same.

A glimpse into another world—the intimate moment where his brilliant works were created.

Also . . . could she circle back to the spectacles?

Allie had never considered how attractive a pair of silver-rimmed glasses could be.

As it had the night before, her traitorous heart thudded in her rib-cage at the sight of him. And just as she had then, she took in a steady breath and reminded herself that she was a realist—despite her restless night's sleep, despite Elation, Hope, and Optimism. If she weren't careful, Ethan's charm would lead her straight to disappointment and regret.

Unlike the night before, she left the door ajar as she entered the room.

Ethan looked up at the sound, rising to his feet, that dazzling smile of his making an appearance.

"Good morning," he bowed, removing the spectacles from his face. "I trust you slept well?" A warm earnestness laced his words.

"I did," she lied, feeling breathless and oddly . . . shy. "You will have to excuse Lady Whipple. Our ordeal yesterday and the dreary weather this morning have left her rather unwell."

"Ah, I am sorry to hear it," he replied, though his grin and cheerful tone said otherwise.

"As am I." Still smiling, she looked about the room, arms swinging against her skirts. "So . . . what shall we do today?"

"I HAVE BEEN pondering what you said last night." Allie reached for another strawberry. "About wishing us to be true friends. The sort who are welcomed into the other's inner life."

"Aye?" Ethan lifted a piece of cheese from a wooden platter.

They sat in their private parlor, dining on a luncheon of ham, crusty bread, a bowl of fresh strawberries, and some excellent Yorkshire Wensleydale cheese. The rain maintained a steady patter against the windows. Though the weather cast a dreary pall, a cheery fire in the hearth brightened the room.

Or perhaps that brightness came from Ethan himself, Allie mused. Even on a rain-soaked day such as this, hours spent with him felt like basking in sunlight.

In many ways, theirs was similar to how her relationship had once been with Kendall—thoughts aligned and opinions flowing freely.

A soul twin, in truth.

But with the added benefit of maturity and euphoric attraction to a man who was most decidedly *not* her brother.

Ethan remained in shirtsleeves and a green waistcoat, his gray coat draped over the back of a nearby chair. The closer she sat to him, the more she noticed the scent of his cologne—sandalwood and something tantalizingly earthy, like a pine-laden forest. Most deliciously, despite the slight chill in the air, he had cuffed his sleeves, revealing a decadent six inches of muscled forearm.

Allie had spent years in the company of brigands, not to mention nearly a decade before that as a citizen of Venice with its abundance of Renaissance paintings and sculpture.

In short, she was no stranger to the male form in various states of *dishabille.*

But those few inches of Ethan Penn-Leith's skin, combined with the heady scent of his cologne, set her head to spinning. Every time his hand lifted to punctuate a point or reach for a slice of cheese, the tendons in his forearm stretched and rippled beneath his skin. Did wielding a pen sculpt such muscle?

"You said there are few you call a friend," she said, forcibly dragging her eyes away from that hint of skin. "So, I wonder . . . who are your true friends?"

Raising an eyebrow, he paused to look at her. "*Och,* jealous already, are ye?"

"Don't let it go to your head."

"Too late." Winking at her, he smoothed a hand down his waistcoat. "A braw Scot *can* be hard for the lasses tae resist."

"Ethan." Allie's voice held a warning note, though she fought a laugh. *Uffa.*

She could scarcely remember indulging in levity before Ethan Penn-Leith. It was as if her life before meeting him had been shrouded in gloom, a bleakness she hadn't noticed until the bright light of Ethan's cheerfulness had shined upon it.

This was the problem, she decided. That despite her misgivings and repeated self-chastisement, it was easy to succumb to the relentless pull of Ethan's warmth.

Could she find the will to resist him? Or to be more precise—could she summon the motivation to care about resisting him?

Pushing back his lunch plate, Ethan's expression turned more serious. "I wasn't exaggerating when I said my circle of friends is rather wee. When all of London claims tae know yourself, ye choose those whom ye *will* call friend carefully."

"I'm flattered."

"As well ye should be, lass," he said with another small teasing glance. "I ken my brother and sister are my closest friends. Ye might even meet them, once we arrive at Muirford House."

Allie experienced a jolt of surprise. "They live near Lord Hadley's estate?"

"Aye. 'Tis why Kendall felt it logical for me tae accompany yourselves to Muirford House. I am merely returning home. Hadley has been the local lord and benefactor all my life."

"And do you call Hadley friend?"

"After a sort. He is more of a fatherly figure than anything else."

A fatherly figure? But what about Ethan's real father?

Abruptly, Allie felt voracious to learn everything about Ethan. About the world that had formed him—the very first pen he set to paper, the lullabies his mother might have sung to him. Perhaps attending the house party wouldn't be such a chore, after all. Not if it gave her a glimpse into Ethan's life and family.

"Tell me about your brother and sister," she said. "Tell me about your family."

"Malcolm and Leah?" A different sort of grin touched Ethan's lips. One she hadn't seen before. *This* smile was a soft, tender affair.

She could see him looking down at his swaddled, newborn child with that precise expression.

Madonna. Her fascination was becoming maudlin.

He sat back, reaching for the pitcher of small ale on the table, that gentle smile still on his face. "Well, as ye can imagine, my older brother and sister love me tae distraction."

As they finished their lunch, Ethan told Allie of his growing-up years. Of his mother's untimely death and Leah's tender care. Of Malcolm's taciturn, brotherly love and his father's support and steadfast character.

"My mother's family, the Leiths, are wealthy gentry from Deeside with ties to the Earl of Aberdeen," he said, moving the bowl of strawberries aside. "So naturally, when my genteel mother, Isobel Leith, fell in love with a lowly gentleman farmer named John Penn, her family devolved into histrionics. My mother would not be swayed. Eventually, my grandfather relented and accepted the marriage, but only after my father agreed to change his surname to Penn-Leith and to use my mother's dowry to build a house commensurate with her place in society. And so Thistle Muir came to be."

"Your family's home?"

"Aye. It's not the grandest of houses, but it has always been home and hearth to me. My happiest memories occurred within its walls."

Allie frowned at his tone. "You make it sound as if the house was lost to you."

"Perhaps it was, in a way. At the age of ten, my mother's brother, Mr. George Leith, decided that I needed to be rescued from the horrors of my father's lowly influence. And so, I was sent to live with my uncle and aunt in Aberdeen, where I was raised and educated as a gentleman."

"Oh!" Allie's frown deepened.

Ten years old.

The same age when she was separated from Tristan.

The identical point in time when her own world had fractured.

"Was that difficult?" she asked.

He paused . . . gaze distant. "I suppose, particularly as I look back at those years. But at the time, everyone only talked about how fortunate I was. How blessed that my wealthy uncle had condescended to help his poor relation. How grateful I must be for that condescension. And I took their words to heart." Ethan sipped at his ale.

"Was your uncle unkind to you?" she had to ask.

He pondered the question for a bit too long. A gust of wind rattled the window panes.

"If you have to think upon it to such an extent," Allie said into the quiet between them, "then the answer is likely *yes*."

Sighing, he shifted in his chair, mouth pulling to one side. Abruptly, Allie could see the boy he had been—wide-eyed and earnest. Painfully open with his emotions, permitting the world to batter him.

"Nae," he finally said. "I cannot say that my Uncle Leith has ever been deliberately unkind. He has never raised a hand against me or been needlessly cruel. He is a good man . . ." He trailed off into silence.

"And yet?"

"And yet . . . he is not a warm man. He is a businessman and shipping merchant, and as such, I ken he saw myself as another of his investments. Therefore, I had to prove worthy of his financial capital . . ."

"But you were a small, motherless boy taken too soon from his family. Not an acquisition to be cataloged and valued."

"Aye. Ye have the right of it. And yet, a part of me will forever be grateful. Without the superior education I received at Uncle Leith's hand, I would not be able to write poetry as I do. I see that clearly. But I often wonder, if I had remained with my family, would life be as . . ." He trailed off.

"Lonely?" Allie offered, unable to stop her tongue from supplying the missing word.

He pinned her with his open gaze. "Precisely. Uncle Leith's generosity has blessed my life immeasurably, but I now inhabit an in-between place. I am considered a gentleman, but many within the *ton* still see me as a Scottish farmer's son. While those of my father's acquaintance consider me to be well above their station due to my upbringing, education, and position within Polite Society. And so I belong everywhere and nowhere all at once."

So like myself, Allie thought.

The eager syllables piled on her tongue, enthusiastically clamoring for release.

Allie pressed her lips firmly shut.

Quiet settled over the room.

Ethan looked at her, a gentle question in his gaze.

And Allie realized in that moment that she was going to do this.

That despite her better judgment, she would let Ethan Penn-Leith know her better. That she would permit this friendship to blossom between them.

And so, she set the syllables free.

"It may seem odd to say . . . but I do understand that sort of liminal existence." She forced the words past her lips. "Though I am the daughter of a duke, I have lived most of my life on the fringes of gentility. Unlike other ladies of my station, I have not been sheltered from the horrors and vicissitudes of Reality. And as such, I cannot relate to other women of the *ton*."

It made the cage Kendall crafted for her all the more difficult to bear.

"It is a lonely place tae be." Ethan nodded. "And what of yourself? Who are your true friends?"

Her friends?

What friends?

Allie struggled to know how to answer that question.

She finally offered Ethan the truth.

"Well . . . I have you, do I not?" she said with strained cheer.

His raised eyebrows said she had not fooled him one whit.

"Was your twin never a friend? Even when you were children?" he asked.

Loss paralyzed her lungs for the space of three heartbeats.

Thump. Tristan squishing into her small bed on a stormy night, his cold hands seeking the warmth of hers.

Thump. Allie racing her twin across the back lawn of Gilbert House, shrieking when Tristan tackled her to the mossy grass.

Thump. Tristan slipping her a biscuit he had nicked from the kitchen, whispering, "Just for you, Allie. I know it's your favorite."

She banished the memories with one deep breath.

"In any way that matters," she said so slowly, the words dripped like cold treacle, "my brother, Tristan, is long dead."

Ethan's fingertips pressed into the tabletop, as if forcibly restraining himself from reaching across the table and touching her, the motion causing a series of muscles to contract in those delectable forearms. Her own hands tingled from the imagined touch.

"And . . . your mother?" he asked.

Allie took in a shuddering breath. The memory of her mother's final moments surfaced—eyes hollow, skin yellow and gaunt, death hovering in the fetid air.

This was always the problem with letting another inside one's armor. Eventually, they wanted *all* your secrets. Even the painful ones Allie had long buried for good reason.

Swallowing, she made a show of rising from her chair and crossing to the paned window. Rain pooled in rippling concentric circles on the flagstone street below.

"From my bedchamber window, I can see the walls of the ruined medieval abbey on the hill behind the inn." She turned back to Ethan. "When the weather lifts, we should explore it."

His eyes said the obvious. *I know ye be avoiding my question.*

And hers replied. *Yes, but I have given you enough of myself today. I cannot share any more.*

Ethan rose and walked to the window, stopping beside her, hands clasped behind his back, his shoulder so close to hers, she could feel the radiating heat of him.

"Aye," he agreed. "When the rain lifts, we should go."

ETHAN BRACED HIS body against the wind. After two days of *dreich* clouds, a stiff breeze had arrived and blown the rain out to sea. The chill air swept in off the ocean, turning the sea frothy and buffeting the ruins of Whitby Abbey that loomed ahead.

"This weather may end us yet," Allie called at his side, a hand clapped atop her bonnet. "I fear the rain might have been preferable." The wind billowed her full skirts, trailing them behind her in a stripe of petticoats.

Ethan had a similar clutch on his own hat.

The abbey remained indomitable before them, its ancient walls having survived nearly a thousand years of pummeling weather on this bluff overlooking the ocean. Where its walls once supported stained glass windows and leaded roofs, they now grew wildflowers and ferns.

"Race you to the ruins," she shouted before taking off at a sprint.

With a huff, Ethan dashed after her.

The entire moment felt like a portrait of their friendship.

Allie, always one step ahead.

Him, running to keep up with her.

It was one of a thousand things he admired about Lady Allegra Gilbert—her clever mind and endless bravery, her acerbic wit and philosophical acuity.

The last three days had been a revelation.

Kendall had been so consumed with repairing the *SS Statesman*, he had utterly absented himself, preferring to dine and sleep aboard ship, trusting Lady Whipple to keep his twin in line.

However, Lady Whipple had taken to her bed with a mild cold . . . or so she claimed. Allie had expressed doubt as to the true state of her aunt's health.

Regardless, Lady Allegra had been left to Ethan's sole care.

Conversation and ideas flowed freely between them.

He had spoken of his time at Oxford and the joy of selling his first book of poetry to a publisher.

She had told him of her adventures with Fabrizio and his cohorts, of the daring exploits they had carried out to raise money for *La Giovine Italia*.

He narrated the whole of Malcolm's betrayal and Viola's defection and how, eventually, it put him on the road in Italy that fateful day.

Allie disclosed the details of her current pact with Kendall and how it might help her regain the Salzi Mine and, with it, her freedom.

And now, after days at her side, Ethan was helplessly caught in the siren song that was Lady Allegra Gilbert.

No matter how many hours he spent in her company, no matter how many confidences they shared, he only wanted more.

More time. More of her secrets. More wee bitty pieces he could stow in his heart.

He knew there was no future for them. Ethan's sworn oaths to Kendall, as well as the duke's expectations of Allie, rendered it impossible.

These hours and days existed on borrowed time.

Yet, he remained in her ambit, hurtling toward certain heartbreak.

The inevitable wreckage would be crushing.

But the current exhilaration of Allie's companionship made that future heartache feel worth it.

What was the Italian expression?

Ne vale la pena?

It merited the pain.

Aye, every minute spent with Lady Allegra merited the pain he would feel when Kendall forced his sister into a loveless marriage, tossing Ethan aside for good.

But for now . . . he reveled in the giddy pleasure of chasing after her.

He caught up with Allie on the leeward side of the abbey's ancient nave. She waited for him with shoulders pressed to the wall, lungs heaving, a devilish smile pinking her cheeks.

He ached to keep walking forward, to push through the mass of her skirts, and press the length of his body to hers. Of a certainty, she would feel like heaven, lush and round where he was lean and firm.

She was not overly tall, his wee *ladra*, but not short either. The perfect height for kissing, as he well knew. He wouldn't have to bend his head down more than a few inches to press his mouth to hers.

But he had meant what he said several nights past. He wouldn't be her plaything—a flitting distraction from the load of Kendall's demands and the pressing weight of her uncertain future.

No. He wanted inside that tightly locked heart of hers. And he wanted her to *want* him there, to plead with him to stay.

And if that meant denying himself the kiss he craved so badly it set his hands to trembling . . .

Well, so be it.

To that end, he stopped a respectful three feet away and smiled.

Allie's returning grin was rueful. "Does that devastating smile of yours ever cease?"

He grinned even wider. "The Swooner, ye mean?"

That earned him a laugh. "The Swooner?"

"Aye, that's what Malcolm calls it." He demonstrated the smile again, the muscles in his cheeks bunching.

She pretended to flinch and held up both hands, as if warding off a curse. "Snuff it out. My eyes hurt!"

"*Och*, The Swooner isn't that bad. You're being a mite dramatic."

"It should be called The Dazzler," she countered, her gray eyes sparkling with vitality against the olive of her skin. "It has a tendency to blind one's good sense."

Ah. He liked the sound of that. At least, as it pertained to her.

"Shall I dazzle ye some more then, my lady?" He leaned forward, her pull so relentless.

"I fear I am only capable of fending off one sun today." She glanced meaningfully at the weak sunlight overhead. "You may have better luck tomorrow."

Laughing, he extended his arm for her to take. She threaded her gloved hand through his elbow, the touch sizzling his nerves. He adored these moments the most, when she leaned her weight into him and he could fantasize about keeping her beside himself forever.

They strolled along the ruined wall, sheltered from the bracing wind that rippled the sea grasses along the cliff top.

"Have you always used The Swooner as a weapon?" she asked as they skirted a patch of nettle growing around a toppled pillar.

The unexpected question startled a laugh from him. "Pardon?"

"Come now." She fixed him with a look. "We both know your charm is as dangerous a weapon as any sword."

She wasn't wrong.

He was merely surprised that she had noticed. But by now, he should have expected her perspicacity.

"Have ye not heard?" he said in return. "The poet is mightier than the sword."

She laughed. "But neither is as mighty as The Swooner, I wager."

"Perhaps not," he agreed.

"But you *do* think of your charm as a weapon, do you not?" she insisted.

Ethan paused. The answer, of course, was *aye*. Aye, he did consider his charm to be a weapon. However, the history behind it was . . . fraught.

Yet if he wanted into that heart of hers, he had to continue to let her into his own.

No boundaries. No secret too intimate.

As if sensing the shift within him to something weightier, Allie slowed her steps, her expression turning inquisitive.

"Ye must understand . . . ," he began, "I was a low-born Scot abruptly thrust into the world of aristocratic English boys at Eton. To say I was a fish out of water is putting it mildly. I was small for my age. I didn't achieve this strapping, tall physique until well into my seventeenth year." He waggled his eyebrows at her, earning him the laugh he sought. "And as ye can imagine, a wee, ill-bred Scottish lad of murky origin attracted bullies and cruel behavior."

He had spent those first few months at school in hiding—under his bed at night, in closets and wardrobes during the day. Ethan had persistent scabs on his knuckles where he had bitten them in an effort to stifle his tears. Homesickness had been agonizing—his stomach clenched and his chest heaved uncontrollably whenever he thought of Thistle Muir and his family.

"My first year at school was particularly harrowing," he continued. "I had no rank or friends to protect me, and I was too small to fight off my tormentors. And so I used the only weapons left me—charm and a clever tongue. I quickly found that if I made a would-be bully laugh—and laugh *with* me, not at me—they were less likely to do me harm."

"And thus, The Swooner was born." Lifting her skirt, Allie stepped over some fallen stones.

"Precisely. I gained allies among a few of the more popular older boys, and they took me into their protection, as it were." An errant gust of wind tugged at his hat, causing him to tamp it down further on his head. "That is also when I realized the power of words—composing silly nonsense rhymes to earn a laugh over dinner, concocting chants to yell during cricket matches. The more people liked me, the more they enjoyed my company, then the safer I was."

He didn't add that, for many years, he had looked anywhere and everywhere for inspiration for those poems. It had taken time and maturity for him to trust his own inner voice.

"I don't know if I am encouraged or disheartened to learn that all your shiny positivity actually originated in loneliness and terror," Allie said.

"Most optimistic cheerfulness does, ye know. Those who are the sunniest have generally suffered the worst storms of life."

"That is a profoundly sad yet beautiful thought, Ethan. Have you considered becoming a poet?"

He laughed. "I just might yet."

They continued in silence, crossing the derelict nave and moving into the tumbled arches of the cloister. The wind battered the cliff face outside and whistled through the occasional hole in the crumbling masonry.

As he had been doing for the past several days, he poked at her armor.

"Are we going to speak of your mother next?" he asked. "And possibly, your long lost twin, Tristan?"

Allie paused, studying a group of poppies huddled around an ancient well in the middle of the cloister.

"My mother? Tristan?" She gave a rueful shake of her head, a bleak expression settling there. "And here I thought the day to be lovely. Let us not spoil it with talk of my family."

Ethan swallowed back a sigh of disappointment. "Someday, though, ye will tell me. It's the sort of thing that devoted friends share."

She walked on for another few steps.

"Someday," she finally agreed. "But simply not today."

14

After five days in Whitby, Kendall darkened the door of The White Horse and Griffin once more—looking far too much like a specter of doom for Ethan's peace of mind—and informed them all that the *SS Statesman* was repaired and seaworthy. They would resume their journey in the morning.

Ethan did not welcome the news.

He had known his time with Lady Allegra would be fleeting. But after days of basking in the glory of her society—or did he dare call it *friendship*?—he struggled to give up the effervescent joy of her private company.

But Kendall made his demands exquisitely clear.

"I shall dine with my sister and aunt *alone* this evening," the duke informed Ethan. "I understand that you have escorted my sister to the abbey ruins and have taken a walk about town with her."

And spent every daylight hour with her in the private sitting room, not to mention visiting the town bakery thrice, taking two turns through a local garden, and enjoying a long stroll along the country lane at the edge of the village.

Ethan wisely kept all that information to himself.

"Such intimacies are now at an end," Kendall said, steel in his voice. "You will cease all association with Lady Allegra. She is none of your affair."

The duke dismissed Ethan with a jerk of his chin.

Kendall must have said something similar to his sister, because Allie closeted herself with Lady Whipple all afternoon, scarcely meeting Ethan's eyes as they passed in the inn's hallway.

For his part, Ethan retired to the public dining room to lighten both his misery and his purse with some honest Scottish whisky.

Of course, he willingly adjusted that plan once the locals recognized who was in their midst. After all, why pay for his own whisky when admirers would happily supply it?

The rest of the evening passed in a blur. Enthusiastic sailors and workmen alike plied Ethan with pints of ale and glasses of amber whisky. The alcohol soothed the jagged edge of Ethan's heartache and blanketed his senses in a numbing fuzziness.

The night was far gone by the time he staggered up the narrow staircase to his room, the walls appearing just as wobbly as his feet and thinking.

Had it only been half a day since he had last seen Allie? Had he ever missed anyone so deeply? Leah and wee Jack? Malcolm and his growing brood?

Ethan rather thought not.

How was he to endure a lifetime of missing Allie?

As if attending to his thoughts, his unsteady feet paused outside her door. On a sigh, he leaned his forehead against it.

This would likely be as close as he would get to his *ladra*, going forward. She truly was a thief. He feared she had stolen his heart and wrapped it in her wee palm.

Or . . . was it currently in her bedchamber? Where *did* thieves hide hearts?

Frowning, he tried to coax his alcohol-sogged brain into providing an answer.

He may also have hit his head against her door a time or three in order to help matters along.

The door abruptly opened, pitching Ethan forward. Panicking, he arched his spine, arms windmilling in an attempt to find his balance. He stumbled backward, only stopping when his shoulder blades bumped against the corridor wall opposite her door.

Lifting his head, he stared as Allie stepped out of her room, wrapped in a dressing gown, hair hanging in a thick dark plait over her shoulder. The soft light from the oil lamps in the hallway burnished her skin to gold and turned her lips into plump, kissable pillows.

The sight obliterated what remained of his brain's ability to operate. Ethan merely gaped at her, unblinking.

"Careful, Poet," she said on a whisper, head swiveling to look up and down the corridor. "You might wake an acolyte or two with your racket. Or worse, my angry ducal brother. And given your current condition, I don't think you could fend any of them off."

"No," he said, voice low and thick with Scotland. "I dinnae think I could either." He leaned forward, causing his feet to stumble. "I fear I am a wee bitty *fou*."

"Is that so?" she asked dryly.

She folded her arms across her bosom, forcing Ethan to note yet again what a magnificent bosom it was. Unfortunately, he was rather slow to lift his gaze.

"Allie," he said, dragging his eyes back to hers, "ye render me *glaikit*."

"*Glaikit?*"

"Idiotic. *Stupido*."

"Ah." A faint grin played at her lips. "I thought it was the alcohol that did that."

"Aye." Ethan attempted to nod and ended up resting his too-heavy head against the corridor wall with a thud. "That, too."

He looked at her, memorizing the pearl texture of the skin just above her collarbone and the hitch in her breath at their closeness in the tight hallway.

Again, he was too slow to raise his gaze back to hers.

She pressed a hand to his chest. "Go to your room, Ethan. You're drunk."

"I am," he hiccupped.

He continued to rest his head against the wall. Also, he may have closed his eyes.

Something tugged on his arm, waking him with a start.

"Come along, Poet. I can't have you sleeping out here," Allie murmured, pulling him up the stairs. "Let's get you to bed."

Och, he very much liked the sound of that.

He let her tug him up another flight of stairs, the scent of her perfume—exotic spices and jasmine—wafting around them. They stopped in front of a door that he vaguely remembered might be his own.

"Where is your key?" she asked.

"In my pocket, o'course."

"Yes, but which pocket?" She raked her eyes up and down his body. "You must have at least seven between your coat, waistcoat, and trousers. And on that note, why are men gifted with such a preponderance of pockets? We women must generally make do with only one."

He fumbled with clumsy fingers for his right waistcoat pocket, producing the key with a startled smile. "It's a conspiracy. We have tae keep woman tied tae us somehow."

"Pardon?" She took the key from him.

Ethan leaned his heavy head against another accommodating wall. "If we have enough pockets, then the lasses have tae stay near us, as we're the only ones who can carry their belongings. I like tae think of it as a 'packhorse gambit.'"

Fitting the key to the lock, she chuckled, breathy and low. "Packhorse gambit?"

"Aye, ye lasses cannae wander too far away from the packhorse carrying all your possessions."

"Ethan Penn-Leith, you are an adorable drunk," she said on a soft laugh.

She swung the door open.

"Thank ye," he replied but made no move to step into his room.

The power of Allie's person held him captive. The rosy pink of her cheeks as she smiled, the dark heft of her braid trailing over a shoulder, the red satin slippers he could see peeping out from beneath her dressing gown.

He liked her like this, he realized—mussed, soft, vulnerable.

But then, he liked every iteration of Allie.

Fiery and determined as she faced down her brother.

Sardonic and teasing as she laughed with Ethan over luncheon.

Thoughtful and reflective as they walked and discussed philosophy.

He even adored the broken bits of her. The parts that lashed out when hurt. The bravado that masked the pain of her past.

And the hidden parts she had yet to reveal? He preemptively loved those, too.

Bloody hell.

He was a shambles.

"I dinnae like being parted from yourself." He shook his head where it rested against the wall, his gaze trailing to her lips. "I miss ye."

"I miss you, too, Ethan." Her expression turned strained. "But you know that Kendall will not allow . . ."

"Aye."

"And he *will* destroy you if you thwart his plans."

"Aye. I ken that, as well."

They stared at one another for a long moment.

Finally, her eyelashes swept down and then up. The tiniest capitulation.

"Here." She took his hand in hers, the warmth of her soft skin licking a current up his arm. "Let me at least tuck you into bed."

ALLIE MENTALLY CHIDED herself as she led Ethan into his bedchamber.

It was a spare, utilitarian space. A bed and table to the right. A washbasin and wooden chair to the left. A fire burning low in the hearth.

Ethan swayed on his feet, patiently waiting as she lit the candle atop the bedside table.

She shouldn't be here.

But then, that was more or less what would ultimately be written upon her gravestone.

Here lies Lady Allegra Gilbertww
Always found where she shouldn't be

Granted, if Kendall discovered her in Ethan Penn-Leith's private bedchamber at one in the morning, that gravestone might be ordered sooner than she would like.

It was merely . . .

For once, being where she shouldn't felt as right as breathing.

And that both alarmed and comforted her.

Ethan stood in the middle of the room—hair askew, neckcloth hanging loosely around his throat—weaving slightly side-to-side and humming off-key. He looked deliciously rumpled and disheveled.

"Sit." She pointed at the mattress. "And take off your shoes."

Ethan shuffled forward and sank onto the bed with an *oof*. But instead of bending to untie his bluchers, he merely pitched himself onto the pillow and lifted his legs—shoes and all—onto the counterpane.

Of course.

Sighing, Allie perched on the edge of the bed and untied his bluchers, tugging them off one at a time.

"Thank ye," he muttered.

"I'm sure I'll devise some diabolical way for you to make this up to me," she countered breezily.

"I cannae wait."

She smiled at the rough timbre of his brogue. All the whisky in his veins rendered him a 'wee bitty more Scottish,' as he would surely say.

"Here." Standing, she tugged on his arm and pulled him to sitting. "You will want your coat and neckcloth off, as well. It will take a week to get the wrinkles out otherwise."

He sat loosely, not moving to help her. Sighing again, Allie nudged one knee between his. She quickly unwound his neckcloth and then proceeded to push the coat off his shoulders. Only then, when she clutched both his coat sleeves in her hands, did she realize the motion had all but pressed her collarbones into his face.

Ethan took ready advantage. He breathed in deeply, his nose touching her neck and sending an electric skitter of goose-flesh down her arms.

"*Och*, the smell of ye, lass," he rumbled against her throat.

Allie swallowed.

Madonna mia, what had she gotten herself into?

Her attraction to this man overwhelmed her senses.

For the tiniest fraction of time, she permitted herself to lean into him. To let him drag his nose up her throat and nuzzle at the hollow underneath her left ear. His hands rose, unerringly finding her waist under the mass of her dressing gown and nightgown, attempting to pull her closer. The heat of his torso scalded her.

She ached to sink into him, to demand more.

But that road led to madness.

Uffa. Enough.

She flexed her fingers on his arms and pushed away. His palms slid reluctantly off her hips, but the imprint of them lingered. Even hours on, she knew she would still feel the burn of each one of his fingers.

Allie finished tugging his coat down his arms and turned to set it on the chair beside the fire.

"I appreciate how ye always save me from myself, sweet *ladra,*" he said, tipping back onto the bed again.

Head on his pillow, eyes glittering in the low light, he appeared a pagan god tumbled to earth. Allie supposed every romantic woman in Britain dreamed of seeing the Highland Poet in just this state—half-dressed, sleepy-eyed, and ever-so-kissable.

And all of their imaginings would pale in comparison with the reality before her.

With every layer of clothing she removed, Ethan's allure only multiplied.

"And why would I continue to do that?" she asked, voice casual.

"Because I'm your friend, o'course. And I ken all your secrets." He paused, frowning. "Except . . . except what happened to your mother. And where Tristan went. Ye willnae tell me those."

Allie froze.

He had asked her the same question at least once a day for the past week. If she truly considered him a friend—no matter how fleeting—she would share that harrowing piece of her history with him.

And yet, still she hesitated.

She never spoke of it. Of those dark days when she had lost her mother and brother in successive blows . . . the only two people in the world who had ever loved her.

Sighing, Ethan rolled onto his back. "Ye dinnae need tae tell me of their loss, lass. Your bonnie heart be injured in that place. I ken how such wounds can be."

Yes, that was also true.

And it was late. And he was drunk and lying half-dressed on a bed. And she was in his bedchamber illicitly and would be ruined were she discovered.

So, actually, as Allie pondered it . . .

. . . now would be the perfect time to tell him.

It made a brilliant sort of sense.

She ticked the reasons off in her mind—she would have to do it quickly, Ethan would have no time to ask follow-up questions, and he was so drunk, he would likely forget their exchange entirely.

In the future, if he asked, she could in clear conscience say she had already discussed it. After all, it wouldn't be her fault if he didn't recall the conversation.

All things considered, she was unlikely to find a better opportunity.

Before she could talk herself out of it, Allie sat down on the edge of the mattress beside his hip, her body facing his head. Ethan's eyes flared in surprise.

"Very well," she said, "I shall tell you the whole sordid history, but do not blame me when you remember none of this come morning."

"Never."

She swallowed, gathering her courage. "It begins with my mother, whose tale is the typical one of woe that befalls any noblewoman who is thrust out into the world unexpectedly."

Allie spoke quickly, breathlessly. She merely needed to get this story over with.

Ethan looked up at her with trusting open warmth, and she had to glance away before the tightness in her throat swelled enough to spill tears out her eyes.

He lifted a hand off the counterpane and touched her elbow. "Lass?"

Focusing on the candle beside the bed, she said, "As you likely already know, my mother received a divorce of bed and board from my father, effectively cutting all ties with the previous Duke of Kendall. It freed us from his cruelty and most likely saved my mother's life. But it left us impoverished, as Kendall—true to his nature—refused to give a single additional farthing for our future support. Additionally, we were ordered not to correspond with Tristan. My mother agreed to my father's terms because she assumed her family back in Italy would not leave us to starve. But in that, she greatly erred."

Ethan watched her as she spoke, his brows drawing down, head tilting toward her on his pillow. His palm had moved from her elbow to rest against her hip. Allie could feel the heated press of each finger.

"Once we arrived in Venice," she continued, "our staunchly Catholic Italian relatives shunned my mother as a divorced woman and refused all help. They insisted she must return to her husband, which of course, was impossible. After much pleading on my mother's part, an aunt granted her the use of a small *palazzo* in the San Polo *sestieri*. But even with a roof over our heads, there was no money. My mother was too proud to abandon the aristocratic lifestyle to which she had been raised. And so, she sold what jewelry she had, and that sustained us for a while. But eventually, she began to take lovers."

By then, Allie had been old enough to understand what was going on behind her mother's closed door at night. Old enough to know that her mother wasn't always eager to welcome a gentleman into her bed but saw no other path.

The guilt still haunted Allie. That her mother had, in essence, prostituted herself in order to ensure Allie had food in her belly and new frocks in her wardrobe.

"Ah, lass." Ethan's hand flexed on her hip, the light from the single candle on the bedside table casting his features in soft shadows. The sheen in his eyes said he understood what she didn't say. That he comprehended the desperate lot of a woman without the protection of a husband, brother, or father.

Allie looked away from his empathy. "My mother protected me as best she could. And to be clear, she didn't take more than one lover at a time. She merely existed somewhere between a kept mistress and a courtesan. And I simply remained in the background, watching . . ."

"A quiet witness tae all she endured." Apparently even copious amounts of whisky could not suppress Ethan Penn-Leith's perceptive soul.

"Yes." Allie bit her lip to stop its quivering.

She simply couldn't say the rest. How at times the gentlemen her mother chose became violent. That Allie, more than once, had tended to her mother's cuts and bruises.

During those dark years, Tristan's vow became a guiding light. He would come for her; he had promised. And Allie's trust in her twin was absolute.

At night, she would look up at the stars and imagine Tristan seeing the same constellations. She would reach a hand skyward, sending her love winging into the heavens and praying he would feel it.

During her longest days, she would replay his words over and over. He would find her. Allie simply had to survive until their twenty-first birthday when they reached their majority. Then, she could finally write him again. Then, he would be free to come join her.

Until that time, she merely had to see their mother through.

"My mother purchased her freedom from Kendall," Allie continued, "but in a sense, she simply exchanged one man's cruelty for that of many others. But as Mamma always pointed out, leaving Kendall allowed her a choice. She could decide which men to let into her life."

"And that is why ye long for freedom of your own," Ethan murmured. "Tae be free from men entirely. Kendall keeps ye captive. Like other men kept your mother, I ken."

Yes, far too perceptive.

Allie refused to follow her mother's path—blindly hoping that some man would solve her problems. No, Allie would never be so naively trusting.

"I thought you were drunk." She dashed an irritated hand across her eyes, banishing away the emotion there.

"Your story sobers me." Loosing her hip, he lifted a finger and caught an errant tear off her cheek. "Ye have said that your twin died in all tangible ways. When did Kendall stop being Tristan to ye?"

"After my mother's death," she whispered.

"When did your mother pass?"

"Six years ago, just after my twenty-first birthday." She attempted to say the words woodenly, but a sob threatened. "A bout of cholera swept through Venice. I survived. She did not."

"And Tristan?"

Allie's chest heaved and a hiccup escaped—a pained keening for the twin she had lost.

"Ye can tell me, lass. I want tae know yourself." Ethan brushed her cheek again, this time with his thumb. Unthinkingly, she leaned into his hand. The heat of his palm seeped into her skin, warming the chill creeping up her limbs. "And it will help me tae know how much to loathe Kendall from here on out."

Allie gave a watery laugh.

"You cannot loathe him as much as I do now," she said, dashing a palm across her eyes. "After my mother's death, I found myself in particularly desperate straits. I went through her effects, looking for things to sell. While doing that, I discovered a packet of letters from my father, ordering my return. Unbeknownst to me, old Kendall had been sending letters to my mother through an uncle for five years. Apparently, he had realized I had value after all as a pawn on the marriage mart."

"The blackguard." Ethan shook his drunken head, his hand slumping once more to the bed quilt.

"Yes, my father was that and more. However, the letters did give me Tristan's direction at Oxford. Stupidly, I wrote to my twin. The first letter I had been able to write him in over eleven years. I poured my heart out, telling him of our mother's death and my dire situation. I pleaded for his help. Tristan wrote back—"

Allie's voice cracked. She swiped away her tears once more.

She hated thinking upon this. Reliving the shattering moment of reading Tristan's letter—the first words she had received from her brother in over a decade. The metaphorical sensation of dirt being shoveled atop the memory of her twin.

"He wrote ye?" Ethan's green eyes glittered in the candlelight.

"Yes." She looked down at the counterpane, tracing its seams with a fingertip, biting her trembling lip. "But he offered no help. No kind words of greeting or sense that he had missed me. Nothing. Instead, my brother railed against my perfidy in refusing to do my duty by our father. He said if I held any love in my heart for him as my twin, that I would . . ."

She trailed off.

Ethan nudged her to continue.

Allie took in a stuttering breath, forcing out the words. "That I would heed our father's demands and marry the man of his choosing. Tristan called me terrible things—cruel, selfish, obstinate."

They had been like a death . . . those words. Every last hope, every last spark that had held her through the darkest moments with their mother . . .

Gone.

Crushed under the weight of Tristan's caustic indifference. In the realization that the boy she had known was gone.

That in every sense that mattered, her twin, too, was dead.

That the memory of her brother would forever be just that—a memory.

And as Tristan's letter had dropped from her bloodless fingers, Allie understood that she was truly, utterly alone.

No one would care for her. No one would rescue her.

She would have to be her own rescuer—her own source of protection and care.

And so she had.

"Worse," she said, "on the heels of Tristan's letter, a henchman arrived, sent courtesy of our father. Not only had Tristan refused to help me, but he had betrayed my situation and location to Old Kendall. My father's thug attempted to abduct me, but I escaped by hiding in a neighbor's wardrobe."

"Bloody hell!" Ethan hissed.

Allie pushed back the memories of those harrowing days. Of her father's man hunting her like a fugitive, tracking her from friend to friend, house to house. Of her own blind grief at losing her mother and Tristan in the same fell swoop.

Finally, she had taken refuge with mere acquaintances, an elderly couple who were supporters of *La Giovine Italia*.

"What did you do then, lass?" Ethan asked.

Allie ran her gaze over his supine body—long legs crossed at the ankle, a hand propped behind his head on the pillow, the intent earnestness in his eyes.

"I left Venice," she said. "I knew my father would be relentless in his efforts to find me. Therefore, I took my mother's surname, became Allegra Barozzi, and disappeared. The elderly couple provided an introduction to *La Giovine Italia,* and I joined their cause. The rest you know."

The revolutionary group had afforded Allie the escape and freedom she craved. Within their ranks, she had been her own woman, able to pick and choose her path, to forge her own purpose. To forget, in a way, that she had ever been Lady Allegra Gilbert.

Ethan reached out and placed his large palm on her dressing-gown-covered knee, the heat of it instantly sinking through the fabric.

"I pity your brother in some ways," he murmured.

Allie lifted her gaze to his, an outraged question mark surely on her face.

He smiled, tired and soft. "I pity Kendall because his actions destroyed a possession that is worth more than gold—your loving heart."

His words battered her armor, knocking away a gauntlet and scratching a greave.

Another bit of herself capitulating to Ethan Penn-Leith's kindness.

Later, Allie would try to piece together what happened next.

She leaned forward to rise . . . perhaps to collect a handkerchief from beside the washbasin?

But Ethan still had a hand atop her leg.

Regardless, in one breathless second, Allie lost her balance as she rose and pitched forward . . .

. . . landing with a quiet *oof* atop Ethan's chest.

She barely caught herself before cracking her forehead on his.

Ethan's palms reflexively wrapped around her waist again, holding her to him.

They both froze.

Her mouth was barely an inch from his.

Allie was acutely aware of the more than six feet of muscled male beneath her. The press of his thigh against her hip. The aching desire in her belly to close that last inch and claim his mouth once more.

"This is verra bad," he whispered roughly.

"Yes," she replied, equally hoarse. "This . . . can't happen."

"Aye."

And still she remained there, atop him, her mouth a fraction from his.

She remembered his kiss—hot, searing, hungry. A sense-obliterating flare of passion.

A kiss like that in this moment would be akin to a torch set to a funeral pyre.

They would both be sent to a blazing death.

"I won't kiss you," she said. "And you insisted you wouldn't kiss me unless I want more than mere friendship."

Ethan squinted at her. "Did I say that?" His eyes fixed on her mouth. "That was a stupid thing tae say."

"You meant it."

"Then I take it back."

"That's merely your whisky-addled brain speaking." Allie fought to come to her senses. "If we ever kiss again, I want us to do it for the correct reasons. I won't take advantage of your drunken state."

She pushed up on her hands, only to have Ethan hold her tight in place.

"Nae, please take advantage," he murmured against her lips. "Take all my advantage. What was it ye said? Sometimes a kiss can just be a kiss. Let's do that."

"Ethan," she pleaded.

"Ye be my wee thief. Steal a kiss, lass."

"I've already done that. Twice, if you will recall."

"Aye, and your sweet kisses haunt my dreams."

Mine, too, she declined to say.

"Please," he whispered.

Allie almost capitulated at that . . . almost closed the last two inches between them and pressed her lips once more to his.

But at the last second, her latent sense of honor reared its head.

A sober Ethan would not kiss her.

She firmly pushed out of his arms.

"You will thank me for my forbearance in the morning," she said, standing upright beside his bed. *If you remember this at all,* she mentally added.

He pouted and rolled to his side, a palm tucked between his cheek and pillow.

"Ye be cruel, *ladra*." He yawned.

"That I am, Ethan," she whispered. Turning, she plucked a wool blanket from the foot of the bed and draped it over him.

"Thank ye . . ."—his eyes fluttered closed—". . . for trusting me with your tale."

She stared at him for one last moment, memorizing the splay of eyelashes fanning his cheekbones, the night whiskers stubbling his jaw.

How could she find even his drunken repose so achingly endearing?

She wanted to keep him. To claim him for herself.

The epiphany rose much like the *acqua alta* in Venice, the 'high water' that swamped the city in winter months. Allie was suddenly drowning in the vision of what a life with Ethan Penn-Leith could look like.

His amused eyes teasing her across a dining table in some cozy, mountain abode.

His whispered words caressing her ear as they watched an opera.

His strong arm flexing under her palm as they strolled along a street in Rome or Paris.

How could *this* be what she yearned for? Hadn't her own sordid family history tarnished the idea of hearth and home forever?

Yes, her heart panged to imagine such a life with Ethan. But she had learned long ago that dreams were just that—dreams.

And so, Allie did as she had always done with something she wanted more than her next breath—her mother's health, Tristan's rebirth, the return of her mines—she blew out the bedside candle and closed the door gently behind her.

E than woke the next morning to sunlight pounding against his eyelids with the force of Thor's hammer.

Groaning, he rolled onto his stomach, pulling a pillow over his throbbing head.

Och, he was never touching whisky again.

Hazy memories of the night before surfaced.

Drinking and laughing in the public taproom.

And then Allie. . . candlelit and mussable, clad in only a dressing gown . . . helping him to his room.

Everything else surfaced like an iceberg toppling sideways, its depths sloshing upward.

Allie removing his shoes and coat . . .

Her husky voice telling him of her mother and Tristan . . .

And then . . .

The decadent feel of her body . . . the soft, lush roundness of her pressing into his every hollow . . .

He took a steadying breath, attempting to quell his pulse.

She had been right not to kiss him, but still . . .

Groaning again, he hit the mattress with his fist.

The rest of the journey to Muirford House would be torture.

First, he would have to resist pummeling Kendall for his actions toward Allie.

And second, Ethan would have to endeavor to forget how close he had come to claiming another kiss from his *ladra*.

THE REMAINDER OF the voyage from Whitby passed as Ethan predicted.

With Kendall in Allie's orbit once more, she was no longer free to do as she wished.

Consequently, Ethan spent most of his time entertaining the ship's crew or closeted with Kendall's secretaries, jotting down ideas in his notebook and ordering himself to be polite whenever he encountered the duke. Granted, that first day back at sea, Ethan struggled to merely remain upright given the depth of his hangover.

Two days after leaving Whitby, their party arrived at Muirford House.

Lord Hadley's residence was impressive. Scarcely thirty years old, the building hearkened back to the architecture of earlier castles in the area with its preponderance of stone turrets and cantilevered ramparts. The entrance hall was paneled from floor to ceiling in dark-stained oak and featured medieval swords hanging above paintings of life in centuries past.

Ethan nodded as he handed his hat to the butler.

Ahead of him, Allie and Kendall finished greeting Lord and Lady Hadley and turned to climb a flight of impressive stairs that ascended to the right. Helplessly, Ethan's eyes followed the sway of Allie's skirts as she ascended on her brother's arm.

"Ethan!" Lord Hadley boomed, dragging Ethan's attention away from the retreating form of Lady Allegra Gilbert. "'Tis a pleasure tae see ye again, lad." Hadley shook his hand firmly.

A tall, handsome man in his late fifties, Andrew Langston, Earl of Hadley exuded bonhomie and good sense. He also seemed the sort who wouldn't hesitate to pound some sense into a *numpty* who crossed his aims.

Consequently, Ethan had always admired and respected Hadley in equal measure.

"It is a delight to welcome you," Lady Hadley agreed in crisp English tones.

Jane Langston, Lady Hadley was a tall, comely woman. The auburn glints in her graying hair and the snap of her bright blue eyes hinted at the great beauty she must have been thirty years earlier.

"Likewise, my lady." Ethan bowed over her hand.

"You have always had the most lovely manners, Mr. Penn-Leith," she said. "As you may have heard, Lady Isolde recently returned from Massachusetts. She journeyed up from London this week to join us and is eager to discuss your latest book of poetry. I fear she finds us dreadfully dull after the mental rigor of her studies at Broadhurst College."

The Hadleys' eldest daughter, Lady Isolde, had sailed off to Massachusetts several years ago to complete a university degree in the United States. No university in Britain accepted female students into their ranks, and so Lady Isolde, with her parent's blessing, had traveled halfway around the world to attend a university that did. Charitable members of the *ton* called Lady Isolde an Original. Less kind individuals preferred the words *termagant* or *bluestocking*.

Regardless, Lady Isolde was a fiery, red-headed lady with strong opinions and an even stronger sense of self. She was rather like his Allie in that regard, Ethan supposed. But where Allie's personality held the vulnerable edge of a battle-scarred woman, Lady Isolde seemed more at ease. After all, unlike Allie, she had been raised in the secure, abundant love of her parents and younger siblings.

"I look forward to renewing my acquaintance with Lady Isolde," Ethan replied.

"Please continue on upstairs. A maid will show you to your room."

Lady Hadley motioned to her left. "The rest of the guests have gathered in the blue drawing-room for afternoon tea and a good *blether*. I know they are anxious to greet you."

Ethan was halfway up the stairs when a familiar voice greeted him.

"Ethan! At last!"

Lifting his head, Ethan found his sister flying down the stairs toward him.

"Leah!" he laughed in surprise.

He caught her in his arms on the first landing, spinning her in a tight circle. The smell of his sister—shortbread and lavender soap—enveloped him. A surge of memories followed.

Leah's pail swinging as Ethan skipped after her to milk the dairy cows.

Leah laughing as she cuddled him on her lap, reading to him from *The Grimm Brother's Tales*.

Leah kissing his cheek and furtively wiping back her tears as she tucked him into Uncle Leith's carriage for the return trip to Aberdeen.

"I thought ye would never arrive," she said as Ethan set her down.

"And miss seeing my favorite sister?" he teased. "Not even the threat of Uncle Leith's disinheritance could have stopped me. But why are ye here? I thought I would need tae ride up the glen tae Laverloch Castle tae see yourself."

"I will tell all. But first, come." She tugged on his arm. "Let us see ye tae your bedchamber."

They had scarcely topped the staircase when another voice greeted them.

"There ye be!"

Ethan grinned as Malcolm walked down the hallway toward them.

His older brother looked like every English stereotype of a Scottish warrior—burly, bearded, taciturn, and intimidating in his great kilt.

The brothers embraced, slapping backs and grunting just enough to express their affection for one another.

"Why are ye both here instead of at home with your spouses?" Ethan asked, looking between his siblings.

Malcolm folded his arms. "*Och*, Hadley thought ye might need a wee bit of reinforcement given the number of your acolytes in attendance."

Once again, Ethan noted that since his marriage to Viola Brodure, Malcolm had lost some of his reticence. His brother would never be a chatterbox, but he no longer impersonated a stone statue, either.

"Aye," Leah nodded, a teasing grin breaking free. "Hadley informed me I needed tae protect your virtue."

"My virtue?!" Ethan snorted.

She shook a finger at him. "Dinnae mock it. Significant dangers lurk about this house."

"Aye," Malcolm agreed. "Ye havenae met the English ladies in attendance. I fear they shall view yourself as a prime specimen of beef tae purchase."

"Given that ye are notorious for your coos, Malcolm," Ethan said, "that seems rather apropos."

Malcolm raked Ethan up and down. "Aye. I can recognize a tantalizing bit of merchandise when I see it."

Ethan felt the tell-tale burn of a blush climbing his neck.

Leah laughed. "We'll simply have tae see to it that no one steals ye, Ethan."

"Or at the very least," Malcolm added cheerfully, "pays handsomely for your sorry carcass."

As Leah walked Ethan to his room to freshen up and change out of his traveling attire, he couldn't help but think of Allie.

How she had admitted to having no friends. How she had lost both her mother and her twin in one gutting blow.

And how he longed for his *ladra* to feel the brilliant sense of belonging that Ethan himself experienced when in the company of Leah and Malcolm.

ALLIE DETESTED AFTERNOONS spent idly chitchatting with strangers.

So did Kendall, thank goodness.

Consequently, her ducal brother stood to one side of Lord Hadley's large drawing-room and censoriously stared down anyone who contemplated striking up a conversation.

Allie plastered herself to his side.

The room was full of people—aging peers and their haughty wives, débutantes giggling in small groups, gentlemen lounging in pairs—none of whom she knew. By contrast, Aunt Whipple, with her eager tongue and gossiping nature, knew everyone. She was already ensconced on a crowded sofa, teacup in hand, chatting energetically with another elderly lady.

People wandered in and out of a pair of tall, glass-paned doors, enjoying the gentle Scottish sun on the terrace and strolling through the Italianate gardens beyond.

Ethan had yet to make an appearance.

"Remember our pact," Kendall murmured beside Allie. "You must give Charswood a legitimate chance if you wish to earn your pin money and months of reprieve. I expect you to act refined, elegant, and most importantly, conciliatory."

"Of course, Your Grace," Allie replied in her sweetest tone.

Given how quickly Kendall frowned at her, he was not the slightest bit deceived.

"I know you have developed something of a tendre for Penn-Leith, but the man is merely a passing fancy, a disgraceful interlude. It is time to shelve him and focus on the reality of your life and future."

"Lord Charswood, you mean?" Allie asked, though given her sardonic tone, she might as well have said, *Don't you mean* your *future, Your Grace?*

"Precisely." Her twin tugged on his waistcoat, ignoring her sarcasm.

Allie said nothing in reply, allowing her caustic retort to burn a hole in her tongue.

She would do nothing to jeopardize her pact with her brother. The promised pin money and increased independence gave her options and time to determine how she would seize the freedom she envisioned.

"Your Grace," a voice said. "Lady Allegra."

Allie turned to see Lady Hadley before them, a younger woman at her side. Given the sharp resemblance between the two ladies, this new-comer could only be her ladyship's daughter.

"May I present my eldest child, Lady Isolde Langston?" Lady Hadley waved a hand toward her daughter. "Isolde, His Grace, the Duke of Kendall and his sister, Lady Allegra."

Lady Isolde dropped a beautifully elegant curtsy. She was a striking beauty—lithe and tall with vibrant auburn hair that glowed against the pale blue silk of her afternoon gown.

Kendall went terrifyingly still at Allie's side, his hands clenching into fists.

He said nothing.

He scarcely breathed.

Allie dared a side-ward glance at him.

Her brother's lips were pressed into a thin line, his nostrils slightly flared.

Mmm, how *very* interesting.

Giving her brightest smile, Allie curtsied and extended her hand to Lady Isolde. "A pleasure to make your acquaintance, Lady Isolde."

Kendall nodded in stiff agreement.

More and more interesting.

Did her brother fancy this woman? Had she left him tongue-tied?

Or did he object to Lady Isolde for some reason and was trying not to offend his hosts?

Either option was fascinating. Allie could barely suppress her glee.

"Likewise, Lady Allegra," Lady Isolde replied in a low contralto. "I understand that, like myself, ye are recently returned from living abroad. I have been living in the United States for the past several years."

Unlike her very English mother, Scotland laced Lady Isolde's words. Her lilting accent sounded similar to Ethan's—a subtle, aristocratic brogue.

"Indeed, how interesting," Allie said.

Lady Isolde smiled widely, the expression taking her face from mere-ly beautiful to breathtakingly exquisite.

Kendall inhaled sharply.

Allie stifled a giggle.

"I should dearly love tae hear about your life on the Continent," Lady Isolde said.

There was a sharp knowing in the woman's gaze.

This was no ordinary débutante, Allie realized. Lady Isolde was also much older than she appeared, likely closer to Allie's own twenty-seven years.

So not a débutante at all.

"And I should like to discuss your life in America," Allie replied, leaning toward Lady Isolde. "I shall make a point to seek out your compan—"

"If you will excuse us, Lady Hadley, Lady Isolde." Kendall wrapped his hand around Allie's elbow, abruptly cutting her off. "I see someone with whom we must speak."

Securing Allie to his side with an iron grip, Kendall ushered her out the pair of doors to the terrace.

"Really, Kendall," Allie chided, hilarity in her voice. "That was abominably rude."

"No, it was abominable of Lady Hadley to force an acquaintance with *that woman* upon us." His voice vibrated with rage. "It was my understanding that Lady Isolde would remain in London for the duration of the house party. I would never have accepted Hadley's invitation otherwise. Your reputation is precarious enough as is, Lady Allegra, without the added taint of associating with Lady Isolde. She may be Hadley's daughter, but she is hardly good *ton*."

Oh! This was too delicious.

Kendall was livid.

And over a woman, no less.

Allie barely caught a laugh. "I *knew* I liked her."

Kendall pivoted to a stop before the terrace balustrade, glaring down at Allie. "Lady Isolde graduated with a degree from a university in the United States, of all places. A woman! At university! Can you imagine?!"

Good for her, Allie thought.

"Ah, yes, an educated female brain," she deadpanned. "The horror. Does it give you nightmares? Do you startle awake at night in a cold sweat, haunted by the images of women spouting Milton and performing algebraic equations?"

Her twin's glare morphed into a dark scowl.

"I was unaware you took such a dim view of the education of women, Your Grace," Allie continued. "Seems rather small-minded of you. Or are you like our sire, and prefer your ladies to be docile, biddable lap dogs? Perhaps you should lobby Parliament to pass a law requiring women to wear collars . . ."

Kendall sucked in a sharp breath. "My objection has nothing to do with the education of Lady Isolde's mind and everything to do with the daughter of an earl sailing halfway around the world to attend university classes with strange men. She was unchaperoned for much of her time in the States. It is ruinous conduct."

"Yes, I have heard tales of gentlemen's scandalous behavior while discussing Plato's *Republic*." Allie leaned toward him, as if to confide a secret. "Is it true? Do you remove *all* your clothing?"

If her brother had been an engine, steam would be billowing from the top of his head.

"Lady Allegra," he bit out, "cease this vulgarity. Remember our agreement!"

"Hah! I would counter that for someone who wishes to be Prime Minister, Your Grace, you should perhaps develop thicker skin and better emotional control than to be overset by one unconventional lady. And the daughter of our host, no less! Moreover, Lady Isolde's behavior pales in comparison to mine. Yet, I am received in Society and—"

"Your behavior is hardly common knowledge," Kendall hissed. "Hadley *celebrates* Lady Isolde's ruinous conduct, and then expects others to—"

"Ah, Kendall," a man said from behind them. "There you are."

Kendall froze and then slowly pivoted around.

An older, bearded gentleman stepped into view. Maybe an inch taller than Allie herself, he exuded the commanding calm of a man who had seen and done much with his life.

Taking in a deep breath, Kendall visibly tamped down his temper, morphing from fuming to collected between one breath and the next.

It was a rather eerie sight, truth be told.

How many years of practice had it taken, Allie wondered, before her twin had learned to swallow back his emotions so ruthlessly? And how interesting that Lady Isolde had caused such an uncontrolled outburst.

"Charswood," her brother said, tone even. "A pleasure to see you again."

Uffa. This gentleman was the Earl of Charswood? The man Kendall intended her to marry?

"And you," Lord Charswood nodded. His eyes drifted meaningfully to Allie.

She forced herself to stand ramrod straight under his scrutiny, feeling far too much like a filly on the auction block at Tattersall's.

"Charswood, may I present my sister, Lady Allegra Gilbert? Lady Allegra, Lord Charswood." Kendall turned to her with a tense smile. *Be polite*, his eyes warned.

Allie obliged. She was not going to risk her pin money and the hope of a future free of Kendall's tether. Obedience was key as she laid the groundwork for her plans.

She dropped Charswood her most elegant curtsy, the one the Duke of Trento had once praised.

Charswood returned with a bow.

"It is a pleasure to finally meet you, Lady Allegra," he said, gaze assessing. "Your brother has often praised your virtues but neglected to mention your remarkable beauty."

Allie pasted on a demure expression. "You are too kind, my lord. I am sure my brother, like most of his kind, fails to see any comeliness in a sibling."

His lordship smiled. "To his own loss, I must say."

Ah, the man could deliver a pretty compliment.

They spoke of inanities after that—their journey and lengthy pause in Whitby, the weather at sea and the possibility of rain here at Muirford House.

Allie was careful to not seem enthusiastic. No need to have Kendall think she approved of Charswood. She would, of course, be refusing the earl.

But that didn't stop her from studying the man—body neither thin nor stout, gray beard and hair, brown eyes. He seemed affable enough, exuding the authority of an aging statesman without excessive arrogance or sneering condescension.

In short, he was not . . . dreadful. He had most of his hair and teeth, which as an endorsement for matrimony, was not quite ringing, but not terrible either.

Not terrible.

How every young lady wished to describe a potential husband.

Charswood and Kendall drifted into discussing the rising price of grain and an amendment to the Corn Laws they were considering, giving Allie a reprieve from the conversation.

Her gaze flitted over the other guests gathered on the veranda. She told herself she wasn't searching for Ethan's buoyant grin, but she recognized that for the lie it was.

After so many days of Ethan's effervescent company, it was difficult to contemplate life with an older, staid gentleman like Charswood. Or even, quite frankly, an afternoon.

A few minutes later, Kendall bid Charswood goodbye and led Allie back to the drawing-room.

"There, you see," her brother said. "Charswood is an excellent gentleman."

"What does *excellence* mean in regard to a gentleman, Duke? Well-mannered and well-spoken? Are those your only requirements for a felicitous marriage?"

"It is a beginning. From here, you will permit his lordship to court you. It is regrettable that our late arrival has diminished your time together."

"Yes. So regrettable."

She and Kendall had scarcely crossed over the threshold when a ripple ran through the room, a face or three turning toward the door.

Allie followed their gazes.

Ethan stood in the doorway, a kilt wrapped around his waist, a tight-cut coat on his shoulders, and The Swooner firmly planted on his face.

Here was the Highland Poet in all his glory.

After Charswood's bland company, Ethan was a decadent feast.

Unbidden, her heart literally skipped and leaped, as if she hadn't seen him in days or weeks instead of mere hours.

Madonna.

She was in a bad way.

Granted, as usual, she wasn't the only one drawn to him.

Like sunflowers rotating toward the sun, every eye canted in his direction. Several acquaintances rushed forward to greet him, pumping his hand excitedly. Ethan's infectious laughter soared over the hum of conversation.

The tall, red head of Lady Isolde sailed across the room, easily cutting through the crowd gathering around Ethan.

His cry of, "Lady Isolde! How lovely tae see your bonnie face once more," easily reached Allie's ears.

"And I, yours," her ladyship said on a laugh, her voice carrying over the din.

The guests parted enough for Allie to see Ethan's delighted expression at Lady Isolde's arrival. The happiness in his eyes as he reached for her hands.

They made a beautiful couple, Allie realized, both lithe and tall with matching wide grins. Lady Isolde's auburn hair brought out the red highlights in Ethan's own.

"Come now. Enough," her ladyship said to the people gathered around him. "I have come up from London specifically tae renew my friendship with Mr. Penn-Leith, and I would beg your forbearance as I claim him."

And with that, Lady Isolde wrapped both hands around Ethan's elbow and tugged him out the door, disappearing into the entrance hall.

Kendall snorted at Allie's side. "Penn-Leith can have that wretched woman. He and Lady Isolde appear to be a matched pair."

Had her brother said those words to manipulate her, Allie wondered? Or was he merely commenting on what he had just witnessed?

The image of Ethan staring into Lady Isolde's face with joy and fondness burned behind Allie's eyes.

A possessive jealousy scoured her veins.

Wasn't that the smile he saved specifically for herself?

Perhaps she didn't like Lady Isolde that much, after all.

But more to the point—

When had Allie begun to think of Ethan as hers and hers alone?

16

Before retiring for the evening, Kendall informed Allie that she would be riding with himself and Lord Charswood in the morning.

"I expect you to display those immaculate manners you keep so well hidden," he said, giving her his stern, ducal stare.

"Like the manners you retain for Lady Isolde?" Allie countered.

Kendall's long-suffering sigh was a thing of beauty.

However, Allie dutifully rose early, though the sun was already high in the sky. The sun scarcely set when this far north and so close to the summer solstice.

After donning her favorite blue riding habit, she met Kendall and Charswood at the stables.

The earl looked presentable in his leather riding breeches and close-cut coat. His lordship wore his age well, Allie could credit him that.

He paled in comparison to Ethan Penn-Leith, but then all men did.

The three of them set off at a canter out of the stable-yard, Allie's head stuffed with thoughts of Ethan.

She hadn't been avoiding him. Not technically.

But then she hadn't *not* been avoiding him either.

It was simply . . . she didn't know how to manage the chaotic, often fevered emotions the Scot inspired. And she had been forced to spend the entire evening watching him flirt with Lady Isolde, which had done nothing to improve her mood.

Naturally, she, Kendall, and Charswood had only been riding for ten minutes when Kendall urged his mount ahead, still within sight but out of earshot, effectively leaving Allie and Charswood alone.

Of course.

Her twin should endeavor to be less obvious.

However, his actions did effectively wipe thoughts of Ethan temporarily from her brain.

Allie and Charswood walked their horses in silence for several minutes, directing their animals around a grove of young Scots pine.

Allie's horse, a spirited mare provided by Hadley's stables, was proving a bit rambunctious and curious. After dancing sideways, her horse paused to chomp on a fern growing out of a stump. Charswood came to a standstill beside her.

"You are an excellent horsewoman," Charswood said. "Another point your brother neglected to mention."

A selling point, you mean, Allie thought dryly. *Besides, Kendall likely does not know the extent of my skill in the saddle.*

"You are too kind," she said aloud.

Pulling her mount away from the fern, she nudged the animal into a walk again.

Charswood followed suit.

Knowing very little of the earl, Allie was hesitant to initiate the chess match this conversation promised to be.

Thankfully, Charswood moved his pawn first.

"I assume Kendall has informed you of his aims, Lady Allegra," his lordship said.

Clearly, Charswood was an aggressive chess player. He had opened with a strong Nordic gambit, intent on cutting right to the chase.

And . . . *aims?* What a neutral word to use when describing the sale of your sister to the highest bidder.

Allie swallowed a sarcastic reply. "Yes, my brother has mentioned that you wish to court me."

He nodded. "I am too old, Lady Allegra, to dillydally around a point. And I appreciate that you seem a rational, sensible sort of woman."

"Thank you."

Charswood was not wrong. Allie *was* rational.

Sensible, however? That might remain to be seen.

"So in that vein," he continued, "let me tell you what I wish from our potential union, and I would then ask you to do the same."

She didn't want to like Charswood in any whit, but she begrudgingly acknowledged that she appreciated his straight-forward manner.

"Very well," she replied.

Allie's mount paused again, this time distracted by a patch of particularly green grass. She permitted the animal to chomp a few bites.

Charswood halted his own mount at her side. "As we are both aware, I am old enough to be your grandfather. In fact, I have grandchildren not far off your age. I have an heir and spare and even more in the wings. I do not need or want more children. Moreover, my countess and the love of my life passed on three years ago."

"I am sorry for your loss."

"As am I. Clara was the best of women."

"Then why pursue a second marriage at all?" Allie had to ask the question.

"Ah, I intuited you were clever, too," he smiled, faint and soft. "Again, if we are to make a match of things, I would have us be completely open with one another. In that vein, I shall be honest with you, though it hurts my pride to do so." Charswood took a long breath, eyes darting over the landscape. "Though I have managed my lands and wealth to the best of my ability, the turmoil of the past several years has taken a toll on my finances. I am considering remarriage because I require the influx of cash your dowry will bring."

"The Salzi Mine," Allie said flatly.

"Precisely. The saltpeter discovery is a phenomenal boon and would see my son and grandson well-settled long after I am gone. Generously, Kendall has also attached thirty thousand pounds to your dowry, in addition to the mines."

Madonna mia. Trust Kendall to do nothing by halves.

No wonder the earl was willing to forgo his distaste for remarriage and take a wife again. He would receive a king's ransom in return. Allie herself was merely a nuisance to tolerate in the deal.

Her heart sank. Given everything at stake, Charswood would be dogged in his pursuit of her.

"There," the earl continued, "I have laid out why I wish for an alliance between us. Now, it is your turn. What do you, Lady Allegra, want from life? What do you wish for more than anything?"

Freedom.

Allie knew her answer.

But what reply did Charswood expect from her? And how much of this conversation would be parroted back to Kendall?

Tugging on her reins and touching the mare's flank with her riding crop, Allie urged the horse into a walk again. Charswood followed at her side.

"I can practically hear the gears turning in your mind, my lady," the earl said quietly. "Please know that I will keep your confidence. Your brother will not learn of this discussion. You have my word as a gentleman."

She believed him. He would keep her secrets.

Drat.

This conversation was not going at all as she had expected.

Charswood did appear an admirable sort of man.

"Please," he repeated. "I would know your wishes."

"Being most truthful, my lord," Allie replied, keeping her voice measured. "I wish for my freedom. The Salzi Mine was my mother's and was always meant to be my own, for me to use during my lifetime and pass along to my first-born daughter, as has been done for hundreds of years in our family. So when you ask what I want, I want my mine returned to me and the liberty to live my life as I wish. To perhaps eventually marry where I choose, should I desire it." She swallowed, refusing to envision Ethan as the other half of that marriage. "Please forgive my bluntness, but I currently do not wish another to command my days. I want the freedom to be my own person and direct my own course."

A long silence met her speech.

Charswood cleared his throat.

"That is not at all what I anticipated you might say, my lady."

"Is it not?"

"No," he said on a short laugh. "I was terrified you would wish for a handsome young husband and a house full of children, two things I absolutely cannot give you."

At his words, another image of Ethan Penn-Leith rose—a pair of rambunctious children, with her dark hair and his green eyes, scrambling onto his lap and demanding another story.

Honestly, this needed to cease.

"I would very much like us both to receive what we want, Lady Allegra," Charswood continued. "Therefore, let us explore how we can compromise. I cannot give you back your mines. The saltpeter is too vital to the financial survival of the earldom."

"But do you need the salt portion?" she asked. "The saltpeter is only found in one small section. It is my understanding that the rest of the mines contain only salt."

Charswood pondered that for a moment. "You are correct, of course. Let us say that I discover a way to legally separate the salt mines from the saltpeter portion. Then upon our marriage, I could return the salt mines to you. I would also be willing to give half of the additional thirty thousand pounds over to your care. This could all be written into the marriage contracts."

Allie said nothing, her pulse a rapid thump under her sternum.

The deal he proposed was generous. More so than most other men would offer.

But Charswood was not done. "In addition, I would make no demands upon yourself as a husband. I would not require you to share my bed. In fact, I would only occasionally need your company in London. Aside from that, you would be free to choose one of my many properties as your home during my lifetime. My only requirement would be that you remain faithful to me. I cannot have lurid gossip of my wife's illicit liaisons dogging our marriage. In all other ways, you would be free to live as you would like. Travel or not. Rusticate or not. You get the idea."

Allie's heart stopped in her chest. As in, her lungs hitched and her breathing ceased.

How tightly laced was her corset?

Of everything she had anticipated from a conversation with Charswood, this reality had never crossed her mind. That the old earl would propose something genuinely appealing.

How to reply?

"You make a remarkable offer, my lord," she began. "But please forgive me for stating the obvious. If we were to marry, you would own me as surely as any horse or dog in your care. I would cease to be a person before the law. Therefore, how can I be sure you will hold to your end of this bargain? You can give me your word, but that is of little comfort when I find myself trading the cage of life with Kendall for the cage of life with yourself."

Smiling, Charswood shook his head. "You are indomitable, Lady Allegra. I find myself surprised at how much I admire your pluck. In some ways, it is a pity I am not thirty years younger. It is not my intention that you should simply have to rely upon my word, my lady. I will happily instruct my solicitor to put our agreement in writing, therefore ensuring that you have some legal recourse should I renege on my promises. Of course, the same document will ensure that I am protected as well, should you not uphold your end of the bargain."

They rode on in silence for a while, Allie's thoughts a whirlwind, fluttering round in her brain.

She had never once expected that she might actually consider Charswood's offer.

And yet, now . . . in a sense, the earl offered her all that she claimed to want—her mines and her freedom.

Without Ethan, of course. But the poet had been lost to her from the beginning.

At least Charswood's proposal was an attainable goal.

"And what about my brother?" she asked. "Would he know of this agreement of ours?"

Charswood scratched his chin. "To be very honest, I believe Kendall is the one who proposed the idea in the first place—that I ask what you desire most and then negotiate a solution."

Allie's eyes narrowed. She considered that . . . very unlikely.

Moreover, Charswood didn't seem the type to bow to her brother's wishes.

"Kendall appreciates control," she said. "I cannot imagine him ceding it."

"Insufferable, is he?"

"You haven't the faintest idea."

The earl chuckled. "I will keep mum on the particulars then. Please know that I would be your partner. You can rely on me."

Allie believed him.

After everything, how could Kendall have been right?

Lord Charswood *did* appear to be a good man.

"I do not require your answer immediately, Lady Allegra," Charswood continued. "I want you to spend time considering my offer. With your permission, I should like to arrange for you and Kendall to visit my primary estate in Derbyshire. Perhaps in six weeks' time? I think it would be beneficial for you to see my lands and estate for yourself. It could be your home as well, you see." He turned in his saddle to look at her. "And then, after you have seen all and pondered how our life would be together, you could give me your answer."

ETHAN PACED HIS room.

A restless creative energy had awakened him with the rising sun. But then he had sat at the wee desk in his room—pen at the ready, words scarce—staring unseeing over the slowly brightening landscape.

Finally, he stood and began walking the floor of his room.

The previous day had been a blur of greeting old friends and making new acquaintances. A familiar sort of dance.

Lady Isolde had certainly grown into a beauty during her time abroad. They spoke of everything and nothing, bickering and laughing in equal measure like siblings.

And then there had been his actual siblings, Malcolm and Leah.

Malcolm urged Ethan to delay returning to London after the house party and spend some time at Thistle Muir.

"Viola may be entering her confinement, but she would welcome your company," his brother had said as the three of them sat in Ethan's room.

Personally, Ethan wondered if it was more Malcolm himself who wished for Ethan's presence. His brother's first wife had died in child-birth. And though he attempted to hide it behind gruff stoicism, Malcolm was terrified of Viola's rapidly approaching delivery. He likely wanted the support of Ethan's presence.

As if to confirm Ethan's suspicions, Malcolm had added, "It will be like old times, yourself and I."

Leah had grinned. "You both intend tae tear holes in your trousers and steal warm shortbread then? Those old times?"

Malcolm had rolled his eyes. "I was thinking more along the lines of throwing stones or perhaps fishing."

Ethan had readily agreed. Hopefully, Uncle Leith wouldn't be too apoplectic over Ethan remaining another pair of weeks in Scotland.

Naturally, he had also told both his siblings *all* the details about his past and present with Lady Allegra Gilbert.

"Ye had tae go and set your sights on Kendall's twin sister," Leah had said, shaking her head.

Malcolm snorted, "Ye have never been one tae do anything by halves."

"Trust ye tae chase after one of the most unattainable ladies in Britain," Leah agreed.

"I am scarcely chasing after Lady Allegra," Ethan replied. "We are friends and nothing more."

Both Malcolm and Leah laughed at that suggestion.

"Aye, keep telling yourself that lie," Malcolm scoffed. "Ye practically vibrate with excitement when ye speak of her. A lass that inspires such a reaction is no mere friend."

Leah nodded, "But please be careful. Kendall will have your head if ye do anything untoward."

Wasn't that the truth?

Ethan was eager to at least introduce his siblings to Allie, but she remained scarce.

He had caught a glimpse of her down the table during dinner the evening before, but when he arrived in the drawing-room with the other gentlemen, she was already ensconced with Lady Whipple and others.

Even worse, she had refused to meet his gaze.

And now, he paced his room and pondered the problem.

What had happened? Had he somehow offended Allie?

Or, perhaps, Kendall had asserted his tyrannical nature and forbade Lady Allegra from even looking at Ethan?

Frowning, he stopped before the window and stretched, looking past the box shrubs of the Italianate garden to the checkerboard farmland and the pines of Ross Muir rising along the horizon.

A flash of movement caught his eye.

He glanced to the right just in time to see Lady Allegra, dressed in a blue riding habit with a jaunty wee hat atop her head, enter the house at the southeast door.

Needing answers only Allie could provide, Ethan reached for his coat.

He raced down the hallway and managed to encounter Allie as she ascended the circular secondary staircase that led from the stables to the guest rooms, long skirts draped over one arm, eyes downcast.

"There ye be, lass," he said without preamble.

Allie startled, her head snapping up.

"Ah, Mr. Penn-Leith." She paused her climb and nodded. "I trust you are well."

"I was until ye began calling me *Mr. Penn-Leith* again," Ethan scowled. "What has happened, Allie? Ye were avoiding my company yesterday."

She bit her lip, glancing away.

"Allie?" he asked.

She looked back up at him, skewering him with her gray gaze. "I have just come from a ride with my brother and Lord Charswood." She hefted the skirt draped on her arm.

"Did ye now?"

"Charswood made me a most unusual proposal."

Ethan froze, unsure how to reply to that.

"And?" he asked.

She shrugged. "He suggests a marriage of convenience between us."

Ethan's brows drew down and down as Allie explained the details of Charswood's offer.

His heart thundered in his ribcage.

Damn Charswood for tempting her so.

"I don't like Charswood for ye," he said when Allie finished.

"You don't have a say in that."

"I ken that, but as your friend, I am going tae express my opinion."

"You sound a bit jealous."

"I *am* jealous—full stop! I detest the thought of ye settling for a loveless marriage. Of committing your life to a man who cares not a whit for the elegant sweep of your neck or the kissable dip of your collarbones. A man who can fall asleep without his arms aching for you. A man who is content to sleep in a different house, for heaven's sake!"

She said nothing, staring intently up at him, her gray eyes turbulent pools.

They studied one another, the dim light of the stairwell casting her features in half shadow.

"Did you enjoy your conversation with Lady Isolde yesterday?" she finally asked.

Ethan rocked back on his heels. "Pardon?"

"Lady Isolde," she repeated, tone crackling with fire. "You know, the tall, beautiful woman that everyone assumes you have a tendre for. The one I expect you will marry and make beautiful Scottish babies with."

Surprise jolted Ethan.

"Ye be jealous, too," he said on a laugh.

She glared and closed the steps between them, as if to pass him.

Ethan would have none of it.

He blocked her path, forcing her to a halt on the step beneath his own.

"Ye be jealous," he repeated. "Like the proper green-eyed-monster variety."

"Good day, Mr. Penn-Leith," she said stiffly, rising onto his step and bumping his shoulder with hers in an attempt to move around him.

Ethan held his ground.

Allie, of course, refused to back down.

They stood shoulder to shoulder, her forehead nearly touching his cheek.

Ethan would only have to bend down a few inches to capture her mouth with his.

"Lady Isolde is nothing more than a mere friend. Not a true friend," he breathed. "Ye have nothing tae fear there."

Allie swallowed, drawing Ethan's eyes to the smooth column of her throat.

"I'm not going tae renege on our friendship," he continued. "And I hope ye won't either."

"Our friendship is futile. Wanting *more* than mere friendship is particularly pointless."

"*Och*, so pessimistic. That's not the woman I know."

"I am a realist, Ethan. *This* is our reality," she shot back. "Are you so sure you know me?"

"Aye, Allegra, I ken who ye are. Ye let me in, remember?" He tapped his breastbone to emphasize his meaning. "That night at the inn."

"When you were drunk?"

"Aye."

"I thought the whisky had drowned your memory of that."

Ethan couldn't hide the heat that flared in his gaze. "Nae, lass. I think I could reach a hundred years and never forget that night."

A dusky blush rose in her cheeks.

A beat of silence.

Ethan leaned even closer, daring to push her.

"Fight, lass," he whispered. "Reach for what ye want."

"Yourself, you mean? I should fight for *you*." Her words were a puff of air against his lips.

"I wouldn't mind that," he countered. "Say the word. I'll be yours."

Another hushed moment passed between them.

She didn't back up.

He didn't move forward.

They remained in the tight stairwell, practically nose to nose.

"I have never been shy to reach for what I want," she finally replied.

"But you wish for the impossible. For me to trust you. To be your *anima gemella.*"

Ethan mentally searched for the translation.

"A soul twin?" he asked. "Aye, I hadn't thought of it like that, but yes. I do wish it."

She was shaking her head before he finished. "I can't. I won't. I don't think such trust exists anymore within me. It has been fractured too thoroughly."

"Do ye truly believe that, lass?" He paused, tilting his head toward her. "Or is it that other men have bruised and tarnished your trust? Such wounds can be mended with time and care."

"Perhaps. But I struggle to find the will to do so. And even if I did, what would come of this, Ethan?" She motioned at the hairsbreadth of space between them. "Kendall has made his position clear. He is one of the most powerful men in Britain. If he decides to destroy you, he *will* do so. After suffering under the heavy hand of two Dukes of Kendall myself, I could not bear to bring such cruelty upon a friend. And so I recognize that Charswood is my best hope for the life of freedom and security I seek. I didn't lie about being a realist."

"Aye, that ye are. But why not give optimism and trust a go for once? Indulge in a wee bit of *carpe diem,* as it were. Make more friends. Embrace your name and be *allegra*—happy. Ye were born for happiness, I ken. Recognize that, if ye are set on marrying Charswood, ye may only have this small space of time to experience the joy of fully living."

"That is the poet in you speaking."

Nae, Ethan thought in reply, *that is the romantic in me speaking.*

His words were sincere—she deserved every happiness, to be encircled by friends. But mostly, he longed for more time with her—days and weeks where he could attempt to win Lady Allegra Gilbert's heart for himself. Was such a thing even possible?

"There is something to be said for 'drinking life to the lees,'" he said.

"Quoting Mr. Tennyson now, I see. You're not even scavenging your own original writings."

"Ye *can* trust me, lass."

Her wide gray eyes stared into his for so long, Ethan wasn't sure she would answer.

Finally, she licked her lips. "Sometimes a wound is too deep to ever heal."

"Allie—"

"I'll think upon it."

She swayed slightly toward him . . .

. . . and then took a forceful step back.

"I shall see you at breakfast,"—a pause—"Ethan."

Turning sideways, she pushed past him in the narrow stairwell, her body pressing fully against his for the most exquisite second.

Ethan stood stock-still, heart a hammer in his throat as he watched the train of her skirts disappear up the stairs, the scent of her perfume resting on his tongue.

The remaining three days of the house party passed in a blur of activity.

Allie took long walks with Lady Isolde (to Kendall's endless annoyance), played chess with Lord Charswood (to Kendall's ecstatic approval), watched guests swoon and laud Ethan *ad nauseum* (to Allie's irritation), and listened to Aunt Whipple's gossip with her friends (to Allie's delight).

And through it all, she scarcely exchanged another word with Ethan. Mostly because others monopolized his time, and her own heart still reverberated with the echo of his words.

Make more friends. Embrace your name and be allegra—*happy. Ye were born for happiness.*

Mmm, Allie generally considered her name to be ironic. She was renowned for many things, but cheerfulness wasn't one of them.

And yet, Ethan's call to action would not let her be—to seize the day and experience the joy of fully living while she still could.

In short—*carpe diem.*

It was a ludicrous sentiment. Melodramatic and hollow. A school boy's chant.

And yet . . . the more time Allie spent with Charswood, the more her future stretched before her in a long, monotonous expanse.

She could clearly see what a life with the earl would entail—a house to call her own, financial security, autonomy during the earl's lifetime, and the freedom to forge whatever life she wished once she was widowed. A life where Kendall would not intrude. One that would require no emotional vulnerability or risks. Charswood would never coax her to place her tattered heart into his open hands.

It was the sort of future she had long desired. Not exact, but close.

Close enough to have Allie tentatively reaching for it.

And yet, she hesitated. Because when set beside the bright warmth of Ethan Penn-Leith, that future appeared lonely, chill, and barren. A sterile existence. One devoid of children and laughter. Of affection and human touch.

What was she to do?

The day before their scheduled departure, Allie joined Lady Isolde for a leisurely stroll along the woodland walk north of Muirford House.

"So ye will be leaving tomorrow?" Lady Isolde asked, spinning her parasol on her shoulder. Warm Scottish sun peeked out between the scudding clouds.

"Yes. Kendall has discussed business and politics with Britain's rich and powerful to his heart's content and is now anxious to return to London and reap the benefits of all that socializing."

Lady Isolde pursed her lips. "May I ask an impertinent question?"

"Of course," Allie grinned. "I adore impertinence."

Lady Isolde smiled widely in return and looped her arm through Allie's. "Hah! That is the answer of someone who is destined to become my bosom friend."

Allie barely stifled a surprised inhale.

Another new friend? Two in as many months? She could scarcely countenance such bounty.

"Is that your question?" Allie asked. "Because your sentence wasn't one. Nor was it impertinent."

Lady Isolde laughed. "Nae, my question is truly an impertinence." She pulled them to a stop along the path. "Is your brother less churlish in private? Or is Kendall's boorishness rather thoroughly ingrained?"

Allie huffed a startled laugh.

Madonna.

How to answer that?

"My brother is . . . complex," Allie began, slowly. "The twin of my childhood was a kind, shy boy. However, the Kendall I knew as a child is long gone. And given the man he has become . . . well, *boorish* is rather the politest adjective I would use to describe him."

Lady Isolde pinched her lips together. "I rather feared that might be your answer."

"Why is that?" Allie asked, motioning for them to begin walking again.

"I was hoping to coax you into staying on at Muirford House. I would dearly love your company."

"And you were wondering if my brother would permit me to stay?"

"Exactly." Lady Isolde slid her a sideways glance. "Would it help tae know that Mr. Penn-Leith plans to stay on at Thistle Muir with his brother and sister-in-law?"

"Ethan?" Allie asked out of surprise.

That sent Lady Isolde's eyebrows nearly to her hairline. "*Ethan*, is it? Well, now ye must stay, Lady Allegra, because I sense a fascinating story that I shall coerce ye tae share."

Allie meant to deflect, to demure, but Lady Isolde's words caught her unawares. And so, to her utter mortification, she blushed instead.

Lady Isolde stopped again and studied Allie's burning cheeks with unholy fascination. "Aye, ye be staying with us. I must know the story between Ethan and yourself."

Allie pressed fingertips to her hot cheeks. "I shall see if Kendall will permit me to stay."

Lady Isolde beamed her approval. "Hah! I should have mentioned Ethan at the outset."

"How did you know his presence at Thistle Muir might convince me to stay?"

"Because he fair says your name every other sentence. Now, ye must tell me all. Do not omit a single detail."

Swallowing, Allie gave Lady Isolde a rather sparse recounting of her acquaintance with Ethan Penn-Leith. Isolde leaned in and listened attentively—reacting with gasps when appropriate and laughing at Ethan's relentless flirtation.

This is what genuine friendship feels like, Allie mused. She recognized the emotion due to her interactions with Ethan—the joy and kindness he exuded and caused her to feel in return.

Allie found it both relieving and terrifying.

Trust, when one had suppressed it for so long, was a difficult emotion to summon.

But having yet another friend in which to confide . . . that was a decadent sweet to be slowly savored.

TWO HOURS LATER, Allie cornered Kendall at the desk in his bedchamber.

"Lady Isolde has invited me to continue on at Muirford House," she said without any preamble. "I intend to stay."

Allie refused to ask her brother's permission. He had said she could have some freedom, and she was claiming that freedom with both hands.

Besides, every conversation with her brother exploded into a heated conflagration. Might as well ignite Kendall's temper from the start.

Her twin did not disappoint.

He slammed down his pen atop his correspondence. "Lady Isolde is not a suitable companion for you."

"Our pact said nothing about you choosing who I claim as friend. Spending time in the company of other young women of my same station is a perfectly acceptable activity. Are you, or are you not, a gentleman of your word, Your Grace?"

"Lady Isolde is a hoyden!"

"Lady Isolde is the daughter of an earl and received in Polite Society. Your personal distaste of her has no bearing on this."

"I suppose Ethan Penn-Leith is staying, as well?" Kendall asked, tone icy and eyebrows raised. "He certainly hasn't requested to return to London with myself."

This, at least, Allie could deflect. "On that, I cannot say. I have heeded your words and not spoken to the man in several days. I assume if he were to stay, he would be at Thistle Muir, not here at Lord Hadley's estate."

"And what of Charswood?" Kendall asked, nostrils flaring. "I know he offered for you. What is to become of that?"

"I believe I have seen enough of Lord Charswood."

"What is that supposed to mean?"

"Just that spending additional time in Charswood's company is unnecessary."

Kendall narrowed his eyes. "So you have already decided against his lordship?"

"Do not put words into my mouth, Duke."

"You pledged to genuinely consider him!" her brother snapped.

"And I am!" Allie sniped in return.

They stared at one another for a long moment, both breathing hard.

Window light raked across her brother's face, painting him in planes of dark and light, haloing his preternaturally gray hair.

He looks tired, she thought.

Dark bags hung underneath his eyes and his skin held a sallow tint.

This man betrayed you. He kidnapped you, she reminded herself. *He has repeatedly attempted to browbeat you to his will.*

And yet . . .

She hated this, Allie realized.

She hated always being at loggerheads with her twin. Hated how they taunted and derided one another.

Hated that their father's cruel hand had forever altered Tristan from the kind, quiet boy he had been.

Begrudgingly, Allie inwardly acknowledged that her own experiences might have changed her, as well. She was anything but the buoyant, affectionate girl her brother had known.

And so . . . for the first time since arriving in England, she extended her brother the tiniest olive branch.

She blamed Ethan Penn-Leith's ridiculous optimism for the change in herself.

Swallowing, she said, "Charswood's offer is tempting. He intends to invite us to his seat in Derbyshire in six weeks' time, so I may give him my answer then." Her voice dropped into the silence between them. She pointed a stern finger at her brother. "Do *not* gloat."

Kendall's expression scarcely twitched, but his eyes did brighten considerably.

He *was* gloating, the reprobate.

"I told you not to gloat!" she hissed.

Her brother dropped his gaze to the desk before him, slowly moving his pen and nudging his inkwell. Gathering his thoughts, she knew, just as he had as a boy.

Abruptly, she saw him as Tristan once more. As the brother she had long loved.

Could they ever return to that place of trust and friendship, the two of them?

Finally, Kendall lifted his eyes back to her, the smugness *mostly* gone from his face. "As I have repeatedly said, Charswood is a good man. He is a fair man. He would treat you with respect and care. I will speak with him about the visit. I know you haven't believed me up to this point, but permit me to say it again—I *do* wish for your happiness, Lady Allegra."

"If that is truly the case, then why force my hand in this manner?" Allie asked, genuinely curious. "Why not permit me to choose my own bridegroom?"

At her question, all traces of Tristan evaporated as so much mist. The imperious Duke of Kendall took center stage.

"A man like Ethan Penn-Leith, you mean?" Kendall said on a sneer. "A lowborn poet who will do nothing to further our family name politically?"

Frustration swelled in Allie's chest. "Not our family, Kendall. It's you—you want my marriage to benefit *you* politically. Let's not ignore the truth."

"The goals are one and the same! I *am* the family. I would not have my only sister debase us all with such a marriage. Beloved poet or no, I would destroy the man first."

"He is a gentleman!"

"Bah! He is a showman. A bourgeois nobody who is a wit with a pen. He wields no real power beyond what we aristocrats ascribe him." Her brother surged to his feet, arms crossed over his torso. "You can put a top hat on a swine, but it is still a pig!"

Uffa! She was an idiot to soften at all on this man. As Lady Isolde had wondered, his boorishness did indeed extend to his core.

Kendall would only ever see things as they pertained to himself.

"Do not refer to my friends as pigs, Your Grace, even metaphorically. Such spitefulness should be beneath you." Fury laced each of Allie's syllables. "Mr. Penn-Leith is a talented, hard-working gentleman. We live in the same world, he and I—both fighting to free ourselves from those who hold our respective leashes."

Kendall rolled his eyes, making his opinion of *that* sentiment abundantly clear.

Allie gritted her teeth, continuing on, "However, Mr. Penn-Leith's intelligence and station are not the relevant bit of this conversation. You claim to want my happiness, and yet, you still see me as a commodity. A thing to be bartered for power, not your twin sister with her own hopes and—"

"You are a woman in a man's world. You do not understand—"

"I have struggled and fought in a 'man's world' for years! I am not some simpering miss, fearful of my own shadow!"

"That is precisely the problem, Lady Allegra!" he all but snarled. "When left to your *own* choices and your *own* perspicacity, you make atrocious decisions. Add in your advanced years, and it's a wonder Charswood will even have you!"

Oh!

Trust Kendall to know where to stab the knife.

Allie took in a deep breath, willing her tone steady.

"If my way of life in Italy bothered you, *Your Grace*"—she leaned on his honorific with heavy irony—"perhaps you should have come to my aid when I first requested it, instead of ruthlessly betraying me to our father. Do *not* attempt to shame me for the life you all but thrust upon me through your callous indifference. I did what I must to survive after being abandoned by the one person who had sworn to love and protect me."

Kendall at least had the courtesy to wince at her words.

"Continuing this conversation is a waste of breath." Allie crossed to the door. "I am staying here as Lady Isolde's guest. If you don't like it, you may drag me from the premises kicking and screaming. I promise to make my exit dramatically memorable for all present." She paused with her hand on the door handle. "Once upon a time, I adored a twin brother who held the other half of my soul. I shall forever hate our father for turning you into a mirror of his own cruelty. Into Kendall. Into this callous, selfish mockery of the Tristan I loved."

As it turned out, she too could deliver a cutting blow.

Her brother paled slightly, lungs heaving, before spinning away to stare out the window, arms folded.

Allie left him like that, slamming the door behind her.

Yes, she recognized that she would likely accept Charswood's offer in the end.

No matter her friendship with Ethan, she would not drag the Scot through the muck of Kendall's vitriol—the destruction of Ethan's career, as well as the livelihoods of his close family members. Nor could she envision resting her threadbare trust in Ethan, relying on the stars and rainbows of true love and friendship to see them through her brother's retributions.

No.

Despite the chill sterility of such an existence, Charswood offered her the freedom she longed for—money and social standing without the weight of emotional entanglements. A purely contractual sort of obligation.

So . . . Kendall would win this round.

But Ethan was not entirely wrong, either.

Allie could still—for a brief, fleeting window—seize all the happiness and joy she could. Embrace Lady Isolde's offer of friendship and bask in the sun of Ethan's light while it still shone in her orbit.

THE HOUSE PARTY ended in a flurry of carriages, trunks, and goodbyes.

To Ethan's purview, the house party appeared to be a success. Conversation had never ebbed, with Kendall's saltpeter mines being a particularly popular topic of conversation among the gentlemen.

Now however, the house guests were eager to return to London and the Season there.

Malcolm and Leah had left for home the previous afternoon. For his part, Ethan had packed his bags the night before and arranged for the local carter to take them to Thistle Muir.

All that remained was taking leave of Allie.

However, he awoke to discover that the Duke of Kendall's entourage—Lady Whipple, secretaries, *et cetera*—had departed in the wee hours of the morning.

Swallowing his disappointment, Ethan slowly dressed in his customary kilt and retreated to the library just off the entry hall. Standing at the window, he watched footmen and grooms haul trunks out the massive front doors of Muirford House.

All the while, attempting to breathe through the sting lashing his chest.

Allie had left without saying goodbye. He had scarcely done more than greet her in passing over the past few days.

Had his words that morning on the stairs truly overset her? Had she so resoundingly rejected his suggestion that she seize joy and happiness that she couldn't bring herself to speak with him again?

Was this how their brief friendship ended?

The sheer depth of his hurt surprised him. Allie's departure pricked him like . . . like . . .

The first stanza of the poem he had written to encapsulate Malcolm's grief after the death of his first wife, Aileen, hummed through Ethan's brain:

> I bear with me always a weight.
> It rests, a heavy knot of stone
> Upon my neck, sinking down straight
> Into the memory of you now gone.

Aye. That fair summed up his mood.

Obviously losing Allie was hardly as ghastly as Malcolm losing his Aileen, but Ethan's sense of grief was still acute.

How had his wee *ladra* ensconced herself in his heart so quickly?

The woman was a menace . . . which thought made him smile and mourn in equal measure.

"*Madonna mia,*" a familiar, sultry voice said behind him. "You look as if someone has kicked your puppy. Or, perhaps, you *are* the puppy."

Ethan let out a yelp of surprise . . . in keeping with the metaphor, he supposed.

He whirled to find Allie standing behind him. Dressed in a sprigged muslin day-dress of reds and blues, she appeared a spring vision . . . one come to shine on the gray that had overtaken him.

It took all of Ethan's control not to sweep her into an overly-exuberant hug.

"I can see why you enjoy startling me so," she continued, an impish light in her eyes. "It's a thrill to hear you squeal like a small child."

Ethan gave her his best mock-affronted look.

"I beg your pardon, Lady Allegra," he said in affected aristocratic tones. "A grown gentleman never squeals."

She laughed and the sound replaced the thump of blood in his veins with effervescing champagne.

"You be here, lass," he said, nodding toward the carriages lined up and down the drive, "but I am quite certain your brother is not. He left hours ago."

"Yes, well, the *SS Statesman* needed to sail with the morning tide."

"And ye were a lazy slug-a-bed?"

"Tush!" She tossed her head. "It is rather that Lady Isolde took pity and offered me a bedchamber for a while longer."

"And Kendall permitted ye tae stay?"

Allie shrugged. "Yes, well . . . I can't say I gave my ducal brother much choice in the matter."

"Did ye stay solely tae spite Kendall, then?" Ethan asked, folding his arms. "Or might there have been other considerations?" And how he hoped there were.

She raised an eyebrow. "I already mentioned Lady Isolde's company."

"And?" He matched her lifted brow. "No one else?"

"Shamelessly fishing for a compliment, are you?" She mimed casting a fishing line.

"Will it get me one?" Ethan winked at her. "I'm particularly fond of my pretty eyes and ravishing physique. Ye can begin your praise there and work downward."

She rolled her eyes skyward, likely praying for patience, but a smile tugged at her mouth nonetheless.

"Why did ye stay, lass?" he asked, voice quieter now.

"As I said, Lady Isolde invited me. It seems I am adding another friend to my small collection."

"I'm right glad of that." Joy for her swelled the space between his ribs. "Ye need more friends. More people to love ye for the fierce, brilliant lass ye are."

She blinked at his words, as if they had struck something within her. Was it his compliment, Ethan wondered? Or the word *love* on his lips with regard to herself?

"Thank you," she said, arms swinging as she crossed to gaze out the window and the carriages amassed there. "Though I feel compelled to tell you that my heart is as distrustful as ever. I intend to studiously consider Charswood's offer of marriage."

Ethan refused to be discouraged by her words. If he and she were here together, he would wear her down. Lady Allegra was going to adore him before she left Scotland. And she would admit to it.

He pivoted and waited until she brought her gaze back to his. "Can ye honestly look me in the eye and tell me that Lady Isolde is the only reason ye chose tae stay?"

Shrugging, Allie brushed her hands over her skirts. "Well, a rather reckless person did urge me to *carpe diem,* and so I thought I might do that, as well."

"Seize the day?"

She nodded. "Or, at the very least, be forced to cast compliments at your knees. Which, I must say, are—" Here she paused, tilting her head to inspect said knees peeking out of the bottom of his kilt. "—adequate, I suppose."

"Adequate?! And *cast?* I would have thought fishing puns tae be beneath ye."

She grinned—wild and mischievous—before her expression turned more serious. "I have thought long about your suggestion, Ethan—to take hold of this small interval of time to revel in the joy of living life to its fullest. But I also need you to acknowledge the reality of my situation. That our time here together—no matter how enjoyable—will be merely a fleeting friendship. It cannot be more than that. Kendall will ensure it."

The genuine sincerity of Allie's tone had a sobering effect on Ethan. Here was the Lady Allegra he yearned to know better . . . the earnest woman behind her bravado.

"I ken that, lass," he said, matching her tone. "Kendall's vindictiveness is well-known, and Charswood offers ye a large portion of the freedom ye crave. I'll help ye seize as many days as I can, even if ye choose to give your future days to Charswood."

Ethan's heart cracked just saying the words.

"Excellent." Relief softened her expression. "I consider it a pact between us."

"A pact it is," he nodded. "Though be warned, I intend to be the best friend ye have ever had."

Such a good friend, in fact, that Lady Allegra Gilbert would toss aside this ridiculous *pact* and insist on staying with him forever, her brother be damned.

But Ethan kept that hope to himself.

"Is that so?" she grinned. "How do you propose to do that?"

He waggled his eyebrows. "Learn all your secrets, of course."

Her grin turned flirtatious. "There is yet much you don't know about me, Ethan Penn-Leith."

He matched her smile with his own. "Baiting the hook for me, are ye?"

"If we are to do this, you *must* stop with the fishing puns."

"Fishing, ye say? That's a brilliant idea." He bowed to her. "I would be right pleased if ye joined Malcolm and myself in fishing on the morrow."

18

Allie sat on the banks of the River North Esk—a mackintosh spread on the ground to protect her skirts from the damp grass—watching Ethan cast his lure into the river.

Lady Isolde had a prior engagement this afternoon—"Tea with the vicar," she had said. "Mamma insists it will bolster my reputation."— and therefore could not join in a fishing expedition with the Penn-Leith brothers. Though Allie would have welcomed her new friend's company, there was something decadent about relaxing outdoors with Ethan Penn-Leith.

As if punctuating her thoughts, Ethan expertly flicked the end of his rod in three successive short bursts before sending the line soaring in a high arc to plink down in the deep pool of water before them.

Here the river eddied and swirled against dramatic cliffs that towered over both banks.

To Allie's left, the waterway closed into a tight gorge overhung with trees, the black stone cliffs glistening with dew and punctuated by rock-cut steps and the occasional tenacious fern growing out of a crevice.

To her right, a grassy bank stretched from the river to the cliff's edge, snaking upstream before disappearing around a bend.

Malcolm Penn-Leith stood on the mossy bank beside his tiny, two-year-old daughter, Kirsty. Ethan's brother had come prepared to fish as well, but his own rod leaned against a boulder behind them, long forgotten.

Instead, Malcolm bent down and handed his daughter a small rock to toss against the stone cliff. He had already patiently explained to her that she couldn't throw rocks into the water, as that would frighten away Uncle Ethan's fish.

Dark-haired like her father, Kirsty ratcheted her arm back and threw the stone with all her might, squealing in delight when it pinged against the basalt cliff-face.

"Again, Papa!" she cried, turning in a circle and surveying the ground beneath her feet, looking for something new to throw.

Malcolm smiled and obliged, scanning for another rock so Kirsty could repeat the process.

Watching the father and daughter together—the cozy happiness of it—sent an aching tendril twining through Allie's ribs.

Would Ethan be a similarly patient, loving father?

She rather thought he might.

Earlier, after arriving at Muirford House to collect Allie, Ethan had claimed uncle privileges and scooped Kirsty into his arms to his niece's eternal giggling delight. When their little band of anglers had reached the river, Ethan had thrown Kirsty atop his shoulder, discussing the birds they could hear as they strolled along the top edge of the gorge to this fishing pool.

Perhaps that was the source of the twinge in Allie's breast.

The thought that in another universe—where cruelty and betrayal hadn't broken her, where she had the freedom to wish for anything—a little girl could belong to her and Ethan . . . a girl he would swing into his arms and point to birds and clouds and flowers.

Or maybe the pang came from the realization that she lived on stolen time. That she would have to renounce Ethan sooner rather than later; Kendall would pull his puppeteer strings and ensure it.

Her pact with Ethan was sincere—she would not fall in love with him. Charswood was still the more sensible choice for her future.

But for now, she was embracing her name and being *allegra*—giving in to the happiness that took winged flight whenever she looked at her Scottish poet.

She scarcely remembered the cool, detached woman she had been in Italy.

Brushing an errant leaf off her skirts, Allie shifted backward, moving deeper into the shade of the cliff face behind her.

Today, the Scottish summer sun had finally decided to shine with true warmth. She had chosen her thinnest petticoats to go under an airy muslin gown and had immediately shed her Kashmiri shawl and gloves upon reaching the riverbank.

Similarly, Ethan had peeled off his coat, hat, and gloves and stood at the water's edge in his shirtsleeves. Allie shamelessly ogled the ripple of muscle in his arms and shoulders as he moved.

Kirsty threw another rock, this one ricocheting with a dramatic *thwack*. She cheered and jumped in place.

"Ye still be scaring away the fish," Ethan groused to his brother, reeling in his line and adjusting his feet atop the boulder where he stood.

"*Och*, the fish cannae hear voices under the water," Malcolm replied far too cheerfully, eyes scouring the river bank for yet another rock. "If anything is scaring them, it be your ugly mug."

Ethan scowled.

Allie grinned, biting her lip to hold back a laugh.

Younger Brother was a role she hadn't seen Ethan play before this morning. It was fascinating to witness the Highland Poet transform into a teasing, grumbling sibling.

"Kirsty, I saw rocks over there . . . by that log." Ethan pointed upriver toward a fallen tree in the distance. "Ye should take your Papa and go see." He punctuated his words by directing a taunting lift of his eyebrows at Malcolm.

Kirsty clapped her hands in delight. "Rocks! Rocks!" she chanted and scampered off upstream, the yellow of her small dress a bright splash of color against the greenery of the riverbank.

Malcolm shot Ethan a long-suffering look that promised retribution and shook his head before turning to follow his daughter.

Allie finally laughed. "You are truly terrible."

"They *were* scaring the fish." Ethan grinned, wicked and unapologetic, glancing at his brother's retreating back. "But I mostly didn't want an audience for this. Come here." He motioned with the hand currently not holding a fishing rod.

Shaking her head, Allie pushed to her feet, setting aside her wide-brimmed straw bonnet and fluffing the wrinkles out of her full skirts.

Grasping his hand, she permitted him to tug her atop the narrow rock where he stood. Given the poof of Allie's skirts, the boulder barely accommodated them both. She had to wrap a hand around his upper arm to steady her feet, pressing her chest against his torso in the process. The hard feel of muscle under her palm and the close heat of his broad body set her head to spinning.

"It's cozy up here," she murmured, her nose practically buried in his collarbones. She resisted the urge to rise onto tiptoe and press her lips to the pulse fluttering beside his Adam's apple.

"Well, that is rather the point, lass," he said, his voice a whisper at her ear. "I need ye close in order to teach ye how to cast a fishing line."

"Cast?"

"Aye."

Leaning back, he gently spun her around to face away, holding her in front of him. *Tightly* in front of him. So close her shoulder blades touched his chest and his strong thighs bracketed her hips.

Allie forgot how to breathe.

Seemingly unaffected, Ethan reached around to place the fishing rod in her right hand.

"Mmm," she said, her fingers closing around the smooth hickory, "this seems like a rather flimsy excuse to embrace me."

"*Och*, it is indeed. One of the many delights fishing can afford." His low chuckle rumbled in her ear. Ethan wrapped his left arm around her waist, his body pressing that much closer. "But ye don't seem tae be overset by it."

Indeed, she was not.

Gracious, seeing The Swooner was bad enough. But feeling it as she could right now, thrumming against her frame . . .

Allie slowly filled her lungs.

Well, she had wanted to seize the day. Though with Ethan's warm forearm banding her waist, she supposed he had done the seizing first.

Kirsty squealed in delight, her piping voice echoing down the gorge. Allie glanced right to see Malcolm hush the little girl before they rounded a bend in the river, the two of them disappearing from sight.

"Something tells me your brother understood your aims," she said dryly.

"Malcolm is no slow top. He's been fishing before."

"Why do I think we are no longer speaking of *literal* fishing?"

A knowing laugh was Ethan's only reply.

He covered her right hand with his, both of them now holding the rod together—skin against skin.

Heat blazed across her nerve endings. Allie nearly trembled from it.

Helplessly ensnared, she leaned her weight into him. Was that his heartbeat fluttering against her shoulder blades?

He clutched her tighter, his left arm circling her waist, fingers splayed across her right hip, his breath brushing over the shell of her left ear.

"Have ye ever cast a fishing rod before?" he murmured.

"No." Was her voice breathy? She *felt* breathy. As if his touch would turn her into so much smoke and, like a hot air balloon, she would simply float away on the currents. "Just fishing in the lagoon of Venice, but that was merely dropping a line over the side of a boat."

"Ah, then ye will enjoy learning this." He pressed her right hand forward, causing the long fishing rod to bob. "The trick with fly-fishing is tae dance the nymph across the water. The fish need tae think it is flying along the surface. Ye simply have to practice the motion."

Here, he demonstrated for her how it was done, his hand still grasping hers—a slow draw back at the elbow and then a quick flick of the wrist.

Silence descended between them as Ethan showed her over and over how to cast the line. Small sounds echoed in the ensuing quiet—the creak of the fly rod, the burble of water lapping over rocks, . . . the *scritch* of Ethan's chin whiskers at her temple.

Allie tried to concentrate on his 'lesson.'

But . . . he surrounded her. The press of his hard torso against her spine, the taut strength in his grip around her waist, the faint brush of his lips across the shell of her ear.

Every point of contact between them hummed, alive and pulsing with a rushing current.

The fire he ignited in her blood turned her thoughts hazy.

Why were they pretending any of this outing was about fishing?

She was rather sure it was about kissing.

Specifically, Ethan Penn-Leith's mouth on hers.

And because Allie was never one to back down from an opportunity, she said as much—

"You needn't contrive a fishing lesson in order to kiss me."

Ethan froze at her back, his hand atop hers going still.

The rasp of his breathing hovered in the air.

And then his lips nipped her left ear, this time deliberate and calculated.

A tremor passed through her body.

"But where is the fun in that, lass?" His breath caressed her skin, sending goose-flesh dancing down her spine.

Flexing his left arm, he pulled her infinitesimally closer, his thumb drawing circles on her hip bone.

"Fun?" she gasped. "This feels rather torturous."

His wicked laugh vibrated her body.

And then, his lips touched her neck, butterfly soft and not nearly enough.

"I seem tae remember telling ye that when I kiss a lady, I kiss her for keeps," he murmured into her skin. "Are ye ready tae take that leap?"

"You know I won't promise that, Ethan. We have a pact, remember?"

Another agonizingly light kiss to her neck was his only reply.

Uffa! He was deliberately driving her mad with desire.

Ethan knew the rules of their agreement, and yet he was choosing this. To toss a torch onto the dry brush of their crackling attraction.

She wanted to inhale him, to consume and be consumed.

"Enough!" She spun around, her eyes surely hungry and eager.

It was the perfect expression to lead to a kiss. Allie should know. She had used it more than once on a gentleman in the salons and ballrooms of Venice.

But then, she had never wanted another man's kiss as much as she wanted Ethan Penn-Leith's.

As she turned, however, she neglected to mind the fishing pole in her right hand. Or the narrowness of the rock upon which they stood. Or the bulky poof of her petticoats.

One moment, Allie was lifting a hand to grasp Ethan's neck and pull his mouth down to hers. To finally, *finally* kiss him again.

The next, the long fishing pole twisted in her skirts, upsetting her balance.

She pitched backward, windmilling her arms . . . once, twice . . .

. . . before toppling gracelessly into the deep pool.

ETHAN, QUITE SIMPLY, panicked.

One moment, he had his arms wrapped around his *ladra*, the scent of her exotic perfume filling his nostrils, his lips at her neck, the intoxicating give of her lush body under his palms . . .

And then Allie whirled around, breaking his hold on her. Her skirts tangled her legs, sending her tumbling into the river with an indelicate screech, her body disappearing under a mushrooming plume of water.

Stunned, he found himself staring at the river and, inexplicably, still holding his fishing rod.

Ethan tossed the rod aside and immediately dove into the pool after her. The shock of the cold water momentarily froze his limbs, panicking him further.

Could Allie swim? And even if she could, would the weight of her wet skirts drag her down to a watery grave?

He surfaced to find Allie treading water beside him, her skirts ballooning and helping to keep her body afloat.

Huh. Unexpected that.

Even more unexpected was the wide smile on her face.

His panic eased.

Shaking water from his eyes, he grinned. "When I asked if ye were ready tae take a leap into kissing myself, I didn't ken ye would act literally."

"You clearly were ready for the plunge, as you jumped after me." Allie slapped the surface, sending water spraying.

Ethan dodged the arc of water and swam toward her.

With a shriek, Allie attempted to stroke away, but her skirts were too bulky and the pool too small for her to escape. He caught her as she attempted to clamber out up the bank, pulling her back into the river.

"Nae, ye cannot escape me so easily, lass." He held her against his chest.

"You and your Scottish heritage," she gasped, elbowing his ribs and paddling out of his arms. "This water is chilling my Mediterranean blood."

"*Och*, lass, ye be too soft. A wild swim is good for the circulation and digestion."

"You Scots are all mad!"

Laughing, she lunged forward and, grabbing his shoulders, pushed him under the water. Ethan reached for her, but the slippery mass of her skirts eluded his grasp.

When next he surfaced, she was scrambling out of the river, dripping wet and laughing wildly.

She had never looked more beautiful.

"I fear you have ice for blood," she called.

"Nae, lass. Merely proving we Scots are made of sterner stuff."

Ethan swam in a lazy circle, merely to make his point. However, she was not wrong.

The water was decidedly Baltic.

Granted, the glacial river *did* help to chill his ardor.

Though as he watched Allie seat herself on the grassy riverbank—hair sodden and skirts clinging to her long, lithe legs—he doubted there was enough ice in the entire Arctic to sufficiently cool the heat of his adoration for this woman. And that was before she bent forward, removed her wet shoes, and proceeded to wring the water from her skirts, showing a delectable amount of pale ankle and shapely calf in the process.

Bloody hell.

She was indeed a siren—as potent as any Odysseus ever encountered—luring Ethan to his doom.

But death had never felt so sweet.

As if finally sensing his gaze, she lifted her head.

Planting his palms on the riverbank, Ethan pushed himself out of the current, enjoying how her eyes widened at the water sluicing off his torso and plastering his shirt to his arms and upper body.

He intended to prowl toward her like a great cat and pounce.

Unfortunately, Fate had other plans.

The water dripping off their bodies had rendered the black rocks lining the bank impossibly slippery.

On his second step, Ethan slipped.

He compensated by staggering toward her, hands instinctively rising to catch himself before he cracked his head.

Allie attempted to assist him, her own hands lifting to meet his, fingers intertwining.

At the last second, Ethan twisted his shoulders to avoid crushing her with the weight of his body, but their hands remained interlocked.

He landed on his back on the soft mossy grass with a loud *oof!*, dragging Allie to sprawl onto his chest crosswise.

Laughing, she pulled her hands out of his and pushed upward on his sternum, her smiling face filling his vision, impish water droplets clinging to her long eyelashes, her mouth scarcely two inches from his own.

"Well done, Mr. Penn-Leith," she giggled. "What a decidedly dignified exit from the . . ."

She trailed off, likely perceiving as he already had, that they were a mere breath away from finally (at last!) kissing again.

He adored her like this . . . soft and tousled, gaze open and unguarded. Just as she had been that night at the inn.

"I ken we have been here before, yourself and I," he murmured, reaching up a hand to cup the side of her head.

"Yes," she breathed. "Though I believe there was more whisky involved last time."

"Ye refused tae kiss me then."

"Because I wanted to respect your wishes." She pressed her own cool palm to his cheek. "Because you said you wished a kiss between us to mean more than just a kiss."

Ethan was starting to doubt the wisdom of his insistence on that point. Perhaps kissing was the next step to winning Lady Allegra Gilbert's heart.

"I think I erred in that." His thumb swept across the petal softness of her cheek.

"Ethan . . . ," she began.

But he was already moving, his roaring heartbeat drowning out all thought. Flexing the hand holding her head, he gently tugged her mouth down to his.

That first touch of her chill lips, the scorching lightning bolt of it—

Ethan's eyes fluttered closed.

His palm reflexively tightened on her jaw, his other hand rising to pin her waist to his chest.

As with everything else, his *ladra* threw herself entirely into the moment.

Like their previous two kisses, this one was hungry.

Unlike their past kisses, this one did not taste of desperation or manipulation.

No.

It felt like a promise.

An assurance that this kiss meant as much to her as it did to him.

He tilted his head and feasted on her mouth, taking every last morsel that she offered up.

With languid, gentle nips at her bottom lip, he soothed the hungry edge of her passion, coaxing a moan from her.

Grasping his head in both hands, she punished him in return, forcing him to chase her mouth and rewarding him with long, drugging kisses that had him growling for more.

It wasn't enough.

No number of kisses would be enough, he realized. There were not enough hours in all of eternity to satisfy his need for her.

It hit him like a thunderbolt—

He loved her.

Ethan Penn-Leith loved Lady Allegra Gilbert.

The knowledge shimmered like fireflies in his veins, golden bright and pulsing with joy.

The force of the revelation nearly pushed the words out of his mouth. A rushing confession—*I love you.*

Thankfully, her lips stemmed the words, inhaling them unspoken into her lungs.

Still, he branded them into every caress of his hands across her skin, every press of his mouth moving from her lips to the silken column of her throat.

I love you.

Ti amo.

Emotions skated through him so quickly, he struggled to label them—

Intoxication. *Kiss.*

Tenderness. *Kiss.*

Wonder. *Kiss.*

Terror. *Kiss.*

Because even as he rolled their positions, urging Allie onto her back. Even as he braced himself on an elbow to look down into her smiling gray eyes. Even as he cupped her jaw and bent to press his mouth once more to her bee-stung lips . . .

He envisioned what their future might be—laughter in front of a roaring fire, walks through cherry blossoms on sunny days, nights quietly tangled together.

Malcolm had always claimed that Life handed everything to Ethan on a silver platter.

But in this he was wrong.

Ethan had never wanted anything—not fame, not accolades, not money—as much as he yearned to keep Lady Allegra Gilbert.

MALCOLM AND KIRSTY returned a short time later, to Ethan's disappointment.

His brother—accurately guessing what Ethan had been up to with his lady—made an unholy racket as he rounded the bend with Kirsty on his shoulders, giving Ethan and Allie sufficient time to pull apart and act as if they had merely been laying out their clothing to dry.

Their air of nonchalance fooled no one.

Malcolm didn't even attempt to hide his knowing grin.

"Fell in the river, did ye?" Malcolm shook his head as he set Kirsty down beside Allie. "I seem tae remember us all getting wet when we took Fox fishing for the first time."

Ethan rolled his eyes. "Aye, but that time, I recall ye made yourself useful and built a fire tae help speed up the drying."

Malcolm snorted and went to look for firewood.

Fifteen minutes later, Ethan was warming his chilled hands over a roaring blaze.

Allie had donned Ethan's coat and was holding wee Kirsty on her lap, the mackintosh wrapped between them to keep his niece dry. Untying her wet pocket, Allie emptied its contents in front of them to survey the damage.

Naturally, Kirsty excitedly reached for each item in turn, her curiosity palpable.

"What this?" she asked in her adorably piping voice, holding aloft a small decorative glass bottle in her chubby fingers.

"Smelling salts," Allie replied patiently.

"Me smell!" Kirsty wiggled her small body in excitement and urged Allie to open the sealed bottle for her.

Allie looked to Malcolm, her eyebrows raised in a question mark.

Malcolm shrugged. "I suspect she needs tae learn about smelling salts sooner rather than later."

"They don't smell nice," Allie warned, taking the bottle and uncorking the stopper. "Only take a small sniff."

Kirsty dutifully leaned over, took a wee snuffle, and coughed.

"That be-sgusting." She wrinkled her nose and pushed the bottle away.

Ethan and Allie shared a glance, both smiling at Kirsty's mangling of the word *disgusting*.

Smelling salts forgotten, Kirsty touched a small gold cylinder. "What this?"

"A toothpick," Allie explained.

Good-naturedly, she showed Kirsty how the narrow point of the toothpick retracted in and out and how to use it between teeth.

With their matching dark heads, Ethan noted, the two could be mother and daughter. It seemed a portent of a possible future . . . Allie wrapping her arms around a daughter of her own, cuddling her close.

Ethan's chest swelled with a heady mix of *joylonginghope*.

Kirsty leaned toward Malcolm to show him the toothpick, and before long, the three of them were in a conversation about how best to use it—did one attempt to slide the thin metal between teeth? or was the blunt tip the most useful feature? Kirsty frowned, lisping that the toothpick looked "scawry."

As Ethan watched Allie laugh with Malcolm over Kirsty's adorable confusion, a burst of understanding illuminated his mind.

Allie claimed she wanted freedom, to have the Salzi Mine returned to her and be permitted to forge her own future. A life on her own.

Ethan didn't doubt that she felt trapped with Kendall, that she wished to be her own woman.

But freedom without connection was its own sort of cage—a lonely, hollow liberty.

What if Allie had confused freedom with belonging?

Surely, she had felt belonging with her twin long ago.

But since that time, had she experienced a place that felt safe? Had she found a home? And not just any home, but one full of people she loved, who loved her in return?

In short—had she experienced true belonging?

Unbidden, the idea swelled and expanded in Ethan's mind, images tumbling free.

He and Allie living in a rambling country house filled with laughter and the pattering feet of the dark-haired children he had envisioned—children they would spoil and scold and adore with fierce intensity.

A refuge of security and devotion where they could build a big, beautiful, messy life together.

A place where Allie would have the freedom of supporting hands, waiting embraces, and words of encouragement.

A freedom only love could supply.

As Allie laughed and planted a kiss on Kirsty's curly head, Ethan wished for that future with all the force of his soul.

19

The weeks that followed their kiss-masked-as-fishing excursion were the most vibrant of Allie's life.

Every day, Ethan would traipse over from Thistle Muir to call upon her at Muirford House. Or he would join herself and Isolde for a drive in Hadley's barouche or go horse riding with them. Sometimes, when Isolde had callers or a prior commitment with Lady Hadley, Allie would slip out through the rear gardens and meet Ethan for a countryside ramble.

And every moment they managed to contrive themselves alone, Allie would find herself kissed senseless.

It was a mad sort of bliss.

Ethan Penn-Leith turned her into a walking, talking cliché of calf love. If she hadn't been so euphoric, Allie would have found it nauseating.

The only dark clouds in her joy were the letters she received from Fabrizio and Kendall.

How her former comrade learned she was still in Scotland, she didn't know. Likely one of Kendall's servants had seized the opportunity to earn a few coins.

Regardless, Fabrizio's clipped Italian had sung one note only—Allie needed to assist him or else.

> *Your brother has attempted to silence my voice through his manipulative antics with Mr. Penn-Leith. However, I have proof that you are the thief in Mr. Penn-Leith's poem. Dispatch us funds, or I will ensure that you are never received in Polite Society again. You may send me word through the innkeep at The Black Crow near Covent Garden.*

Allie had tossed the letter aside in exasperation.

Proof? What proof could Fabrizio possibly have aside from his word?

It wasn't as if there had been a photographer along that highway, instructing them to put down their weapons and sit still for five minutes in order to capture a daguerreotype.

The problem, of course, was that Allie couldn't just ignore Fabrizio's demands. Not with Lord Charswood's offer on the table and her contract with Kendall still in force. Not with her reputation at stake.

When she presented the matter to Ethan, he suggested she wait a week before penning a reply.

"Let our Italian friend fret and then send him a brief missive casting doubt on his claims," he advised. "As ye have said, Fabrizio cannot have any true proof. He is merely bluffing."

Allie agreed. Fabrizio was a known *chiaccerone*—a big talker. Surely this latest message was just another ploy to get Allie to capitulate.

"Besides," Ethan winked, "ye could just decide tae be with myself, and then it won't matter what Fabrizio says or does."

"Ethan," Allie sighed, "you must remember our pact. We are seizing happiness at the moment. Let us not darken it with thoughts of the future."

He had chuckled and kissed the back of her left hand . . . and then had bent to kiss the soft skin above her collarbone before moving on to her mouth . . . successfully obliterating every other thought from Allie's head.

As for Kendall, he had been his typical autocratic self.

> *I have arranged a stay with Charswood for the first week of August. Hadley informs me that you are welcome to remain at Muirford House until then. I cannot say I am pleased with your recalcitrance in lingering there, particularly as you continue to associate with Lady Isolde and Ethan Penn-Leith. I adjure you to shun the poet's company. It is rather obvious that he has developed a tendre for you, but nothing will be permitted to come of it. I have already taken steps to ensure it. I expect you to spend your time in quiet reflection and recognize that Charswood is the best choice for your future.*

To that end, her overbearing brother had enclosed a note from Lord Charswood himself.

His lordship's letter had been all that was polite and conciliatory, inquiring after her health, her past in Italy, and specific wishes for her future.

Allie had set down the foolscap with a sigh.

Charswood *was* a decent, honorable man, and he offered her the life she had long envisioned—the return of her mother's Salzi Mine and freedom from Kendall's control.

It was just . . .

The colorless monotony of that life paled when placed before the vitality of Ethan Penn-Leith. Any lady, Allie concluded, would struggle to settle for *good* and *honorable* and *safe* when she basked in the blinding light of the Highland Poet's regard.

Allie merely needed to remember that, no matter Ethan's potent allure, her future *would* lie elsewhere.

Kendall had made this abundantly clear.

And Allie herself still doubted she could piece her tattered heart back together enough to trust Ethan with it.

Life, she knew, was better unencumbered—free of entanglements that inevitably ended in hurt and betrayal.

ON A SUN-DRENCHED Thursday in July, Lady Isolde urged Allie to slip away to meet Ethan.

"I shall tell Mamma you have a megrim," Lady Isolde had said with a wink.

Though Allie rolled her eyes at Lady Isolde's obvious matchmaking, she had still dutifully raced out the door.

She found Ethan along a wee burn that bordered the far end of Thistle Muir's property. They easily fell into step, strolling alongside the stream, speaking of everything from her adolescent years living on the fringes of genteel society in Venice to his career as a poet.

"Did you always want to write poetry about Scotland?" she asked, tipping her head back, her skin once more seeking the sun. "A modern-day Robert Burns, as it were?"

"Nae, not precisely." Ethan shook his head, pausing to pluck a wild pink rose from a bush growing along the burn. "Rabbie Burns wrote poetry in Scots for the Scots. He wanted tae elevate our maligned native dialect tae something more noble and artistic. For myself, I didn't start out intending to focus on Scotland at all. But as Scotland has my heart, inevitably my words turned there. In the end, I think I merely wished my readers tae see Scotland as I see her—vibrant, wild, free. So perhaps ye could say that Burns wrote poetry for our native countrymen, and I write poetry for the *sassanach*." He began to strip the rose of its thorns.

"So you are evangelizing Scotland through your words, as it were?"

"Hah! I like that, lass." He shot her his signature grin, continuing to pick at the thorns. "I should write a poem about that. Title it 'The Evangelist' and describe bonnie Scotland. They would love that one in Edinburgh salons."

"Looking to gain even more devotees, are you?"

"Hardly. I feel I have sufficient for my current sanity."

"I read a critic's article about you yesterday in a journal that Lady Isolde lent me."

Allie didn't add that Isolde had loaned her the journal strictly *for* the article about Ethan.

"Pardon? And ye only be telling me this now?"

"Of course. I didn't want it to go to your head. It's already swollen enough."

"Lady Allegra, ye could never say too many flattering things about myself." He twirled the rose in his fingers.

"Yes, well, the author of this article went on at great length trying to decide if you were truly a poet or merely a performer."

Ethan used the flower stem to mime a knife stabbing his heart. "What sort of question is that?"

"I think they felt you aren't tortured enough to be a true artist. Your steady, sunny disposition and dashing persona are at odds with the melancholic appearance and unsociable behavior of other poets. I believe Milton and Burns himself were posited as examples."

"And so because I am not a raving lunatic for at least part of the time, I cannot truly be artistic?" Ethan scoffed.

"Precisely. You are, simply put, far too congenial to be an effective poet."

"What twattle." He stopped, a hungry look in his eyes Allie had come to recognize. "In fact, I think I feel inspired to prove that author wrong right this instant."

Five minutes later, Allie found herself lying on her back, staring up at Ethan propped on an elbow beside her as he composed a poem.

"I believe I would begin by comparing love to a religion." He leaned and drew the rose down her face, its petals silken on her cheek. "Something like . . .

> My love rings like the echoing aftermath
> of evensong. An unbroken hosanna
> rising to heaven . . ."

He punctuated each line with a caress of the rose . . . across her cheek, over her chin, down her throat . . .

The entire scenario should have been ridiculously maudlin.

Instead, Allie was quite sure it was the single most romantic moment of her life.

Like the rose across her lips, Ethan Penn-Leith drew every sincere emotion out of her heart.

How had she gone from the cynical woman robbing coaches with her colleagues in the *Südtirol* to this saccharine English lady tumbling head-over-heels for a Scottish poet?

Worse, she treasured every second of it.

Particularly when Ethan tossed the rose aside and repeated its caresses with his lips.

"I ALWAYS ADORE seeing the place you call home," Allie said, looking around the front parlor of Thistle Muir.

"I always adore seeing ye in the place I call home." Ethan smiled, unable to stem the lovestruck look on his face.

It had become, more or less, his permanent expression over the past two weeks.

As the days passed, Ethan feared his heart would expire from sheer happiness. The poor organ skipped and danced and raced every moment he was in Lady Allegra's company.

So it was no surprise that his heart had leaped when, an hour past luncheon, Hadley's barouche had rolled to a stop before the front door of Thistle Muir and a footman handed Allie and Lady Isolde down.

"Thistle Muir has that lived-in feeling." Allie ran a palm over the window seat cushion where they sat. "The sense that love has forged it into a true home."

She was not wrong in that.

The house with its tall windows and symmetrical construction had been a love letter from Ethan's father to his mother. A way for John Penn to demonstrably express his adoration for Isobel Leith.

Of course, Thistle Muir was no longer quite the same house Ethan had grown up in. Viola and Malcolm had made the home their own.

There were several new bookcases along the walls, and the sagging sofa with its well-worn fabric had been replaced by a new one upholstered in a satiny velvet. Malcolm, however, had managed to retain his favorite armchair and footstool—battered and well-used—which still rested before the fire.

Despite the changes, the room exuded the same homey warmth of Ethan's childhood.

Again, he thought of his epiphany—that Allie wished for belonging more than freedom. How would she respond if he confronted her with the idea?

A laugh from across the room drew their attention.

Lady Isolde was ensconced with Viola on the sofa before the hearth, chatting amiably. Beowoof, Malcolm's dog, shuffled from his bed before the fireplace to rest his chin in Viola's lap. Ethan's sister-in-law scratched the pup's curly head, setting his tail to thumping.

Poor Viola was well into her confinement and near to bursting with child. How the tiny, blonde woman had room to carry a babe was a mystery of biology. And given her wee stature, Ethan understood why Malcolm was beside himself with worry over his wife's looming childbed. It was nearly the only topic of conversation Malcolm could discuss at the moment—what if Viola's body was too petite to push out the babe? what if the midwife was unable to stem the bleeding?

But if Viola was to be believed, Kirsty's birth had been a straight-forward affair. She had faith that this next baby's arrival would be the same.

Viola and Lady Isolde both bent to study a gilded copy of Mr. Coleridge's poems, Beowoof now curled at their feet.

Seeing an opportunity, Ethan quickly brushed Allie's lips with his. Instead of blushing or looking scandalized, his wee *ladra* grasped his lapel and insisted on a decidedly more thorough kiss.

The tell-tale patter of Kirsty's feet in the hallway forced Allie to release him.

"Laggie!" Kirsty burst through the parlor door, running headlong for Allie and setting Beowoof to yipping in excitement.

Allie had quickly become a tremendous favorite of his niece.

Malcolm and Viola had given up trying to teach Kirsty to pronounce

Lady Allegra properly and had agreed that *Laggie* was the best their daughter could manage.

Scrambling onto the window seat, Kirsty crawled into Allie's lap.

"Pocket?" she asked, eyes bright and curious.

This was a game they played—Kirsty begging to see what was in Allie's pocket and Allie surprising Ethan's niece with some unexpected trinket.

Today, Allie dug into her large pocket and pulled out a wee carved frog.

Kirsty clapped her hands and the two of them set to examining the small toy.

This, Ethan realized.

This was Lady Allegra Gilbert.

A woman surrounded by friends and family who adored her.

A woman who gave love and accepted it in equal measure.

Allie simply hadn't realized it yet.

Kirsty slid off the window seat—giggling as Beowoof tried to lick her face—the frog clutched in her dimpled fist.

"Look, Mamma." She raced to Viola and waved the toy under her mother's nose. "Look. A fwog! Laggie gots a fwog."

Viola, like all mothers everywhere, dutifully inspected the toy and made appropriately impressed noises.

Ethan took advantage of the distraction to wrap Allie's hand in his.

Her returning look of contentment, eyes wide and shining, sang joy to his soul.

If only she would pull a love for him out of her pocket, as well.

Then his happiness would be complete.

But even that thought did not dim the joy that lingered long after Allie and Lady Isolde had taken their leave.

It still lingered the following morning when Ethan received a dire letter from his publisher, warning him that the Duke of Kendall had threatened to purchase and dismantle the publishing house if His Grace found Ethan's behavior questionable.

Ethan had stared at the letter for a solid five minutes, trying to summon a sense of fear or outrage. Instead, love for Allie pulsed through him. She fought Kendall at every turn. Ethan would happily join her in that struggle, if only she would remain at his side.

Of course, on the heels of his publisher's warning, Ethan received yet another letter from Uncle Leith demanding to know how things had progressed with Kendall and when Ethan would be returning to London.

The answers, clearly, were *not far* and *when Allie herself quits Muirford House.*

Not the replies his uncle sought.

Ethan did not know what to do about Kendall. Given his actions with Ethan's publisher, there seemed no feasible way to salvage a contract with the duke now. It was more likely Kendall would chain Ethan's bloodied carcass to a dank dungeon wall for daring to court his twin sister, and then set about laying waste to Ethan's life.

The lease was nearly up on his uncle's London townhouse for the Season, and so, Uncle Leith would be returning to his home in Aberdeen soon. As usual, he wished Ethan to join him and spend the autumn and winter wooing potential investors and ensuring that Uncle Leith was invited into every home of influence.

But this year, Ethan wanted nothing to do with that social whirl. He wished to remain right where he was—close to Allie.

Uncle Leith would finally disinherit him in all likelihood.

Kendall would ruin him.

But in the light of Allie's happiness, Ethan struggled to care.

AFTER THREE WEEKS at Muirford House, Allie received word in the morning post that Kendall desired her to return to London in advance of their visit to Lord Charswood's estate. Her brother would arrive on the *SS Statesmen* in Montrose in two days to retrieve her, as he wished to "ensure her comfort on the return journey."

Allie rolled her eyes at his words.

More than likely Kendall wanted to ensure she spurned Ethan's advances and was bludgeoned into accepting Lord Charswood's offer. As if her brother's threats would be the sole reason she decided to marry a gentleman.

No. She intended to go into marriage more clear-minded than that. She was a realist, after all.

Over the past weeks, she had looked at her life from every angle.

And though thoughts of Ethan stuffed her head near to brimming, each path she considered led to the same conclusion—

Lord Charswood's offer of marriage was likely the best choice for her future.

She simply did not see a way forward with Ethan. He had told her of Kendall's threats to his publisher. Allie believed her twin's warnings—he would destroy Ethan Penn-Leith before he would have the man as a brother-in-law.

Ethan himself appeared unconcerned about the prospect of Kendall's retribution, but Allie suspected that attitude would rapidly change once her twin expanded his reach to harm Malcolm and Uncle Leith.

And even if Allie could embrace the chaos of a life on the run from her brother's cruelty—could stomach the vitriol he would rain down on everyone connected to Ethan Penn-Leith—she couldn't summon the will to place her soul in Ethan's hands. To trust him with both her heart *and* her future.

It was simply a bridge too far.

After all, Tristan had changed into Kendall.

Ethan could change, too.

Regardless, the Scot needed to be told of her imminent departure.

Muirford House was in a bit of an uproar—maids airing guest bedrooms, footman polishing silver—as a small group of Lady Isolde's intellectual acquaintances from London was set to arrive later that afternoon.

However, the chaos ensured that no one noticed as Allie tucked Kendall's note into her pocket, donned her bonnet, and slipped out the front door, walking the three miles to Thistle Muir.

But when she knocked on the front door, Ethan himself answered, not the housekeeper or maid of all work.

"What is wrong?" Allie asked, taking in Ethan's missing coat, cuffed shirtsleeves, and general sense of disarray. "You look as if you didn't sleep last night."

"I *didn't* sleep last night," he said, voice harried and weary.

Ethan stepped out onto the front stoop, closing the door behind him.

She had never seen him like this . . . exhausted and depleted. As if clouds had rolled in and shrouded the light of his optimism.

It tugged at her. She yearned to clasp her hands tightly around his waist and promise all would be well. Which, given the weight of the letter currently resting in her pocket, would be a heartless lie.

A scream rent the air.

Allie startled in alarm.

"Blast." Ethan looked back at the house.

"What has—"

"Viola's time has come. She has been laboring since late last evening." He scrubbed a tired hand down his face. "I meant tae send word to Muirford House, but Malcolm has been—"

Another wrenching scream sounded. Viola. In agony.

The front door burst open and Malcolm Penn-Leith barreled out, tears wetting his beard.

"I cannae bear it. I am the worst sort of coward," he said, voice hoarse. "I'm never touching her again. I cannae go through the terror of childbirth another time." He startled, finally noticing Allie. "I beg your pardon, Lady Allegra."

"None needed, Mr. Penn-Leith."

"Malcolm," Ethan touched his brother's elbow, "ye know this was Viola's decision as much as your own."

"But we both experience so much pain and terror, and if I were to lose her . . ." Malcolm choked.

Another cry rang out—slightly different this time. Was it in agony? Joy? Allie couldn't tell.

A terrible silence followed.

The brothers stared at the house, Ethan placing a comforting hand on Malcolm's shoulder.

Abruptly, a newborn's squall sounded, angry and strong.

Malcolm froze, eyes wide and stunned, before rushing back into the house—throwing the front door wide, feet pounding up the stairs.

Allie and Ethan stared at the open door.

They both spoke at the same time.

"I should leave you," she said.

"Please, come in." He waved her into the house.

Hesitating, Allie placed a hand on his arm. "You're exhausted."

"Aye, I'm fair knackered," he nodded. "But hopefully all will be well now that the babe is here. Malcolm has been beside himself with worry, as ye saw." Ethan finally looked at her properly, a faint smile touching his lips. "However, ye be a welcome sight for my poor, weary eyes, lass. Come inside. Let me at least enjoy the pleasure of your company for a few minutes."

And so, Allie agreed, stepping into the small entrance hall, her gaze drifting up the main staircase.

Feet bustled overhead, the midwife and maids seeing to Viola, surely.

Malcolm's soft chuckle carried down the stairwell.

Ethan visibly relaxed, a broader smile on his face.

"Laughter must foretell good news," he said, motioning for her to step into the parlor. "I would offer you some refreshment, but . . ." He trailed off.

"There is no need." Allie crossed to sit on the sofa. "I won't intrude for long."

"Ye can stay all day, as far as I'm concerned." Ethan sat down beside her, taking her hand in his and stealing a kiss.

The man was shameless.

The letter in her pocket burned through her petticoats. How could she discuss its contents with him exhausted and yawning?

"Malcolm and Viola will be too busy cooing over their new babe tae even notice your presence here," he continued. "In fact—"

He cut off at the sound of heavy feet on the stairs.

Malcolm entered the parlor, a tiny bundle cradled against his chest. His joyful smile spoke volumes of hope, love, and happiness. "Ethan, Lady Allegra, would ye like tae greet my son?"

"A son?" Ethan jumped to his feet and instantly crossed to his brother. "Congratulations! I trust Viola is well?"

"Aye," Malcolm's voice went hoarse again. "My wife is a goddess among women."

"And this one?" Ethan peeled back the blanket to look at the babe. "*Och*, he's a *braw* lad, Malcolm. Viola, bless her, ensured the boy avoided your ugly mug."

"Aye," Malcolm agreed far too cheerfully. "As I said, my wife is a goddess. Here, ye should give your new nephew a wee cuddle."

Malcolm gently shifted the small bundle into Ethan's arms.

With a soft smile on his face, Ethan carefully held the babe to his torso, slowly swaying. Allie caught a glimpse of the babe's bald head and adorable tiny nose.

Uffa.

Allie's heart had not been properly prepared for this sight. To witness Ethan Penn-Leith tenderly rocking a newborn. The quiet trill of a lullaby on his lips. The cords of his forearms flexing as he lifted the bundle to press a kiss to his nephew's forehead.

It was the stuff of every maiden's fantasies. If Allie could somehow bottle and sell this moment, she would have no more worries about her future.

Ethan paced over to the bow window that faced the front drive, studying the baby in the daylight.

"He's bonnie," Ethan said, eyes soft and looking back to Malcolm. "Ye be the luckiest of men."

"Aye." Malcolm crossed to his brother.

"Have Viola and yourself decided on a name?"

"Robert," Malcolm replied, "but I am sure we will call him Robbie."

"A sound Scottish name."

The brothers bent their heads over the babe. A wee fist escaped the swaddling, waving in the air until Ethan offered a finger for it to grasp.

Malcolm said something too low for Allie to hear.

Ethan chuckled.

It rushed over Allie then.

An unexpected tidal wave of *adorationdevotiondesireyearning* that robbed her of breath and threatened to drown her.

Madonna mia.

No.

No!

She was in love with Ethan Penn-Leith.

Wildly, madly, headlong in love.

So in love, the force of the emotion filled her lungs, stinging her eyes and choking her throat in an attempt to escape. It frothed and foamed under her sternum, expanding outward until she feared it would overfill the room if loosed.

The space of that love stretched vast within her. Fathomless. As if she could spend a lifetime exploring it and never reach its end.

It was simply . . . too much.

How could she have been so heedless, so stupid?

What was she to do?

Panic shuddered—a giant's fingers wrapping around her ribcage and slowly squeezing.

The same panic that had gripped her as she watched Tristan's tear-streaked face fade into the distance all those years before.

The same panic that had lanced her as their mother took her last breath.

The same panic that had chased her from house to house in Venice, barely two steps ahead of her father's hired thug.

Allie couldn't keep Ethan. Not like this. Not with only love and trust knitting them together.

If keeping Ethan required some feat of great strength or courage—climbing a mountain, facing an unruly mob—Allie would gladly embrace it.

But placing every last shred of her battered soul on the altar of trust? To have faith that Ethan would not eventually discard her as every other man in her life had done? To believe that their love could endure Kendall's vindictive destruction of Ethan's career and family?

No. She feared that was bravery she did not possess.

But how could she give Ethan up?

That thought, too, felt unbearable.

That she would leave Fettermill in two days' time, journey to Charswood's estate, and agree to become his countess. Never again to bask in the warmth of Ethan Penn-Leith's regard. To let this vast, new horizon of love in her breast dim and recede, eventually snuffing out all light within her.

It was too much.

Too much feeling.

Too much pain.

The world went black at the edges; the room turned suffocating. The panic in her breast shuddered along her limbs, agitating them into motion.

Allie surged to her feet and raced out the front door before consciously thinking to move.

20

Allie raced down the gravel drive of Thistle Muir, heart pounding. The turmoil in her chest bubbled over, spilling tears down her cheeks.

Was is possible to run far enough to escape the pandemonium exploding within her?

Could she sprint away to join a revolutionary group as she had after losing Tristan? Perhaps some band in the Caucuses might—

A shout sounded from behind her.

"Lass!" Ethan called.

Allie ran faster.

Feet pounded, coming closer.

A hand wrapped around her elbow, pulling her to a stop.

Allie pivoted into Ethan, collapsing onto his torso, her elbows tucked between their bodies.

Heaving sobs escaped her.

She didn't *want* to love him. Love had only ever caused her anguish and grief.

Ethan enveloped her in his strong arms, which somehow only made everything worse.

She couldn't bear his caring right now.

Not when her heart was in pieces, torn between options that felt untenable. How could she choose between the terror of keeping him or the pain of losing him?

Pushing, she broke free of his embrace, dashing a palm across her eyes.

He stared at her—hatless hair mussed, eyes bloodshot, forehead furrowed in confusion.

"What is it? What has overset ye?" He reached for her again.

Allie stepped back, wrapping her arms around herself.

His brows fell lower.

"Allie?"

ETHAN STARED AT his *ladra*—the taut line of her mouth, the rigid set of her shoulders, the faint tremor where her hands clutched her upper arms.

In this moment, she seemed more akin to the woman he first met in the *vetturini* in Italy—cool, withdrawn. A fortress unto herself.

Clearly something had transpired to shatter her, to force her to retreat into a protective shell.

He blinked, his exhausted brain trying to parse the sequence of events.

One minute he was holding his new nephew. The next, Allie had bolted from the house as if lit by a lucifer match.

"What occurred tae upset ye so?" he repeated.

She bit her quivering bottom lip. That wee sign of distress nearly did in the remains of Ethan's heart.

"*Mia ladra.*" He reached for her again . . . anything to ease her pain.

She skittered back, tears spilling down her cheeks . . . tears she brushed furiously away.

"This wasn't supposed to happen," she said, voice watery, lungs hiccupping.

"Pardon?"

"This!" She motioned between them. "I wasn't supposed to fall in love with you!"

She said the words with such vehemence, such anger, it took Ethan's weary thoughts a moment to catch up.

He stilled.

And then shook his head.

Had he heard that right?

"Pardon? Ye love me? Ye be, as ye said, *in love* with me?"

"Of course!" Allie wailed, throwing her arms up in misery.

Hope ballooned so quickly, Ethan's ribcage could scarcely encompass it.

This brilliant, brave, beautiful woman loved him, just as he loved her.

"I adore everything about you," she continued, tone anguished. "Your caring heart. Your quick wit. Your absurdly handsome face. And that ridiculous smile—" She glared, pointing an accusing finger at his face. "Yes! That smile right there."

Ethan was quite sure The Swooner had never shone so bright. "This one?"

"Yes. You need to wipe it clean. It hurts!" She put her palms up to shield her face, as if he were an attacker.

Laughing, Ethan closed the distance between them, gathering her in his arms once more. "Ye be absurd, love."

Her eyes snapped to his at the endearment. "*Love!* Don't call me that!"

"Why wouldn't I? I love ye, too," Ethan confessed.

And then he kissed her. Softly. Tenderly.

A kiss of promise. A kiss of beginning.

This would be the birth of their life together. He was certain of it.

She would stop dithering and refuse Charswood. Together, she and Ethan would take on Kendall.

Yes, they faced obstacles, but surely they could overcome them. If they loved one another, they *would* find a way.

But Allie returned Ethan's embrace with anything but tenderness.

She kissed him like a wanderer in the desert, thirsty and desperate, hands threading into his hair and holding him tight.

She tasted of despair.

Pulling back, Ethan attempted to gentle the kiss.

"Hush, lass," he whispered, voice husky. "I am here. I'm no' going anywhere."

She hiccupped again at his words, moving her head out of his immediate reach.

"*Sì*, you will remain here. But I must leave." She stepped fully out of his arms. He immediately mourned the loss of her.

"Pardon?" He frowned.

She swiped at her cheeks once more. "I received word from my brother this morning. Kendall arrives in two days' time to fetch me."

Oh.

His tired brain was struggling to understand the implications of her words. Kendall arriving did not seem to merit her tears and distress.

"Naturally, I had thought tae have more time," Ethan nodded, "but 'tis no matter. I will simply return tae London as well, and we can continue our courtship there. Or I could just ask ye now if . . ." He trailed off as Allie tipped her head into her hands, shoulders shaking with emotion.

She said nothing.

An icy chill skated down Ethan's spine.

"What am I missing here, love?" he finally asked.

Drawing in a stuttering breath, Allie dug into her pocket for a handkerchief. She wiped her cheeks with belligerent strokes.

Splotchy and red-faced, she had never looked more beautiful.

"I will not be in London long," she replied. "We will leave almost immediately for Charswood's estate in Derbyshire, as Kendall has planned."

"Kendall is forcing ye tae go?"

"He won't be forcing me." Her shoulders slumped. "I will go willingly."

The icy chill along Ethan's spine expanded toward his heart.

"What?" He looked out over the drive of Thistle Muir before returning his gaze to her. "Why?" He heard the bafflement in his voice.

She stared, her lovely gray eyes admonishing him to *stop being an eejit*.

"I've been up all night, lass," he said, "and I'm afeart my thinking is a wee bit sluggish. I don't understand why ye be traveling willingly to visit Charswood."

She continued to stare at him, unblinking.

No.

She couldn't—

"Nae." He shook his head, head rearing back in dismay, his accent slipping into the brogue of his youth. "Ye cannae still think tae entertain Charswood's offer. To cling tae that harebrained pact we made weeks ago. We've moved beyond that. Ye love me. I love your fair self. Why would ye choose tae—"

"That is just it. I don't know what to choose!"

"You choose me! You choose us!"

"How can I? Kendall will hurt—"

"Why would ye let that bastard of a brother of yours dictate our happiness? Let us fight him together. We arenae powerless, yourself and I."

Allie made a scoffing noise. "Kendall is already threatening your publisher over the vague *possibility* that I may run off with you. Imagine his vitriol if we were to actually do it? He would never forgive me for such defiance. Like my father before him, he will plot something Machiavellian to ensure our destruction."

"I say let him try! For yourself—for the sake of our life together—I would endure it."

"But that is the point, Ethan!" She gestured wildly. "I don't want to watch you *endure* Kendall's punishment for my sake. That is why I insisted on our pact in the first place. Because I am a realist and always will be. Kendall will never release my dowry to your care. Instead, the mighty Duke of Kendall will ruin your uncle. He will destroy Malcolm and his coos. He will demolish your own career. Neither you nor I have any skills to see ourselves employed. How will we live?"

A loud buzzing began in Ethan's ears.

"We'll find a way, lass. I could take a position at a university. We could immigrate to the United States and forge a life there. The options are legion. Yes, Kendall could perhaps hurt us financially, but I would deem any struggle worth it tae have you at my side. I know my brother would say the same," he said, voice rising. "But *you* have tae want to join me in battle. Where is the indomitable woman I know and love? Where is the woman who held my own gun to my chest on that Italian highway? *That* woman would choose love, consequences be damned!"

"That woman is a survivor! She is afraid and untrusting and heartsore. She survived losing her mother. She survived losing her twin. She would survive losing you, too!"

"Aye. I ken that. Your wee heart has been ill-used in the past. But dinnae punish me for others' sins! Ye can trust me, lass. Be brave enough tae let me love ye. Choose us!"

"I have never lied to you, Ethan! I told you from the beginning this would only ever be a fleeting friendship." She motioned to the space between them. "I have reminded you repeatedly of my wishes for the future."

Ethan had to agree. She had been forthright in that regard.

He had simply hoped she would change her mind. He had believed he could persuade her otherwise.

"Aye, lass. Ye have." He caught her gaze and held it. "Ye have told me over and over that ye wish for freedom. But I'm not so sure that is what ye truly want."

She folded her arms, her wee jaw sticking out stubbornly. "Oh yes, please tell me what I wish for instead!"

"Belonging," he retorted. "Ye dinnae want freedom. Ye want tae belong."

"Belong?"

"Aye. As I see it, ye consider freedom a way tae buy yourself a place of your own. But what would ye be part of? A house? A fleet of servants? Ye dinnae need money to purchase the freedom ye feel in belonging. When ye belong, ye can spread your wings. Ye can fly high and know ye will always have a home waiting for ye. We could have that freedom together, yourself and I. We could belong tae each other, love and be loved in return. Make a family that would be ours alone. Kendall could try tae break us, but if we truly belong . . . *that* he could never take."

Allie stood in stunned silence. As if his words had ricocheted within her, knocking aside long-held assumptions.

Ethan took that as encouragement.

Stepping closer, he looped an arm around her waist and pulled her against him once more.

"Ye cannae marry Charswood. A man who will take your best years and leave ye wealthy, aye, but alone in the end. An old man who willnae appreciate the fire and joy—the love!—that ye are." Here, Ethan ran a hungry hand from her ribcage to her hip, tugging her that much closer. "Choose me, Allie. Make a life with myself. Be my wife. Let me show ye every day the true meaning of freedom."

For one flickering eternity of a moment, Ethan thought she would capitulate. She swayed toward him, their lips brushing in the lightest of touches.

But then she pressed a hand against his chest, forcing him to step back.

"Your words are hopeful, Ethan, because that is what you are—an optimist. But I am a realist. I will *always* be a realist." Tears glittered in her eyes, at odds with her hard tone. "And the reality is, I am not sure I can choose *us*."

And with that lethal shot, she turned and walked away.

21

Allie raced from Thistle Muir, wind tugging at her bonnet and scattering her tears.

Ethan called after her, but she refused to turn around.

She *should* be brave and fight for them. She knew this.

It was just . . .

The thought of choosing Ethan—loving him and letting him love her in return—set a shaky tremor to vibrating her very bones until running became the only logical response.

She knew her brother and her father before him—ruthless men who would permit nothing to stand in the way of their aims. Men who tormented wives, separated children, kidnapped siblings and held them captive.

Charming poets, in particular, were to be obliterated.

Yet even as she ran, the memory of Ethan's voice nipped at her heels.

Ye dinnae want freedom. Ye want tae belong.

His words resonated like a struck gong.

The man was more prophet than poet.

Panting from her exertions, Allie slowed to a walk, forcing her lungs to take in measured breaths.

Think.

She needed to think. To somehow untangle the knot of *terroragony-fearlovelovelove* that pounded against her sternum.

If Ethan were to be believed, she had been chasing *belonging* all these years.

She turned the idea over and sideways in her mind, poking it to see what truths might tumble out.

A wish to belong could explain her eagerness to ally herself with *La Giovine Italia.* And perhaps it clarified why Tristan's transformation into Kendall had so thoroughly devastated her. She had assumed that she would always belong with her twin, and when that bond broke, she was cut adrift.

We could belong tae each other, love and be loved in return.

She *did* wish that. Of course, she did.

Who didn't want to love and be loved in return? Particularly by a man such as Ethan Penn-Leith?

Allie closed her eyes at the pain of the revelation, stumbling and nearly pitching herself face-first onto the narrow lane. Regaining her feet, she continued onward.

As she rounded the last bend down the long drive to Muirford House, Allie noted several carriages gathered before the open front door, footmen moving in and out with luggage.

Frowning, she belatedly remembered the friends of Lady Isolde from London who were to arrive today.

Uffa.

Surely Allie looked a mess—tear-streaked, red-eyed, and rumpled from running. She would simply slip in the front door and escape to her room to freshen up. Perhaps she could even claim a megrim in order to beg off the evening's activities. Burrowing her head in a pillow and sobbing her anguish for a night held a certain maudlin appeal.

Slipping past two footmen carrying a heavy trunk through the front door, Allie kept her head bent, eyes intent on the stairs.

"Lady Allegra!" a decidedly familiar aristocratic voice called.

Allie froze, one foot on the bottom step.

Porca miseria.

"Where have you been?" The voice was closer now.

Spinning round, Allie scowled up into the stern, handsome face of her twin brother.

"Kendall." She bobbed a curtsy.

No need to ask *why* he was here. Apparently, her twin had decided to follow immediately on the heels of his letter, likely realizing after the fact that if she were forewarned, she might bolt.

His reasoning was not wrong.

A burst of laughter sounded from the open doorway to the drawing-room . . . Lady Isolde with her friends.

Kendall seemed not to hear them. Instead, he stared at her, gaze flitting over her face and likely cataloging the aftermath of her weeping. His brows drew down. "What on earth has—"

"Lady Allegra, it is a pleasure to see you again." Another voice joined them.

Allie looked past her brother to see a smiling Lord Charswood hand his hat to the waiting butler.

Of course.

Of course Kendall would bring Charswood along.

The earl's smile faltered as he, too, noted her face. He darted an apprehensive glance up at Kendall.

"Are you well, my lady?" his lordship asked, his eyes so very kind.

She hated that Charswood was a good man. That she couldn't find him odious and loathsome and, therefore, easy to dismiss . . . for practical reasons, that was. Which once upon a time were the only kind of reasons she believed in. Now, however . . .

"I fear I have the beginnings of a headache," she said, pressing fingertips to her temple.

It was not a lie. A steady hammer was picking up pace behind her right eyeball.

Another round of laughter came from the drawing-room, a group of newcomers stepping into the doorway. From the sound of things,

Lady Isolde's intellectual friends seemed just as likely to reach for a glass of brandy as a copy of Descartes.

A dark-headed man separated from the group, meeting her gaze.

Allie's heart sank to her toes.

Fabrizio smiled, nodding his head in her direction.

How the hell was he here?

She could guess why. But *how*?

His smug expression intimated he was up to no good. His carefully tailored superfine coat and silk waistcoat declared he had come prepared for diplomatic war. The confident set of his shoulders said he had a plan.

This did not bode well.

"You are staring rather fiercely at that foreign-looking man, Lady Allegra," Lord Charswood's voice intruded upon her thoughts. "Are you acquainted?"

How to answer that?

"Somewhat," she replied, voice too weak to be convincing.

"Interesting." Charswood looked to Fabrizio who had the good sense to join another gentleman in conversation. "I do believe Lord Hadley said he is Italian, but I have already forgotten his name."

"An Italian?" Kendall said, frown deepening. "Do you recall his name, Lady Allegra?"

"Fabrizio Sacci." She saw no point in lying.

Kendall's chin inched up, the slightest acknowledgment that he recognized the name.

Allie held her brother's gaze, hoping her expression communicated that the Italian was precisely who Kendall thought he might be.

As far as Allie knew, Fabrizio and Kendall had never met. But they had surely corresponded to coordinate her kidnapping . . . before her brother had forbidden the man from contacting him again.

Did 'accidentally' attending the same house party as the duke count as an attempt at contact?

"Mr. Sacci is a colleague of Mr. Mazzini, the leader of *La Giovine Italia*," Allie continued. "Mazzini is the sort of idealistic man that Lady Isolde would entertain sympathies for, and she certainly would have crossed paths with him in the literary salons of London earlier in the Season. I presume Mr. Sacci is here at Mazzini's behest."

No doubt Fabrizio had manipulated events to ensure his invitation here, knowing Allie was still in residence. Kendall's arrival was merely an unexpected bonus.

"Lady Isolde and her ridiculous friends," Kendall scoffed, turning his attention to Charswood. "Yet one more reason why women should be permanently barred from our universities. Permit them to be educated, and next you know, they are supporting revolutionaries and promoting forms of government they scarcely understand. If we are not careful, someday they will demand the vote, as well."

Allie bit back an irritable response to *that* medieval opinion.

Not that it mattered now.

All her troubles had come home to roost today.

THIRTY MINUTES LATER, an impatient knock sounded on Allie's bedchamber door, forcing her off her bed to answer it.

She had been lying down, attempting to convince her lacerated spirit that she could leave Ethan behind tomorrow. All she had received for her efforts was a pounding head and even sorer heart.

Kendall's angry face greeted her from the hallway. Her brother barged into her bedchamber, shutting the door with a *clack*.

"You must come downstairs for tea," he commanded. "I require your assistance to help me entertain Charswood and avoid Lady Isolde."

Allie turned away from him, crossing to the window. "That seems rather cowardly, Kendall. I didn't realize one helpless woman would overset you so."

"That woman is anything *but* helpless," he shot back.

"Methinks the duke doth protest too much," Allie muttered under her breath.

"Pardon?"

"*Niente.*" She waved a hand at him.

He stared at her.

Allie ignored his stony presence and sat at the small vanity table before her bedroom window, attempting to repair her hair.

"I assume this Fabrizio Sacci is the same reprobate I corresponded with in Italy?" her twin finally asked, tone sharp.

"You mean the man you hired to drug and kidnap me?" she asked far too innocently, meeting her brother's gaze in the mirror. "That man?"

"Yes."

"*Sì*. He is that Fabrizio Sacci."

"Do I want to know how *well* you know him?"

"No," she replied far too blithely.

"Will he be a problem?"

"Oh, most definitely."

Kendall's irritated grunt pleased her to no end. "Is there anything *else* you would like to tell me about Signore Sacci?"

"Well, let's see," Allie sighed, making it woefully dramatic. "Fabrizio and I are old acquaintances. He was the leader of our small gang the day Ethan Penn-Leith was robbed. Therefore, he was an eyewitness to those events. Fabrizio has spent the past several months threatening to reveal my past unless I give him money for his revolutionary cause. Obviously, he has gotten nowhere with that, mostly because I have no money and loathe Fabrizio for the betraying, backstabbing blackguard that he is." She tapped her lips. "I believe that sums up everything."

Kendall sucked in a long breath. "And why did you neglect to tell me any of this?"

"Because I didn't care if Fabrizio ruins me." Allie finished smoothing her hair. "And as men of your ilk are wont to do, you would most assuredly have punished me for Fabrizio's perfidy instead of helping me in any material way."

She frowned at her reflection in the mirror. No amount of primping would ease her puffy eyes. She poked at the dark circles underneath them.

Finally, she noticed Kendall's stony silence behind her.

Again, she met his gaze in the mirror.

Her twin appeared troubled—gaze stormy, mouth drawn into a tight line. Or was he perturbed? Constipated?

She hardly knew.

"Do you truly believe that?" he asked. "That I would do nothing to help you?"

Allie dropped both hands to her lap, eyes rolling back in her head.

"Of course, I do," she retorted. "Why would I think otherwise? When I needed you most, you not only refused to lift a finger to help, but betrayed me in the most brutal way possible. Why should this situation with Fabrizio be any different?"

"Because if you had bothered to speak with me, I would have told you that Sacci has already attempted to blackmail me!"

She swiveled around in her chair, looking up at her twin.

"Pardon? Fabrizio told me you forbade him, on pain of severe retribution, to ever contact you again."

"He lied."

"That seems like . . . ," she paused and then sighed, ". . . precisely something Fabrizio would do. Were you stupid enough to comply with his blackmail attempts?"

Her twin appeared affronted. "Of course not. A Duke of Kendall does not succumb to blackmail. We counterattack."

"Ah." *Of course.* "Like requesting Ethan Penn-Leith to accompany us north? Threatening journalists? That sort of counterattack?"

"Precisely."

Allie pressed two fingers to the bridge of her nose.

"Given that his past attempts have failed, why would Sacci be here now?" Kendall continued.

"I cannot say with any confidence. In his last letter, he claimed to have proof that I was on that road in Italy with Mr. Penn-Leith."

"What proof?" her twin retorted. "It isn't as if you paused the robbery long enough for a local photographer to take a daguerreotype."

"Exactly!" She pointed a finger at him. "I had the same thought!"

"Clever." Kendall was pacing now.

"Thank you. Fabrizio is a menace."

"Agreed. He almost certainly has a plan to weasel money out of us."

"Yes. He finagled an invitation from Lady Isolde for a reason."

"Clearly."

"He needs to be stopped."

"Yes."

"Why are you agreeing with me?" Allie frowned. "It's unnerving."

Kendall paused, spinning to peer at her. "I'm . . . sorry?"

"You are disrupting our hateful equilibrium. I hardly recognize you like this . . . so . . . so rational and . . . understanding."

She didn't add that she saw shades of Tristan in their repartee. That this was precisely how she would have imagined an adult conversation with her brother to progress.

It was . . . unsettling.

"Never fear," he snorted. "I am certain this accord is merely temporary."

"It needn't be."

We could become Tristan and Allie again, she thought.

Madonna, but she would give almost anything to have her brother back.

"Ah. So you're willing to tame that shrewish tongue of yours?" he said sharply. "Agree to my plans for your future? Realize that I do know what is best for you?"

A less power-hungry man might have said those words as a joke, but not Kendall. He meant them as seriously as the first time he had said them.

So . . . a reconciliation was clearly not in the cards.

"Hardly. I rather hoped you would finally recognize that I understand my own mind and wishes for my future."

"Charswood is a good man."

"Yes, he is. But that does not automatically mean I will be happy as his wife."

That I will feel as if I belong, she did not dare add.

Drat Ethan and his poet's perception.

"Bah! We have had this conversation *ad nauseum.* I am done with it." Kendall turned for the door.

"Done with *me,* you mean?"

Her twin flinched, the slightest twitch of his shoulders.

"Charswood is here for you, and I expect you to dance attendance on him," he said, tone chilly. "We have an agreement, after all."

"There is the despotic brother I know only too well." Allie pushed to her feet. "Lead the way, my gaoler."

AN HOUR LATER, Allie sat sandwiched between Kendall and Charswood in Lady Hadley's drawing-room—sipping tea, nibbling shortbread, and feeling generally miserable.

If she chose Charswood, scenes like this one would be her future, soulless gatherings of meaningless chatter.

Though . . . the guests around her this afternoon didn't appear soulless, per se. They talked and laughed and engaged in spirited, intellectual discourse.

Perhaps it was Allie who lacked a soul?

Ye dinnae want freedom. Ye want tae belong.

Or perhaps she simply didn't belong here.

But if she didn't belong here, then where did she belong?

It was not as if she could move into a wee Highland cottage with Ethan and subsist on gruel and the power of love.

Though, as she imagined it—Ethan seated before a homey fire of an evening, pen scritching in the firelight, his gaze lifting to meet hers and promising all sorts of wickedness . . .

Allie took in a stuttering breath, blinking her eyes and biting her bottom lip to stymie the emotion that clogged her throat.

Where is the indomitable woman I know and love? Ethan's entreaty echoed in her ears.

Why *did* fear hold her in thrall? Why did she hesitate to embrace the life she wanted with Ethan, Kendall be damned?

Opposite, Fabrizio turned to look at her, his eyes widening slightly as he realized she was upset. He likely assumed he was the reason, the *idiota*. He lifted his eyebrows in challenge—as if to say, *ready to spar?*—before turning back to banter and flirt outrageously with Lady Isolde.

The man was a never-ending annoyance.

And given how often Kendall tensed beside Allie, her twin found Fabrizio equally irritating.

So . . . the man's presence wasn't entirely unwelcome.

But what was the bandit's agenda?

And how was Allie to antici—

Snick.

The door to the drawing-room opened, admitting the butler.

"Mr. Ethan Penn-Leith," the man intoned.

Oh!

Her Ethan.

He was here.

Allie sat up straighter as a coal lit in her chest, hot and aching.

The butler stepped aside as Ethan walked through the doorway. He had washed and changed into a well-fitted dark blue coat and gray trousers, his wavy hair damp around the edges. However, he still looked exhausted, his eyes as red-rimmed as her own.

He scanned the room until finding her, their gazes locking.

Adoration and yearning took up a steady drumbeat beneath her sternum.

All of her longed to rush across the room, throw herself into his arms, and beg for his forgiveness. To shout, *Yes, I choose you!* To promise that she would claw, fight, wrestle . . . anything so that they could be together.

But Kendall shifted at her side and Ethan looked away and the moment was lost.

Lady Hadley crossed to Ethan, hands outstretched. "Mr. Penn-Leith! How delighted we are to welcome you."

"Lady Hadley," he bowed.

"Lady Isolde has invited some friends up from London." Her ladyship took his arm. "Permit me to make introductions."

Ethan dutifully followed in Lady Hadley's wake, nodding and smiling amiably.

But The Swooner was strained today, Allie noted. Ethan performed the requisite niceties without any of his usual sparkle.

And aside from that first glance, he avoided Allie's gaze.

"Your Scot appears a little worse for wear," Kendall murmured in her ear. "I wonder what has tarnished him so. Did someone criticize his poetry? Mock his smile? Terrorize his cat?"

Allie gritted her teeth.

"Must you always be so disagreeable?" she whispered.

Kendall grunted.

They both watched as Fabrizio greeted Ethan.

"Mr. Penn-Leith," Fabrizio said in heavily-accented English. "Such a pleasure to finally be *properly* introduced."

Fabrizio's eyes darted meaningfully to Allie as he spoke, taunting.

Beside her, Kendall let out a heavy breath.

"And yourself, Mr. Sacci," Ethan replied, voice giving nothing away.

"Your poem about the *banditi*, the highwaymen, in Italy has been a success here in Britain, no?" Fabrizio asked. "You shall have to tell us about it."

Ethan's smile turned even more strained. "I believe the poem says all that need be said."

"And yet, you are being *molto riservato* in hiding the lady's identity. Who is she? The English ladies in Italy . . . they are not many. Perhaps I know her?" Fabrizio's eyes flicked Allie's way as he spoke.

Honestly, the man was about as subtle as a stagecoach horn.

Charswood, on Allie's other side, stirred to life. "I must say, Mr. Sacci, I do not like your line of questioning. Mr. Penn-Leith has been a gentleman in refusing to divulge the lady's identity. Perhaps you should follow suit and respect her privacy."

Fabrizio swung his gaze toward Charswood. "Perhaps. But the lady is a criminal, is she not? She robbed Mr. Penn-Leith and others of their money and possessions. Perhaps it would be best *per tutti* to know her identity. Who is to say she isn't currently robbing other members of the *ton*?" Fabrizio framed that lovely jab with a cherubic smile.

"At gunpoint?" Kendall scoffed. "I fear you have an Italian flare for the dramatic, Mr. Sacci. Does Mr. Mazzini approve of you spending your time investigating literary gossip?"

"How charming." Fabrizio narrowed his eyes at Allie's twin. "Your mother was Italian, was she not, Your Grace? Perhaps you have something to hide?"

It took all of Allie's self-control to bite her tongue and not respond in a stream of blistering Italian.

Kendall merely gave Fabrizio his icy, ducal stare. The one that said he did not suffer fools.

"Charming, indeed," he intoned, tossing Fabrizio's own word back at him.

The entire conversation felt like a chess match. Each player jockeying for position. Though Allie was unsure if she was the queen in this analogy or an easily-sacrificed pawn.

Regardless, the exchange with Fabrizio had garnered attention. Every head in the room had turned their way.

"I must agree with Lord Charswood," Lord Hadley said, tossing his hat into the ring. "'Tis a wee bit gauche tae be attempting tae ferret out the lady's identity, Mr. Sacci. Let's let the topic rest, shall we?"

Fabrizio bristled at Hadley's paternal tone, like a cat with its fur standing on end.

"You do not care, my lord, that you may have a viper in your midst?" he countered, darting another pointed look at Allie.

His meaning was unmistakable.

Hadley's eyes narrowed.

Allie didn't know the earl well, but that expression on a nobleman's face never presaged gentle words or kind behavior.

Hadley rose. "Might I have a wee word with yourself, Mr. Sacci?"

"I believe I shall join you, Hadley." Kendall stood as well.

"Count me in," Ethan quipped.

Without thinking, Allie rose to her feet.

Kendall gave her a repressing look. Allie returned with a slight shake of her head.

As if she would permit her brother, her beau, and Lord Hadley to question a former colleague and—well, whatever else Fabrizio had once been to her—without herself being present.

"Shall I come, as well, Your Grace?" Charswood asked at Allie's elbow.

Allie met her brother's gaze at the question. She could almost hear the calculations whirring in his brain. If Charswood learned of Allie's career as a highwaywoman and involvement with *La Giovine Italia*, how would that affect Kendall's political stratagems?

Her brother turned to Charswood with a tight smile. "I believe you had best remain here, my lord."

Ah.

Turning, Kendall offered her his arm.

Moments later, they followed Hadley, along with Ethan and Fabrizio, into the seclusion of his lordship's private study.

22

Ethan stood to one side of Hadley's study, shoulder blades resting against the window casement, carefully observing each person present.

The room was a pleasant one with rich wood paneling and bookcases, two large windows, and an enormous desk situated in the middle.

The palpable strain between the room's occupants, however, rendered the atmosphere as fraught as a sheriff court session.

Fabrizio lounged against a bookcase opposite the doorway.

Allie stood beside Kendall just inside the door, her back ramrod straight as if facing a firing squad. The set of Kendall's mouth and his steady glare at Fabrizio said he wished to tear the Italian limb from limb.

Hadley leaned a shoulder into the fireplace mantel, expression curious.

For his part, Ethan crossed his feet at the ankle and shoved his hands into the pockets of his trousers. He had slept for an hour—just enough to prevent himself from collapsing on his feet—before bathing and hurrying to Muirford House to see Allie.

They were hardly done with their conversation from earlier. Ethan just hoped he could keep himself on his feet until then. He took in a deep breath, trying to clear the cobwebs in his brain.

"It pleases me to see you all here," Fabrizio began, grinning confidently. "Perhaps we can dismiss pleasantries and move on to discussing how you will ensure my silence?"

No one else moved, but Hadley's eyebrows rose. "Well, my afternoon just became more interesting," the earl said, standing upright and folding his arms. "Silence on what?"

Fabrizio's returning grin was wicked. "Lady Allegra is the woman from Mr. Penn-Leith's poem."

"The highwaywoman he kissed?" Hadley asked.

"Sì, the very same."

Hadley whistled. "That is quite the claim."

"Careful, Sacci. I do not like allegations being made against my sister," Kendall said, low and threatening. "Such idle words threaten her reputation as a lady."

Allie's eyes rolled ceiling-ward at her brother's sentiment, eliciting the first genuine smile Ethan had given since she admitted she loved him.

His *ladra* would never care too much what others thought of her. And she certainly didn't require her brother's protection.

"Hear, hear," Hadley agreed. "Ye make a dangerous accusation, Mr. Sacci."

Fabrizio snorted. "I make no accusation. It is the truth. I was there."

"Pardon?" Hadley's head reared back.

"I was there that day," Fabrizio repeated, "as a colleague of Lady Allegra."

"So . . . ye be a highwayman, too?" Hadley asked.

The question was said mildly enough, but even Fabrizio heard the steel in Hadley's voice.

"Why was this miscreant even permitted to enter your house, Hadley?" Kendall interrupted.

"Lady Isolde's invite. Bit of a rabble-rouser, my daughter," Hadley replied, far too cheerfully. "A trait inherited from her mother."

"It seems ill-advised to indulge Lady Isolde so. She has rather poor discernment in gentlemen." Kendall motioned a hand toward Fabrizio. "As we can see."

"I'd be careful how ye speak of my eldest daughter, Kendall." Hadley's bonhomie vanished, expression darkening. "Lady Isolde and her siblings are the light of my life, and I won't have anyone, even a lofty English duke, speaking ill of them. As ye said, idle words can be damaging."

Kendall managed to hold Hadley's stern glower for a few seconds before looking away.

"I have proof of my claims," Fabrizio said into the silence.

"What proof?" Kendall retorted. "What could possibly prove you were there?"

"I have Mr. Penn-Leith's revolver."

Shock straightened Ethan's spine. "My revolver?"

"Sì, with your name clearly engraved on it."

"Ye could have gotten the revolver from the true thieves," Ethan countered. "That proves nothing."

"Ah, yes." Fabrizio held up a finger. "But I also have this." With a flourish, he produced a rigid copper daguerreotype from his coat pocket and handed it to Hadley.

Glancing at the photograph, Hadley raised his eyebrows.

"And do not think to mangle the plate or destroy the image with fire," Fabrizio warned. "The photographer took multiple frames, so I have two more such photographs in my possession."

Hadley passed the copper plate to Ethan.

The edges of the metal felt cool against Ethan's palm. The image showed Fabrizio in the center of a group, a piece of parchment in his hand with *La Giovine Italia* written on it. Allie stood to his right, a hand on his shoulder, stalwart and brazen. Four other men were positioned around them.

Ah, his *ladra*. She appeared so resolute in the photograph—stern-faced, staring directly into the camera. So determined to do her part. To belong.

Absently, Ethan rubbed his sternum, attempting to assuage the ache there.

Kendall crossed to peer over Ethan's shoulder.

With a sniff, His Grace plucked the photo from Ethan's grasp, took four steps to the fireplace, and promptly tossed the daguerreotype on the fire smoldering in the grate. The heat instantly warped the metal backing, obliterating the image.

Ethan glanced at Allie, still standing rigidly just inside the doorway, hands clasped before her. If she felt a pang at the image burning, her face didn't show it. And when she shifted her gaze to Ethan's, he found her gray eyes to be stormy and unreadable.

"As I said," Fabrizio grit out, "destroying the photograph will not prevent me from publishing the other images I possess."

"Perhaps not." Kendall stalked toward him. "But it is one less thing I will have to extract from your bloodied body."

The duke towered over Fabrizio.

To his credit, the Italian attempted to hold his ground, but as Kendall had at least six inches of height on him, Fabrizio had to crane his neck back to avoid staring at Kendall's shirt buttons.

"No one threatens my sister," Kendall said in a tone so menacing, it set the fine hairs on Ethan's neck flying to attention. "You would do well, Sacci, to remember that."

Fabrizio swallowed but jutted out his chin in bravado. "I am happy to accept payment in return for my silence regarding her involvement with our *gruppo*."

"I do not cave to blackmailers!"

Fabrizio retorted in sharp Italian.

Hadley watched, his expression inscrutable.

Ethan used the distraction to cross from the window to stand beside Allie.

"How fare ye?" he murmured.

Her red-rimmed gray eyes lifted to his. Ethan read the turmoil there . . . her indecision, her fear.

She shrugged. "Heartsore and hating the choices before me." She turned to look at her brother.

Ethan studied her for another moment, the ache in his lungs tightening.

Something had to be done. Allie required more choices than merely Charswood or himself. There had to be a solution that freed her from Kendall's machinations without a man attached. Ethan didn't think he could bear to watch her fierce spirit be slowly crushed under the weight of her brother's heavy authority and Charswood's neglect.

Ethan slipped his hand into Allie's.

Hadley noted it with a lift of his eyebrows.

Ethan was beyond caring who knew of his regard for this woman.

Kendall's raised voice intruded. "Try publishing this information and see what happens to your precious *La Giovine Italia*. Two can play at this game, Sacci. What salacious thing might you find broadcast about yourself or Mazzini? Do not think to intimidate me."

Fabrizio spat something in Italian, hands gesturing wildly.

Kendall lifted the man up by his lapels, shoving him against the woodwork of Hadley's study.

"Come, lass," Ethan whispered, bending to Allie's ear. "Let us fight Kendall together."

ALLIE STARED DOWN at Ethan's hand wrapped around her own. She felt it then . . .

Belonging.

An almost overwhelming sense of being linked with something larger than herself.

Tears pricked once more.

As if responding to her emotion, Ethan planted a tender kiss on her knuckles.

"What is going on here?" Kendall's voice whipped her. "Unhand my sister, Penn-Leith!"

Allie lifted her head to see Kendall scowling, his eyes locked on the back of her just-kissed hand.

Ethan didn't so much as flinch. Instead, he clutched her palm and pulled her tight to his side.

Kendall sucked in an outraged breath.

"I thought you were a gentleman of honor, Penn-Leith! Will you now follow the path of this miscreant here?" Kendall stabbed a finger at Fabrizio behind him. "Attempt to blackmail me, too?"

"My intentions toward your sister are most honorable, Your Grace," Ethan said.

"Bah! No man's intentions are honorable when a dowry such as Lady Allegra's is in the offing. What man would marry her without it?"

Kendall's denunciation landed like a blow to the solar plexus, leaving Allie breathless.

She looked at Ethan . . . and stilled.

Over the past few months, she had seen Ethan Penn-Leith exhibit every emotion—from cheery optimism to thoughtful musing to pained heartbreak.

But for the first time in . . . ever . . . he did not appear charming or good-natured.

No.

Jaw clenched, eyes narrowed, brow furrowed . . .

Ethan Penn-Leith was angry.

Furious.

Apoplectic, even.

"Ye may be a duke, Kendall," Ethan snapped, "but how dare ye accuse me of monstrous conduct toward a lady I admire and respect as much as your sister."

"Hear, hear," Hadley raised an imaginary glass in agreement.

"I love Lady Allegra, Your Grace. For herself and herself alone." Each word left Ethan's mouth with the force of a gunshot. "If she would agree, we would ask your blessing for our union, dowry or no."

"That will *never* happen," Kendall replied, tone dripping aristocratic certainty. "You would only marry over my cold corpse."

"That can be arranged," Fabrizio offered dryly.

"*Cold corpse*? Truly?" Allie asked in exasperation. "Must you be so melodramatic, Kendall?"

"You cannot agree with Penn-Leith, Lady Allegra," Kendall returned.

"I do."

"You love *him*?" Kendall pointed a finger at Ethan. "This lowly-born Scot with no political connections to further our family name? A man whose only credentials are a charming smile and a witty pen? A poet whose current popularity will be fleeting at best?"

Allie knew Kendall meant his words to be insulting, but they brought a smile to her face. The first true smile all day.

"Yes, that precise man. But you neglected to add that Ethan—"

"Ethan is it?!"

"—is kind and funny and clever and kisses with such sweet—"

"Kisses?!" Kendall's brow became a thundercloud. He whirled on Ethan. "You have been kissing my sister when I expressly forbade it?!"

"Aye." Ethan's jaw remained set. He likely resembled his Highland ancestors, eager to snatch up a broadsword and hunt down invading Englishmen. "Aye, I have. And I hope tae kiss her again."

"Penn-Leith—"

"What will it take?" Ethan asked.

"Pardon?" Kendall reared back.

"What will it take to set Lady Allegra free? I ken that ye want tae use her as a puppet in your play for power in Her Majesty's government. But as we both know, everything has a price. So I am asking ye, Duke . . . what is the price for her freedom?"

"So she may marry you?" Kendall sneered.

"Aye, if that is her choice. However, I love Lady Allegra enough tae want her freedom. To take possession of her dowry now, with or without a husband attached to it."

"Have you gone mad, Penn-Leith?"

"Perhaps." A small smile touched Ethan's lips. "Love has a way of doing that, I am finding. So what is your price, Duke? Do ye wish for more money? If so, I will sign over the rights tae my poetry. Is it power? Let me play Virgil to your Augustus. I shall use my 'witty pen,' as ye called it, to laud your fame. Tell me and if it is within my power, I will do it. Just grant Lady Allegra her freedom in exchange. Let her choose her own path."

"Ethan," Allie began, "I cannot permit you to—"

"Hush, lass." He pressed another kiss to the back of her hand. "I will not see ye leg-shackled tae suit your brother's whims. Not if I can prevent it. I love ye enough tae want your happiness over anything else. Even myself."

Allie leaned toward him, lost in the sincerity brimming in his eyes, reveling in the grounding weight of his hand in hers. For the briefest moment, she glanced back at her brother, noting the disdain and fury in his eyes.

And *justlikethat*—

She made her choice.

Allie could not give up Ethan Penn-Leith.

It flooded her in an instant, wave after wave of love and adoration. The same overwhelming emotions that had scoured her hours earlier as Ethan cuddled his wee nephew.

Only this time . . . she welcomed them.

Mentally, she spread her arms wide and allowed the powerful surge of *devotionyearningdesirelove* to wash over and through her, cleansing all doubt and fear.

Ethan was right.

He had been right all along.

She wanted to belong to him. She wanted to place her trust in him—to love and be loved in return. To choose a life together.

She yearned for the future he envisioned for them.

She was his.

Just as he would be hers.

She merely needed to join him in the fight.

If they united, together they would find a way to—

"As touching as this is, you are delusional, Penn-Leith," Kendall snarled. "My sister is not a horse to be sold off to the highest bidder!"

Allie couldn't stop her incredulous gasp of laughter. "That is *precisely* what I am to you, Kendall! Do not pretend otherwise!"

"I will not stand here and be so slandered by—"

Crack.

The sound of a gun cocking reverberated through the room, fracturing their argument.

Everyone froze before turning to look at Fabrizio still standing with his back against the bookcase.

The Italian pointed a revolver toward them.

"This is all so very touching," he said, "but it would please me if we could discuss how I will be paid."

"Is that . . ." Ethan began. "Is that *my* revolver? Here?"

"Perhaps," Fabrizio hedged. "It does have six chambers, so I could easily put a bullet in each of you and still have two left."

"That's my weapon," Ethan said incredulously.

Fabrizio shrugged. "It might be yours, Penn-Leith, but you will have to pry it from my hands."

His tone suggested that said hands would have to be dead for that to occur.

"Fabrizio, you might like to gamble, but this is *ridicolo*, even for you," Allie said. "If you murder us, you will swing for it. What good would all our deaths do?"

"I do not care. I am as good as dead," he replied, gun trembling in his hand. "As you said, I am a gambler, and this is *la mia ultima scommessa*—my ultimate gamble."

Understanding illuminated her mind.

Of course.

"You have gambling debts. Money lenders."

"Oh, our Mr. Sacci has plenty of debt," Kendall said, drawing Fabrizio's attention. The Italian pointed the revolver at Allie's twin. "Once he began contacting me, I made sure to investigate him. I may have convinced a few of his debtors to call in their markers."

"It is you then who I have to thank for my current predicament?" The gun shook in Fabrizio's hand, his handsome face contorting in rage as he aimed the revolver at Kendall's heart.

Allie's world slowed, as if everything were moving through sticky honey.

She knew Fabrizio.

She had seen him kill more than once.

The Italian's finger twitched on the trigger.

He was going to fire at Kendall. At this close range, it would likely kill her twin.

And Allie knew, as sure as her own heart beat in her chest, that she could not—she *would* not—let that happen.

Allie raced forward before Fabrizio even finished speaking.

Ethan cried out.

Allie crashed into Fabrizio's shoulder, sending him staggering backwards.

Fabrizio fired—once, twice—as he fell into the bookcase, books tumbling.

Allie hit the ground. Hard. Breath left her body in a loud *oof!*

Fabrizio rolled, shaking off books, attempting to rise.

Hadley and Ethan pounced on him.

Ethan pinned the Italian's right hand to the floor, wresting the revolver from his grasp, while Hadley flipped Fabrizio onto his stomach and pressed a knee into his spine, twisting the man's arm behind his back.

Gasping for breath, Allie pushed to her knees and turned to look for her brother.

The Duke of Kendall lay on the floor, a bright red stain spreading across the white of his neckcloth and pooling beside his gray head.

Allie's soul left her body.

"Tristan!!!" she shrieked.

On a sob, she lurched to her feet and staggered the few steps to him, collapsing beside his head.

"No! Tristan! NO!!"

She couldn't lose him. Not like this.

Not angry and fighting.

Not unreconciled and hateful.

"No, no, no!" she wailed, fingers frantically untying his cravat and wrenching at his shirt buttons.

Where was the wound? Was he breathing? Was she too late—

Tristan moaned and pushed her hands away.

"Stop," he muttered.

Coughing, he rolled to his left side.

OH!

He wasn't dead.

Tristan was alive.

He's alive! The words stampeded through Allie's brain. *Alive, alive, alive.*

Her twin looked at his right shoulder and then let loose an impressive string of curses.

Alive and swearing!

How much better than merely alive!

Her mind clearing, Allie finally noted the hole in the right shoulder of his coat where the bullet had grazed him.

Her brother wasn't lethally wounded.

Sobbing in relief, she scooted forward on her knees and began patting down his torso, trying to ascertain if the second bullet had struck him anywhere.

"I said stop," he growled, pushing her hands away and flopping onto his back again. "I shall be fine."

Uffa!

Her stubborn, obstinate, overbearing brother.

It scoured her heart—

She loved him.

She had loved the quiet, kind boy he had been.

And, despite everything, she still loved the irritable, arrogant, overprotective man he had become.

More's the pity.

It was as if opening her heart fully to Ethan had lifted the floodgates, allowing love and belonging to pour in.

Allie sat back on her heels, tears blurring her vision.

And in that moment, she knew . . .

She didn't want to be Kendall's adversary or tormentor any longer.

No.

Hating him was exhausting.

She wanted to forgive him for his betrayal and kidnapping. For the wrongs he had committed over the past eight months.

More to the point, she wanted to be his twin—his sister, his friend—again.

They had been born together—Allie and Tristan, Tristan and Allie.

They *belonged*, as Ethan had intuited.

Why had she automatically conceded that their sire had irrevocably changed Tristan? That he had irreparably molded and morphed the loving boy she had known into this cold, austere man?

That boy had to be inside him somewhere. She caught glimpses of him from time to time.

Allie vowed that she would find that Tristan, free him, and force him back into the light of their belonging. Kicking and screaming, if necessary.

Tristan thought she had been vexing up to this point?

That would be nothing when compared to her fight for his soul.

And then, once he remembered his brotherly love for her . . .

He was going to escort her down the wedding aisle to marry Ethan Penn-Leith.

23

Ethan guided his horse up the lane to Thistle Muir, so very soul-heavy and weary he sagged in the saddle.

He hadn't slept in over thirty-six hours, and all of him—body, thoughts, heart—felt sluggish and dispirited. He stared sightlessly at the sun where it hung low in the sky and painted the clouds in brilliant shades of pink and lavender.

He had not spoken to Allie after Fabrizio fired the gun and injured Kendall's shoulder. Understandably, she had been distraught by Kendall's wound and refused to leave her twin's side.

For his part, Ethan had joined Hadley in detaining Fabrizio. And then, once the sheriff and procurator fiscal arrived, he had recounted the events of the afternoon and answered questions.

But now, returning home, Ethan had to wonder when, or even if, he would see Allie again.

Kendall had intended to return to London tomorrow. But would his wound permit a departure? The duke's injury hadn't seemed too serious once the bleeding had been staunched. And if Allie did leave with her brother, what would she decide regarding Charswood?

Matters between Ethan and his *ladra* were anything but settled. And likely to remain so if Kendall had any say in the matter.

Ethan rounded the final curve to Thistle Muir.

His heart sank.

Bloody hell.

His day had only needed this.

A familiar traveling coach was pulled up before the front door.

Uncle Leith.

No need to wonder why his uncle was here.

Ethan's lack of reply to his letters had undoubtedly spurred Uncle Leith northward, intent on forcing Ethan to heel. And his uncle, being an old-fashioned sort who eschewed locomotive travel, had made the journey by his habitual carriage.

Sighing, Ethan handed his horse off to a farmhand and turned for the house.

"I HAVE QUIT my lease in London," Uncle Leith announced a quarter hour later, a teacup and saucer balanced in one hand, a biscuit held in the other. "I have heard word there is an importer in Aberdeen who might be interested in a shipping contract. So I am returning home."

Ethan sighed, reaching for his teacup.

Malcolm glared at their uncle, his own teacup untouched before him.

The fact that the household could produce a tea tray and shortbread at such short notice when Viola had given birth less than twelve hours previously was a testament to Thistle Muir's efficiency.

"And ye couldnae write tae us of your intentions?" Malcolm asked.

Uncle Leith's eyebrows rose at Malcolm's tone.

Ethan shot his brother a warning look. No need to rile their uncle. Ethan would prefer to not be on the receiving end of the man's irritable tongue for the journey to Aberdeen.

"I saw no need," Uncle Leith replied. "Besides given how unreliable

Ethan has been as a correspondent, I didn't suppose my sending ahead a warning would have mattered."

His uncle likely intended the remark to sting, but it only ruffled Ethan's testy mood.

He did not want to return to Aberdeen with Uncle Leith. He didn't want to be forced to woo and charm another investor.

He was so tired of this Catherine wheel.

But could he flat-out refuse?

"I hear congratulations are in order, Malcolm," Uncle Leith continued conversationally. "Your wife delivered a fine baby boy, I understand."

"Aye." Malcolm folded his arms. "This morning."

Every line of Malcolm's body communicated his aggravation at their uncle's presence.

"This morning?!" Uncle Leith sounded scandalized. As if Malcolm were at fault for permitting visitors at such an inauspicious time.

Ethan mentally rolled his eyes, setting down his teacup.

"Well, I certainly cannot spend the evening here then," their uncle frowned.

"Nae, ye cannae," Malcolm agreed.

"Ethan will see us to an inn in Fettermill tonight," Uncle Leith decreed. "We can leave from there tomorrow morning."

Ethan pressed two fingertips to the bridge of his nose.

He couldn't leave Allie, not without knowing how things fared with Kendall. Not without having one final conversation about themselves and what their future might be.

Uncle Leith rightly read Ethan's hesitation.

"I have permitted you to gallivant about this business with Kendall, but it is apparent that nothing has come of it," his uncle said. "We must retrench and consider other options. You will return—"

"Kendall was wounded this evening," Ethan interrupted, "so I cannot say what will come of your shipping request."

"Pardon?!" Uncle Leith set down his teacup with a *clink*.

Sitting back, Ethan related the series of events, from Kendall's unexpected arrival to Fabrizio's firing of Ethan's revolver.

"Ye have had quite the day," Malcolm said. "And Kendall . . . ?" He drifted off into a question.

"I believe His Grace should make a full recovery. The bullet wound appeared superficial, thankfully."

Uncle Leith frowned into his teacup.

"If anything, this turn of events strengthens my resolve to return to Aberdeen. You will be coming with me, lad." He pointed a finger at Ethan. "I will not be refused in this. Now that Kendall is wounded and recuperating, he will be in no position to receive visitors or make decisions about shipping. It is imperative that I pursue other opportunities. We leave at first light."

"And if I refuse?" Ethan had to ask it.

Uncle Leith narrowed his eyes. "Then you will regret your choice."

24

It was well past midnight before Allie found herself standing at her brother's bedside.

The doctor had come and gone, tending to Tristan's wound and leaving instructions for his care.

Now clad in a clean linen shirt and trousers, her twin lay in the middle of the bed, his chest rising and falling in deep breaths. Whiskers stubbled his jaw and his gray hair was akin to a haystack, poking out every which way.

He appeared so . . . young. His eyelashes fanned across his cheeks and his nose twitched just as it had when he was a boy.

Sitting on the edge of the mattress, Allie pressed a hand to his forehead.

Did he feel feverish? Infection was the greatest danger now, the doctor had warned.

"Stop touching me." Tristan pushed her hand away without opening his eyes. "You're hovering, and it's insufferable."

"For a few moments, I thought you had died, Tristan." Allie purposefully put her palm back on his forehead. "You shaved a solid decade off my life. I'm permitted to hover."

The image of Tristan bloodied and lying so still would haunt her to her own deathbed.

Over the intervening hours since his injury, her resolve to reconcile matters between them had settled into a hardened sense of *rightness*.

She would coax and wheedle and provoke her twin until he found the boy he used to be. They *would* love one another again and celebrate their belonging in each other's lives.

But first, Tristan needed to stop being such a curmudgeon.

"I'm scarcely wounded." He shoved her hand off again, his dark eyes flaring open. "The bullet did little more than scrape my skin. I shall be right as rain by tomorrow."

"Scrape?!" She pulled back to gape at him. "Your shoulder bled like a gutted pig and required twelve stitches! It is so like you to be testy over a wound."

She stood up and leaned to fluff the pillow behind his head.

He grabbed for her hands. "Lady Allegra, you must cease. Do not make me summon a footman and have you removed!"

Allie froze, aghast. "Tristan! You wouldn't!"

"I would!" he shot back, eyes bloodshot and threatening.

"You can try, I suppose." She stared down at him, hands on her hips. "Hadley's footmen—and quite frankly Hadley himself—prefer me over your surly carcass, so your chances of winning their assistance are slim."

Tristan scowled at her.

She ignored him and returned to fluffing his pillow.

His long-suffering sigh of annoyance buoyed her spirits to no end.

"Since when have I become *Tristan* to you?" he growled.

"Since I saw your supine form covered in blood, you dunderhead."

"Now you are simply being histrionic."

"Stop being hurtful. If you had permitted the doctor to give you laudanum as he recommended, you wouldn't be so peevish."

"You know I hate laudanum."

"Mmm, that is true. You hated it even as a boy."

"Exactly, and now, you are attempting to coerce me into approving Penn-Leith's absurd marriage proposal."

"Is it working?"

He clenched his jaw in reply.

"I *do* intend to marry Ethan," she said, casually . . . cheerfully, even. "I love him and he loves me and we will be blissfully happy together. And though we would appreciate your blessing, we do not require it. I would, however, ask you to not sabotage our plans."

Tristan rolled his eyes. "How have my wishes regarding Penn-Leith been unclear to you, Lady Allegra? You are usually not quite so dense. I have been excessively consistent in my refusal of his suit and OW!!"

Her brother stared down at her finger where it had just poked his wounded shoulder.

"Merely a scrape, eh?" Allie cocked an eyebrow at him.

"That hurts!"

"Are you going to agree to my terms?"

Tristan looked up from his bandaged shoulder in confusion. "Terms?"

"The terms where you decide to love me again and accept Ethan Penn-Leith as your brother-in-law with open arms."

"Lady Allegra, you need to relinquish—OW!!"

He caught her finger that time. "Stop that!"

"What? This?!" Allie poked his wound a third time with her unshackled hand.

Tristan grabbed her other hand, holding both of hers in one of his. "Dammit, that hurt, Allie!"

Allie.

The name resounded like a struck gong.

Finally!

He had called her *Allie*!

She couldn't stop a bright flare of hope as her name reverberated . . . *Allie, Allie, Allie . . .*

Progress. She was making progress with her twin.

She twisted, trying to free her hands.

"Stop being so ill-tempered!" he grunted, holding her fast.

"I will when you stop being such a controlling arsehead!"

Tugging hard, she redoubled her efforts to free her hands, to no avail.

Uffa but he was strong.

She changed tactics, falling forward to drive an elbow into his solar plexus. The breath left him with an *oof!*

Tristan groaned in pain, releasing her fingers.

Allie braced her palms on the counterpane, one to either side of his head.

She glared down into his chocolate-brown eyes.

Their mother's eyes.

Eyes that were so dear to her.

Enough of this resentment and anger. They had already spent too many years as adversaries.

It ended now.

"You listen to me, Tristan Gilbert," she declared. "I watched you be shot today. I experienced whole seconds where I thought . . . I th-thought . . ." Her bottom lip trembled uncontrollably. "I th-thought you had d-died."

A tear spilled onto her cheek.

And then . . . another.

Her twin's gaze softened.

She took a deep breath, allowing her emotions to tumble out, exposing her soft underbelly.

"I realized then that I love you, Tristan," she continued. "I have always loved you and will never stop loving you. And you, damn you, are going to love me, even if I have to smother you in affection for the rest of our lives. We're going to be best friends once more and support each other and tell each other things and listen to each other's disappointments and wishes. We're going to belong to one another. To become *Allie* and *Tristan* again. I won't let you refuse me in this!"

Stunned silence met her tirade.

Tristan swallowed, the sound loud in the quiet.

"You love me?" he whispered, tone incredulous.

As if the thought were a novelty.

As if love were so scarce in his life, he couldn't fathom it.

The last of Allie's anger toward him crumbled.

"Of course, I love you, you lumbering oaf! It's *you* who have forgotten your love for *me*!"

"Never. I could never forget." He was shaking his head now, looking so much like her Tristan, Allie feared her heart would give out. "I never stopped loving you. I never stopped missing you. I never stopped—OW!"

This time, Tristan's yelp resulted from Allie having dropped her body onto his torso, sobs wracking her body.

Gently, her twin wrapped his one good arm around her. Allie assisted him by climbing fully onto the bed and curling against his uninjured side.

He held her as she wept.

Crying for the years they had lost.

Crying for herself and the aching loneliness of missing her other half.

Crying for the pain her brother must have suffered at the hands of their father to change him so.

Tenderly, she felt his hand in her hair and the soft press of a kiss on her forehead.

"I wish I had a handkerchief," he murmured. "You were always a messy crier."

She elbowed him in the ribs without any real force.

"Ow," he said anyway.

"You were always such a b-baby about pain."

He snorted. "Only because it annoyed you. Here, use my shirt to dry your tears." He handed her the long tail of his shirt.

She obliged.

"If you l-love me, as you claim, then why have me k-kidnapped?" she asked, still sniffling.

"Because if I had sent a polite letter, you would have tossed it into the fire. I *do* know you." He jostled her.

Allie stilled.

He was right, of course.

She *would* have spurned him.

"Well, you could have *tried*," Allie countered, voice perhaps a little too plaintive.

"I know now that I should have." A heavy sigh left him. "It's just . . . I assumed you hated me after that business with Father and would react accordingly."

Again, he was correct.

She *had* hated him for that.

"Why did you do it then? That 'business with Father'? Why side with our sire after Mamma died? Ordering me home like you did, betraying my location to his hired henchman? That was . . ." She bit back tears again. "That was so cruel, Tristan. It still hurts me." She pressed the heel of her hand to her sternum, as if to ease the ache there.

"With all of my heart—though it is woefully inadequate as you have claimed—I am sorry, Allie."

"You promised me! You promised that you would come for me. And then when I reached out, you abandoned me to an uncertain fate!"

"Hush. It wasn't me. Not entirely. Father monitored my post, even at Oxford. He forced me to write that letter to you. He watched everything I did and said . . ."

"You could have done *something*, Tristan. You're too intelligent to be that helpless."

"Berate me if you must. Hate me, too." His lungs deflated. "I don't think you can despise me any more than I despised myself after sending that letter." She felt him swallow. "He was so cruel, Allie. He thrived on hurting me, on finding any small weakness to exploit. I just didn't . . ."

No need to clarify who *he* was. "I know. I remember."

"Father became worse after you left. Angrier. Harsher. More determined to regain everything he had lost after his bigamy was exposed. He controlled my every move, allocated every penny I spent. There was simply no way to reach you. Not without him knowing. And if he had understood how I cared for you, he would have used your safety as a bargaining chip. Yes, I abandoned you. But at the time, I reasoned that you were safer outside of Father's purview. Or perhaps . . ." He let out a shuddering breath. ". . . after so many years suffering at the hands of his malice, I simply hadn't the courage to fight him head-on. Compliance was easier."

They breathed in silence for a few moments, lungs rising and falling in harmony.

Allie chewed on her bottom lip, trying to accommodate everything Tristan was telling her. She had never considered that their father would have used her safety as a bludgeon to bruise Tristan. But now, she could see clearly how that would have been the case.

"The day after Father died, I hired investigators to find you," Tristan continued. "I never forgot my promise, and they did eventually track you down. But I was . . ." He swallowed hard again. "I guess . . . I was a coward. I feared that even if I asked, you wouldn't come back to England. I knew how badly my rejection must have wounded you, and your hatred of me was certainly justified. But I simply.couldn't bear it. I couldn't bear knowing you were out in the world—alone, in danger, and refusing my help. And I suppose I have, to an extent, learned the ways of our sire. If I want something—even a person—I possess the power to take it."

She elbowed him again. "Then why not tell me all this when you kidnapped me, you idiot?! Why deposit me at Hawthorn for nearly six months without a word? Why these past weeks of combative words and commands?"

"You haven't exactly been the warm, affectionate sister of my memory," Tristan replied on a sigh. "And I did try. I asked if you wanted to be allies the night of Lord Aberdeen's soirée, remember? But I thought my actions had irreparably destroyed any regard you may have ever held for me. Enduring your disdain became my penance. All your comparing me to our bastard of a father didn't help."

Oh.

It was Allie's turn to swallow.

"I have been so concerned about your future," he continued.

"Not concerned enough to permit me to forge my own path."

"I know that is how you see it, but I have been looking at the problem from a gentleman's point of view. I know the world isn't kind to unmarried women of a certain age—Ow!" He rubbed his ribcage where Allie had poked him.

"No uncharitable comments about my age. You love me, remember? That means saying nice things." She cuddled closer.

He grunted softly. "As I was saying, marriage is the best opportunity for a lady to achieve financial stability. I examined nearly every unmarried man in the *ton* before selecting Charswood as a potential partner for you.

He is an honorable man. One who would grant you lavish pin money and liberty without forcing you to share his bed. Most significantly, he is an *older* man. Therefore, you would be widowed rather young, giving you all the freedom you crave."

"Charswood said as much when he proposed," Allie harrumphed. "That you were the one who proposed our marriage as he had outlined it."

"He spoke the truth. I *have* been listening to you. I do understand what you want, and I have been endeavoring to gift it to you. You simply haven't been listening to *me*."

"Perhaps," Allie conceded, "or maybe you have been rather poor at communicating your thoughts."

"Well . . . maybe, that too," he admitted begrudgingly.

"And you must confess that my marriage to Charswood would benefit you politically and financially, as well. So it isn't as if your behavior has been entirely altruistic. You are still our father's son in some ways."

"I do acknowledge that there are secondary advantages to such a match, but had Charswood proved a man like our father, I most certainly would not have promoted a match between you. I have always held your interests first and foremost. Why do you continue to refuse him? He would give you the life you claim to want."

"Yes, but I have since realized that I want more than Charswood can give."

"More?" Tristan huffed a disbelieving laugh. "Like what, pray tell?"

"Children, for one."

That silenced her brother for a solid fifteen seconds.

"You want . . . you want children?" he asked.

"Yes. I do." Allie pushed out of his arms to sit up. "I want a husband I love. And I want us to fill a ramshackle house with children that we love. And we will all belong together and play and bicker and make up and be an enormous, messy family." Her hands were waving now, the yearning for her vision so strong. "And when you come to visit us, we will force you to join in with our messy, chaotic, wonderful life. The children will shriek with joy and race down the drive to welcome their favorite uncle and bury you under the force of their happiness. There will probably even be a large dog to lick your face."

Tears pricked her eyes once more.

With a grimace, her brother offered her the use of his shirttails again.

"How is any of that freedom?" he asked. "It sounds . . . confining. And, frankly, unsanitary."

"Don't you see, Tristan?" She dabbed at her eyes. "It's *belonging*. I've thought all this time I wanted freedom, but in actuality, I merely want to recapture what you and I once had—*true* belonging. When you belong to others, you don't need to escape."

He lay in silence, as if needing time to accommodate her revelations.

Finally, he released a deep breath. "Somehow, I already know Ethan Penn-Leith is the husband you are envisioning in this scenario?"

"Hah! Yes!" She pointed a finger at him. "I think your twin sense is returning."

He rolled his eyes. "We never had a twin sense, whatever that is."

"Hush. We did. And you're ruining this moment."

"Allie—"

"As I said earlier, I am going to marry Ethan, Tristan, with or without your blessing. But I would very much like you to sanction our union, as I want you to be in my life, just as I want to belong in yours."

Tristan pressed the fingers from his uninjured hand to his brow bone, eyes shut tight. "I swear you're only asking this because I am injured and weak and you rightly understand that I cannot say *no* to you." He opened his eyes and looked at her. "Very well, I will agree to support your continued courtship with Mr. Penn-Leith."

Allie lunged to hug him.

He placed a staying hand on her shoulder. "But one thing first. Do not think that I will immediately abandon my political goals and become some paragon of domesticity. I still intend to see our family name restored. Not because our ghastly father desired it, but because I want to forever remove the stain of his cruelty from our name. I wish my own star to shine so brightly that others forget our father ever existed."

"Oh, Tristan. You say the most delightful things," Allie laughed, sitting back once more. "You know I will assist you however I can in obliterating the memory of our father's existence."

"I probably should have led with that explanation months ago."

"True! Had I known you wished me to marry Charswood to spite our sire, I very well might have agreed to it." She patted his chest. "Maybe next time."

They stared at one another, the clock on the hearth ticking.

"I cannot believe you are forcing me to accept Ethan Penn-Leith, of all people, as a brother-in-law," Tristan moaned. "It just feels so . . . so . . ."

"Wonderful? Exciting?"

"Hah! I was going to say cliché. Of course, the immensely famous Highland Poet would marry the beautiful, wealthy daughter of a duke. The man is a living fairy tale."

"Ah. You called me *beautiful*."

Tristan gave her arm a playful punch.

"Ow. Now who's being mean?"

He chuckled, low and warm.

Allie smiled at the sound as she scooted off the bed. "I'll leave you to get some sleep."

"I love you, Allie," he murmured.

Her heart skipped and danced to hear those words on his lips.

"I love you, too, Tristan." She bent down and kissed his forehead. "Now, I'm off to bed. After all, I have a Scottish poet to woo tomorrow." She wiggled her eyebrows at him. "I cannot wait to return and regale you with every last detail."

The delightful noise of his long-suffering groan followed her from the room.

25

Ethan stared out the window of his uncle's carriage. The landscape crawled by, a patchwork of green and brown fields giving way to pine forest, the purple hills of the Cairngorms rising in the distance. The dusty road and lush scenery were reminiscent of that highway in *Südtirol* nearly a year past.

Each mile traveled from Fettermill and Allie felt like another nail in Ethan's coffin.

He had left a letter for her to be delivered to Muirford House. In it, he had pleaded for her patience. To give him a week to extricate himself from his uncle's clutches and return to her.

Last night, exhausted after nearly two days of no sleep, he had been unable to think clearly, to formulate a plan. It had been all he could do to pitch headlong into bed.

But now, as he journeyed north with his uncle, it felt the veriest madness. How could he leave Allie? How could he abandon her with an injured brother and her future in limbo? No—*their* future in limbo.

Agitation buzzed through Ethan's veins, a swarm of wasps desperate to escape.

His knee bounced. And then his whole leg.

He should have stayed.

He shouldn't be here.

They had only been on the road for an hour. It would be a simple matter to order the carriage to a halt. He could walk back to Muirford House before luncheon.

"Uncle," Ethan said, looking to his side, "I don't ken that I can go with ye."

"Pardon?" Uncle Leith's forehead furrowed.

"I have unfinished business in Fettermill. I need tae return."

"Now?"

"Yes, now."

His uncle sighed. "Let me guess. This involves a woman?"

"A lady, yes. You see, I have gone and fallen in love with—"

The pounding of horse hooves approaching from the south at a gallop cut off Ethan's words.

A mare passed them in a cloud of dust.

But instead of carrying on, the rider veered in front of their carriage, forcing the coachman to pull their own horses to a stop.

What in heaven's name—?

"Stand and deliver!" a familiar female voice rang out.

Uncle Leith shrieked in alarm.

A spark of hope lit in Ethan's chest.

Laughing, he reached for the door handle.

"Ethan!" Uncle Leith grabbed his shoulder. "Dinnae be daft! There's a highwayman . . . ehr, highwaywoman—"

"This isn't a robbery, Uncle." Shrugging off his uncle's hand, Ethan stepped from the coach. "I ken what's happening here."

Or, at least, Ethan hoped he did.

His wee *ladra* sat atop a lathered horse, breathing hard. She appeared a goddess, fierce and determined.

She was the most lovely sight.

The ember of hope burst into a full conflagration.

"Ye must be mad, lass!" He crossed to her, still laughing. "Ye cannot raid carriages in Scotland."

"Hah!" She tossed her head, causing her mount to whinny restlessly. "There is only one thing I need from this coach."

"Please say it is my dashing self?" Ethan grinned, patting her mount's neck.

"Shameless as ever, Mr. Penn-Leith."

"I believe ye meant 'magnificent as ever,' my lady."

She laughed, a bright trill of sound.

He held up his arms and she placed her hands on his shoulders, permitting him to lift her from the saddle.

Once she was on the ground, Ethan refused to release her, his arms banding her waist. Her mare tossed its head but remained standing at Allie's back.

How had it been only yesterday morning that he and Allie had pledged their love to one another? It felt a lifetime past.

"I was just moments from stopping the coach and returning to ye," he murmured against her lips. "But I'm liking your own thinking much better. Please tell me ye gave Charswood his walking papers and have come tae steal me away."

"Yes," she murmured.

"Yes?" Ethan said incredulously, pulling his head back. "To both my requests?"

That seemed almost too much joy to encompass.

And yet, she nodded in agreement. "I had a conversation this morning with Lord Charswood and politely informed him that I would not be accepting his offer of marriage. He was gracious and understanding and waxed eloquent about his great love for his previous wife."

Relief—sweet and liberating—washed through Ethan.

"And . . . myself?"

"I wrote you a poem."

Ethan paused, blinking at her.

"Ye wrote *me* a poem?"

"Yes." She reached into her pocket and produced a sheet of foolscap, flapping it for him to see. "It took me hours, so I expect you to properly appreciate it."

Unable to stop a sultry grin, he pressed a kiss to her temple. "I'm verra good at appreciating things, lass."

"No, you cannot distract me." She braced a palm against his torso, waving the paper with her other hand. "The poem took me the better part of the night and—hey now!"

Allie's horse snatched the paper from her hand, chewing and swallowing it in one gulp.

"That was my poem!" Allie stared up at the mare, aghast.

Ethan was torn between laughing uproariously and cuddling his *ladra* in consolation.

"It was tae be the best love poem I ever received," he said.

She swiveled back to him, her eyes narrowing. "Something tells me it was to be the *only* love poem you've ever received."

"Well, that too." Ethan kissed her cheek. "Tell me what it said, lass."

"First, you must know it was absolutely brilliant." She clasped her arms around his neck, sagging her weight back into the cradle of his hands.

"I don't doubt it."

"That smirk on your face, Mr. Penn-Leith, says that perhaps you *do* doubt it."

"Nae. This smile declares I'm *fou* with happiness that ye be here, talking with me in my arms. What did the poem say? Did it start, 'There once was a Scot named Penn-Leith'?"

Her brows lifted. "Are you truly suggesting I composed you a *limerick* as a love poem? Perhaps it is for the best that the horse ate my poem. My tastes are certainly more sophisticated than that."

He laughed.

"If you must know," she continued, "the poem—*not* a limerick— spoke of my lonely existence before finding yourself and even rhymed *strife* with *life* to explain how brilliant the world has become now that we have found one another."

"Did ye profess your undying love for myself?"

"Naturally. It was the most beautiful poem. You would have been jealous."

"I don't doubt it."

"And the masses would not have clamored to know who my true love is, since I wrote it outright in the title—'To Ethan, My Love.' Because as you said yesterday, we belong together, you and I."

"That we do, lass."

"Most importantly, my brother sends his regards."

"The poem said that?"

Breathless, Allie laughed. "Don't be ridiculous. Tristan has finally acquiesced to my demands."

"Tristan, is it?" Surprise cemented Ethan to the ground.

"My brother's scrape with death forced us both to realize how much we care for one another. We reconciled, Ethan," she said, her eyes going suspiciously glassy. "I'm Allie again to him. And he is Tristan to me. I truthfully think that my brother has a good heart. He just needs to remember that fact and recover the boy he once was. It will take some time, I am sure, but I refuse to allow his current behavior to calcify and turn him into our father. Tristan, for his part, is committed to changing, too."

"That is wonderful."

"Most importantly, he has granted us his blessing. Though I had already decided to marry you regardless."

"Are ye stating the truth? This must be a jest."

"No jest, my love." She cupped his jaw with her gloved hand.

"But what about your mines? Ye will be giving up—"

"Tristan has agreed to my dowry, Ethan. I give up nothing."

"But that means . . ."

"We shan't be paupered. In fact, I would say our prospects appear—"

Ethan caught her words with a kiss.

It was simply too much, too glorious, too longed for—

Her mines, returned. Her heart, in harmony with his own.

Just as they had on that dusty road in Italy, she grasped his head, hungrily kissing him.

But that first kiss had been desperate and punishing, whereas this one . . .

It was a homecoming.

A kiss that spoke of lazy afternoons basking in some sunny grassland while bees buzzed overheard. A kiss that promised wintry nights curled together under a down counterpane, a fire crackling in the hearth.

A kiss that vowed a lifetime of belonging.

Allie pulled back first, but Ethan chased her mouth, nipping at her lips.

"I say! Is that Lady Allegra?!" Uncle Leith's voice interrupted their embrace.

Ethan turned, his arm still around Allie, to see his uncle step from the carriage.

"It *is* Lady Allegra." Uncle Leith blanched and pressed a trembling hand to his forehead. "Ethan, my boy, what have ye done?"

"Fallen in love, Uncle," Ethan replied with almost frightening happiness.

"Kendall will have your head."

"Not if I have any say," Allie chimed in. "My brother has given his blessing, Mr. Leith."

Uncle Leith darted a gaze from Allie to Ethan and then back to Allie again. "Truly?!"

"Yes," she nodded.

Ethan's uncle pulled out his pocket watch, checking the time. "If we hurry, do you ken we could convince the local sheriff to marry you afore nightfall? I would hate for Kendall to change his mind."

Allie looked at Ethan in astonishment and then burst into laughter.

"I don't think that Kendall will change his mind, Mr. Leith," Allie reassured him. "I won't permit it. Though he might disown me if he is denied the chance to walk me down the aisle."

Uncle Leith looked between them, head swiveling back and forth once more. Ethan nearly laughed at his uncle's look of astonishment.

"And the . . . shipping contract?" Uncle Leith asked rather weakly.

Ethan shrugged. "We'll have to put the matter to Kendall."

"I will certainly encourage him to keep business in the family," Allie said, smoothing a hand down Ethan's chest.

"Family," he laughed, pressing a kiss to her temple. "I adore the sound of that."

"Me, too, *amore mio*," she whispered in return.

EPILOGUE

Allie stretched her arms overhead, admiring how her gold wedding band caught the window's light.

"Preening, Mrs. Penn-Leith?" Ethan asked lazily, rolling onto his elbow beside her in the bed.

The voice of a gondolier and the calls of seagulls drifted in through the open window of their bedchamber. The salt sea air of the Lagoon of Venice wafted in behind and ruffled the lace curtains.

"Always. I shall never tire of any reminder that I am your wife," she said.

Just as she would never tire of this view of him poised above her—the muscles in his bare shoulders bunching and flexing, her own radiant happiness reflected in the pupils of his green eyes.

Ethan's grin turned wicked.

Allie ran her right hand through the thatch of his hair, fingernails grazing his scalp. His gaze went hooded.

She adored The Swooner. But this smile? The one that spoke of nights curled around one another in their marital bed? The one he saved for her alone?

This smile was her favorite.

But then, everything about the past ten months of marriage to Ethan Penn-Leith had been blissful.

They had married in early September in a ridiculously grand wedding ceremony at St. George's in Hanover Square. The church had been packed to the rafters with the *hoi polloi* of London.

Allie had worn a lavish white pearl-and-lace crusted dress that Tristan had ordered from Paris because he said, "You must put every other bride of the Season to shame." Her brother's arm had trembled under Allie's fingertips as he walked her down the aisle to a waiting Ethan, devastatingly handsome in a great kilt woven in the red and gold Leith family tartan.

Allie's twin had become more open with her after his injury. That wasn't to say Tristan had reformed himself entirely. He still barked orders, grew insufferable when his aims were thwarted, and climbed the political ladder like a man obsessed.

But with her, his demeanor had decidedly softened. And true to his word, Tristan had granted Allie the entirety of the Salzi Mine as her dowry.

Uncle Leith had been ecstatic. The shipping contract had been easy for Allie herself to award to him. They had signed the documents over glasses of champagne.

Once Tristan had accepted the inevitability of Ethan as a brother-in-law, the duke had thrown his support behind the couple. After all, if the mighty Duke of Kendall saw no problem with his only sister marrying a low-born Scottish poet, then no one else could either. Her twin had even spoken of it in his last letter to her:

> *It appears that having Ethan Penn-Leith as my brother-in-law is not quite as deleterious as I had anticipated. Her Majesty, in particular, appears enamored of your match. She has asked me to dine next week. I hope to*

woo her into considering a cabinet position for myself.
Though I fear she will spend the entire dinner speaking
of Ethan and trying to decide if she will knight him
when you finally return to England. Try not to gloat,
will you?

The gentle teasing of his words had conjured a smile on her lips.

Of course, Tristan's support hadn't stopped gossiping tongues. Many within the *ton* (rightly) believed Allie to be the anonymous Italian highwaywoman from Ethan's poem and castigated her reputation accordingly.

For her part, Allie failed to care. Others could believe what they would. None of it impacted her love for Ethan. Or the joy of their life together.

She and Ethan had decided to spend the first years of their marriage abroad. There was so much of the world to see, and Allie couldn't wait to explore it all with Ethan.

Granted, they only made it as far as Venice before the lure of her roots had called. Though they had already spent a month in the city, neither of them wished to quit it anytime soon.

For her part, Allie was appalled that she had once aspired to a future alone, to a crippled idea of freedom. Nothing was more freeing than resting in the arms of one you loved and trusted so implicitly.

A gentle breeze stirred the gauzy curtains once more, holding the worst of the scorching Venetian sun at bay.

Ethan bent and pressed a soft kiss to her lips. Sighing, Allie ran her palms up his chest.

"I wrote ye a poem yesterday, lass," he murmured against her mouth.

"A poem?"

"Aye. To commemorate our meeting almost two years ago today."

"Is that so?" Allie frowned, thinking over the timeline. "I daresay you're right. It has been two years."

"I always am," he replied.

Allie laughed and nipped his shoulder.

"Our visit to the *Basilica di San Marco* yesterday inspired me," Ethan continued. Rolling onto his back, he reached for the bedside table and the leather-bound notebook there.

Over the course of their courtship and marriage, Ethan had written Allie a number of poems. In fact, she was currently encouraging him to submit them to his publisher—a volume of love poetry that would be sure to set his female acolytes to swooning.

But that didn't stop her own stomach from swooping at the thought of hearing her husband's words addressed directly to her.

Notebook in hand, Ethan turned to her, propping himself once more on an elbow, the notebook resting on the sheets as he flipped through the pages.

Allie ogled him unabashedly—the fan of lashes across his cheek, the lopsided purse of his mouth . . .

He lifted his head and gave her that grin—her favorite one. "If ye keep staring at me like that, wife, ye will distract me from reading this."

Allie ran her fingertips along his jaw. He turned his head and kissed them.

"Read to me, Ethan," she whispered.

Smile turning softer, Ethan read from his journal.

> "My lady,
> To begin, I will lay a stone.
> A tow'ring bulwark of bright hope
> Placed 'neath the growing cathedral
> Of our love."

The lilt of his brogue threaded between each syllable. Allie sighed, resting her temple against his forearm. "You compared our marriage to building a cathedral."

"Aye. Hush, now. Let me finish."

Clearing his throat, Ethan continued:

> "We will build.
> Each gentle touch, a mason's grace,
> Each whispered word, a statue fair
> The arches formed, our arms outspread,
> Encircling our love.

We will create
A hallowed sphere of mind and soul
Bathed in light from windows above.
A hosanna ringing to eternity,
My love."

Allie closed her eyes, savoring the beauty of his words.

"*Bellissimo*," she murmured. "It will be the capstone of your new book."

Ethan shut his notebook. "I decided that I don't wish tae publish a book of love poems."

"Pardon? Whyever not?"

"Because I'm selfish." Ethan cupped her cheek, gaze so open and earnest. "Because I do not wish to invite the world into our private lives. Because I want to treasure the love that flows between us, not wrap it in a leather binding to be sold for four shillings."

"That's the loveliest sentiment, Ethan—a poem all on its own. For me." Tears stung Allie's eyes. She tapped his notebook. "You should record your beautiful reasoning, too. Just for us."

"Writing down our interactions is how we landed here, ye ken." Ethan bent and pressed a soft kiss to her mouth. "Tell me, of all the travelers ye accosted, was mine the most memorable kiss?"

"The most memorable kiss?" she asked on a startled, watery laugh. "Do you suppose I made a habit of kissing handsome men at gunpoint?"

"I shouldn't blame ye if you did."

"No, my love. That was never my way, even then." Tears tumbled in earnest now. She cupped Ethan's face in her palms. "I never kissed another traveler. There was only ever yours."

"My kiss?"

"Yes." She pressed her lips to his. "Merely that one kiss, alone."

AUTHOR'S NOTE

The process of writing *One Kiss Alone* was tumultuous to say the least. The book itself—its characters, its plot—was a joy. My personal life, however, was shambolic.

Right as I finished the book before this one, *Adjacent But Only Just*, my husband and I realized that, due to family pressures, we needed to leave Scotland and return to the USA. We were devastated, to say the least. What followed was months of packing, planning, moving, and then moving again. Obviously, finding time to write was challenging, as my days were consumed with the logistics of transporting a family and our belongings halfway around the world. The difficulties of the housing market in the Rocky Mountains meant it took six months before we were able to purchase a home and truly begin to feel settled again.

And somehow, in the midst of all of this upheaval, I managed to write the book you are currently reading. Though to be fair, the characters of Ethan and Allie practically wrote themselves. Their combined energy crackled from the first words I put to page. I have rarely enjoyed writing a love story as much as I did this one, and I hope you felt the same enjoyment as you read it.

So . . . on to a few historical notes.

La Giovine Italia was an actual political group, led by Giuseppe Mazzini, whose aims were as described in the book—they wished to see Italy reunited again. That said, there is no historical evidence to suggest the group resorted to robbery to fund their aims. That concept was entirely my own fiction. Though Giuseppe Garibaldi, another active reformer of the time period, did spend some time in Brazil associating with rather shady characters. The *Risorgimento* eventually succeeded, and Italy united as a single country once more in 1871.

Alfred, Lord Tennyson, did write the first dramatic monologue, "Ulysses," in 1833, though the poem wasn't widely published until 1842. You will note, however, that Ethan does not refer to him as Alfred, Lord Tennyson or Alfred Tennyson, Lord Tennyson, as Queen Victoria didn't create Tennyson's baronetcy until 1884.

Steam travel was just starting into its heyday in 1849. The *SS Great Western* was the first steamship built specifically for transatlantic travel, with her maiden voyage occurring in 1838. Trains and rail lines also connected every major city of the UK by 1849.

Whitby is a lovely seaside town in Yorkshire. The ruins of a medieval Benedictine abbey overlook the town and the ocean. The town is also the place where Anne Brontë spent the final weeks of her life before succumbing to tuberculosis. She is buried in the local churchyard.

Broadhurst College, the university in the United States that Lady Isolde attends, is fictitious. However, there were schools in the US at the time that accepted female students, most notably Wesleyan College (not to be confused with Wesleyan University) in Georgia and Bradford Academy in Massachusetts.

I know I've mentioned this before, but for those reading one of my Scottish books for the first time, allow me to also comment on the Scottish language. I've used modern spellings of Scottish pronunciations and, even then, restricted myself to a few key words to give a Scottish flavor to the text. So at times, the accent as written is not perfectly consistent; this was done to help readability.

I have created an extensive board on Pinterest with images of things I talk about in the book. So if you want a visual of anything—including the Dolomites, Grosvenor Square, steamships of the era, fishing in Scotland, etc.—pop over there and explore. Just search for NicholeVan.

As usual, writing a book is this bizarre mix of working long hours alone while simultaneously rallying a village to help get the novel to publication.

A HUGE thank you to all my ARC and beta-readers who read, give suggestions, and post about my books.

Also, I cannot give enough thanks to my two primary editors—Erin Rodabough and Shannon Castleton—for their tireless efforts and brilliant suggestions. They always help me take what I see as a so-so manuscript and turn it into something far beyond my own meager efforts.

And lastly, I lavish all my love and appreciation on my children and husband. Thank you for your endless words of encouragement and for listening to me ramble my way through a thorny plot issue. When I am with you, I am precisely where I belong.

READING GROUP QUESTIONS

Yes, there are reading group questions for this book. They exist mostly as a ploy to encourage readers to congregate and discuss the book, preferably with lots of good chocolate and laughter.

1. As a character, Lady Allegra Gilbert is fiery and determined to forge her own path. How did you feel about this? Did you admire her tenacity and refusal to accept anyone else's nonsense? Or did you find her reckless and selfish? Why or why not?

2. Both Ethan and Allie struggle with loneliness, despite being surrounded by people. What are the causes of their loneliness? Have you ever felt similarly?

3. The book discusses belonging and equates it to freedom. How can love and belonging be a type of freedom? Is this an accurate portrayal of what belonging can mean?

4. How did you feel about Lord Charswood's proposal? Did its terms surprise you? Do you think Allie could have found happiness in such an arrangement?

5. Obviously, Tristan Gilbert, the Duke of Kendall, is a complex character. He functions as the villain for most of the book. However, he does reconcile with his sister in the end. How did your feelings toward Kendall change over the course of the book? Do you feel he is redeemable as a character?

6. At the end of the book, Allie tells Ethan she wrote him a poem. As a reader, you never see that poem. However, the poem exists; it was merely edited out. Why do you think the author chose not to include the poem, in the end? Here is the poem:

> One kiss alone, and all my anger fades.
> My heart now filled with love that ne'er ages.
> For years, I roamed the earth with bitter strife,
> Until at last, I found my love, my life.
>
> It seemed to me that happiness had fled,
> And left me cold and lonely in its stead.
> But now I know that love is worth the pain,
> For with one kiss, my heart is whole again.

7. Allie mourns the loss of her twin brother, equating his betrayal to a death. Did you find this portrayal to be accurate? Have you ever experienced something similar in your own personal relationships?

8. Clearly, this book contains a lot of information about Scotland and Scottish culture. Did you learn something new or unexpected? If so, what was it?

9. Consider how this book would be as a feature film. Who plays Ethan? Who plays Allie? Kendall? etc. In the movie version, what aspects of the book should be thrown out, condensed, or altered?

OTHER BOOKS BY NICHOLE VAN

THE PENN-LEITHS OF THISTLE MUIR

Love Practically
Adjacent But Only Just
One Kiss Alone
A Heart Sufficient (February 2024)

THE BROTHERHOOD OF THE BLACK TARTAN

Suffering the Scot
Romancing the Rake
Loving a Lady
Making the Marquess
Remembering Jamie

OTHER REGENCY ROMANCES

Seeing Miss Heartstone
Vingt-et-Un | Twenty-one (a novella included in *Falling for a Duke*)

BROTHERS *MALEDETTI*

Lovers and Madmen
Gladly Beyond
Love's Shadow
Lightning Struck
A Madness Most Discreet

THE HOUSE OF OAK

Intertwine
Divine
Clandestine
Refine
Outshine

If you haven't yet read *Love Practically*,
please read on for a preview.

LOVE PRACTICALLY

It is a truth universally acknowledged that a single lady in possession of no fortune must long to marry a duke's son.

Unfortunately, Miss Leah Penn-Leith feared she had inadvertently killed one instead.

She stared down at the unmoving form of Lieutenant Lord Dennis Battleton illuminated in the firelight. He lay slumped beside her bedroom door, eyes closed, head tilted toward the left shoulder of his red regimental coat, blood trickling from his nose.

What have I done? Whathavedone?!

Panic tasted acrid, drying her throat.

This might be her first time attending a house party, but even Leah knew an evening of whist and laughter did not typically end in homicide.

Clutching her night rail to her chest, Leah nudged Lord Dennis's Hessian boot, jiggling the tassel.

"My lord?" she whispered.

Nothing.

Snick.

The door to her bedchamber opened.

Leah stifled a startled scream and jumped back, meeting the gaze of Mr. Fox Carnegie, Lord Dennis's close friend.

Mr. Carnegie peered into the room, skimming over her surely terrified expression, before spotting Lord Dennis's supine form beside the door jamb.

"Blast," he muttered and mumbled a string of profanity that Leah supposed would make a gently-bred lady swoon.

As she was not *quite* a gently-bred lady, she withstood the swearing with equanimity.

After all, the situation quite merited it.

Mr. Carnegie stepped into her bedchamber, quietly closing the door behind himself. It was scandalous for him to be in her room, but then so was killing a duke's son, so Leah figured the horse had already bolted from the barn.

"I-I didnae mean tae hurt him," Leah stammered on a whisper, her Scottish brogue deepening in her distress. "I awoke as he was trying tae climb into my bed. I just . . . reacted." She mimed a kicking motion.

It had been a terrifying few seconds.

First, waking to feel large hands on her hips, the smell of brandy, and murmured slurred words, "I sh-shink you've been waiting for me, love."

Then, her instinctively violent reaction, balling her body and kicking the unknown man with both feet, much like a bucking horse. Her aim had been true.

The man had staggered back, his head and shoulders hitting the wall with a resounding *thud* that rattled her bedchamber door.

Leah had scrambled out of bed, finally getting a good look at her assailant, horrified to realize she had attacked a duke's son—Lord Dennis Battleton.

Now she watched as Mr. Carnegie stooped and placed an ear to Lord Dennis's chest.

"His heart is strong," he said, voice low.

Leah nearly sobbed in relief.

Mr. Carnegie pulled back one of his friend's eyelids, studying the pupils for a second, and inspected Lord Dennis's head for more injuries.

"Why is he yet unconscious?" Leah whispered.

"I fear Lord Dennis was exceptionally deep in his cups tonight." Mr. Carnegie pulled out a handkerchief and wiped the blood dripping from his friend's nose. "The bump to the head simply sent him to sleep a mite sooner than the brandy."

For his part, Mr. Carnegie did not appear inebriated, though the smell of alcohol lingered on him as well.

"I simply need to remove Dennis from your bedchamber with no one the wiser and leave you with my most abject apologies for this unwelcome intrusion." He flashed her a grim smile, the world-weary expression at odds with his youthful face. "We must ensure this mishap does not damage your reputation nor set gossiping tongues to wagg—"

A scuffle of footsteps in the hall outside had Mr. Carnegie turning his head and muttering another low oath.

Moving quickly, he straddled his friend, wrapped his arms around the man's chest, and heaved him upright. Not unlike Leah's father hefting a fat ewe for sheering.

In short, it was an impressive feat of physical strength.

Mr. Carnegie pivoted, spinning himself and Lord Dennis around, stopping just behind Leah's bedchamber door as a knock sounded.

Leah didn't know whether to be impressed by Mr. Carnegie's quick reaction or appalled at the smooth, practiced nature of it. This was clearly not the first time Mr. Carnegie had lifted the leaden weight of a drunken friend.

Mr. Carnegie jerked his head toward the door, indicating she should answer it.

Nodding, Leah snatched a shawl from the foot of her bed, wrapping it around her shoulders. She cracked open the door.

Miss Smith and Miss Wells—two fellow guests—stood in the hallway wearing elegant London wrappers, night caps, and matching expressions of faux worry.

"Are you quite all right, Miss Penn-Leith?" Miss Smith asked, her blond braid gleaming even in the dim light.

"Yes," Miss Wells added. "We heard a *terrible* thump."

The ladies peered beyond Leah's shoulders, searching the room as if they somehow knew there were two young gentlemen concealed behind Leah's bedchamber door.

"I apologize if I gave anyone a fright." Leah pulled the shawl tighter around her shoulders and mentally grasped for a plausible lie. "I was up reading late—Miss Austen's works are so captivating, ye ken—and I stumbled over my own *muckle* foot as I was getting into bed."

As a falsehood, it wasn't particularly good.

"*Muckle?*" Miss Smith wrinkled her dainty nose. "You Scots use the oddest words."

Miss Wells giggled, standing on tiptoe, unabashedly craning her neck to see more of the bedchamber.

In Leah's peripheral vision, Mr. Carnegie made a rolling motion with one hand. *Get on with it.*

"I thank ye both for your concern," Leah began closing the door, "but all is well. I shall bid ye goodnight."

The ladies murmured a reply, and Leah shut the door fully, throwing the lock.

Now what?

Turning back to Mr. Carnegie, she watched as he eased Lord Dennis back to the floor.

"Clever," he whispered, chin gesturing toward the door. "You are a quick study."

Leah blushed. The unexpected praise sent a jolt of pleasure through her still-racing heart. Until this moment, she had never considered that her good sense and quick thinking could be used to conceal an illicit assignation and attempted homicide.

She wasn't sure whether to be proud or appalled.

Oblivious to the uproar he had caused, Lord Dennis emitted a blissful, sleepy snore.

Because . . . of course, he did.

Mr. Carnegie stepped past Leah, placing an ear to her bedroom door.

"They're still nattering on," he murmured. "We'll have to wait."

Miss Smith and Miss Well's breathy giggles sounded outside as if to emphasize the point.

With a sigh, Mr. Carnegie sank down beside Lord Dennis, shoulders against the wall, wrists resting on the raised knees of his white breeches. Lord Dennis—dark-haired, stubble-cheeked, flush-nosed—snored again, snuffling in his sleep.

Leah stared down at them, unsure of the social mores when entertaining two gentlemen in her bedchamber.

Two gentlemen.

In. Her. Bedchamber.

Her mind stuttered. Surely this exemplified the sort of lascivious behavior Aunt Leith had warned her abounded in London.

Leah busied herself, stirring the fire to life and lighting a lamp on the wee writing desk. She rotated the desk chair—a worn wooden Windsor—to face Mr. Carnegie and sat gingerly, pulling her shawl tight around her shoulders and tucking her toes under the hem of her night rail.

Mr. Carnegie watched her, the lamplight flickering in his pale gaze and turning his blond hair into molten gold. His eyes were intensely blue, she noted. The color of Loch Muick on a cloudless day.

Unlike Lord Dennis, Mr. Carnegie no longer wore his coat. Instead, he sat against the wall in the red waistcoat of a regimental officer, his white shirt sleeves cuffed to the elbow. Swallowing, he tugged at his dark neckcloth, loosening and mussing it. Leah tried (and failed) not to stare at the shadowy outline of lean muscle rippling under the fine linen of his shirt as he moved.

No wonder gentlemen were required to remain precisely dressed at all times. A disheveled man invited all sorts of salacious thoughts. At the moment, Leah was hard-pressed to concentrate on anything other than the marvelous flex and pull of tendons across his bare forearms.

But then, Mr. Fox Carnegie had been drawing her eyes all week.

Leah was attending the house party—hosted by an English cousin, Mrs. Gordon—as Aunt Leith's companion. It was all part of the campaign to lift Leah out of the 'unfortunate circumstances of Isobel's marriage.' That, of course, referred to Leah's deceased mother, Isobel Leith, who had married John Penn, a Scottish gentleman farmer well below her aristocratic station.

This meant that while more refined young women were stitching samplers and perfecting their posture in a side-saddle, Leah had been darning her younger brothers' socks and galloping across the Angus glens astride her favorite gelding, helping her father and his shepherds track lost sheep.

Unfortunately, sock-darning and sheep-wrangling were not activities that gentlemen appreciated in a well-bred young lady.

But that did not deter Aunt Leith. She ruthlessly polished Leah's manners, intending to find her niece a more appropriate husband than 'some half-drunk Scottish blacksmith.' Though if Aunt Leith had actually *met* the blacksmith in Fettermill with his bulky muscles and charming wink, she would not so cavalierly dismiss the idea.

Regardless, at scarcely eighteen years old herself, Leah was at a loss as to what men *did* want in a bride. Well, aside from a large dowry and, perhaps, an equally out-sized bosom—facts she had gleaned from Miss Wells and Miss Smith as they sat giggling over luncheon.

Leah possessed none of those things—a dowry, large bosoms, or a preponderance of giggles.

But this obvious lack had not stopped her from noticing Mr. Fox Carnegie.

He had arrived in a burst of ribald laughter and youthful scuffling—Lord Dennis's, not his own. Mr. Carnegie had stood behind his friend, arms folded, expression wry and watchful. There had been a quiet sense of *noticing* about him, a steadiness that had instantly drawn Leah in.

Granted, it hadn't hurt that he looked remarkably dashing in the red coat of the 64th Regiment of Foot. The crimson wool caught the auburn highlights in his blond hair and accentuated the sharp line of his jaw. Her eyes had stubbornly followed him—noting the liquid grace of his walk, the way his shoulders tilted toward a person as he listened, the kind gentleness in his tone.

Not that Mr. Carnegie had spared a glance for the awkwardly shy Scottish lass Leah knew herself to be. None of the gentlemen in attendance did.

Though . . . Mr. Carnegie appeared to be noticing her now.

In the lamplight, his gaze skimmed her, likely taking in the unadorned linen of her night rail, the homespun wool of her thick stockings, the tattered edge of her shawl. She pulled the garment closer.

Leah knew her features were a study in nondeterminate mediocrity—bland and vacillating. Her hair was not quite blond, nor brown, nor auburn, but some unflattering mix of the three. Her hazel eyes changed color with her moods—brown to green and back again. The rest of her—body, bosom, height—remained stubbornly average.

If Mr. Carnegie found her lacking, his expression didn't show it.

He cleared his throat. "You seem to have the advantage of me, Miss . . ." His voice drifted off, a ruddy flush climbing his cheeks. "I know we were likely introduced, but my memory for faces is not the best, and I fear with all that has happened, your name has plum slipped my mind."

He said the words kindly, but Leah experienced a sinking sensation nonetheless.

She was forgettable. She knew this, and yet . . .

"Miss Leah Penn-Leith, at your service, Mr. Carnegie."

He winced. "Of course, you have the manners to remember my name."

"As your Christian name is Fox, it does have a tendency tae stick."

He smiled at that, teeth flashing and sending a zing of pleasure chasing her spine. The sensation was akin to winning first place in the jam-making contest at the Fettermill Summer Fair. (Which she had done. Twice.)

More to the point, his grin rendered him boyish and young, too young to be in a soldier's uniform. Was Mr. Carnegie even older than herself?

"I must apologize for Lord Dennis." He nodded toward his friend, sleeping beside him. "I fear he mistook your room for . . . another's."

"Another lady?" The thought was rather shocking. That Lord Dennis would have entered a woman's room, crawled into bed with her, and the lady would have . . . welcomed it?

Lascivious, indeed.

"I shall say nothing more upon the matter, as it involves some delicacy, as you might imagine."

Well, Leah *hadn't* been imagining it, but now . . .

Her eyes dropped to the long fingers dangling over his knees. What if it had been Mr. Carnegie's gentle hands reaching for her? Would she have pulled away so quickly?

She looked away, a blush scalding her skin.

"Regardless," he continued quietly, thankfully oblivious to her wayward thoughts, "I noticed when we parted that Lord Dennis had gone down the wrong corridor, so I followed hi—"

Wham!

Another door banged down the hallway, causing them both to jump. Someone giggled.

Mr. Carnegie frowned and sent a speaking glance toward the door. "I fear it might be a while before we can make an escape unseen, Miss Penn-Leith." He nudged Lord Dennis's prone body with his foot.

Leah nodded.

They sat in silence for a moment. It was a companionable sort of thing, as if they were comrades in arms, waiting to complete an important tactical mission.

Having been raised by a stoically silent father, Leah understood that silence was often a conversation unto itself.

Sometimes it could be as soothing as an embrace, as understanding as a long *blether*.

Other times, silence was a noisy thing—loud and shouty and demanding attention.

Not everyone was fluent in the language of silence, but Mr. Carnegie appeared to have mastered it. Quiet felt peaceful in his presence.

Leah liked him all the more for it.

The scent of shaving soap and sandalwood drifted over her. It was a remarkably masculine smell, the sort that rendered a young woman weak-kneed and pliable, willing to make all sorts of poor decisions.

Keep your wits about ye, Leah!

"So . . ." she began, floundering for a topic, "uhmmm, *Fox* . . . that is an unusual given name."

"I suppose," he snorted. "My father was quite fond of Mr. Charles Fox's politics. I was named in his honor."

Leah was unsure how to respond. The name *Charles Fox* was vaguely familiar. Hadn't Mr. Jamieson, the town glazier, once said something rather crude about Mr. Fox when he thought no women were present?

"He was always a bit of a radical, Mr. Fox," Mr. Carnegie continued as if he, too, were eager to have a topic to discuss. "He championed revolution, hated imperialistic warmongering, and detested our current Hanoverian kings. My father was rather passionate about Mr. Fox's pacifistic views and democratic principles."

Something caught in Leah's chest at that.

My father was. Past tense.

She understood something about a past-tense parent.

"Do ye share your father's views then?" she asked, looking pointedly at the brass buttons on his regimental waistcoat, at the monarchy and imperialism they represented.

He followed her gaze, plucking at the sturdy red wool.

"It hardly matters now, I suppose." He shrugged and looked away, the lamplight casting his profile in stark shadow upon the wall behind.

Footsteps echoed down the hallway, drifting away from her door. Lord Dennis muttered in his sleep.

"How did ye end up as a commissioned officer then, if I may ask?"

Mr. Carnegie rested his head against the wall with a soft *thump*, as if the question troubled him. "I was orphaned last autumn, but I will not reach my majority for another two years. Worse, my father lost most of his fortune due to poor speculation, leaving me with little."

Leah's heart gave another wee lurch. So he *was* young . . . only nineteen.

"My uncle became my guardian after my father's death," he continued. "Unlike my pacifistic father, my uncle believes a man must do his duty and go to war when needed. I cannot say I relish the thought, but I must provide for myself and I have no interest in the Church. Therefore, the military is the only choice left. Uncle purchased me a commission in the 64th Foot, and here I am."

Living a life I never really wanted.

He didn't say the words, but she heard them nonetheless.

Leah knew that in-between feeling. When the smooth sailing of life crashed into a hard, unforgiving calamity.

"I ken a bit about change. My mother died two years past when my youngest brother was born—" She blink, blink, blinked before swallowing back her grief. "—and my father is still heartbroken over her loss. My younger brothers are too wee tae be without a mother, so I've had tae become their mamma."

Leah let out a slow breath, thinking about Malcolm and Ethan back home at Thistle Muir. How Malcolm, barely five, had *greited* and clung to her skirts as she walked to Uncle Leith's waiting carriage. How Ethan, scarcely two, had wailed his distress, reaching for her, fighting to get out of Cousin Elspeth's arms.

It had been too much. Leah had nearly turned back and stayed.

"Get on with ye. Go tae London," Elspeth had urged, holding Ethan tighter. As a lifelong spinster, her father's cousin had spent her years being passed like a parcel between relatives. "Get yourself a husband, lass."

Leah's father had stepped forward and pressed a soft kiss to her forehead.

"Aye," he said, voice gruff and eyes suspiciously bright. "Your mother wouldnae want ye tae be here. Go have a wee adventure. And if ye come back tae us married to some braw, young gentleman, so much the better."

Well, Fox Carnegie certainly fit the definition of a 'braw, young gentleman.'

"How challenging for you, to be raising your brothers," Mr. Carnegie replied, hair glinting in the firelight. "To take on so much, so young."

"You are kind tae say so, but we do what we must."

He sighed, a weary, body-worn sound. "You speak truth."

Silence descended.

A silence of kinship this time. A sense that, despite the differences in their upbringing and experiences, she and Fox Carnegie saw the world through a similar lens.

That they were, perhaps, cut from the same cloth.

He angled his head toward the door, listening intently. "We might finally be in the clear."

"Let me check."

Leah approached the door on light feet, pressing her ear against the dark oak.

Nothing.

Cautiously, she turned the lock and peered out into the hallway.

No one.

"How does it look?" he asked, his words close to her ear.

Leah jumped slightly, looking to him. Mr. Carnegie was scarcely a foot away. So close, she could see a faint mole to the right of his nose and count his individual eyelashes. So close, she could feel the heat of his body. So close, she would only have to lift onto tiptoe to press her mouth to his.

She blinked.

What had he asked?

"Good." Was her voice breathless? She *felt* breathless. "The coast is clear."

Nodding, he stooped down and hefted Lord Dennis upright once more. His lordship's eyes fluttered open and closed. Mr. Carnegie adjusted his hold, draping Dennis's elbow over his own shoulders and wrapping another arm around the man's waist.

"Thank you again for your kind company, Miss Penn-Leith," Mr. Carnegie whispered. "We shall remove ourselves, and let you see to your slumber."

He saluted her with his free hand and then he was gone, slipping out the door with his burden as soundlessly as he had entered it.

But the *feel* of Fox Carnegie lingered. A whiff of sandalwood. A sense of adventure in the air.

Sleep was decidedly long in coming.

Visit www.NicholeVan.com to buy your copy of
Love Practically today and continue the story.

ABOUT THE AUTHOR

THE SHORT VERSION:

NICHOLE VAN IS a writer, photographer, designer and generally disorganized person. Though originally from the Rocky Mountains, she has lived all over the world, including Italy and the UK. She and her family recently returned to the US after spending six years in Scotland. Nichole currently lives in the heart of the Rockies with her husband and and three children.

THE LONG OVERACHIEVER VERSION:

AN INTERNATIONAL BESTSELLING author, Nichole Van is an artist who feels life is too short to only have one obsession. In former lives, she has been a contemporary dancer, pianist, art historian, choreographer, culinary artist and English professor.

Most notably, however, Nichole is an acclaimed photographer, winning over thirty international accolades for her work, including Portrait of the Year from WPPI in 2007. (Think Oscars for wedding and portrait photographers.) Her unique photography style has been featured in many magazines, including Rangefinder and Professional Photographer.

All that said, Nichole has always been a writer at heart. With an MA in English, she taught technical writing at Brigham Young University for ten years and has written more technical manuals than she can quickly count. She decided in late 2013 to start writing fiction and has since become an Amazon #1 bestselling author. Additionally, she has won a RONE award, as well as been a Whitney Award Finalist several years running. Her late 2018 release, *Seeing Miss Heartstone*, won the Whitney Award Winner for Best Historical Romance.

In 2017, Nichole, her husband and three children moved from the Rocky Mountains in the USA to Scotland. They lived there for six years—residing on the coast of eastern Scotland in an eighteenth century country house—before returning to the USA in 2023. Nichole currently lives in the heart of the Rockies, miles up a mountain canyon.

She is known as NicholeVan all over the web: Facebook, Instagram, Pinterest, etc. Visit http://www.NicholeVan.com to sign up for her author newsletter and be notified of new book releases.

If you enjoyed this book, please leave a short review on Amazon. com. Wonderful reviews are the elixir of life for authors. Even better than dark chocolate.

Made in the USA
Monee, IL
31 March 2024

55362374R20196